ADVAN

THESE ARE THE FIREWORKS

"If you've ever looked at your family and thought, 'who are these people?' then Vicki Grant's delightful new novel is for you. *These Are the Fireworks* is a twisty, funny, and ultimately warm-hearted mystery."

ELIZABETH RENZETTI,
co-author of *Bury the Lead*

"Sharply plotted, tender, tense, and hilarious, *These Are the Fireworks* turns the fallout from one man's apparently accidental death into an irresistibly readable tangle of lies, loyalties, and long-buried truths. Readers who love Liane Moriarty and Celeste Ng will devour this."

TOM RYAN,
bestselling author of *We Had a Hunch*

PRAISE FOR VICKI GRANT

"One of the funniest writers working today."

VANCOUVER SUN

"Quirky, fully fleshed characters and a tender third-person narration accompany themes of grieving, making amends, and living a full life in this winning novel."

PUBLISHERS WEEKLY, on *A Green Velvet Secret*

"There's heart and hope in this slightly zany book that sensitively deals with death and grief."

KIRKUS, on *A Green Velvet Secret*

This book is dedicated to whoever coined the term
"spousal death fantasy."
VG

Vagrant Press is an imprint of Nimbus Publishing Limited
3660 Strawberry Hill Street, Halifax, NS, B3K 5A9 | (902) 455-4286 nimbus.ca

Nimbus Publishing is based in Kjipuktuk, Mi'kma'ki, the traditional territory of the Mi'kmaq People.

NB1839
Editor: Whitney Moran
Design: Bee Stanton

Library and Archives Canada Cataloguing in Publication

Title: These are the fireworks : a mystery / Vicki Grant.
Names: Grant, Vicki, author
Identifiers: Canadiana (print) 20250320177 | Canadiana (ebook) 20250320185 |
ISBN 9781774715109
(softcover) | ISBN 9781774715116 (EPUB)
Subjects: LCGFT: Detective and mystery fiction. | LCGFT: Novels.
Classification: LCC PS8613.R367 T54 2026 | DDC C813/.6—dc23

Nimbus Publishing acknowledges the financial support for its publishing activities from the Government of Canada, the Canada Council for the Arts, and from the Province of Nova Scotia. We are pleased to work in partnership with the Province of Nova Scotia to develop and promote our creative industries for the benefit of all Nova Scotians.

THESE ARE THE FIREWORKS

THESE ARE THE FIREWORKS

a mystery

VICKI GRANT

Vagrant Press

PETRA

BEFORE

Petra Fforde's husband was doing the dishes. She wanted to kill him.

Kill him, she thought, leaning hard into the k.

She closed her book over a finger so she wouldn't lose her place and stared past the tiny sparks stippling her vision. No use trying to read when she was like this. When *he* was like this. That's what she really meant. She couldn't even look at the man.

Although, of course, she did. Malcolm was as grimly irresistible as a three-car pileup. She took a quick peek over her shoulder. Her stomach lurched.

He was so infuriating. Even the way he was standing—chest out, shoulders back, Rockports ergonomically planted a manly three feet apart. Honest to God—who stood like that? Who stood like that to do the *dishes*? He looked like some sorry excuse for an action figure.

G. I. Schmo.

That just came to her. She was amazed she hadn't thought of it before. Malcolm to a goddamn tee. Poseable limbs, yes, but a hollow core and no genitalia whatsoever. She'd have laughed if it wasn't so sad.

She remembered as a kid, holding a magnifying glass over a plastic soldier until the sun melted its face. For a brief moment before succumbing, its mouth had twisted up into a smile as if she'd done it a favour by putting it out of its misery. She wondered how long it would take for Malcolm's face to melt.

Enough.

She closed her eyes and inhaled deeply. She relaxed her shoulders, teeter-tottered her neck from side to side and gave herself a little talking-to.

Malcolm was just being Malcolm. Nothing had changed, *would* change, so suck it up, buttercup. She had a very good life, all things considered. Three beautiful daughters, money in the bank, and of course, this gorgeous house.

Petra let her eyes drift across the sunroom. Her lovely, calming sunroom. There wasn't a thing she'd do differently: the wide-plank floors, the clean-lined furniture, the fireplace she'd refaced in a vintage tile she'd spent months scouring the internet for. The glaze was exquisite—a muddy greenish grey with a slightly bubbly texture that reminded her of fudge on the simmer. A small part of the overall design, but it made the room, it really did.

She felt briefly righteous, but then she thought, *No.* She was being unfair. Malcolm wasn't totally inert. At least he didn't whistle anymore. She'd asked him to stop, and he had—graciously, too, even though he'd clearly enjoyed it and was, she had to admit, pretty good at it.

But so what?

A good whistler was even more annoying than a bad whistler. All those trills and crescendos. The bird sounds. What was she supposed to do? Clap? Sing along? Smash her face against the wall in time?

Petra let out a small snort of derision. Malcolm may very well have stopped whistling, but he was still—absolutely, utterly, and to the very core of his hogtied little soul—the type of person who whistled.

Stop.

She was being terrible. She adjusted the shade of her mid-century copper reading lamp. Here she was, comfortably ensconced with the latest bestseller and a steaming hot cup of oolong tea, while the poor man did the dishes. She really had nothing to complain about.

Petra looked at her husband again in what she hoped was a kinder light. She was pretty sure by now he'd have moved on to the terracotta dish she'd baked the cannelloni in. He'd have saved it to last. It was going to take some work. He'd probably been looking forward to it.

Who wouldn't want to kill a man like that?

Her vision went blurry. Everything became clear.

She'd stab him with the four-hundred-dollar Japanese chef's knife he'd just patted dry, hold his head under water until the bubbles stopped breaking through the grease, then feed him—bit by quivering bit—into their new ultra-quiet garbage disposal unit.

She pressed her nails into her palms and let that idea play out.

She'd need lye, she realized. The new garburator was good, but not that good. Even German engineering wasn't up to disposing of 178 pounds of bone and sinew, not to mention those clamshell-thick toenails of his.

Plastic sheeting, too, because things would get messy. Petra remembered the first time she'd cut into a living body. The gore. The pulsing. She'd had to struggle to stay conscious, but she'd gotten used to it. Come to like it, in fact.

Bleach—bottles of it. There'd be a lot to do. Walls, ceiling, counters—the knife, too, of course. (How often in one of her detective books had a cop identified the murder weapon after noticing a knife missing from a set? She wouldn't make *that* mistake.)

Gloves. Her first thought was to use Malcolm's dish gloves, but no. The squeak they made just about drove her up the wall. Disposable latex would be better. She could pick some up at the pharmacy. Everyone used them these days. No one would bat an eye.

And, of course, a power saw of some type. Malcolm had one in his workshop. She'd just tell him she had a little project to do. A home improvement project. *Not untrue*, she thought with a smile.

Malcolm gave the casserole dish a quick rinse, then whipped a linen tea towel off his shoulder to dry it. He scratched at something still stuck to the inside lip and frowned gravely. Churchill reading the dispatches.

Teatowel back on shoulder. Dish back in water. More goddamn squeaking.

Didn't bother him, of course. He was listening to one of his favourite podcasts. He'd told Petra what it was called, but she'd instantly forgotten. Some political history thing. He'd put in his earbuds so as not to disturb her, but even that infuriated her. Malcolm was always so fucking worried about disturbing her. As if that was the worst thing that could happen. *Had* happened. The man lived in denial.

He stopped scrubbing, cocked his head to the side, and froze like a special ops agent who'd just heard a twig snap in the jungle or a well-preserved professional man who'd just heard some fascinating fact about the origins of the Sino-Japanese War. A murmur, a little nod of appreciation, then back to the terracotta dish. He'd no doubt be telling her about it later. It was like waiting for a Pap smear.

She tapped the armrest in lieu of screaming and stared blindly at the fireplace. What had gotten into her? Petra Fforde was sixty-six years old. She'd had decades of this.

Why was she so angry now?

She didn't know. It wasn't the big stuff that set her off anymore, not like those first horrible few years. Significant dates, the screech of tires, a tiny sneaker turned on its side—she'd worked hard to neutralize the obvious triggers. It was the little things she had to be careful about now. The stuff she barely noticed. Microscopic but pernicious. Like dust mites accumulating unnoticed that set off a fatal asthma attack or wisps of methane seeping into a mine shaft. One spark would be all it took—then kaboom. Utter carnage.

She needed to get out before she did something terrible. She did a quick search on her phone. There was a group meeting that night near Lakeview Mall.

"Malcolm?" she said. "Sweetheart?"

He popped out an earbud and turned toward her, smiling. Always smiling. How she pitied Mr. Rogers's wife. She'd have taken that little blue sneaker of his and beaten him bloody with it years ago.

"Sorry," he said. "Almost finished. You ready to chat?" That night they'd planned to nail down dimensions of the backyard pond he wanted to put in.

She didn't need her coat. Her purse was on the hall table. "Yes." She smiled sheepishly. "I mean, no."

He raised one eyebrow in an exaggerated question mark. There was often something a little 1970s-sitcom to their interactions: corny, good-natured, false. He wiped the counter and waited.

"Could we talk tomorrow?" She grimaced in mock embarrassment. "I'd love to nip out to a little shop I just heard about in—"

He waved his dishcloth at her, laughing. "Yes! Geez. Be gone with you. There are some numbers I should go over first anyway and—"

"Sure you don't mind?" She was already putting on her lipstick.

"One hundred percent. You're happy, I'm happy." He winked, then started working on the casserole dish again. He'd missed a spot.

She came up behind him, kissed him quickly on the cheek. "Back in, oh, a couple hours?" He turned around for a hug, but she was already heading for the foyer.

Petra stepped outside, clicked the door behind her, and sucked in a lungful of air like a parolee experiencing her first taste of freedom after decades of hard time. All she was hoping to get out of that night's Grief-Share meeting was a brief reprieve from her rage.

Instead, she was finally going to find a man strong enough to share it with.

NINA

THREE YEARS LATER

We had no inkling what our mother was capable of. My sisters and I accepted her at face value. Pampered wife, devoted mother, dedicated volunteer, and a woman of exceptional style and grace. We loved her but had clearly underestimated her. I feel badly about that now, but I'm sure she doesn't. Our collective blindness allowed her to do things she never would have gotten away with otherwise.

On the day this all started, Jesse and I were working as live-in help for an elderly professor in the town where we'd gone to university.

Don was down for his siesta. (He found the word "nap" infantilizing. Even Hemingway, he claimed, took siestas.) I was sitting in what he called his reading chair, a low-slung Danish number in burnt orange, with matching ottoman and standing lamp. A copy of *The Cuisine of France* was open on the arm, emitting a slight but comforting pong of vintage damp. My knees were tucked up inside one of Jesse's old Mount Heber U sweatshirts. I raked my toes over the nubbly upholstery and considered dinner options.

A soufflé? My last one had been a triumph—light, savoury, and the even golden-brown of a perfectly roasted marshmallow—but we'd been feeding Don a lot of eggs recently.

Bifteck Diane? No. Don's ability to chew had gotten iffy and, as Jesse observed after our last near-death experience, "nothing casts a pall over a nice meal quite like the Heimlich manoeuvre."

I flipped a few more pages and came upon a photo of a pale larval blob, garnished with an optional sprig of parsley. I read the caption: *A delicate creamed fish dumpling served in a shrimp or lobster sauce.*

"How about quenelles?" I said.

The main floor of Don's home was low-ceilinged but expansive. Original teak kitchen open to a sunny dining area, then three steps down to the unbearably hip "conversation pit." Jesse—picture Gumby with a beard and thrifted T-shirt—was at the kitchen island, reviewing Don's medical appointments for the week. He didn't look up. "Never heard of them but, hey, go for it." No surprise there. Jesse was generally game for anything. (I either loved that about him or hated it, depending where I was in my cycle.)

I turned back to the recipe. I hadn't heard of quenelles either. I'd only become a cook since starting at Don's. The first couple of months, everything I'd made for him looked like it was meant to be eaten in a high chair or snorted through a feeding tube. I'd stuck to the low-salt, mulched-meat recipes the dietician had xeroxed and presented to us on three-hole paper. Then, one evening, Don mentioned his late wife's quiche Lorraine with such enthusiasm that I hunted down the recipe and made it. It wasn't perfect—we killed ourselves over the automotive upholstery I tried to pass off as pastry—but we could see how much happier real food made him.

That quiche was the turning point. Jesse and I pledged never to let Donald R. Meisner, distinguished professor emeritus of law, end his days with a bib and a sippy cup. At 6:00 P.M. on the dot, Jesse brought Don downstairs with combed hair, a clean cardigan, and pressed trousers. A single martini lite on the deck was followed by full dinner service: flowers, wine, beeswax tapers in Dansk candleholders, the whole bit. We discussed philosophical questions and current events, with an occasional foray into Russian literature. Tiramisu or crème caramel, a shot of decaf espresso, then Don shakily dabbed his lips with his napkin, thanked me for the lovely meal, and allowed Jesse to escort him back to his room, a happy man. Despite whatever humiliations the rest of the day meted out, for those ninety minutes at least, we all inhabited the grown-up world.

Quenelles looked like a potential addition to my repertoire. At the bottom of the page in her impeccable handwriting, Don's wife Ruth had written, *Visiting Scholar Dinner, 12 April 66. Everyone raved. USE FULL CREAM.*

I read the instructions, took a mental inventory. We had haddock and shrimp in the freezer, eggs, nutmeg, but no cream. It wasn't good for Don's cholesterol. I was debating how much the recipe would suffer if I used low-fat milk instead when my phone rang.

I picked it up absentmindedly. Don was almost ninety-seven. His legs barely worked. His eyesight was just about gone. So were most of his friends. He liked cream. Would it be such a crime to give him some? What makes life worth living?

Jesse and I pondered that daily. Partly because we were looking after an elderly man and we were concerned about him. Partly because we were looking after an elderly man and we were concerned about ourselves. How the hell had we ended up here? What were we doing with our lives? What had happened to our dreams, ambitions, self-respect, etc.? Planning elaborate dinners provided me only occasional refuge from my real concerns.

"Hello," I said into the phone and thought, *Greek yogurt might work.*

"Nina? This is Wayne Dudek."

"Hey." A startled chuckle. "Wayne."

It felt immediately odd, him calling me. Not crazy-odd, just weird enough to set off a small questioning *ping* in my head. I'd known Wayne forever, but only the way I'd known most of my parents' friends. Long, but not well. Dad and "The Dude" had been business partners since I was a baby.

A surprise party, I thought. That was the only thing a direct call from Wayne Dudek could mean. But for what? Dad's seventieth had been the year before. Retirement wasn't happening. (His standard line was, "Oh, good Lord, I'd drive your mother over the deep end!" and he'd have been right. That's obvious now.) We'd already done a big thing for their fortieth anniversary.

"What's up?" I tried to convey both 'great to hear from you' and 'I'm kind of busy at the moment.'

"Is your man there? I need to speak with him."

My chest thumped. I realized the party might be for me.

But no. Couldn't be. My birthday was months ago. It had been twelve years since I'd graduated from university. Eight since I'd done anything of note. An intervention, while deserving, seemed unlikely. My parents had always insisted they were proud of me. For what, I couldn't imagine.

"You mean Jesse?" I said.

"Jesse. Yes. Sorry." Wayne obviously didn't remember his name despite meeting him hundreds of times. "Could I have a word?"

"Sure. One sec."

I put my hand over the phone and hissed like I was calling a cat. Jesse was busy doling out Don's pills into an ice-cube-like tray. He raised his finger, as in *wait.*

I walked into the kitchen and whispered, "It's Wayne Dudek. He wants to talk to you."

"Wayne?" Jesse squinted at me suspiciously. "You mean, like..." He mimed a crazy accurate off-the-cuff imitation—the rooster-ish stance, the fingertip adjustment of his glasses, the side-talking.

"You got it." I handed him the phone.

He shrugged like *too weird,* then exclaimed, "Why, Mr. Dudek!" It always amazed me the way Jesse could pull bonhomie out of his ass. "How you doing?"

He listened for a while then said, "What?" He stopped smiling. "When?"

He sucked in his breath and massaged his forehead. Jess was obviously worried but, unbelievable as it sounds now, I was still thinking *party.* Life had not prepared me for anything more catastrophic than that.

I double-checked Don's pills and thought about the male strippers Wayne had hired for his wife's sixty-fifth birthday. They'd strutted into the Dudeks' great room, wearing bowties and satin thongs filled with what appeared to be lightly sedated hamsters. Everyone screeched with laughter, the women covering their faces with fanned-out fingers, the men wincing. The show quickly ramped up to full-bore bumping and grinding. A bad call. With the exception of The Dude himself, the crowd was made up of the type of glowing, active seniors seen in vitamin commercials. Dry-humping the birthday girl was way outside their comfort zone. One of the men switched Tom Jones off mid-growl. Mum brought in a giant leopard-print birthday cake. Everyone turned and watched Debbie Dudek blow out the candles while Dad discretely ushered the Chippendale boys to the door. I hated to think what Wayne had in mind for us now.

Jesse walked onto the deck and slid the glass door closed behind him. He stood looking out over the backyard tennis court, the phone at his ear.

He hung up a few minutes later but stayed outside, his hands gripping the railing, his neck sunk deep into his shoulders. It bothered him that we'd let the court get in such bad shape. I figured he was just contemplating how to resurface it. (As if Don was ever going to play tennis again. But that's Jesse. Ever hopeful.)

I headed out after him.

"The Dude himself. Calling *you*?" I leaned against the door jamb, feet crossed, arms crossed, fingers tapping elbows. "What's up? He looking for a new line-dancing partner or something?"

I expected Jesse to parry. Toss a quip my way. Inane banter was our love language. Instead, he turned, dragged a hand over his beard, and said, "C'mere."

"What?"

I swear I heard blocks falling. A tower collapsing in my brain.

"Nina."

"No."

I took a step back into the house.

"Neens."

He walked toward me. I rammed the door closed and hit the lock.

"Neens...Nina. C'mon." He tugged at the handle a few times, then slumped against the glass, arms above his head as if he was being frisked. "Let me in. Please. I have to talk to you."

I stood there staring at him, my hands clasped in front of my chest like a nun, a doubting nun, my head vibrating more than actually shaking. "No...No. No. No. No. No."

Jesse kept banging at the glass. I focused on how white the undersides of his arms were. The sharp vertical line where the course dark hair stopped growing. Things I knew and loved and could count on.

"Nina," he said again. "I'm sorry. I'm really sorry, but it's your dad."

NINA

It was late. All day long, there'd been a rolling barrage of friends, colleagues, and graciously efficient neighbourhood ladies bearing casseroles with reheating instructions neatly taped to the lids. The house was finally quiet. Clary and I should have been exhausted but we weren't. We left our menfolk sleeping in our childhood bedrooms, tiptoed down the hall, and crawled into bed with Libby.

"Go away," she whimpered. It had taken her twenty-eight long, fuggy hours to make it home from Iqaluit. She whacked her hand at us bonelessly, like a drunk disturbed on the subway. "Seriously. Get out!"

"No," I said, cuddling up next to her.

"We missed you." Clary mussed her hair.

"Leave. Me. Alone." The arm again, coming at us from all directions. "I mean it."

"No, you don't. You wuvs us!" I grabbed her wrist and started making kissy sounds. Clary muscled into bed behind me.

People talk about the various stages of grief—disbelief, sadness, anger, something, something—but they never mention idiocy. That's the stage Clary and I were at. We'd cried and cried and would cry again but it was after midnight, Mum was asleep, and our brains were still sputtering along on the last few drops of trauma juice. We couldn't help it if we were being assholes.

"Push over," I said, thrusting my pelvis into Libby's bum.

She went, "I hate you guys," but she moved. I nuzzled her neck. She smelled of anxiety and other people, but I didn't care. Lib was nothing like me, but she was my twin, my wombmate, and I loved everything about her. She pulled my hand up under her armpit and kissed my fingers.

"Damn." She started to cry. "Dad."

"I know." I started to cry.

Clary threw an arm over both of us and started to cry too. We lay together juddering miserably for who knows how long until I felt wet on my back and jerked upright. "Oh, my God. Claaaaraaaa."

"Already?" Clary sat up and turned on the light. "Shit. I just fed him." Her pink T-shirt had a maroon splotch capping each breast.

"Gross." I pinched the damp fabric away from my skin. "Is it weird having food just squirt out of you like that?"

Lib said, "Why is the light on?"

"Of course it's weird!" Clary pulled off her shirt. "I'm like a fucking milk machine, just churning out product 24-7. Plus I'm hot. Like, *so hot*." She kicked frantically at the duvet until it slipped off her legs. "Is this new?"

"No one cares," Libby moaned. "Turn off the light."

"I don't know." I rubbed the duvet fabric between my fingers. "Probably." I didn't recognize the pattern, a subtle cream on ecru print, but I didn't *not* recognize it either. Mum had a pretty established style. Clean, neutral, understated. Think expensive spa at a heritage inn. She was always remodelling but nothing ever looked substantially different, just sort of subtly better.

"It's nice. Really kind of—"

"Clary! Turn off the light and shut up."

"I was talking!"

"*Please.*"

"No. C'mon, Lib. We're awake. Talk for a while." Clary leaned against the linen headboard and crossed her legs pretzel-style. Her bra was enormous. Her belly button had developed an overbite. The pad in her underwear was roughly the size of a baguette. I barely recognized her. "Krish is going to have the baby here one second after he cries. I need adult company. How are you? Just tell me that."

Libby rolled onto her back. She looked like hell—exhausted, pasty, pissed. The self-inflicted pixie cut wasn't helping either. "Well...my father was just killed in a freak cycling accident, but otherwise I'm fine. You?"

"Ditto," I said, snuggling back down beside her. Our parents, in their wisdom, had encouraged us to go to separate universities. Learn to stand on our own two feet. Libby had wobbled for a while but then righted herself. I'd met Jesse in Romance Literature 101. Best friends by RoLit 201. Lovers by, we can never remember exactly when. Jess says Easter. I think early June. (It just sort of happened. A leak in his bedroom ceiling. A wet mattress. I said, "May as well sleep with me." Done.) Who needs to stand on their own two feet? Four is much more stable. When I wasn't with Jesse, I had Libby to prop me up.

"And Clara?" Libby wiped congealed drool off the corners of her mouth with a thumb. "If we're doing this, let's do it. What about you?"

"Yeah, ditto. I mean, I guess." She opened the trap door on her nursing bra and picked at a thick, chocolatey scab on her nipple. Her breast was as round and veiny as the head of a cartoon alien. (Any other time I would have pointed out the similarity, but I let it go. Our father had just died after all.) "My husband's a bit of an entitled douchebag at the moment, but I'm okay."

Libby and I both went, "We love Krish!" We weren't just saying it. Krish was great. Funny, smart, and despite an occasional emotional boneheadedness, utterly devoted to Clary, which ain't easy. She's funny and smart too—and would run into a burning building for any of us—but entitled is kind of her thing.

"I didn't say he wasn't lovable. I said he was a douchebag. Arlo's his baby, too, you know."

"Do we though?" Lib said.

Clary shrugged coquettishly.

We let her vent about Krish—the workouts he hadn't cancelled, the meals he hadn't made, the sleep he hadn't lost—until we'd had enough; then Libby said, "How's Mum?"

Mum had been awake when Libby arrived that night, but just barely. They'd kissed and hugged and made it through half a glass of wine before staggering off to their separate beds.

"She's all right," I said. "Not smiling much but, like, *Mum,* right? When did she ever? She seems like herself only on Ativan or something. Slightly...fuzzy around the edges."

Jess and I had been the first to arrive. We called Jesse's parents to look after Don, threw our funeral getups into his ancient Saab, and took off. We made it home four hours after Wayne's devastating call. The whole way there I kept thinking: *Mum.* This was going to kill her. No one to look after her. Protect her. Love her.

We were barely in park before I was out of the car, charging up the front steps. I was going to save her. I was going to do what Dad would have wanted me to do. She was my responsibility now.

But the big oak door had opened before I'd even made it to the porch and Mum had run out and thrown her arms around me. Next thing I knew, I was sobbing like I was five and had lost Libby at the playground. Mum stroked my head, murmuring, "Oh, sweetheart. Lovie. It's all right. It's going to be all right."

Shameful. I'd managed to be the grown-up for less than five minutes.

I turned to Clary. "How do *you* think she's doing?"

"Fine? Or at least 'rising to the occasion.' You know. As per."

She shrugged then hoicked up her bra and snapped it shut. I couldn't help staring at it. All the stitching, the hooks and pulleys, the dingey utilitarian white. It looked like a piece of Victorian fencing gear. La Perla had always been more her thing. Who was this person? Another stab to the heart. I couldn't lose my father and my big sister too.

"We should go to bed," I said.

"We are in bed. How long do you think before Mum starts dating?"

"Oh my God!" I whacked Clary with a pillow. "Dad's not even cold!"

"I'm not talking now. I'm talking whenever. She's young. Young-ish. She still looks good. You want her to be alone forever?"

"Yes. We want her to be alone forever, don't we, Lib? Spend the rest of her life mouldering away in a dark room. Why would you even say that?"

"Because I thought it and I understood this to be a safe place. But, hey. Guess not."

Lib and I were used to Clary's provocations. We ignored her.

"Poor Mum." Libby got up on her elbows. "I try to picture her life from here on but all I see is this giant hole. How's she going to survive without Dad?"

I had no answer for that. (Clary did, of course, but it would be a while before she'd show her hand. She was still sussing us out.) We lay down flat, arms at our sides, staring at the ceiling. Bereavement Barbies.

I spent the silence that followed thinking about losing Jesse, what would happen to me. It wouldn't be nice, but at least I had sisters. Mum didn't even have that. Her brother had died years ago. She'd married young. Never worked outside the home. She had tons of acquaintances but very few real friends. She hadn't needed them. She'd always had Dad.

At some point, we realized Libby was crying again.

Clary scrambled over me to get to her. "Aw, honey. Libbo. Mum'll be fine. Really. She's not going to fall apart. She looks fragile, but she's actually pretty tough. Right, Neens?"

"Absolutely. Jackie O." That's what we'd called our mother since high school. The reasons were obvious. "You should have seen her today. House all done up. Making everyone feel comfortable—"

"Oh, come *on*." Libby wiped her nose on her wrist. "That Martha Stewart shit? You think that's the real her? She's just going through the motions! Mum's sixty-*nine*. Her world has fallen apart. What's she going to do now? Renovate the house again? Like all she needs to fill the emptiness is the perfect fucking—"

I think she said "backsplash," but she was sobbing too hard to tell.

"She'll be okay." Clary held Libby close and talked into the nape of her neck. "It'll be tough for a while, but we'll keep an eye on her."

"We will," I said.

But how? Clary lived in Toronto and had a husband and a baby and a boss who called every afternoon begging her to come back early from mat leave. Libby was principal of an elementary school, pretty much at the North Pole. I was only three hours away by car, but I had Don to look after.

"I can't talk about this now, guys." Lib tried to smile. "Can you go? Please?"

Clary was leaking. I needed to pee. We kissed Lib goodbye and headed down the hall to our respective bedrooms.

At the landing, Clary said, "Look." The window was open. Mum was sitting on a boulder next to the backyard pond she and Dad had put in a few years earlier. She was in bare feet and silk pajamas, her legs squeezed up to her chest like a kid left out of a game. The white fairy lights in the willow tree lit her up from behind.

"It's almost two," I said. "Should we go get her? She's going to feel like hell tomorrow."

"No. The funeral's tomorrow. She's going to feel like hell anyway. She's fine. She's probably communing with Dad's spirit or something."

Mum had never seemed like the type to commune with spirits, but what did I know? They'd both loved that pond.

PETRA

BEFORE

Petra was so relieved to have escaped another conversation with Malcolm about the goddamn pond that she wondered if she even needed to go to the meeting. But she'd driven all the way to Lakeview. She was here now. She figured she might as well.

She took the elevator to the third floor and walked halfway down the brightly lit hall to Room 326. A glass plaque attached to the door said: *The Jaxon McDonough Room. Gratefully funded by Mark and Angela McDonough, in loving memory of their son. Always and forever.*

The McDonoughs had bought their son naming rights to a small multipurpose room in a five-storey institutional building with an aspirational parking lot and a view of the off-ramp. Petra hoped, she really did, that it worked for them. No judgment. Different strokes for different folks. It just didn't work for her.

She peeked through the brick-sized window in the door. Taupe carpet tiles, stacking chairs arranged in a circle, a dozen people studying their fingernails. The same sorry mix she'd come to expect. Early to late middle-age. Unhealthy, or maybe just unhappy. The full range of skin colours but all a bit faded.

Not necessarily a bad sign. *We contain multitudes,* she thought optimistically. *Who knows what they're hiding?* She stepped inside.

A large woman in a drape-front cardigan and wide-legged trousers was writing an uplifting quote on a portable whiteboard. She turned at the sound of the door opening, took the marker cap out of her mouth, and smiled warmly. "Metro Grief-Share?"

Petra nodded.

The woman swept her hand to the side and said, "Welcome!" An oddly opulent gesture for such a utilitarian room. "Help yourself to coffee then come join us. We're just about to start."

Petra whispered thanks and headed to a wood-patterned folding table in the back. The coffee smelled strongly of several hours on high, but she poured herself a cup anyway. Not as if she was going to drink it. It was a prop. Something to hide behind if her cover slipped.

The circle parted. A man reached back and dragged another chair in for her with one hand. Quite a bit younger than her. Late forties maybe? She couldn't tell anymore. He was beefy in an athletic way, although going to fat around the waist. Something about the way his shoulders slumped made her think of a football player getting a verbal drubbing from Coach at halftime. Contrite but manly.

She nodded a thanks to him and sat down.

"It's five past," the woman at the front said. "How about we get started? My name's Lucretia Upshaw—but please, call me Lu." She opened her eyes wide and shook her head. "*Lucretia.* Honestly. What were my parents thinking?" An old joke.

Everyone chuckled or at least smiled. Politeness is a hard habit to give up. In her more charitable moments, Petra thought that was Malcolm's problem—too well brought-up to actually show his feelings—but she knew that was wrong. Malcolm was too afraid to even have them. She'd always been braver than he was.

Lu brought her hands together under her chin. "I'd like to start by congratulating each of you for coming out tonight. This is probably the last place you want to be. But you *came.* You got dressed, got out of your house, showed up. You took the first step towards personal renewal. You are truly phoenixes. All of you."

This is when Petra had to call upon her famous iron will. *Do not react. Do not roll your eyes. Do not in any way let on that you smell feathers burning.*

As usual, after congratulations came the confidentiality blurb, a short warm-up about the commonality of grief, the dissipation of painful feelings, the blah-blah-blah of blah-blah-blah. Then, finally, a little icebreaker to show that we're not just survivors, we're thrivers.

We gotta lotta livin' to do.

Tonight, it was, "Give us your first name, followed by your favourite snack and then the reason you're joining us." Petra would fudge the last one. That was one thing forty-some years with Malcolm had given her: the ability to fake it.

"Who wants to start?" Lu settled into her chair as if she had all the time in the world.

No one answered. No one made eye contact. People held their breath so as not to draw attention to themselves. Eventually, a skinny woman with prominent eyes raised a hand to her shoulder and said, "I will...I mean, if no one else wants to." She looked embarrassed, as if she was taking the last doughnut. A few people smiled back, relief dressed up as encouragement.

"Okay. Well. I'm Rondelle...and, um, I guess pizza is my favourite meal. I mean snack. Whatever. I'm here because I lost my son last year. A car accident. Night of the prom." She raised her eyebrows like *crazy, eh?* then scratched her forehead, her hand obscuring her face.

Everyone could hear her swallowing. Smacking her lips and swallowing as if, with a little effort, the death of a child could be masticated, digested, and expelled from her system. They felt her agony in their own throats. The man beside her piped up, if only to make it stop. Cheeseburgers. Lost his son to blastoma. That got the ball rolling.

A woman. Sweet-and-salty popcorn. Lost her daughter to medical error.

A man. Frosted Flakes. Lost his son to suicide.

A man. Dill pickle chips. Lost his grandchildren in a housefire.

A couple. Mac 'n cheese. Lost their kids in a drowning.

Their stories were tragic, but their voices were calm, unemotional, almost apologetic.

This wasn't what Petra had come for. *Oh, well.* There'd be other meetings, other days. She'd buy herself a new murder mystery on the way home. Something gruesome. A little emotional aspartame. Nowhere near as satisfying as the real thing but as close as she was going to get for the time being. She slid her coffee cup under her chair and prepared to leave, but just then the next woman started to speak.

"I'm Natalie, and you can probably tell—I love anything fried." She spread her hands as if to say, *Look at the size of me.* "I can't stop. Just eat, eat, eat. Especially since I lost Olivia. She was—"

"You…lost her?" The athletic guy, the one who'd gotten Petra the chair, sounded confused.

Natalie managed a small smile. No one else had been interrupted. "Yes. Last year. She—"

"You *lost* her. Wow." He sat up a little straighter, one hand cupping his knee. "What was she, a puppy?"

"No." Natalie's face had gone deep pink and moist. "She was my—"

"Your keys? Your glasses? Your—what?—joie de vivre?"

Natalie didn't laugh but made a noise as if she was trying.

Lu said, "Excuse me. Sir?"

He turned toward her like a teenager who'd been warned about his attitude before. "Yeah?"

"We don't all express ourselves the same way."

"Really? Well, *they* sure do. *Lost him. Lost her. Lost the whole fam-damily.* You people are downright scatterbrained. Seriously. You're in the wrong meeting." He pointed his thumb over his shoulder. "Alzheimer's is two doors down."

Despite themselves, some people laughed.

"What's your name?" Lu said gently.

A pause. "Gord." Said with a smirk but no eye contact.

"Gord. So glad to have you with us."

"Bet you are." He nodded at the floor.

"We are. Really and truly. But in group, it's important to validate—"

"Validate." He tapped his foot.

"Yes. It's important to validate the individual experience of—"

Gord jumped up, roaring like a Viking in one of those big-budget epics Malcolm secretly enjoyed, and hurled his chair over his head. It bounced off the back wall and on to the snack table, before landing on the floor. The powdered creamer followed.

People froze, fists to their chins, eyes wide. Gord stood with his back to them. Blue-grey dots of sweat speckled his white shirt. His ribs heaved.

Yes, Petra thought. *This* was what she'd come for.

Her heart was beating so hard it hurt. To feel it beating at all seemed like a small miracle. There were times over the years when she'd been convinced it had stopped altogether, and she just hadn't fallen over yet. Like those stories about people who die in packed streetcars and stay propped up and lifelike until everybody piles out at the station, then they slump to the floor.

Gord turned to the group. "You think all you need is a little heart-to-heart with a bunch of strangers then, poof! All better? Sorry, folks. You can't talk your way out of this one. This is a life sentence."

Corny, Petra thought, *but effective.* The guy knew his audience. It's what, deep down, they all wanted to hear. That their pain is endless and unbearable.

"Where are your balls? Where's your—"

"Now, Gord," The grandfather took a step toward him. "Why don't we just—"

"Why don't we just *what*? Apologize for our 'loss'? Behave ourselves? That your plan?" Gord turned away in disgust.

There was a long, uncomfortable moment when the only sound was the hiss of the coffee pot finally boiling dry, then Gord kicked Lu's whiteboard. The bang was shocking. Markers shot out like shrapnel. The board skidded into the wall.

People screamed. Gord stomped out of the room.

Petra listened as his footsteps disappeared down the hallway. She put her hand on the back of Lu's chair and whispered, professional to professional, "I've had experience with this type of thing before. Why don't I go see how he is?"

Lu pinched her bottom lip. Gord was her responsibility, but the other participants were upset. They needed her help, too, and this woman seemed legit. "You're comfortable doing that?"

"Absolutely." It came out a little too perky, but Petra was desperate. She couldn't lose him.

Lu gave a small smile, then flicked her eyes toward the door as if to say, *He's all yours.* "Much appreciated."

Petra nodded like it was nothing, then slipped out of the room.

She found Gord in the parking lot, leaning against a dark blue sedan and swearing at the pavement. She introduced herself. Lit a cigarette for him. Lit one for herself. Why not?

After all these years, she'd finally found a fellow traveller.

AL-HADDAD

THREE YEARS LATER

Detective Ryan Al-Haddad retrieved his gym bag from his car, then slammed the trunk shut, exposing the early morning sky. It was still navy velvet at the crest, but a startling band of bright yellow satin now outlined the horizon. Its unexpected splendour stopped him, but only for a moment. He clicked the doors locked. He actually preferred the harsh fluorescent lights of the police station. The sunrise cooed, *slow down, enjoy this.* The overhead lights barked, *get to work.* More his vibe. He'd just made detective and wasn't going to blow it.

At the building entrance, he clamped the edge of his travel mug in his teeth so he could tap his ID card, then ran upstairs to Major Crimes. The room stunk of leftover pizza and indigestion, but at least it was quiet. He nodded hello to a few guys still there from the graveyard shift and headed to his cubicle. He sat down, switched on his computer, then allowed himself a sip of green tea while it woke itself up.

He should have got a coffee. It was going to be a hell of a day. Court at ten, then interviews with witnesses on the bank job, then pinning down the goddamn firearms examiner about the Whitson case. She'd promised the report weeks ago. He was hamstrung without it.

And those were just the urgent matters. He had twenty other open files, all screaming for attention. His insides clenched at the thought.

They clenched at the thought of his lonely old dog, too. And at the thought of Alex. First thing he had to do every day was decide who he could get away with neglecting and for how long. Absolutely necessary if he wanted to get any work done, but it always made him feel like shit.

"As it should," Alex had said before he'd snuck out that morning.

As if someone who toiled in "content creation" could comment on workplace pressure. And in that tone too.

"Asshole," he muttered into his tea.

"You talkin' to me?"

Al-Haddad turned and saw the puffy red face of Blair Zinck looming over his cubicle wall. "Not always about you, Sarge. What's up?"

"Can't I just be popping by to chat?"

"You can but you aren't." Zinck was a good supervisor and a hard worker but not a 5:00 A.M. type of guy. He was too close to retirement for that nonsense.

"You hear about Henderson?" He plunked himself on the edge of Al-Haddad's desk. Binders fell over. "Went into labour last night."

"Seriously? I thought she wasn't due until August."

"She wasn't."

"That's not good."

"It is for *her.* Got the baby out early *and* got out of here. Sounded thrilled when I talked to her." Zinck lifted a buttock and removed a large red stapler. "Not so good for us though."

Al-Haddad knew where this was going.

Zinck handed him a bundle of manilla files. "Sorry, pal. I know you're up to your armpits but, hey. Staff shortages. What can I do?" A practiced grimace. "I tried to give you the easy ones. Plus, you know Henderson. Meticulous notes."

"Well, piece of cake then." Al-Haddad gave his boss a thin smile. "I'll get to them as soon as I can."

"All you can do." Zinck stood up to go. "Although, be nice if you could give a quick look-see at the Fforde case..."

"The who?"

"Malcolm Fforde?" Like that should mean something.

Al-Haddad shrugged.

"Dudek & Fforde? The engineering firm responsible for the new arts centre? The Osterlich mansion? The sportsplex?"

"Yeah. Okay." He recognized the buildings, the name not so much.

"His body was found off Highway 3 on Sunday. Went out cycling that morning and didn't come back. Everything's saying accident but I'd love to confirm that sooner rather than later. Give the widow some closure."

"I got a few widows looking for closure, Sarge. Any reason this guy gets bumped to the head of the line?" *Other than he's obviously rich?*

"Personal favour. My wife was on the hospital board with him. She's really broke up about it. Says Malcolm was a saint. That's the word she used. I told her I'd put my best detective on it."

"Well, I'm flattered."

"Joking!" Zinck squeezed his shoulder and walked out of the cubicle. "You've been a detective for three months and think you're the best? Got a ways to go yet, buddy."

NINA

In retrospect, there were signs as early as the funeral that something was up with Mum.

For starters, her lipstick. She'd worn the same shade forever, a Bobbi Brown beige. Went with everything. Just enough colour to give her a healthy glow. Her trademark lip.

For Dad's funeral, she wore red.

"I wouldn't call it *red*," Lib said.

We were at the yacht club, a Victorian-era pavilion prized for its spectacular views and shabby pedigree. White shingles, dark green trim, a bank of ancient four-paned windows held open by iron hooks screwed into the underside of the eaves. People were drinking wine on the wraparound veranda and laughing. At seventy-one, Dad had been old enough that his funeral wasn't expected to ruin anyone's day. It was a social event that just happened to include a corpse. Women held back their face-framing layers with one hand so they could get the glass to their mouths with the other. Gulls sat on weathered wooden posts, watching servers in black vests dispense oysters. Sailboats clanged at anchor. It reminded me of Clary's wedding. That was the last time we'd all been here together.

Mum was standing inside, near the front of the main hall. A mob of well-dressed people—sympathizers? Grim greeters? We'd debated what to call them—waited for their chance to tell her how very, very sorry they were to hear about Malcolm. We sisters were standing shoulder-to-shoulder some steps away. The B-list reception line. After the initial rush, we were in a bit of a lull.

"You wouldn't call that *red*?" Clary snorted. Libby and I craned our necks around her to look at Mum, modified Three Stooges–style.

She was wearing a gorgeous dove grey summer suit. Chic, but not too showy, perfectly appropriate for the modern widow. She looked good, like Diane Keaton in one of her later rom-coms or Blythe Danner with better hair. She reached out to embrace an older man in yacht club blues, her face a perfectly calibrated mix of pleasure at seeing him and sadness at the occasion.

"I *like* the colour," I said. "What do you expect her to do? Put on the bombazine and go into deep mourning? Dad wouldn't want that."

"I didn't say that." Clary faked a smile. "I just find it surprising that today's the day she'd want to experiment with a new shade." A rusty red. A good choice with her blue eyes and expensive antique-blond hair, but really. Now? Clary had a point. I wondered how many other people had noticed. Women raising their eyebrows and whispering in the ladies' room. Men reluctantly admitting on the ride home that Petra *had* looked good for someone who'd just lost her husband.

Libby shrugged. "Maybe it was a mistake. Maybe she just grabbed the wrong lipstick."

Clary and I let out little *pffts* of laughter. Lib could be kind of clueless, although I sometimes thought not without trying. Being conspicuously out-of-it about that sort of thing was her way of quietly drawing attention to her anti-consumerist values. She'd come home with a backpack full of thrifted hiking gear and a bamboo toothbrush. She'd had to borrow a dress from Clary for the funeral.

"Please," I said. "Mum just had all the window trim repainted because the white 'leaned a little too buttery.'"

"So?"

"So she'd notice."

Clary laughed. Libby shook her head like *you guys...*

A sweaty man in a suit and loosened tie barrelled up to us. He barked, "Rod Bonnar," and grabbed my hand. "Now which one are you?" No shame. His wife—any of the women there—would have pretended to know. When I said "Nina," he opened his mouth in a wide "Ahh...," and I knew what was coming. "The one who 'works with the elderly.'"

Those were The Dude's words. His valiant attempt to put a positive spin on my so-called career. He'd meant well, but it was killing me.

Wayne Dudek had given a lovely eulogy, he really had. (Nothing is more moving than a professional man of a certain age trying to describe his deep feelings for another man without having to resort to the word "love.") He talked about Dad's unflappability. His quiet generosity. His self-discipline. He mentioned how proud Dad was of us all. Of his beautiful wife, Petra, and the exquisite home she'd created for him. Of his eldest daughter, Clara, setting the investment world on fire. Of Elizabeth—Libby—three times a National Educator of the Year. And of Nina—the dark-haired twin—for "her selfless work with the elderly."

At that, Clary had slapped her hand over her face, her eyes skittering toward me in a kind of abject terror. She managed to mouth *selfless* but that's as far as she got. She flopped over in the pew, rocking helplessly, tears streaming down her face, laughter escaping in thin squeaks and seal-like sobs. Mum reached across to rub her back. I covered my mouth, squeezed my eyes shut, and started laughing too. Jess said later that the congregation had seemed touched by the depth of our despair.

I spent the rest of the afternoon saying, "No, not a geriatrician." Or, "No, not a social worker. I actually provide home care for a retired law professor."

"Oh!" people would say, scrambling to cover their embarrassment. "I bet he's lucky to have you!"

I'd smile modestly but think, *hardly*. If anything, Jess and I were the ones who'd lucked out. Room, board, and a living wage for two over-educated, underqualified people? Nice work if you can get it.

Wayne's heart had been in the right place but, frankly, I wished he'd spared me the agony and just come out and said it: "Nina's an unskilled personal-care worker. Her father loved her anyway." That's what really made me cry. That Dad loved me anyway.

I glanced across the hall and found Mum again. At least I still had her. She was speaking with an old neighbour of ours. Mr. Harris is a deeply loathsome man, but she greeted him with the same poise and apparent goodwill she showed everyone else. She didn't even wince at his breath, which was as notoriously foul as his politics.

I had no idea how she managed to do it, but I certainly didn't think of it as an act. At least not yet.

PETRA

As a teenager, Petra had been a very good ice dancer. Not national-level good, but close. When she wasn't at school, she was at the rink. She practiced until her feet bled, her quads ached, and she could perform every jump, spin, and forward-inside death spiral effortlessly. Put in enough hours, and it became almost like flying. Fluid and joyful. The audience had no idea how hard she'd worked to make it look that easy.

Gary Schneider was offering his condolences when she realized that's what this reminded her of. Ice dancing. Why had she been dreading the funeral? What had she been so afraid of? That she'd mess up? Give something away? This was a breeze. She'd practiced her whole married life for it. "Now enjoy it," she remembered her coach saying as she stepped onto the ice to compete. "You deserve it."

So she did. She relaxed her shoulders and let muscle memory do the rest.

"Petra." Gary looked her dead in the eye. "Promise you'll call if you ever need anything. Anything at all. Okay?"

She arranged her mouth into an appreciative frown and squeezed his arms in thanks. His biceps were deliciously meaty. *Life,* she thought. She resisted the urge to throw herself into them. She had to hold back, just a little while longer. She was almost there. She hoped life would wait for her.

She turned to the next person in line and presented her best funeral smile.

The woman was short and thin and wearing a purple crimplene dress. Her no-nonsense hair was white, and her face so deeply wrinkled, that Petra didn't recognize her at first. Last time she'd seen Sharon, her hair was an extravagant tangle of dark curls and she'd had the pale, flawless skin of a silent movie star.

"I hope you don't mind me coming. When I heard about Malcolm. Oh, honey—what can I say? I'm just heartbroken."

Petra took in the Sears-era dress, the sensible shoes, the unforgiving lines across Sharon's cheap trifocals.

She's not even trying. That's what hit her first. *Sharon's just given up. Thrown in the towel.*

Petra had never had that option. She'd had to get up every morning, put on her face, put on her self, carry on. But Sharon seemed to feel she'd gotten a pass. Like her tragedy somehow trumped Petra's. *Poor thing,* Petra imagined concerned friends saying, *let me do that for you.* Sharon, the victim, taking it as her due.

Petra could have slapped her.

But then she recalled the look of love she'd had to manufacture for her teenage skating partner. Darrell was arrogant, acned, and deeply in lust with the guy who drove the Zamboni, but Petra's look had been so convincing people often assumed they were dating off-ice. It was all in the body language: the angle of the chin, a softness in the shoulders, an openness to the eyes.

She turned it on now and listened.

"Malcolm meant the world to me. And now it's too late. I missed my chance to make amends. I don't want to miss the chance with us, too, Petra. Couldn't we...couldn't we try and—" Sharon picked at her collar, moving her lips to say more, but tears overwhelmed her.

Petra could see how much pain Sharon was in. Could actually feel it in her own body. Petra's heart swelled, crowding out her lungs, her tongue, her resolve. She'd loved this person once. They'd been family. She knew how much Sharon had suffered and how much courage it must have taken for her to show up here after everything that had been said and done.

And not done. That was the worst part.

Petra couldn't bear it any longer. She pulled Sharon into a hug. Ken Arnold was standing only a few feet away, waiting to give his condolences. He no doubt could see the sobs racking Sharon's puny frame. He never would have guessed she'd been a beauty once.

Petra rubbed Sharon's back and whispered into her ear, "Get the fuck out of here before I drag you out myself."

She wasn't going to be sucked down into that cesspool again. Malcolm was dead. Petra was finally free.

She deserved this.

NINA

A tearful ex-con gave me a truly exhaustive account of a public housing project he'd worked on with Dad, then mercifully said his goodbyes. Clary and Libby were busy talking to Mrs. Rhinehart, a teacher we'd all had at The Academy. I scanned the hall and spotted Jesse.

I remembered Wayne on the phone asking for *my man* and had to bite my lip to keep from smiling. "Man" was such a hammer of a word. Jesse was more of a hand-cranked eggbeater. A charmingly inefficient maker of whipped cream and meringue, not roofs and sheds. I had a roof. Who needs a shed?

He was wearing one of Don's old suits and holding Arlo. Krish, meanwhile, had a glass of wine in one hand and a scallop kebab in the other. I wondered why Krish was getting to eat and drink while my guy got stuck looking after his baby.

A couple of jellyfish, I thought.

That's what Clary had called us once. She'd been on the deck, talking to Dad about our lack of direction. It was early morning. She'd just come back from some ridiculously long run. Jess and I were still lolling in bed, awake if barely. (We were on holiday. No one but ourselves to wash and change and feed that day. Why get up?) Her words buzzed in through our open window like hornets, insistent and bloodthirsty, but Dad just murmured, "Oh, now, Clara. They might not be as driven as you, but jellyfish? Really, sweetheart?" Jesse and I laughed into our pillows.

We started to refer to each other that way. *Coupla jellyfish.* We even thought about getting matching tattoos—two wobbly red hearts trailing flagella—but we never got around to it.

Another thing we never got around to. The tennis court, the tattoos, life.

Mrs. Rhinehart kissed my sisters, then moved on to me. She hadn't changed much. Her face was still pretty and animated, although not as defined as it had once been. It was as if she'd accidentally left it out on the porch all winter.

She asked what I was up to. She did her best to conceal her disappointment at the flatlining of one of her most promising students, then launched into some close-talk about how much she'd enjoyed Dad.

"The school would never have gotten the new wing built without him leading the charge. But he got the job done—on time, on budget, and cheerfully too! We all just adored the man."

For some reason, that undid me. I let out a loud sob. She hugged me for an admirably long time, then stepped back and squeegeed the tears off my cheeks with her thumbs.

"He led a good life, Nina. You can take comfort in that. He really did, honey."

She patted my face and left. I cried some more. Not, I realized with horror, over my father and his life but over myself and mine. The life I wasn't living. The one I might never get around to, given the way things were going. I hoped nobody was counting on me to get their new wing built.

I stood there in the inoffensive navy blue dress Don had bankrolled so I'd have something appropriate to wear to his friends' funerals and dabbed at my eyes with the pulpy remains of a tissue.

Lib put her arm around my shoulder and cooed, "Neens. Why don't you go and tidy yourself up?"

I headed to the washroom. People touched my arm on the way past and gave me sympathetic pouts I didn't deserve. I couldn't even do grief right.

I peed. I splashed water on my face. I reapplied my lipstick—my usual one, my own non-colour—and wondered if I shouldn't try something different too. The single step that starts the journey. Maybe all it takes is a new shade.

By the time I'd cleaned myself up, the crowd was thinning out. In the lobby, I stopped and watched a Malcolm Fforde retrospective with Dave and Andrea Marcoux, a couple our parents occasionally golfed with.

The slideshow hit all the highlights. Dad in spandex, biting medals from his various Gran Fondos. Walking Clary down the aisle. Travelling with Mum to Sweden, Australia, Brazil. Dressed up as Dorothy on Halloween with a tiny Scarecrow, Tin Man, and Lion hanging off his legs.

"Oh, my," Andrea said when their wedding photo popped up. "Look how plump Malcolm used to be." We all laughed.

"Wouldn't have recognized him," Dave said. "The man's been a goddamn greyhound long as I've known him."

"But your mother!" Andrea shook her head, smiling. "Wasn't she adorable?"

Mum's mouth was open wide in delight. Her wedding dress was white and lacy but super-short and way off the shoulder. You could practically see the sparks flying off her. Dad gazed at her in adoration.

"Whoa," Dave said. "Did Malcolm ever marry up."

Andrea slapped his arm.

He went, "What?" Then, "Oh. God. Sorry, Nina." He'd forgotten he was talking about a dead man.

"Dave. Please! Dad said it all the time." I jerked my head toward the hall. "I should go. My sisters will dock my pay if I'm not back soon. Say hi to Melanie for me." Their daughter and I had spent a summer working at the golf course canteen. Back then, Mel couldn't reliably make change from a twenty. Now she was a cardiologist. What had she figured out that I hadn't?

Andrea squeezed my hand. "It's a sad, sad day, sweetheart. But this too shall pass."

"I know," I lied.

I left them and grabbed a glass of white from the nearest server. I thought of Dad on his wedding day. Years younger than me but with a real job, babies on the horizon, a house. What a colossal waste of space I'd turned out to be.

"Life is fleeting," Don would say, and I'd think, *Really?* He'd been around for almost a century. That never sounded very fleeting to me.

But Dad dying—happily pumping up a hill one minute, then gone the next—put a whole new spin on it. Life could be all over in an instant. I was thirty-six. Time I got off my rapidly sagging ass.

I downed my drink and got another. Jess saw me standing alone and came to join me.

We bumped elbows. "You look good in that suit," I said.

"I know. Makes me look like I actually have shoulders." He took a step back and gave me the once-over. "You look good in that dress."

"I know. Makes me look like I actually have a career."

"High-powered position working with the elderly. That's what I'm seeing." He mouthed, *Ver-y sex-y.*

"This our version of role-playing? Getting all hot and bothered by putting on big-people clothes?"

"Middle-management porn."

"Our own sub-genre."

"Yeah. Who says we've never done anything!" He laced his fingers through mine. Warm, slightly sticky fingers. It was like the laying on of hands. He'd always had that effect on me.

"You lost Arlo." I took a drink of wine. It was a pretty nice Sauv Blanc for a funeral. Tea or sherry in the church hall was the best I could expect with Don's friends.

"Not lost. Wrenched from my arms! These middle-aged women have serious bloodlust for the babies. Like something from a David Attenborough documentary. Predators of the High-End Suburbs. I think Deb Dudek has him now."

"What about you?"

"They managed to keep their hands off me, though they did like the suit."

"I mean, baby-lust-wise. How you doing in that regard?"

"Whoa. Surprise question."

He waved at a couple who was leaving. "C'mon." I elbowed him. "Babies, how do you feel about them?"

"Generally positive." As in *who wouldn't be?*

"Do you want them?"

"*You* were the one who didn't want them."

"No I wasn't."

"Okay. Didn't want them *yet*. You said you wanted to get your career established first. Write that novel. Start that heritage food emporium. Et cetera. Et cetera."

"And how's that going for me?"

"Hey, it's not the destination. It's the journey."

"Can it be called a journey if we've been at an utter standstill. For *years*?" I thought of an aspic recipe I'd found in one of Ruth's cookbooks. Hunks of greying meat suspended in gelatin. Almost too on the nose.

"So what?" Jesse slipped his arm around my waist. "There's no one I'd rather stand still with."

"Awwww," I went, very faux.

"Plus, Don's our baby."

"You know how much he'd hate to hear you say that?" I took a swig of wine to keep my heart from breaking.

"Yeah. I hate myself for even thinking it. I just mean he takes up a lot of our time and our love. Plus, I'm not sure my gag reflex could survive changing diapers at both ends of the life cycle."

I sighed. Seven years ago, we'd thought, Professor Meisner's great, it's free room and board and it'll be a chance for us to concentrate on our manuscripts/theses/business plans, before we burst forth onto the world stage to universal acclaim. We were thinking a year. Two, tops. "It was only supposed to be short-term."

"He decided to live a little longer than planned." Jesse shrugged like The Pink Panther. "Whaddya going to do?"

I had a sudden memory of driving to the regional science fair with Dad. I wasn't a science kid, but I'd worked really hard on my presentation. (*Genes Make the Dog: Growing a Pugglier Pug!*) It was snowing. We got stuck. My presentation! The ticking clock. We were never going to make it. Dad opened the trunk and got out the sand, the salt, the shovel. He shoved the driver's seat forward, put me at the wheel, then he pushed and pushed and pushed until the car lurched free. He jumped back in and gunned it, his shiny bald head dripping with sweat, his grey trousers pompommed with slush, his face beaming. When we got to the school, he ran in ahead of me, waving my presentation and hollering, "Nina Fforde! Nina Fforde!" so the judges would know we'd made it in time.

Whaddya going to do?

You just do what you have to do, lambchop. The number of times I'd heard him say that. It takes on a whole new significance, of course, knowing what we know now about our parents' lives, but back then I just thought he was being a good dad. The best.

"You okay?" Jesse said.

"I need another glass of wine." I handed him the empty.

"*Need?*"

I shrugged.

"I shouldn't enable you." He kissed my forehead. "But I shall."

Jesse wasn't gone a minute before a large woman bustled up to me.

"You must be Nina," she said.

"I am." I found a smile. "And you are...?"

"Bonnie Peters." She had an odd voice. High and slightly strangulated as if she was trying not to sneeze. "Devastated to have missed the funeral. Had a meeting I absolutely could not escape."

There was a sort of appealing dishevellment about her. She wore a blocky blue dress, big wooden beads, and enormous statement glasses I suspected were left over from the last time they'd been in style. Her burgundy lipstick was a nice contrast to her grey hair, although she'd had a little trouble staying within the lines.

My first thought was she must be one of Dad's clients. He'd worked on the new Arts Centre. Professor on the design committee, maybe. She gave off that energy.

"What a mensch Mac was." She leaned in close, her lips wriggling as if she was remembering something slightly naughty. "And a ton of fun too!"

"Aw. Thank you." I smiled, despite feeling slightly weirded out by her enthusiasm. Dad was a stellar human being but hardly the life of the party. Plus, nobody ever called him Mac. I rethought the client thing.

"How'd you know my father?"

"Petra and I were university roommates."

"Really?" She had my full attention now. Mum and Dad had never regaled us with stories of their youth. They were both "forward-thinking." That was how The Dude had described Dad in his eulogy. He no doubt meant it in regard to structural engineering, but it was true in his personal life too. Yesterday was of no interest to either of my parents.

In fact, yesterday was off-limits. I don't remember any specific prohibition against it, but we girls somehow knew not to inquire into their past. It would have felt a little like asking about their bowel movements. *Let's talk about something else, shall we?* I wasn't going to miss this opportunity to find out more.

"Wow," I said "So you were at U of T together."

"No. McMaster."

We looked at each other quizzically.

Mum had gone to the University of Toronto. I knew that for sure. We'd talked about it when I was trying to decide on a school myself. She thought I'd like living in the big city, but I wanted something smaller. Leaving Lib was going to be challenge enough.

Bonnie's dishevellment suddenly seemed less charming and more pathological.

"My mistake!" I touched my forehead. "Long day." Don didn't have Alzheimer's—"still sharp as a tack"—but we'd prepared for it. Jesse and I had taken a course at the local hospital. Don't fight the delusions, they'd told us. Embrace your loved one's world view, regardless of how bizarre it might be. "Have you kept in touch?"

"Not as much as I'd like. Emails, the occasional catch-up call but, you know. Different cities. Busy lives. We haven't seen each other in years. I just happened to be in town for a conference and saw the obit in the paper." She sniffed loudly. "Oh, sorry. Allergies."

She started digging in her enormous straw bag. "All the perfumes in here. People are so odd about their natural smells, don't you think? Dousing themselves in chemicals rather than—God forbid!—letting someone in on the shameful secret that they're human. I'd take a whiff of good old unwashed crotch over some toxic body spray any day."

By now, I was thinking nutcase. Dad had been on the board of St. Alban's for decades. (Chair. Head of the Building committee. Official timekeeper of the Sunday school three-legged race.) The church had an outreach program for the mentally ill. I took in the size of Bonnie's purse and figured that was the connection. You only needed a bag that big if you're dragging around all your worldly possessions.

"Ah. There." She pulled out a hankie and swabbed her nose. "Yes, Petra and I were at med school together."

"Med school?" *Whoa. Go big or go home. So Mum's a doctor now? Of what? Feng shui?*

"Met on our first day and were joined at the hip from then on. In fact, I was with her when she first spotted Mac." Bonnie's mouth curled into a tight, delighted U. "She took one look at your father letting loose on the dance floor and said, 'I have to have him.' And Petra being Petra, of course, she got him."

I pressed my tongue hard against the roof of my mouth to keep from laughing. Dad letting loose on the dance floor? There's one good reason not to think about the past.

"Unfortunately, that was just before Petra and I were heading off to Congo—"

"Congo?" *Oh, dear. Here we go.*

Bonnie babbled on about derring-do in the jungle. An Ebola outbreak. Men with guns. Wild rides in ancient Jeeps. I was pretty sure I'd seen the same movie. I was hoping my sisters would get back before she finished—this was excellent material—but Bonnie suddenly stopped and said, "Oh. She's free!"

I turned and saw Mum waving goodbye to the Riordans. Bonnie squeezed my elbow. "Better grab her while I can. Sorry I didn't get to meet the others. Whirlwind trip! Got a plane to catch."

She lumbered away. Her ankles spilled heavily over the top of her shoes. I remembered Dad talking about the problems homeless people have with their legs. Always on their feet, nowhere to sit. Everything the woman said may have been nonsense, but I was moved by the effort she must have made to get here. If nothing else, her affection for Dad was real.

She called out, "Pet!" and waved. Mum looked up, a startled half-smile on her face. I wondered if I should step in. Deflect Bonnie somehow. Mum was no doubt exhausted after playing mourner-in-chief all day. The last thing she needed was to deal with a crazy person.

But then I thought no. I'd just make it worse. Jackie O was a pro. I knew she'd handle it with her usual poise.

But she didn't.

Mum saw Bonnie and she ran to her. Dropped her jaw and ran, like a woman sprinting wide-armed to a grandchild in the airport arrival lounge. They hugged. Squeezed each other hard. Stepped away. Did the whole little dance again.

I couldn't process what I was seeing. Mum was holding Bonnie's face in both hands, and they were laughing. Gleefully. Unabashedly. Two twelve-year-olds and a fart joke.

It wasn't right.

It wasn't right for my mother to do that, not at Dad's funeral.

Not when she'd never laughed like that with us.

PETRA

Malcolm's response to tragedy had been to lose weight and find God. Petra had been fine with the weight loss—by his thirties, Malcolm's exuberant appetite for life had started to show around his middle—but she could never stomach the God thing. Malcolm was a smart man. How could he believe that garbage? Especially after what they'd been through.

She remembered screaming at him—this is when she still did that sort of thing—"God treats us like shit, but we're supposed to say thanks? Like, *hit us again, Lord, because we fucking adore Thee?* What's the matter with you?"

Malcolm gazed back benevolently and started talking about divine mercy.

That did it. Petra said a few truly unforgivable things about the size of his balls, then slammed the door and took off. They were done.

He found her a couple hours later and brought her home. Three little kids. A broken heart. What choice did she have?

She'd shut her mouth but her opinion about religion never changed. She bowed her head reverently enough at the funeral, but that was simple ice dancing. Paint a story for your audience. Make them believe. She could do that.

At least until Sharon had shown up. Petra probably hadn't handled it as well as she could have but oh, well. She'd said what she'd said. Ken Arnold, one of Malcolm's golf buddies, had graciously led Sharon outside and got her a cab. "Malcolm's sister-in-law," Petra whispered sadly to people waiting in line. The poor woman was understandably upset.

Wayne Dudek had come by with a glass of wine—"Drink up, sweetheart. Doctor's orders"—but Petra doubted anyone else had noticed her shaking. She'd smiled as the Riordans paid their respects, murmured the right things back, but all she could think was *Sharon.*

Did Petra really need some ghost from her past showing up now? Was that fair? Hadn't she done her time? She was tough and proud of it but seeing the person largely responsible for destroying her life had pushed her dangerously close to the breaking point.

And then, out of the blue, Bonnie appeared.

Bonnie, who Petra hadn't seen in years. Bonnie, who somehow always knew when Petra needed her and what to do.

Her dearest friend.

Her only friend.

Thank God, Petra thought, then ran into her arms.

NINA

"Excuse me? Miss?"

Someone was trying to get my attention. I pulled my eyes away from Mum and Bonnie's little lovefest to see an older man standing in front of me, not quite smiling.

He was trim, and his suit and haircut were expensive, but there was something crude about his face. A character actor's face. Small-mouthed and pouchy.

He cleared his throat and introduced himself. "Keith Osterlich."

I leaned in. "I'm sorry. Keith...?"

"Osterlich."

He looked slightly annoyed that I didn't immediately drop to a deep curtsy. At the time, though, I had no idea who he was and I was too tired to care. I'd spent a day smiling dry-toothedly at people I didn't know.

Plus, who the hell did he think he was?

"Are you a colleague of Dad's?" I at least had to be polite.

"Actually, Malcolm restored a heritage building for me."

"Interesting." *So he worked* for *you, not* with *you. Thanks for clarifying.*

"I was impressed with his attention to detail. An excellent engineer. No complaints at all. I'm sorry to lose him." And then, almost as an afterthought, "You must be too."

"Yes. We—"

"Right. Well, my deepest sympathies." He nodded, Prussian officer–style, then strode off, duty done. I almost made a face behind his back, before remembering this wasn't junior high. (Alcohol never brought out the best in me.)

I shook a few more hands, heard a few more anecdotes, and then the reception was over. It was after seven. In the back of the hall, Clary was sitting on a folding chair, drinking wine and nursing Arlo. Krish was on the floor beside her, also drinking wine, his back against the wall, black dress shoes forming neatly pointed serifs at the end of his slim outstretched legs. Jesse and Lib were circling a table, picking through the scraps of hors d'oeuvres left out on large silver trays. Jesse had forgotten to bring me my wine. Probably just as well.

I looked across to see what Mum was doing. She was standing alone, adjusting her cuffs, dusting off her shoulders, very much her old self again. Maybe the Bonnie thing had been nothing. Mum just mirroring another person's behaviour to make them feel comfortable. The perfect hostess.

I headed over. "You survived all right?"

She tipped back her neck and brushed hair off her forehead. I noticed a smear of Bonnie's burgundy lipstick by her ear. "Yes, darling. Of course. It was actually kind of wonderful, don't you think? Everyone saying all those nice things about your father? People really were so very, very fond of him."

"I met Bonnie," I said because, frankly, that passionate little PDA wasn't nothing and I knew it.

"Bonnie?" she said. A flicker of what may have been panic.

Or maybe confusion. Mum had talked to a lot of people that afternoon. Could have been more than one Bonnie. I gave her the benefit of the doubt. "Yeah," I said. "Bonnie Peters."

A server bustled by with a tray of empties. Mum waved at him like she was hailing the last cab out of war-torn Paris. "Any of those available?"

"Mother. You are not drinking other people's slops."

"I've been on my feet all day. I don't care who had a go at it first."

The server, a balding guy with a tattooed vine curling out of his collar, proffered his tray with a bow. "I just happen to have a lovely untouched Sauvignon Blanc with your name on it." No doubt an out-of-work actor. My age and apparently doing no better. Maybe worse. I smiled at him.

"Oh, thank goodness." Mum plucked up the glass and took a swig. She'd never been a swigger, a gulper, a wolfer-down of drink or food or life. But, hey, *Dad,* I told myself. She was suddenly teetering on the edge of a very deep abyss. Sipping wasn't going to soften the fall.

"Delicious. Sorry, Nina. You were saying?"

"Bonnie Peters."

"Who?...Oh, right. Bonnie. Such a doll. Haven't seen her in ages."

"She said you went to med school together."

Mum swivelled her neck back, then kind of slumped forward. "She did? Oh, for heaven's sake. Why would she say that?" She shook her head. I felt better. *Nutcase,* just like I'd figured.

"Have you eaten?" Mum said.

"The odd morsel."

She took my arm. "Come. I have to get something into me before I expire." We joined the others to graze on cold kebabs and deconstructed "sliders," then we headed home, too exhausted even to be sad anymore.

By the time I thought of Bonnie Peters again, I'd forgotten her name.

GORD

Gord was on automatic. He was tired and jet-lagged and wary about letting himself look too closely at what he'd come here to do. He got off the elevator and walked down the dim hall until he found the apartment. He keyed in the access code and opened the door. A blast of sunlight hit him in the face. Gord covered his eyes with his elbow and groaned. He was reminded of the many times he'd been shaken awake after a lot of drinking and a little sleep. He coughed out a laugh. Small mercies. That was one part of his old life he didn't miss. He blinked the world back into focus and went inside.

The apartment looked exactly like the photos in the AirBnB listing. Accent wall, big-box décor. A small but superficially high-end kitchen, open to the living room. A balcony with—from a certain angle at least—the promised lakeview. The place was sparkling clean, no doubt perfectly comfortable, and totally devoid of character. He hadn't been prepared for how much it would depress him.

He dropped his backpack onto the linen-look couch, knocking one of the throw pillows onto the floor. *BE GRATEFUL* was printed on it in pale blue script.

A tiny mushroom cloud erupted in Gord's head.

A pillow telling him how to feel.

A pillow—not to sleep on, not to cradle the head of a dying man—but to throw out of the goddamn way when you wanted to sit.

Millions of kids are hungry, cold, and abandoned, but you know what we need? A decorative pillow.

He rubbed his hand over his mouth, his heart pounding, his muscles twitchy, his whole body on high alert. Three years working at the orphanage had convinced him he was past all that, but he knew the signs. He pulled his St. Jude medal out from under his T-shirt, kissed it, then dropped to the floor and started doing push-ups. He couldn't let the beast out yet. He'd be needing it later. His anger was too valuable to waste on throw pillows.

And, anyway, who was he kidding? Hypocritical asshole. He'd had his share of throw pillows in his day.

He made himself do a hundred push-ups, then stood up, wiping the sweat off his bristly scalp. He'd come home for one thing—justice—and that was going to take every second he had left. He owed it to his two dead boys.

He collected the pillows and put them neatly in the hall closet. Other people had made them. Maybe even delighted in them. He would treat them with respect.

There was a bottle of wine and a welcome note from the host propped on the kitchen counter. Gord put the card into the recycling bin and opened the wine. A Malbec. He inhaled deeply. It was so thick and jammy he could almost taste it. He and Aziza had spent their honeymoon in Argentina. A week hiking in Patagonia, a week refuelling in Mendoza. Argentine Malbec was his favourite wine. It could be absolute cat piss and it would still be his favourite wine. Those weeks were sacrosanct.

He poured the Malbec down the drain, then leaned his hands on the counter and stared into the sink. The high arc of the black matte faucet, the multi-function nozzle, the ergonomic handle. He was suddenly hyperaware of how vulnerable he was here. Mali had been easy. There'd been nothing there to spur his memories, cloud his head, sweet talk him away from the edge. Alone, unmedicated, his brain clear and sharp, he'd finally been able to see what he had to do. It scared the shit out of him, but he knew the rightness of it. The honour in it.

That made him think of his grandfather and, despite everything, he smiled. Good old Bix. Half-cut and crotchety, on his way out, but more man than Gord would ever be.

Ernest (Bix) Bickerton had been in Bomber Command, not an ideal situation if you planned on living past twenty, especially if you found yourself crammed into a glass bubble at the arse-end of a Lancaster with a gun in your hands.

"Were you scared?" Gord had asked him once. He was twelve or thirteen at the time, with a school project on World War II to do.

"Goddamn right I was. If I hadn't been scared, I'd have been a goddamn idiot." Bix took a drag on his cigarette and pointed at Gord with two yellowed fingers. "And I'm no idiot. Write that down."

Gord rinsed out the bottle. He realized scared made sense in his present circumstances too. He apologized to the universe for the waste of water (and wine), then threw the bottle into the recycling bin.

His host had also generously provided cheese and crackers. Gord put the cheese in the fridge, then made the practical decision not to check the label to see if any animals had been harmed in the production of the crackers. He hadn't eaten in hours. He took the box into the living room for dinner.

He sat on the couch, took out his laptop, and got to work.

Gord didn't have much good to say about his time practicing law, but it hadn't been a total waste. It taught him to do his research. It taught him not to be cowed by an expensive suit. (They're usually empty.) And it taught him you don't have to be right to win. You just have to *sound* right.

Or maybe it was Bix who'd taught him that. Gord chuckled. Of course it was Bix.

Gord tore open the box of crackers and stacked a thumb's length of rosemary thins on the coffee table. He remembered something else his grandfather had said. He'd just finished describing a nighttime raid on Essen.

"Put this down." He motioned at Gord to open his scribbler again. "Say I wasn't scared of dying. I was scared of dying *in vain.* You know what that means? It means 'for shit'—although if your mother asks, I said 'for nothing.' Guys I knew over there got drunk and spun out on their motorbikes or died because their pilot hadn't learned to fly, or died of the flu just like they coulda done if they'd never left their nice little bed back home in Debert. One poor sucker I knew got dysentery and shat himself to death. *That's* what I was scared of. Croaking before I'd made my life count. If I died in my turret taking down a Jerry, at least I knew, by Jesus, I'd gone out doing what I was supposed to do."

And then Bix had cleared his throat, and his rheumy, red-rimmed eyes filled up, and he poured himself another tumbler of rye. By the time he'd wiped his mouth on the back of his hand, he was Bix again, tough as nails, taking no shit. He told Gord not to slam the door on his way out.

A few years later, Bix slipped away, slumped in his leatherette La-Z-Boy, mouth open and pants pissed, The Weather Channel chattering away in the background, his glory days long behind him. His wartime service took up just a single line in his obit, less space than they'd given the job at the dockyard he'd hated for thirty-seven years.

Gord wasn't going to die in vain. He owed it to Bix. He owed it to his boys.

He opened his laptop and clicked on the file marked *Keith Osterlich.*

PETRA

Petra stubbed out her cigarette on a rock and flicked it into the pond. This was torture.

Worse than pregnancy, she thought. A woman can stand anything until her due date—the nausea, the fatigue, the imposed sobriety—but one day over and it's unbearable.

That's how she felt. Like she'd gone full-term, taken all her vitamins, choked down all her calcium, done her goddamn Kegels until her labia were toned enough to sing the national anthem. She'd done everything she was supposed to do. She couldn't take a second more.

She loved her daughters—her smart, beautiful, funny daughters—but when in hell were they leaving? She had places to go, people to see, forty-plus years to make up for. The funeral was over, the body disposed of, everything that needed to be said had been said. Why was nobody packing their bags?

"I'm going to lose my mind," she said out loud. "Lose it." She checked over her shoulder, despite knowing the girls were asleep, the backyard empty. If they heard her talking to herself, she'd never shake them. She couldn't crack now.

She dipped her toes in the silky water and brought her emotional temperature down a few degrees.

They were concerned about her, that's all. She should congratulate herself! Proof she'd done a good job. (She *and Malcolm* had done a good job. He was an excellent father. Credit where credit's due.) And wasn't that the whole point of this little charade? Making sure her kids were okay?

She rolled up her pantlegs and dangled her legs a little deeper in the water.

They were good girls. They were only trying to help.

Okay, but sorry. She didn't want their help.

Anybody's help. Anybody's anything. Not their casseroles. Not their condolences. Not their goddamn amends. Petra just wanted everyone to get the fuck out of her way.

She lit another cigarette. She'd never really liked smoking, but she did like the look. She remembered the tough girls at school, tilting their heads back on the inhale, exhaling through half-open mouths, then scraping shreds of tobacco off their tongues with long frosted nails. So bad. So sexy. The boys practically wet themselves. Petra had been too much of a goody-goody back then to give it a try, but everything was on the table now. Carte blanche. No holds barred. The world was finally her goddamn oyster. She wondered if you could still buy unfiltered cigarettes or if she'd have to roll her own.

She attempted a smoke ring and resolved to ask her daughters to leave. They'd protest—she had to be prepared for that—but secretly they'd be relieved. They had their own lives. Staying here wasn't making anyone happy.

She put her feet on the rock and rested her chin on her knees. She was badly in need of a pedicure. Her face had held up okay, all things considered, but her callouses betrayed her. These were old-people feet. *The Podiatry of Dorian Grey.* She snorted out a little laugh. Bonnie would love that one.

She took another drag. Who was she kidding? She was never going to tell the girls to leave. They were grieving. She kept forgetting this was supposed to be a sad time. Being home was good for them. They needed each other. They may even have needed her, or at least the illusion of helping her. Having a purpose can make any pain almost bearable. Petra knew that first-hand. They wouldn't be here forever.

Fine. She'd just have to keep busy until then.

Her first baby had been nine days late. It hadn't killed her.

She tilted back her head and inhaled.

AL-HADDAD

Detective Ryan Al-Haddad had driven way the hell out to Murchyville for nothing. He'd gone to interview associates of a suspected drug dealer, but Google had never heard of the dirt road he was looking for and neither, conveniently, had any of the locals. The associates weren't answering their phones. It was pissing him off.

He tapped the steering wheel of his unmarked car and considered the tiny purple house across the road. The paint was peeling, and one windowpane was more duct-tape than glass, but someone had gone to the trouble of planting pansies in a broken toilet in the front yard. An act of civic pride. A sign they might have a more favourable opinion of the constabulary than their neighbours? He decided to give it one last try. He got out of his car, reached over the chain link fence to open the latch, and a massive Rottweiler charged at him, barking and snarling. A canine meth head.

Al-Haddad quickly closed the latch, got back in his car, and headed home. Freaked out, frustrated, but alive. To hell with the drug dealer.

Murchyville was forty-five minutes behind him before he noticed it was actually a nice day. Hot but not scorching. Sunny. A light breeze. His running gear was in the trunk. He wasn't far from Sawyer's Beach. He could squeeze in a half-hour run, shower in the changing room, and be back in the office by one. Clear his mind. Salvage the day. Maybe even make some goddamn progress on something for a change.

He took the next exit onto Highway 3 and felt his spirits rise. Even the sudden clog of traffic didn't bother him. Happy people heading to the beach! Some part of his brain started thinking he had a day off.

He'd just passed the sign for Larry's Truck Stop when it hit him.

Highway 3. That case Sarge had dumped on him a few days earlier.

Bicycle accident.

Weird name.

Al-Haddad had read the file, but it took him a few seconds to retrieve the details. The hellhound had shaken him up.

Fforde. That was it.

He pictured the extra f and the e. Fuh-for-day. *Well, excuse me.* The affectation annoyed him.

Or maybe he was just annoyed because he knew his run wasn't going to happen now. Sarge had asked him to make the case a priority. Al-Haddad was right here. He was obviously going to check out the scene, go back to the office, call a few people, write up his notes, and miss out on another day's exercise. No wonder Alex had lost interest in sex. Al-Haddad was turning into a dough ball.

He located the area where the body had been found, about twenty metres past the crest of a long hill. He pulled onto the narrow shoulder, slowing traffic. Lots of honking and middle fingers. So much for happy people. He had to wait until an older couple took mercy on him and stopped before he could even get out of his car.

He ran his hand over the dent in the guardrail. Red bike paint from Fforde's bike was still embedded in the silver metal. Clearly a hard hit. Looking up the steep hill, he wasn't surprised. This would be a treacherous descent, especially with all the gravel scattered across the asphalt. There must have been a little spill. He kicked some pebbles onto the shoulder and clicked his tongue. All credit to the old guys still on the road, but how many seventy-somethings really have the strength or reflexes to react fast in bad conditions? This wouldn't be the first death by delusion he'd heard of.

He stepped over the guardrail, waded through a thicket of wild rosebushes, and shuffled down a small embankment to the shallow stream where Fforde had been found face down. He crouched to check the depth of the water with his fingers. Maybe three inches. Not much to drown in, but with a broken neck, that's all it would take. The victim wouldn't have been able to lift his head. With any luck, the poor bugger had been unconscious and missed the worst of it.

The coroner put Fforde's death at around noon, but the body wasn't found until four. Reading the file, the time it took to make the discovery had bothered Al-Haddad, but from his current vantage point, it made perfect sense.

The rosebushes.

The Department of Transportation pruned them annually but, for some reason, they'd obviously missed this stretch of road. The roses only came to Al-Haddad's knees but with the ditch, that could easily be high enough to obscure a body.

A weekend warrior going too fast loses control, hits a guardrail, and lands face down in a stream, hidden from passing cars by bushes. Al-Haddad rubbed the back of his neck. That tracked.

He climbed over the guardrail, feeling relatively certain he could offer the wealthy widow closure. No run, but his day hadn't turned out to be a total writeoff. He stood on the shoulder and waited for a break in traffic.

A tour bus gave him a little toot. Al-Haddad waved thank-you and hurried into the driver's seat.

The car was scorching. He rolled down the window, hoping to get back a little of that day-off feeling, but something wasn't sitting right.

The Number 3 is a narrow two-lane secondary highway and the only road to Sawyer's Beach. On the day Fforde died—a hot, sunny Sunday in July—it would have been packed with cars. Al-Haddad's theory explained how people had missed the body. But how had they missed the accident?

A six-foot-tall man in neon spandex on a bright red bike flipping over a guardrail.

How *could* they have missed it?

He idled on the shoulder for five minutes before a minivan let him out. He drove back to the city still mulling that question over.

NINA

The day after the funeral, Mum cleared out Dad's closet.

My sisters and I were downstairs in the kitchen. The morning sun made hot white rhomboids on the floor. Dogwoods showed off in the backyard. A pair of doves cooed. I felt incongruously happy. My heart may have been broken, but we were together.

I'd just warmed up some pastries a neighbour had dropped off. Clary was stretched out in the window seat, nursing Arlo. She took him off her breast with a pop and draped his limp body over her shoulder. Something thumped overhead. We looked at the ceiling in unison.

"She's really going at it," Lib said.

"No kidding." Clary walked over to the table, pulled a chair out with her foot, and sat down beside me. She was wearing a pair of Krish's boxers which gaped widely at the fly. She'd left her bra open for her nipples to air-dry. It seemed at once like any other day at home with my sisters and a creepy dream about it. "A little hasty, don't you think?"

I was trying not to. Jesse's father, The Right Reverend Ed Whynacht, had called the night before to check in. "People grieve in lots of different ways," he'd said in the course of a long, enlightening conversation. "Just relax and let the process do its thing. There's a beauty to it. An at times terrible beauty, but a beauty, nonetheless. You'll all get where you need to go if you let it."

That's why I said "No" to Clary now. "Mum's just being practical. No point hanging onto his clothes. It's not as if he's coming back."

Lib went, "Geez, Nina," as in *did you have to?* She put two cappuccinos on the table, took Arlo from Clary, and sat down herself. "But I agree, keeping busy is good for Mum. Takes her mind off the grief." She cupped the baby's bottom in one hand and patted a burp out of him with the other.

Clary took a sip and sighed. "Oh, my God, Lib. You are *wasting* your talents moulding young minds. This is seriously the best cappuccino I've ever had. Don't ever leave me." She ran her fingers through Libby's hair. "Or you," she said, doing the same to me.

A joke at first, then not. Clary's eyes went glassy. She pulled us together hard. She smelled of coffee and sweat and something sour which I presumed was baby-related. "I mean it. *Never.*" The sudden emphasis made Arlo cry. Lib jiggled him.

Clary let go. We pulled apart, all on the verge of tears again.

"I don't know what I'd do if something happened to you guys. But I'll tell you one thing." Clary wagged her spoon at us. "I sure as hell wouldn't be purging you from my life the day after we buried you."

Lib laid Arlo on the kitchen table to check his diaper. His little thigh was curved and plump, a Pillsbury Crescent Roll on the rise. "Mum is not *purging* Dad," she said lightly, as if it was almost too ridiculous to comment on.

Clary raised her eyebrows. "The sun has just peeked over the horizon, and she's already got five boxes ready for the St. Alban's Jumble Sale. But purging? Heavens, no."

I shrugged. "She was up early." I'd staggered down the hall to pee at around four and seen her sitting by the pond again, smoking. (I'd never known her to smoke. I was trying not to let this bother me either.) "She and Dad always said they needed to do a big clean-out. It's probably just stuff they'd planned to get rid of anyway."

"Fine. Fine. It's perfectly normal." Clary dipped a croissant into her cappuccino and took a bite. "But it sure don't look good to me. Dad dies from this weird accident on a busy road that *nobody* witnesses, then five days later Mum—cheery red gloss still staining her lips—is seen gleefully offloading all his stuff. Excuse the cliché but, what will the neighbours say?"

Lib's expression had gone flat. "Don't even joke like that."

"Who's joking?"

I huffed. "Oh my God, Clara. As if you ever cared what anybody said." I realize now she was trying to find out how much we knew. At the time, though, I just thought she was being annoying. We all have our ways to avoid difficult feelings. Hers was to provoke them in others. I flicked a crust at her.

"What are you suggesting?" Lib glared at Clary. "That Mum's happy Dad's dead? That she—what? *Did* something to him?"

"I'm merely pointing out the optics. If this were an episode of *Cold Case Files*, we'd all be thinking the same thing. Who wouldn't be suspicious of an attractive widow who—"

"Take your baby." Lib shoved Arlo at her. His little arms flew out as if he was falling backwards off a high building.

"Oh, come on. I'm just saying—"

Lib leaned in close and pointed her finger at Clary. "Don't feel obliged to blurt out every piece of shit-crap that pops into your head, okay? Don't...*sully* us with your sick mind."

Clary tried to grab her finger, as if this was all fun and games, but Lib batted her hand away and stormed out.

We were quiet for a while, then Clary said, "She's pissed."

"You think?"

"But since when do we censor? Since when do we not tell each other our shittiest thoughts?" She shrugged, then picked at something crisp and yellow on Arlo's eyelid. "And anyway, admit it, there *is* something unseemly about the way Mum's acting. She's practically whistling."

"She is not." She wasn't.

"Okay. But she's awfully energetic for someone who just lost her husband."

"How do you know?"

"Well, look at her."

"No. I mean how do you know what's normal? This is foreign territory for all of us. We don't know what we're doing or what we're supposed to be doing, or feeling, or anything. Plus it's pretty rich, *you* making a big deal about how Mum's behaving. You were the one laughing your face off at the funeral."

"True."

A lengthy pause. She took another bite of her croissant, then blew away the crumbs that had fallen on Arlo's head. He laughed, so Clary did it again. I laughed, too, and wished more than ever that Dad were here. He'd have blown crumbs off that baby's head all afternoon just for the simple joy of it.

"My turn for some love," I said.

Clary handed me the baby, then pulled her feet up onto the seat and squeezed her knees into her chest, extruding side-boob. Insane side-boob. The colour and sheen of a fish belly.

I'd become semi-obsessed with her breasts. None of us had ever really had breasts before. Small sensory mounds, not without their charms, but that was about it. I'd thought big womanly boobs would be a perk of pregnancy but seeing them up close—heavy and sore and Lucien Freud–bulbous—I wasn't so sure. Maybe I didn't want to grow up after all. Maybe I just wanted to live here with my sisters forever. Never have to be, or prove, anything.

"Okay but seriously," Clary said. "Do you think Mum's hiding something?"

"What? No. What are you talking about?"

"Look, I take your point—grief, foreign territory, etc.—but something doesn't feel right. I'm not getting 'bereaved' from her at all."

"Mum's always been reserved. What did you expect? Gnashing of teeth? Ululation?"

"No. But something real would be nice. Everything about the way she's acting just seems so..." She looked around for the word. "...faux."

I squinted at Clary pointedly. She'd known all along what she was going to say. "Faux" was just too perfect. Not quite calling Mum a liar but ensuring that's what I understood.

"I mean it, Neens. It's like she's this lovely neighbour you've known for years, and suddenly strange noises start coming from her house in the middle of the night. You don't say anything because she's still tending her tulips and waving at the neighbourhood kids, but you do start to wonder..."

"What? If there are bodies in the basement?"

Clary shrugged. "Maybe."

I kissed Arlo's head. "Your mama's cray-cray."

I wasn't going to let her drag me into this.

There was a commotion at the back door, and the guys came in from their run, Krish with the healthy glow and high-tech gear of a dedicated athlete, Jesse with the deathly pallor and canvas shorts of someone who would have preferred to sleep in.

"How far did you go?" I asked, gesturing at Clary to shove her nipples back into her bra. I was annoyed I had to tell her.

"Just ten K," Krish said.

Jesse mouthed, *Just! Fuuuuuck*, and collapsed into a chair. Krish did a month's worth of crunches, then put on a fresh pot of coffee. Mum must have smelled it, because a few minutes later she came down for a break. Clary crawled up the stairs in penance and managed to lure Lib back into the circle too.

We spent the rest of the morning hanging around the kitchen, laughing, talking, telling Dad stories.

It was great. Mum was great. I briefly felt like we had nothing to worry about.

NINA

The guys only stayed a couple more days. Krish and Jesse both had important work to get back to: managing a multi-billion-dollar fund and babysitting an old man. Lib had responsibilities, too, but her school insisted she take another week off. She needed a break. They promised to call at the first sign of kids going feral.

The night before the boys left, we hung out in the sunroom, drinking wine, being stupid. Clary lay on one big white sofa while Krish massaged her feet. Jesse and I were curled up on the other. Lib sprawled on the floor. Clary was midway through an old story about a Tinder date who'd tried to turn her on to "snake-milking" when Mum came in carrying a large cardboard box. Everyone stopped laughing and scrambled up to help her, as if her new status as widow had suddenly rendered her feeble.

"Honestly," she said, blowing hair out of her eyes. "Sit. Sit." She'd done at least an hour of hard exercise every day since forever. She dropped the box in the middle of the room and wiped her hands on her thighs.

She was wearing stained yoga pants, a torn T-shirt, and mismatched socks. A perfectly reasonable outfit to clean house in but jarring on the impeccable Petra Fforde. It was like seeing the Pope in a mesh tank top on a hot day. Hard to argue with but, still. Weird.

Libby pretended it wasn't. "What you got there, Mum?" All smiles.

"Presents."

A round of "oohs."

"You're first, Jesse." Mum grinned and took a grey cashmere sweater out of the box. "I thought this would look great on you."

"Mother. What are you doing?" I uncurled my legs and sat up straight. "Don't."

"Don't what?"

I remembered the scene in *A Christmas Carol*. Scrooge's cockney maid gleefully selling the nightshirt she'd stripped off his still-warm body.

"Don't, like...*pawn* off Dad's clothes. We just had the funeral!"

"Oh. Sorry, darling." Mum's face fell. She dropped her hands. The hem of the sweater pooled over her feet. "Is this inappropriate, Jess?"

"You're asking *me*? Petra." He guffawed. "I'm a minister's kid. I grew up *literally* wearing the underwear of deceased parishioners. Can I see?"

Mum looked at me for approval. Maybe Clary was just getting to me. I thought of Libby using the word "sully." I shrugged. "Fine."

Mum tossed him the sweater.

Jesse held it up to his shoulders and raised his eyebrows. "It's pretty fab, Neens...Feel it."

I knew exactly what it felt like. Only weeks earlier, Dad had hugged me in it. I'd leaned my head against his chest and heard his big, beautiful heart.

I realized the sweater might be nice to have. Like a seashell on a windowsill that still sounds of the ocean. A bit of Dad when I needed it. I told myself that was probably why Mum wanted Jess to have it too.

I touched the sleeve. "Super fab," I said. "It'll match your eyes."

Mum reached into the box again. "This something you could use, Krish?" She pulled out an electric green jersey. "You're a cyclist."

My head jerked. No. Now *that* was not okay. She'd crossed a line. How could she be so insensitive? Even mentioning *cycling*? What's the first thing any of us in that room was going to think of?

Dad's crumpled body in the ditch.

I turned, open-mouthed, to Clary. She shrugged and took a sip of wine like *what did I tell you?* Lib looked back and forth between the two of us, hard-eyed. The teacher letting the talkers in the back of the class know there'd be hell to pay once assembly ended.

Krish got up and took the jersey from Mum. "I'm. Um. I'm honoured." He sat back down, his fist bouncing against his lips. Clary put her arms around his shoulders and whispered into his cheek. It felt like a bona fide moment. An award-winning commercial. I could see the tagline—*Love. Pass it on.*—as a family gathered around a bucket of KFC in memory of the dear departed.

Maybe this was just what people do when they lose someone. Maybe this was normal. How was I supposed to know?

I told myself, *Grief is weird*, and let it go. Weird, I could handle. In fact, I always kind of liked weird.

In the end, we pretty much emptied the box. I even took a couple of things. I tried not to let it bother me that Mum hadn't kept anything for herself. "No. No," she'd insisted. "You take them. I've got to get rid of this stuff!"

NINA

The days after the boys left felt oddly like Christmas holiday. The sisters all together. Lots of food in the house. Nowhere else we needed to be. It was easy to pretend Dad was just out on an errand somewhere. He'd been the procurer, the facilitator, the shoveller, the shopper. The one to jump up when someone needed eggnog or bristol board or tampons. He'd be back any minute. If we didn't examine the thought too closely, it still felt true.

I tried my best to believe Mum was fine too. By now, everyone had noticed her late-night wanderings, the cigarettes by the pond, but I resolutely sided with Libby. Mum's life-partner, her soulmate, had just died. If a little nicotine helped her cope, so what?

"Yeah, so what?" Clary said, but not like she meant it.

During daylight hours, Mum still busied herself clearing out Dad's stuff. She'd rebuffed all our attempts to help, so we mostly just left her to it. But one afternoon I found myself at loose ends. Lib was tutoring a kid online. Clary was nursing the baby while walking her boss through a presentation he had to give in her absence. There was no Don-based emergency demanding my attention. It felt wrong to read a book or watch a rom-com while everyone else was working, so I offered my services to Mum.

She was sitting on the floor in Dad's office, a cardboard banker's box between her legs. *MDF 2*—a.k.a. Malcolm Duncan Fforde—was neatly printed on the side in black marker. Dad's office was the only room in the house that didn't have Mum's distinctive stamp on it. Desk, chair, credenza. A bank of file cabinets. Not so much ugly as shamelessly utilitarian.

"Hello, darling." Mum shoved the lid on the box with a squeak.

"You've been busy."

She glanced behind her at a wall of boxes, all labelled *For Dudek & Fforde*. A mound of bulging recycling bags loomed in the corner.

"Haven't I, though. I feel like I'm cleaning out a Nazi commandant's office."

"Mum!"

She gave a startled laugh. "Sorry. That sounded terrible! I just mean as far as record-keeping goes. Your father didn't buy a pencil without logging the expenditure in triplicate. Poor Wayne. I'm trashing the obvious garbage but I'm afraid I'm sending the rest to him."

"Can I help?"

"Oh, thanks, Nina, but no. This is something I have to do myself." She leaned her elbows on the box in a modified yoga stretch and sighed. "Speaking of which, you girls shouldn't feel like you need to stay home to help your widowed old mother. I'm fine!"

I sat down beside her on the floor. "We don't need to. We want to."

"Well, that's very sweet, but please. You have your own lives to live."

"Ha. Not me."

She frowned. "What are you taking about?"

"I'd hardly call what I'm living 'a life.' I take care of an old man."

"Seriously? That's how you feel?" She rubbed a smear of ink off her thumb. "I…I thought that was all part of the plan. You said a low-stress job is exactly what you wanted. Something to pay the bills but keep your brain free to create."

"Yeah…" I had said that. Mortifying but true.

"And wasn't it 'grist for the mill' too? The novel you were so excited about. The retired prof. The young couple. What happened to that?"

I shrugged. How far had I gotten? Sixty pages? I'll give myself the benefit of the doubt and say seventy. Seventy pages of lumpy sputum.

"Nothing happened to it," I said bravely. I'd never talked about this with anyone other than Jesse and Lib. (Clary would have just told me to get to fucking work.) "Writing a novel would require me to actually do something, and I'm just not disciplined enough. The only thing I'm doing these days is taking care of Don. That's what my life has become. His."

Mum slapped the box. “Stop that immediately!”

I jerked back in shock. “Geez, Mum. Trying to give me a heart attack or something? You *scared* me.”

“Good. Do not live another person’s life. You hear me?”

“Hard not to.” She never raised her voice, and she didn’t this time either, but her tone was alarming. So was her face. Way too much nostril.

“You’re in charge of your life, Nina. You and no one else.” She jabbed her index finger at me. “Make it count.” Her eyes stayed open a bit too wide for a second, but then she chuckled. “In the meantime, darling, could you get my X-Acto knife? It’s in my office.”

“Sure.” Sooner I got out of there, the better. I didn’t want her going all Maleficent on me again.

“If it’s not there, try the garage or your father’s workshop. I need to cut up some stuff for recycling.”

I headed up to the third floor. Mum’s office was a gorgeous space open to the rafters, with a big old arched window on the back that threw morning light across the pine floor and another one in the front that caught the afternoon sun. An antique refectory table acted as her desk. Glassed-in bookcases lined a wall. Teak file cabinets did double-duty as lampstands. Everything was stylish, irreproachable, one hundred percent Petra. This was her sanctuary. I was almost surprised she’d allowed me up here on my own.

I started looking for her knife. The bookcases yielded nothing. The file cabinets were full of fabric swatches and warranties. The desk drawer was locked, but it was always locked. (When we were kids, that’s where she’d squirrelled away any documents she didn’t want us chopping up into craft projects.)

Next, I checked the cupboards under the eaves. I opened the first door and saw stack after stack of precisely labelled bankers boxes. (My parents were pathologically well-organized.) I opened the next door. More of the same. The cupboards ran the whole length of the north wall and were all neatly stuffed to the gills. There must have been dozens of boxes in there. I sighed, then made an executive decision. If Mum had left her X-Acto in there, too bad. I wasn’t rifling through a lifetime of documents for something she could easily pick up at the hardware store. My time was worth more than that. (Really? Okay, maybe not, but

I still wasn't doing it.) I closed the cupboard doors and headed down to the garage workshop, but the search was equally fruitless there.

Thirty minutes later, I was back in Dad's office. "No luck," I said.

"With what?" Mum was sitting at the desk organizing stationery into piles.

"Finding your X-Acto knife."

"Oh, sorry, darling. I found it! I should have told you."

She went back to purging. I went back to the kitchen.

On my way out, I noticed that the box marked *MDF 2* was gone but thought nothing of it. Why would I? At that point, it was just another box.

PETRA

Petra was giddy. Today was the day. The girls were finally leaving. Doors opening. Light pouring in. Music swelling. Let the games begin!

She gazed out her third-floor office window at the blue, cloudless sky. When had she last felt this way? When had life offered so many possibilities?

She pushed her chair aside to get at the storage space under the eaves.

Never, she thought. There'd always been something in the way: parents, school, marriage, children. And then, of course, death. She picked up the box marked *MDF 2* and shoved it into the cupboard.

She wondered again if she should have burnt it. Nina had barged into Malcolm's office the day before and, for one terrible moment, Petra thought she'd been caught. It rattled her. She'd sent Nina on a trumped-up errand so she could pull herself together, then hid the box behind the pile going to Dudeks'. She'd planned to destroy it when the girls went out for a walk that morning but couldn't bring herself to do it. Instead, she'd smuggled it up here.

Petra kissed her fingertips and touched the top of the box. Someday she'd be ready to deal with its contents, but not yet. Now was her time. She was going to be happy.

She closed the door, slapped the dust off her hands, and bounded downstairs.

AL-HADDAD

Detective Ryan Al-Haddad had a headache. He took a long, hopeful glug from his fancy water bottle but knew dehydration wasn't the problem. It was work. It was frustration. It was Alex.

He checked the time: 17:25. Twelve hours since he'd clocked in. Why was he still here? He'd been spinning his wheels for the last two hours. Three, if he was honest.

Frig it. He was going home.

He switched off his computer and grabbed his gym gear. He didn't bother straightening his desk or organizing his priorities for tomorrow. He had to leave before he came up with another reason not to. He'd pick up something from that restaurant Alex liked. A peace offering. A couple of beers on the deck. Take the dog to the lake. All would be well. He felt the tension behind his eyes abate.

He texted: Sushi?

Four pulsing hearts appeared.

Home by six, he answered. He wasn't an emoji guy but what the hell? He threw in some hearts too. Fake it till you make it.

He turned to go.

"Not so fast, buster." Blair Zinck was leaning, mock-seductively, against the cubicle divider. He'd been at a conference in Toronto for a few days. Everyone at the shop had been hoping he'd take some vacation time and make a week of it but no such luck. "Pay up," he said.

"For what?" Al-Haddad huffed. "You still owe me for the hockey pool." A point of contention.

"Not hockey. Henderson. Baby present. She'll be back from mat leave if we don't get a move on."

"Oh, right." Al-Haddad retrieved his wallet from his back pocket. "What are we getting her?"

"Don't know. Some high-tech blanket-warmer? Bottle-warmer? Something. My wife's organizing it."

They shrugged at each other. Sarge had four kids but didn't know anything more about childrearing than he did. Al-Haddad handed him a twenty.

"Speaking of my wife, any headway on the Fforde case while I was away? She was asking me about it this morning."

Al-Haddad's headache returned.

"Not much." He explained about stopping by the site and seeing the unpruned rosebushes. "I figure that's the reason it took so long to find him."

Zinck scratched his belly. "Sounds plausible."

"Yeah, accounts for why no one saw the body. But why didn't they see the accident? Road would have been busy then."

"So what are you thinking?"

Al-Haddad actually hadn't been thinking about it at all. Too many real crimes to deal with. He winged it.

"It's not an accident? Someone attacked Fforde elsewhere and left him there to die?"

Zinck pooched up his lips and nodded slowly. He wasn't buying it.

Neither was Al-Haddad. He'd read the comments on Fforde's obit page. He'd read the op-ed Wayne Dudek had written about his partner in the paper. There was always a certain amount of gushing in those sorts of tributes, but these were over-the-top. Malcolm Fforde seemed to be deeply committed to doing good. Zinck's wife wasn't the only one to refer to him as a saint.

"But that strikes me as unlikely," he said. "No apparent enemies or ongoing disputes. Unless the guy was leading some seedy secret life, I don't see any reason someone would want him dead. Plus, who'd deposit a body beside a busy road in the middle of the day? Kind of asking to get caught."

"Any notes in Henderson's file about drag marks, suspicious bruising?"

"No. There's also a pretty convincing dent on the guardrail with his bike paint all over it."

"So, accident then?"

"Well..." Al-Haddad sucked his teeth. He wanted the case off his desk, but not enough to rubber-stamp it. "I'm still scratching my head over the no-witness thing."

"Probably some totally reasonable explanation."

"Agreed."

"So why don't you drop by the widow with your findings then."

"'Findings' might be a bit of an overstatement, boss..."

Zinck shrugged like Al-Haddad was splitting hairs. "Your theory, then. People are concerned about Mrs. Fforde. My wife said she's not acting herself. A few words from you might ease her mind."

And yours, Al-Haddad thought. "Sure," he said, if only because he had to run.

This little convo had only held him up for a few minutes, but these days that was all it took. Alex would be pissed if he wasn't back by six.

NINA

My sisters and I kissed and hugged and cried like we were never going to see each other again, then Mum drove them to the airport. I stood in the driveway waving, my hand arcing over my head like a sweetheart catching the last glimpse of her soldier sailing off to war. Almost everyone I loved was crammed into that car. That never would have occurred to me before.

I was heading the other way, back to Jesse. Mum had handed me the keys to Dad's Volvo on the condition we never again drive Don's 1982 olive green Saab. I'd agreed. I'd reached the point in life where safe trumped cool, plus Dad's car had a heated steering wheel. I hated how much that appealed.

I filled my travel mug with coffee, then locked the front door of the house with Dad's key. It was still on the handmade wooden fob we'd carved his initials into for Father's Day one year. I remembered us finding instructions for it in some crafty tween magazine we'd briefly been addicted to. Clary had been almost too old for that sort of thing, but Libby and I were feverish with excitement. We'd spent one of his golf afternoons making it, terrified it would rain and he'd come home early and ruin the surprise. Dad still had some brown in what was left of his hair then. Libby and I had matching elastics on our braces. Clary's nipples stuck out like Hershey's Kisses on her flat chest. It was ages ago and yet it was yesterday.

All those years gone, just like that.

"Life is fleeting," Don always said.

I unlocked the door to the house, went back inside to FaceTime Jesse. Something had to change.

~

"One of us should stay." That was my excuse. "It just seems too early. Leaving her alone."

"I get it," Jesse said.

I was in the sunroom. I'd waited until I was sure Don was down for his siesta and Jesse would be alone. He was sitting spread-legged on the lawn, leisurely weeding the grass with the help of a kitchen knife and, my guess, a little weed. He had that look. Not baked, just pleasantly buzzed. He put his elbows on his knees and gazed down at me like I was a Borrower trapped in a jar. The skin on his face pouched forward. His mother's jowls. When had that started?

"Petra needs you. Stay as long as it takes. You're right. She's probably still in shock."

Shock. I'd gone too far with that one. Never had a woman seemed less in shock.

"You guys okay on your own?"

"Yes! We're loving it." He laughed "Boys' night, every night. It's kind of fun."

"What are you eating?"

"Crap."

"Jess-seee."

"Low-sodium crap. No chewing required. Don't worry. I'm looking after Don. I think he kind of likes the change."

"Thank you very much."

"No, no, no. He misses you. We both do. But you know. He's got that old-fashioned thing about ladies and decorum and all that. You're gone so he feels like he can let his hair down. Yesterday, he said, 'Let's forget the shave, shall we?'"

"You didn't shave him?"

"Nope. He wanted a short-sleeved shirt too."

"He'll be wearing dungarees next!"

"He's a happening guy."

Another possibility hit me. I put my hand on my chest to calm my heart. "You don't think he's giving up, do you? This isn't the beginning of the end?"

Jesse shook his head. "He's just kicking back! We've actually had some *in-teresting* chats while you've been gone..."

"Okay..."

"Did you know Ruth was his student?"

"No way."

"Yup. Way. They had an affair. He left his first wife for her and, not coincidentally, his tenure-track position at McGill. That's how they ended up here."

"Gasp. Seriously?"

"I know. It was a huge scandal. Don and his wife had a big society wedding and a big house and plans for a big family, but he threw it all aside for this 'mousy little girl from the Prairies.' His words, not mine, so holster your sidearm, bucko."

I didn't know Ruth except in pictures—she'd died the year before we started at Don's—but the pairing had always seemed strange. Don had been a hunk. A young Warren Beatty. Tall, broad-shouldered, with a roguish tendency to wink that never left him. Ruth was small and tidy with severe cats-eye glasses and dirndl skirts. Today in pictures, she looks oddly hip, but in the 1960s? Pretty mousy.

"When did he tell you that?"

"Yesterday. We were just sitting around talking about love."

"As men do."

"Okay. Sex and love."

"I can't leave you guys alone for a minute. Did he impart any pearls of wisdom?"

"'Sex is one of life's great gifts. Get it while you can.'"

"Noted."

"It's one of the few things he misses."

"Yikes. You don't think he'll be wanting us to procure...*services* for him now, do you?"

"No. He said it in particular reference to Ruth. They were—his words again—'deeply, deeply in love.' That was why he was willing to give everything up for her."

"This mousy little girl from the Prairies."

"Yup. And he never regretted it. The euphoric sex was just a bonus."

"Damn. He said that?"

"Yup...Oh, and another thing. It apparently wasn't all talk in the so-called conversation pit..."

I squawked. "Details!"

"Sorry. That's all I got. A gentleman is discreet."

We floated some scenarios as to what Don could have been implying, then talked about practical stuff for a while—changing his physio appointment, where to find Ruth's galette recipe, septic issues.

"Come back soon," Jesse said. "I can hardly wait to have a—dot, dot, dot—*conversation* with you."

"Me neither," I said. "Very much looking forward to a little parry-and-thrust."

"Many salient points to be made by both sides."

"Only one of us has a point that can be made salient, but I get what you're driving at."

We beat that joke into the ground, then said our I-love-yous and hung up.

I didn't move. I tried to tell myself that the call had gone well, but it hadn't. It was too fun. Too comfortable. Too much like every other day for the last fifteen years.

Is that what I wanted? More of the same? To be stuck in a buddy movie for the rest of my life?

I wished Jesse hadn't told me about Don and Ruth.

What was this half-assed shit I was trying to pull off?

I called Jesse back.

NINA

"Hey."

"What's up?" Jesse seemed to be working on the same dandelion. Maybe he was more buzzed than I'd thought.

"I'm just going to say it."

"What?" He stabbed the knife into the ground and went still.

"I think we should take a break."

"A break?" He laughed like this was some joke he didn't quite get. "What does that mean?"

"Not see each other for a while."

"We aren't. You're there. I'm here."

"I know, but I mean…on purpose."

He picked up the phone to hold it closer to his face. "You mean like, what? Break up?"

"Yeah. Well. Sort of."

"Sort of? Nina. Just say what you mean."

"Do our own thing for a while. Be on our own."

Jesse's shoulders went up, his neck forward. "Why?"

"Because…I don't know…we never have. We should probably try it." I smiled weakly. I hadn't expected this to be so hard. Jellyfish aren't supposed to have backbones.

"You mean the way we should try gochujang? Salsa dancing? What are you saying?"

"No, no."

"Did you meet someone?"

"Jesse. Where would I have met someone? When would I have had the time?"

"So you've just been too busy?"

"No. Of course not."

"Then what? Five minutes ago, we were laughing. You were telling me you loved me. What's going on? Are you unhappy? How long have you been unhappy?"

"It's not about that."

"Is this about your dad?"

I didn't want to blame Dad, but I didn't want to take responsibility for it either. "No. Not really."

"So what's it about then? You want a baby? I'll give you a baby. Two? Five? How many you want?"

"No. I mean, I do. I want babies. Just not like this."

"Not like what? Not like with me?"

I didn't know what I meant. "That's not what this is about, Jess. I just think you've got to live your life for a while and I've got to live mine, and that's the only way we can know if we want to live a life together."

"No. Wrong. I know. I've known for years. *You're* the one who doesn't know. So fine. If that's what you want, Neens, there's nothing I can do about it."

"Are you mad?"

He jabbed the knife into the ground. So, in other words, yes.

"I'm sorry, Jess."

"Yeah, well, me too."

"You know I love you."

"Not sure I do, actually. Right now, the one thing I know is that you want to leave me."

"I don't want to. I have to."

"You're making it worse. You're making me sound like I'm psycho or contagious or something and escaping is the only thing that's going to save you."

"That's not it at all. I—"

"Mind if I sign off? I'd love to get a few beers into me before reality sinks in."

"Jess..."

"You've got my number. Call if you need me. Give my love to Petra. See ya."

He hit the *off* button with his gloved hand. It took him a couple of tries before he realized he had to hit it with a bare finger to hang up. His angry face was the last thing I saw. I couldn't remember the last time I'd seen Jesse angry.

It scared me, what I'd just done to my life. I looked around the kitchen, blinking, my breath loud and ragged as a horror movie soundtrack. I felt like I was waking up in a room I didn't recognize, with no idea how I'd got there. It felt sinister and dangerous.

But right too.

I covered my mouth, not knowing if I should laugh or cry. Not knowing what I should do at all.

GORD

It was a fluke Gord had ever connected with Keith Osterlich. Years ago, in the long days and nights waiting for his son Luke to die, Gord had read every article in every magazine in the critical care parents' lounge. He knew how and when to prune cherry trees. He could recite the ten steps to vaginal health. He knew about political unrest in Ethiopia, the best investing strategies in the Bitcoin age, and who Hayden Panettiere is.

When the nurse came to get him, he was in the kitchenette, waiting for his toast to pop, flipping through an old issue of *Our Town*. It was a local publication, a rag, the type of thing you only read after you've exhausted everything else.

The cover article was a puff piece about sixty-eight-year-old Keith Osterlich moving back to his hometown after a high-flying career as CEO of PhiTex Inc. It described the landmark Victorian mansion he'd had moved at great expense to a high point overlooking the harbour. Photos showed him delivering the newspaper to that very house as a boy, laughing with George Clooney at a recent black-tie event, squatting to play marbles with neatly dressed children at an orphanage he founded in Mali. Call-out quotes highlighted his twin passions for antiquities and philanthropy.

Gord, of course, had known who Osterlich was before reading the article. He'd invested early in PhiTex and had done extremely well with it—but that didn't mean he liked the guy. Gord had come a long way from his grandfather's Insulbrick bungalow, but there was still a bit of

Bix in him. Rich guys flaunting their wealth bugged him. Or maybe it was just guys richer than him that did it.

"Blah, fucking, blah," he muttered, noisily flipping pages. He skimmed the article, looking up every so often to see what was taking so long with his goddamn toast.

He jumped when the nurse touched his arm.

"Sorry, Gord," she said. "I'd come right now if I were you."

Gord stared at her. He'd always been decisive. Nothing made him crazier than the guy at the deli counter agonizing between pastrami and corned beef, the opposing counsel requesting another week to weigh options. Gord's approach had always been to jump in headfirst, work out next steps later. It had served him well. He'd married Aziza three weeks after laying eyes on her at a climbing gym. She was hopeless—no upper-body strength at all—but he liked her tenacity. And her ass. He figured he could make it work. But now, with the nurse's hand on his elbow, her kind but insistent eyes, he couldn't figure out what to do. He'd already opened the jar of Cheez Whiz. He'd stuck the knife in, got out the paper plates. The toast was almost ready.

"Aziza," he said, as if he'd been getting it *for* her, not to get away from her.

"Leave the toast." The nurse rubbed his back. "C'mon now."

Gord sucked on his lip, shoved the magazine into the pocket of his hoodie, and followed her out.

The magazine stayed rolled up in Gord's hoodie for almost two years. When he saw it next, it was February—dark and cold and hopeless. He'd been drinking. Pretty much drinking non-stop since Luke died. The hospital had a restraining order against him. (Gord was convinced the doctors should have done something earlier.) His law firm, "reluctantly and with great sadness," had asked him to step down. (His files were a mess. He'd told a judge to fuck off.) The Barristers' Society had revoked his licence (professional misconduct, incompetence). His best friend had agreed not to bring charges against him (broken nose, damage to vehicle) on condition Gord not come within five-hundred metres of him. The only person Gord felt he could talk to was Petra, a woman he'd met at a grief session Aziza had forced him to go to. But, after several months of clandestine meetings, Petra was gone now too. (A trip to Turkey, a daughter's wedding, life.)

All he had left was Aziza, and as of that moment, she'd had enough. Enough of his anger, his self-abuse, the stink of him. When she'd left for work that morning, she'd asked him yet again to at least have a shower. She'd come home ten hours later, her briefcase bulging with files, and found him lying in a fug on the couch, a half-empty bottle of Grand Marnier on the floor beside him, harness racing on TV.

Aziza put down her briefcase and clicked off the television.

"Hey!" Gord barked, as if he'd actually been watching it.

"Out." She didn't scream. She didn't dramatically fling her arm towards the door. She clasped her elbows and quietly said, "Now."

"What?" He ground his palm into his eye. The tone she'd been using on him lately was incredibly irritating.

"You heard me."

He wobbled to his feet. "You're kicking *me* out? It's my house too."

"Too bad. You're leaving."

"Oh, yeah? Make me." He said this laughing. Genuinely almost happy. He remembered the way they used to be when they were first together. The arch sparring, the horseplay. Like teenagers flirting outside a convenience store. He put up his dukes, hoping she'd remember that time, too, but her eyes were cold. She was going all tough-love on him.

Well fuck you then, he thought.

"Make me," he said again, only uglier this time. She pushed him backwards toward the door. He could have easily stopped her—her upper-body strength was still shit—but he didn't. Each slap to his chest felt like a win to him. He wanted her touching him, didn't matter how. They lurched down the hall.

She opened the front door. "Out."

"No."

She lunged at him, her arms locked at the elbows, her hands flat.

He laughed.

Aziza was little, a mere wisp, but she was enraged now, and he was drunk. His heels caught on the threshold. He stumbled out. The steps were icy. (She'd asked him twenty times to salt them.) He fell backwards and thumped comically down the stairs and onto the sidewalk.

She slammed the door. He lay on the snow, his filthy grey T-shirt ruched up over his belly, his arms out wide, his legs flipped one way and his head the other. A washed-up modern dancer interpreting heartbreak.

"Shit." He gingerly fingered the lump rising on the back of his head. The outdoor light turned on. The door opened. Aziza threw the hoodie at him. The hoodie he'd left hanging on a kitchen chair for months, that she'd asked him to put away a million times. The magazine, still rolled up tight, fell out of the pocket and onto the front porch. She picked it up and biffed it at him too. It landed in a snowbank like a javelin. She slammed the door again.

"Zizi!" Gord screamed, hefting himself up onto his elbows. He heard the lock click shut. "Christ." He fell back down. The lump on his head pulsed like a living thing. He thought of Luke, the first time he'd held him. His tiny heart beating.

He remembered lying next to Aziza, and feeling her heart beat too. *Two hearts beating as one.* Who sang that? Why had he never realized what a great song that was?

Gord got onto his hands and knees, then onto his feet, and staggered up the stairs. He'd beg forgiveness. He'd hang up the hoodie. He'd salt the steps. He banged on the door. He wailed her name.

After a while, the mail slot opened and his wallet dropped onto the porch, but the only response to his apology was the sound of Aziza's footsteps clip-clopping away. The light in the kitchen came on. Gord smelled soup, toast. The light went off. He pounded on the door again, called her name, swore at her, pleaded.

She didn't come back. He knew she wasn't going to. This was the end. He picked up his wallet and headed down the steps. He noticed the magazine, still jabbed in the snow. He picked it up too. It was open to the page he'd been reading in the critical care lounge. There was a quote from Osterlich, set in bold, that said something about how witnessing the resilience of the orphaned kids in Mali had made him a better person.

That was the push Gord needed. He indulged a brief fantasy about coming back home in six months a better person, but he was drunk, not stupid. He just had to get as far away as possible. He owed his wife that much.

He waved down a cab, then texted Aziza to courier his passport to the airport hotel. She didn't ask why he wanted it or where he was going. By the time he'd checked into his room, his passport was waiting at reception and so was a duffel bag full of clean clothes, shoes, his shaving kit, money. Aziza wanted him gone. He got the first available flight out. Four days after touching down in Bamako, he began volunteering at Osterlich Children's Village.

Now, three years later, Gord was back in town again. A better person?

He laughed at that, then popped a rosemary cracker into his mouth whole. Maybe not better than he'd been before, but certainly better than Osterlich.

That evil piece of shit.

NINA

I waited a few days to tell my sisters about the breakup. My commitment to bold life changes was still too wobbly to withstand an onslaught of concern.

"How are you doing?" Lib was sitting on her sad little single bed in Iqaluit, laptop on her knees. She smiled at me the way a teacher smiles at a kid who's wet her pants. *That's all right. Nothing to be embarrassed about. Why don't we clean you up?*

I was in the sunroom. I could see Mum out by the pond, talking to a tradesperson.

"I'm okay," I said, almost truthfully. Add "excited" to "terrified," divide by two and the average is probably "okay," although it was a state I only glimpsed on my rush to either extreme.

"Well, I think it's fantastic." Clary was in the bath, arms dangling over the sides, hair pulled sloppily into a scrunchie. Her breasts bobbed in the soapy water. *Coupla jellyfish,* I thought. "Might turn out to be the boot in the arse you both need," she said. "Lord knows, Jesse was never going to take the initiative."

"How's Mum with it?" Lib asked.

"I dunno. She was a little surprised when she got home and found out I hadn't left."

"Ha!" Clary stepped out of the tub and treated us to a close-up of her ungroomed vulva. It reminded me of Fagin's glue-on beard in our junior high's production of *Oliver!* "Happy-surprised?" she snickered. She'd already guessed the answer.

I wiggled my head. I thought of the look on Mum's face when I'd told her. The tight smile. The barely concealed panic.

"You're staying?" she'd said lightly.

She'd just walked in the kitchen door after dropping my sisters at the airport. She had a long pink dress in dry-cleaner plastic flopped over one arm and a bag from Angelo's Wig and Hair Centre dangling from the other.

She said, "But why? You and Jesse seemed to be getting on so well."

I reminded her of the conversation she and I had had in Dad's office, the one about me living my own life. I explained how shaken I was at the funeral by the passage of time, the sense of missed opportunities, of unfulfilled potential. She listened quietly, nodding at all the right spots.

"Well, not *un*happy," I said to Clary and Lib now. "But she did have some new house rules for me." The girls became very alert. I knew this wouldn't go over well.

Mum had put on the kettle, got out the milk and mugs. She took a box of waxy store-brand cookies out of the wig bag and put it directly on the table, no plate. I noted that the box was already opened, a row half-gone. A tiny thing but unsettling, nonetheless. My mother did not snack, did not snack on high-sugar no-name products, did not snack straight out of the package. I told myself she was allowed the occasional weak moment. I let it go.

"It's time I stopped procrastinating." I grabbed a cookie for emotional support and picked off little shards of brown coating. "I just feel like I need some time alone to figure out what I'm doing with my life." I smiled flimsily. "Do you understand?"

Mum filled the teapot and brought it to the table.

"I do." Her face, at that moment, was the one I remembered from my childhood. Engaged. Empathetic. A haven of a face. I briefly felt as if everything was going to turn out fine. I could wrestle with big life choices in the safety of my family home with my mother there as guide and mentor.

She poured the tea. "Now, I'm going to tell you a few things, and I hope you'll understand too." She held up the carton. "Milk?"

I shook my head. After I'd talked to Jesse that afternoon, I decided to give up dairy. I was starting fresh. I was going to do all the things I'd been telling myself I should do forever. Refusing milk now, though, was more about nausea. Mum was not giving off mentor vibes.

"I'm sixty-nine, seventy in four months, so I know a thing or two about the passage of time and missed opportunities. I'm happy you're here"—she reached across the table and squeezed my hand—"but I'm afraid you're here as a guest. This is my life. *Finally*, my life. I apologize in advance if I make some choices you don't like, but they're my choices. The ones that work for me."

"Which means what exactly?" Clary said when I gave them an abbreviated version of the exchange. "'Choices you might not like'?" She bared her teeth as if she was expecting the answer to involve fecal matter.

"I don't know. I asked her the same thing. All she said was, 'I'm not sure.'"

"Oh, my God." Lib put a hand over her mouth. "Maybe it's because Dad just died, or maybe it's because all of us—as in 'everyone'—has a deep-seated need for their parents to remain constant and known, but that sounds scary. Why wouldn't we like something if it was good for her? We want what's right for her. We all do."

"Has she done anything yet?" Clary was standing with one foot on the tub, slathering cream onto her thigh with both hands.

Through the window I could see Mum by the pond, talking animatedly to a guy in a green uniform.

"Not really," I lied. "She's still cleaning. She seems to be sleeping in later than usual, but she probably needs it. She's eating a lot more carbs, too, but that's what we've got in the house. People keep dropping treats off."

"Right," Clary said, "Because you can never have too many Hello Dollies."

"True. They make me miss the funerals Jesse and I used to take Don to."

"Nina." She stopped rubbing her thighs and squeezed her eyes shut. "Do you have any idea how tragic that is?"

"They're good."

"So?" She put her hands on her hips. A nudist gym teacher, pissed at my lacklustre performance. "You're thirty-six and single. You should be missing raunchy sex with nameless strangers or the incredible cavatelli al funghi from that little hole-in-the-wall off Piazza di Whatever. Not the Hello Dollies at Shirley's funeral. Seriously. It's like you went straight from university keggers to seniors' bingo."

"It's my life."

"Don't you mean 'life'?" She made air quotes. "You deserve more than that."

"Yeah, well, we're not talking about me. We're talking about Mum." *Save yourself. Push* her *onto the tracks.* "Speaking of which, she's getting the pond filled in."

"What?" the girls squawked in unison.

"Yup. There's a guy outside with her now."

"Why?" Lib sounded hurt, no doubt on Dad's behalf.

"She said it's too serene."

"Too *serene*?" Clary hauled on her underwear and glared into the screen. "Mum's redone the house ten times. She has never once strayed from 'calming neutral.' Does 'too serene' sound reasonable to you?"

I shrugged. "She said we might not like some of her choices."

"It's not a question of liking, it's a question of understanding what the hell she's thinking. His clothes. The pond they both loved. Anyone check to see if she's photoshopped Dad out of all the family pictures yet?"

"Give it a rest, Clare." Lib didn't take the bait.

"No. I want to know. What other weird shit has she been up to?"

Mum sang show tunes in the shower. She left half-smoked joints smoldering on Majolica plates. She sunbathed nude in the backyard—although to be fair, I wasn't supposed to see that. I'd told her I was going out for a coffee, then realized I'd forgotten my wallet. I was in my room searching for it when I noticed something move in the backyard. I looked out the window and there she was. Totally naked, mid Sun Salutation.

I walked to the café in a daze. Mum was an adult, in the privacy of her own backyard, hidden by trees. She could be nude if she wanted. Why did it make me feel ill then? Widows don't need to wear black, but surely they should wear something. I told myself that was my only concern. Simple propriety. I stayed at the café for hours. When I got home, Mum was fully dressed, curled up in an armchair, and watching an old Marilyn Monroe movie. She didn't look depraved at all.

No need to tell my sisters about any of that. Everyone grieves in their own way.

"She's just being practical," I said. "The pond's a lot of work. Dad's not here to help so she's getting rid of it. It's not a crime."

Clary said, "Maybe not," but in a way that strongly suggested the opposite. Libby rolled her eyes.

The doorbell rang. Mum was still out back with the tradesman. My sisters and I air-kissed and signed off.

I ran downstairs and opened the front door. A police officer said, "Ms. Fforde?"

NINA

"That's me," I said.

The cop flipped open his black leather wallet and held it beside his face. A badge and ID, just like on TV. "Detective Ryan Al-Haddad." He compressed his lips and nodded.

The look on his face. The world wobbled. I put my hand on the door jamb. Don was dead. I knew it instantly.

I pictured him bent over his dinner plate, face grey, eyes wide, flecks of vol-au-vent spraying across the table as he struggled to bring his napkin to his mouth. Jesse never cut his food up small enough. How many times had I said that? How many times had I said not to make Don laugh when he was eating?

I was going to kill Jesse.

No, I wasn't. The truth hit me like a softball to the solar plexus.

Jesse was the one who'd died. It had to be. If Don had died, Jesse would have come himself. He wouldn't have sent a cop.

I sucked back a sob. I'd broken his heart. I'd killed him.

The cop said, "Ms. Fforde?" and touched my arm. "Is this a good time to talk about the investigation into your husband's death?"

I realized how much I loved Jesse, what a terrible mistake I'd made.

"He's not my husband." I could barely say it. "We're not married."

I shouldn't have left him. I should have just married him, started having babies. He would have been happy. I would have been happy. Happy enough.

"Are you speaking about Malcolm Fforde?"

"Oh." I slumped, my hand on my throat, and laughed, just a little. "You mean my father! I thought you meant my..." I suddenly saw how bad that must look, me laughing. I went serious. "Yes, Malcolm Fforde is my father. Was. You're looking for my mother."

As if on cue, the back door opened, and Mum breezed in from the kitchen, raking her hair into place with her fingers. She was wearing a short pink-and-yellow sundress, no bra. Flagrantly, no bra.

"Sorry. Sorry! I was out back with a landscaper. I forgot you were coming." She approached the cop smiling, her hand out. "I'm Petra Astbury."

Astbury? I flinched. The cop's eyes slid discretley from me back to my mother.

"Formerly Fforde," Mum explained. "I'm using my maiden name again." She chuckled winningly. "People always had trouble with the spelling."

"You're changing your name?!" I gawked at her.

"Oh, Nina." She turned to the cop, smiling. "As if she hadn't pestered her father for years about all those silent letters."

"I was a teenager!"

"Well, yes, and I'm a grown-up and I'm calling myself Petra Astbury now." Tossed off, as if it was no big deal.

"Well, either way, you sound like the person I need to speak with. Detective Ryan Al-Haddad." He handed us each a card.

"Come in. Come in." Mum led him to the living room. "Can I get you some coffee?"

"If it's no trouble."

"None at all." Mum looked at me. "Darling? Would you mind?" And then, "Maybe a little something sweet too?"

"We having a party or something?" I had no intention of trotting off to get goddamn bonbons to go with the autopsy photos.

"Please? I'm starving and I bet Detective Al-Haddad is too." Mum's voice was tinny with false cheer, a regular Blanche DuBois.

She was making me look bad. I managed a service-industry smile and left the room.

Dad wasn't dead three weeks, and she was already deleting him from her ID. Not that I in any way believed a woman should be required to take her husband's name. It's a tradition I'd happily see go the way of the droit du seigneur, but still. Mum suddenly going all Independent Woman was just so unbelievably...

Suspicious.

The word flashed in front of me like a neon sign for a seedy bar. Clary had clearly got to me.

I leaned one hand on the kitchen counter and rubbed my forehead with the other. *This is your mother. She's just been through something terrible. Give her a break.*

I slammed a couple of K-Cups into the machine, threw a few Hello Dollies onto a plate, and brought them into the living room for our gentleman caller.

Detective Al-Haddad was on the couch, a manilla file folder on the coffee table in front of him. The tab read *M. D. Fforde*, followed by what I presumed was a case number. He'd written *Petra Astbury* on the cover with two little lines under the almost silent T, as if he was worried he'd spell it wrong next time. ("Astbury" wasn't that easy to spell either, so there goes that argument.)

Mum always said every well-designed room needs a hit of black, and he provided it. Black hair, black jacket, black shoes polished to a high shine. Al-Haddad was crisp and fit and extravagantly handsome in a charity calendar kind of way. Undo his shirt to the belly button and you'd have Detective September.

Not my type at all, I thought.

And then I thought, *I have a type?* How could I have a type when all I'd ever had was Jesse. Mere minutes ago, I was thinking how much I loved him. My id had once again galloped off ahead of me.

I put the squares on the table and gave the cop his coffee. He took it with both hands—one on the handle, one underneath, holding it up for a moment like an offering. If he'd been Jesse, I would have made the sign of the cross and mumbled some Pig Latin, and he would have got the joke immediately. Al-Haddad just thanked me.

I sat down across from him.

"You don't need to stay, Nina. This might be upsetting." Mum didn't look upset. She was already nibbling on a square.

"That's okay." I was just doing my duty as an adult daughter. Sharing the burden. Not letting her get away with anything. "What did I miss?"

Al-Haddad glanced at Mum for approval; she gave a tiny nod, and he continued. "I was just catching your mother up on our investigation. As you know, Mr. Fforde's body was found off Highway 3 near Sawyer's Beach."

He took a photo of the scene out of the file. "Stop me if there's anything you don't understand or if it becomes too much."

I nodded and shook my head, a dashboard bobblehead going over a rough patch. He took that as "okay."

"Our working theory is that Mr. Fforde crested the hill and was on the downward slope when he spun out on a small gravel spill, flipped over the guardrail here," he tapped the picture, "and landed face down in a stream on the other side of the shoulder."

"Did he die instantly?" Mum asked. A catch in her voice would have been nice.

"I'm afraid not. Water was found in his lungs, indicating he was alive at the time of impact. Given his injuries, he wouldn't have been able to lift his face out of the stream."

I felt ill but Mum leaned over and studied the photo as if she was considering fabric swatches. *Calming neutrals*, I thought.

"Poor thing," she said but, again, her delivery could have used some work.

Al-Haddad turned to the next photo.

"These wild roses would usually be cut back, but the DoT must have missed them. They obscure the view of the stream from the road. We think that's why the body went unnoticed. The coroner estimates death occurred several hours before it was discovered. But that's just an estimate. We have no witnesses to the accident as of yet."

Mum made a little humming sound like, *oh, interesting.*

I said, "How could no one have seen the accident? Highway 3 would have been bumper-to-bumper the day Dad died." I knew this for a fact. I'd been on it many times. My sisters and me, gauzy sleeveless dresses thrown over bikinis and Doc Martens, the car jammed with friends, music blaring, a bag of Stacy's Pita Chips making the rounds. *We*, no doubt, would have sailed right past, but I can't imagine everyone else would have. All those SUVs and minivans full of families playing car games? Somebody would have noticed. *I spy with my little eye someone who just died.*

"Yes. It is a bit surprising." Al-Haddad nodded. "Either the timing of the accident was extraordinarily unlucky or there's more to this than is immediately apparent."

Mum sat up very straight. "By which you mean?" Concerned at last.

He was silent for a couple of beats. "Would you have any reason to believe Mr. Fforde was meeting someone that day?"

Mum shook her head. "Malcolm usually cycled alone. Not many of his friends could keep up with him. He was in excellent shape."

"Maybe not for cycling. For another reason, perhaps?" Al-Haddad took a small black notepad out of his jacket pocket.

I'd probably watched too much TV since we'd started at Don's, but I got the sense the cop had an answer in mind. As if he only needed to gaze at us long enough with those liquid brown eyes and we'd feel compelled to blurt out the truth.

Dad was having an affair.

Dad was extorting money.

Dad was dealing crystal meth from the paniers of his spanking-new Trek Madone.

Mum stared out the window and thought for a moment. Her nose was a little broad head-on but exquisite in profile. She may have struck that pose on purpose. "I don't think so."

"Any enemies?"

I actually laughed at that. One loud indignant *ha*. "Dad? No. He was a highly respected businessperson. A tireless volunteer. He went to church!" I said, then thought *serial killer.* Who else would have a CV that spotless? I shut up.

"I wouldn't think so," Mum said. "I can't imagine Malcolm having any enemies. He was known for being a fair dealer."

"What about family?"

"Just his three daughters and me. Oh, and our grandson, but he's still a baby." A tinkle of what used to be referred to as gay laughter. The merry widow.

"No extended family?"

Her smile vanished. She took a performative sip of coffee. "His parents are long dead, of course. He has a brother, but we haven't seen him in years."

"Any reason for that? A dispute of some type?"

"A dispute?" She looked away, as if parsing the meaning of the word. "No. No. I wouldn't say that. Malcolm and Randall didn't fight. Just different interests, I guess. Chalk and cheese, as my father used to say. And, of course, Randall had lots of family matters to deal with."

"Such as?"

She gave a little moue as in *pas important* but Al-Haddad waited her out.

"Um. Addiction issues... Not Randall himself. One of his children."

"Randall had children?" I said.

Mum laughed. "Of course, he did! You knew that." She turned to Al-Haddad and said, "See? We really had very little contact with that side of the family. None in fact."

Did I know he had children? It didn't feel like the type of thing I'd forget, but maybe? I'd only met my uncle once. I was little. He'd been in town for something, and Dad had taken us girls out for lunch with him. Mum wasn't there. Randall looked like Dad, only older and fatter. When they saw each other, they shook hands and nodded. My sisters and I played in the children's area at the back of the restaurant while they talked. They hugged for a long time when they said goodbye. Randall mussed my hair and called me Libby. After that day, he'd never crossed my mind. He was old and boring and got my name wrong. What was he to me?

"Not all families are close," Mum said, trying to sound sad about it. "And, of course, Randall lived so far away and his kids were so much older than ours. Nick must be in his late forties and, gosh, Sarabeth might be over fifty now, if she's still alive."

"She was the addict?" Al-Haddad was taking notes and didn't look up.

"Yes."

"What was she addicted to?"

"Drugs of some type. By high school, my sense was she was into the hard stuff." Mum closed her eyes and inhaled, as if the thought appalled. "Randall and Sharon certainly had their hands full...but so did we, for that matter. Although in our case it was about keeping up with school and sports and drama for three bright, active girls."

Such a snotty, un-Petra thing to say. The horrible druggies versus the lovely middle-class family. I'd bet Al-Haddad had had plenty of run-ins with kids from our fancy private school, but he just smiled pleasantly. "They must have kept you busy."

He wrote something in his little notebook, then said, "Ms. Fforde, do you remember what you were doing the day of the accident?"

"Me?" I put my hand on my chest. Not that long ago, there would have been two Ms. Ffordes in the room.

He nodded encouragingly. He had magnificent eyelashes. Long and black and thick.

"Um, I was at home? Working? I live about three hours from here. In Hazelton. Not too far from the, um..." I realized I was babbling. It was those eyes. I dribbled to a stop. "...like, ballfield."

"Would anyone be able to vouch for you during that time?"

"Oh. Yes. Yup. My boyfriend. My former boyfriend. Jesse Whynacht? He was there. He was with me the whole time."

One hundred percent true but my palms were sweaty and my heart pounding like maybe I'd murdered my father and just forgotten.

"And you, Ms. Astbury?" He pronounced the T. "Where were you that day?"

"Here. Malcolm goes to church—went to church—but I never do. He usually attended the 9 o'clock Eucharist but that day he did the early service because he'd planned a long bike ride. He got back from St. Alban's around 8:30. We had a quick breakfast together then he headed off. I spent the day gardening. I already explained that to the other officers."

"Never a bad idea for us to hear it again. Did anyone see you?"

"I doubt it." Mum gestured towards the window like an aging Vanna White. "We've got a large lawn, mature trees, so it's very private. No one would have seen me unless they'd come right into the yard, and even then, the rhododendrons. They're quite dense." A small smile. A woman remembering the sun on her nude body.

"And you were there all morning?"

"Most of the afternoon too. It's a big job."

"When did you notice Mr. Fforde was missing?"

"I didn't think in terms of him being *missing*. He'd just gone for a long ride. He had some sort of training schedule he stuck to religiously. Certain routes on certain days for certain amounts of time. Some scientist he followed online had apparently figured out the optimal way to train."

"So you weren't worried when your husband didn't return?"

"No. He'd packed energy bars and energy drinks, so I wasn't expecting him for lunch. Around mid-afternoon I texted to see what he'd like for dinner, but he didn't reply. That was unusual for him. After the fifth or sixth time, I called Wayne Dudek, his business partner, to see if he might have heard from Malcolm. He hadn't, but they had the same cycling app so Wayne was able to check where Malcolm was. That's how he found the body."

"Yes. The police have spoken with Mr. Dudek...Otherwise you didn't see or speak to anyone that day?"

"No. But that's not unusual for me. I don't work outside the home. My days are often quite solitary. I wish I could provide a better alibi." She smiled apologetically.

Alibi.

Who says "alibi" if they aren't guilty?

Detective Al-Haddad shook his head as in *not to worry.* "And your other daughters. Any idea where they were that day?"

"Clary—Clara—was in Toronto with her new baby, and Libby was in Iqaluit. She's a principal at a school there."

"They both had excellent relations with Dad." I was in danger of crying. "They were crazy about him. We all were."

Mum reached out and touched my arm. I looked at her hand and thought, *Were you?*

Al-Haddad slipped the two photos back in the manilla folder and stood up. "I think I've got all I need for today. We'll continue looking into this matter. Feel free to call if you have any concerns or questions."

"Yes, of course." Mum thanked him for coming, then urged him to take a square. "A big, tall man like you needs to eat."

"I shouldn't," he said, "but I will."

When he picked up the Hello Dolly, the icing pulled away in flame-shaped licks from the square beside it. Mum somehow managed to produce a napkin. He held it just under his sculpted chin and took a bite. "Oh. Wow." He licked a crumb off his perfect lip. "Did you make these?"

"Afraid not." Church squares were not Mum's thing. Too much gluten, too much sugar, too back-of-the-box easy. "A neighbour. People have been so kind since the funeral."

Al-Haddad seemed to remember why he'd come. He reined in his smile. "Well, they're very good." He placed the square on the napkin. "I'll save the rest for lunch. Thanks for your time. I'll get back to you as soon as I have any developments to share."

We stood in the doorway, watching him walk to his car. Before getting in, he smiled and gave us an oddly jaunty wave. He was used to women looking at him.

Mum waved back, just as jauntily. "Amazing, isn't it," she said as he pulled away, "that no one saw it happen."

PETRA

Petra hadn't realized Malcolm had still been alive. Her heart hurt for a moment, but then she thought it through. The force of impact, the broken neck—in all likelihood, he'd have been unconscious. He wouldn't have suffered. Plus, Malcolm would have had his God there to comfort him. She stood up and flushed the toilet.

Speaking of gods—that detective! What a face. *He can take me into custody anytime.*

She chuckled at her little joke. She could picture herself in her twenties Mae-Westing a line like that to Bonnie before undoing a couple of buttons and hitting up some young stud on the other side of the bar. She felt a happy little shiver of possibility.

Then, washing her hands, she was struck by a sudden memory of Malcolm's face at that age. Those beautiful teeth. The green-brown-grey-yellow eyes. The effect they'd had on her. She'd always been susceptible to male beauty. She'd just buried it along with everything else. She patted her hands dry and made a mental note to get a manicure. Something bright and fun. Summery.

She'd spent many hours sourcing just the right sconce for this bathroom, but she still found the light unforgiving. She dotted an expensive French eye cream into her crow's feet. It wouldn't do much at this stage, but she'd keep trying.

Unlike Sharon. Toddling in like some old lady. A life wasted. The nerve! Petra screwed the cap back on angrily. She doubted Randall had held up any better. Last time she'd seen him, he'd looked like hell. Living with an addict had aged him. She wondered if he was even still alive. Sharon hadn't mentioned him at the funeral, although to be fair, Petra hadn't given her much of a chance. She had no interest in how they were doing. Petra learned early not to think about them at all.

She stepped back and studied herself in the mirror. The sundress might have been a mistake. Her cleavage wasn't the crowd-pleaser it had once been. Petra had fought like the devil, but life had taken its toll on her too.

AL-HADDAD

Al-Haddad pulled into a McDonald's parking lot and dumped the Hello Dolly into the nearest garbage can. If he didn't get rid of it immediately, he'd eat it. Bad enough he wasn't running. He needed to maintain some definition, at least until beach season was over.

He took a wet wipe out of the glove compartment, cleaned his fingers, and thought about his visit with the Ffordes. Blair Zinck had pretty much convinced him that Malcolm's death was accidental. After meeting Petra, though, Al-Haddad wasn't so sure. There was something off about her demeanour. Like she couldn't have cared less about the man.

Sarge always said, "If only well-loved people kicked the bucket, my mother-in-law would be alive today." Al-Haddad knew that, but still. The dress, the name-change, the hand on his arm when she gave him the square. The "big, tall man" comment. Petra didn't have to be sad her husband was dead, but most people knew enough to keep their glee under control until the cop left the premises. It just looked bad. The daughter clearly thought so too.

He was going to do a bit more digging into this Petra Astbury-Fforde.

And he was going to get out of this parking lot. He couldn't be trusted around a Big Mac either.

NINA

Nina: a cop just came by
Libby: what about?
Nina: just updating us on the investigation
Clary: anything new?
Nina: mum's going by her maiden name again
Clary: WTF
Libby: why?
Nina: Fforde is too hard to spell
Clary: after 45 years? Think she'd have mastered it by now
Libby: it IS too hard. I go by ford at school now
Clary: since when
Libby: since I realized none of the kids could spell it. The cop came by because mum changed her name?
Nina: no but that's new
Clary: I meant what's new in the investigation
Nina: not much. Dad landed behind some rosebushes. That's why no one saw the body. They're still trying to find witnesses. He asked us if dad might have been...wait for it...*meeting someone*
Clary: what does that mean?
Nina: he was up to no good
Libby: the cop said that?!?!?
Nina: reading between the lines
Clary: they're suggesting dad was murdered?
Nina: *suggesting* is too strong

Clary: but not ruling it out?
Nina: idk. The cop acted like dad might have been doing something he shouldn't have
Libby: dad? are they crazy?
Nina: cop may have been bluffing. I think he was just trying to find out what we knew
Libby: clearly more than he does
Clary: was Mum there
Nina: yup
Clary: how did she take it

My thumbs hovered over the phone. I looked out my bedroom window. Mum's car was gone. She'd raced off minutes after Al-Haddad left, hair pulled into a rough ponytail, those crepey legs still on show, a postmenopausal teenager. I knew what Mum had said to the cop, how she'd occasionally tittered when she'd said it, but I couldn't bring myself to tell my sisters. It felt weirdly disloyal.

Nina: mum? Jackie O. Poised to a fault
Clary: don't know why I even asked
Libby: would you drop it Clary. You want her to cry?
Clary: maybe a little
Libby: I'm signing off. I don't need this. I've got work to do
Nina: don't go yet. I need to talk to you about something else. Did you know Randall had kids?
Clary: who's Randall?
Nina: dad's brother
Clary: a while since I heard that name and no
Libby: I knew
Nina: you did? How?
Libby: just did. I really got to go sorry
Clary: me too. The succubus howls. Love you
Libby: love you
Nina: xoxoxo

I stared at the blank screen. I didn't like withholding stuff from my sisters, but something had changed. Clary and Lib had jobs, goals, passions. I didn't. I sensed I had more in common with Mum now. We both had new lives all of a sudden and no idea what to do with them. I didn't want Mum looking ridiculous (Clary) or needy (Lib). I'd keep the nude sunbathing to myself for a while longer.

The nude sunbathing, though, was just the tip of the crazy-berg. There were the packages arriving daily from Sephora and Lovehoney. Tuneless singing of old Marilyn Monroe songs. A complete twelve-piece set of Limoges wedding china tossed to the curb. The wholesale dismantling of her/our life.

It felt overwhelming. I sat on my bed, alone for the first time in my life. My father, my mother, my big sister, my twin—all, in one way or another, gone. I felt incomplete. A puzzle with half the pieces missing. A car on blocks. I didn't know what to do, what I wanted, who I was.

I called Jesse.

NINA

"Hey," Jesse said. "What's up?"

We'd spoken semi-regularly since our breakup. Nothing substantive, of course, but substance had never been our thing. We approached conversation the way toddlers approach Christmas presents: more interested in the shiny wrapping than the contents. He'd call to ask where Don's amber cufflinks were or what issues he should discuss with the geriatrician. I'd call to tell him about a Bollywood rom-com I thought he might like or pass on an update about Arlo's budding humanhood. ("If he keeps this up, he'll be producing fully formed stools in no time!") The rest of my universe had been rocked by massive catastrophic change, but on the phone, we were the same old us.

Or had been, until that moment. Jesse always opened with "What's up?" but he sounded different this time. Annoyed would be overstating it, but he certainly sounded less than delighted to hear from me.

"Just wanted to check how things are going." I kept the tone light. "Don okay?"

"I would have called if he wasn't."

"Even if he was a little not-okay? Like, he had an itch or the hiccups or was running dangerously low on English Leather aftershave?"

Jesse didn't laugh, didn't counter. Not that it was all that funny, but he'd always been happy to go along for the ride before.

He said, "Yeah, well, I'm relatively confident I could handle those scenarios on my own."

"How are you?" I said when the dead air became uncomfortable, which was almost immediately.

"Not really your concern anymore, Nina...Anything else you need?"

You, I thought.

"Yeah. I, ah, wanted to talk to you about Mum." I was shameless.

"She all right?" A glimpse of the old Jesse. I sensed him stopping whatever he was doing—fixing the back door, defrosting the freezer—to listen.

"That's what I don't know."

"You still worried about her cleaning out closets? Because it's totally normal. Dad says widows like to stay busy. Keeps the void at bay."

"Did you tell him about the red lipstick?"

"Yeah. He preferred the beige."

"Seriously?"

"No, I didn't talk to Dad about the lipstick." All business again. I heard a clunk. A tool of some sort. "What else are you worried about?"

I went with the clickbait. "She was sunbathing nude. In the backyard."

Silence.

"Did you hear me?"

"What am I supposed to say? Did she get a chill? A nasty burn?"

"No, but, c'mon. Don't you think that's weird? She's almost seventy. It wasn't that hot. She's always been worried about sun exposure. If it's not weird, it's at least seriously off-brand."

"I don't know your mother well enough to comment."

"You've known her fifteen years!"

"So? Petra's never been one to reveal much of herself."

"Well, she's sure revealing much now!" No laugh, no rim shot. I changed my tone. "Are you suggesting she's hiding something?"

"Aren't we all?" Jesse snorted.

"You don't hide stuff. I don't."

"You do so."

"I do not."

"Nina. You broke up with me. Totally out of nowhere. Clearly, you hide stuff. And Petra does too. Even my mother noticed that."

"*Roz* noticed? They barely know each other. What did she say?"

"I don't remember exactly."

"Do so."

He hesitated.

"Jesse. Tell me for Christ's sake."

"I dunno. She just wondered why a woman as smart as Petra would spend so much time frantically redecorating if she wasn't in some way troubled."

"She actually said 'frantically'? Ooh. Meow. Minister's wives aren't usually that critical. And it's not redecorating, anyway. It's renovating."

"She wasn't being critical. I think she felt sorry for Petra."

Shabby, hair-on-her-chin, never-been-to-Europe Roz Whynacht felt sorry for *my* mother? "May I ask why?"

"Bird in a gilded cage–type thing."

"As in Dad trapped her or something? Held her against her will? Sweetest guy in—"

"No. Petra trapped herself. The whole perfectionism thing. That's what she meant. Now can we just drop this?"

I pictured the cluttered mess of hand-me-down furniture Jesse's parents called home. I considered mentioning that Roz's standards might have been the real issue here. "You look at the life my mother built and that's what you get? Something's wrong with her?"

"No comment."

"I beg your pardon?" Jesse and I had always commented on everything.

"Look, Nina. You and I aren't together anymore, so this really isn't my business."

"It is so your business. Why are you just...trashing everything? Acting like we're not even—"

"*I'm* trashing everything? You're the one who nuked our life!"

"I never said I wanted to expunge you. I just suggested we needed a break."

"Suggested. Ha."

"You could have argued with me."

"When has that ever worked?"

"Lots of times. You—"

"Sorry, Neens. Didn't mean to upset you. I'm very fond of Petra. But, look. Don's going to be up soon, and I still haven't started dinner. I got to go."

He was leaving me. Everyone was leaving me.

"What are you making?" I said. Happy, sweet, good old Neens.

"Salisbury steak and home fries."

"No greens?" Still light, but with a hint of concern. *Don will die of scurvy without me. You'll be arrested for elder abuse. See how Roz likes that.*

"Thanks for your interest, Nina, but it's not your problem how these two old bachelors choose to eat anymore."

That was ridiculous.

"I should come back."

"No, you shouldn't."

"I mean, I want to come back. I miss you. I miss Don. Forget the Salisbury steak. We've still got all those condolence casseroles in the freezer. Mum won't care if I take a spinach lasagna or two. If I leave now, I can be home by six."

"I don't want that."

"Okay. There's a chicken Marbella, too, but the prunes? With Don's tummy?"

"Nina."

"I'll bring both! I'm sure—"

"No. Nina. I mean, I don't want *you* coming back."

"What? No. Why?"

"You said you needed time to figure your life out. And you do. You're troubled, too, you know."

"Am not."

"Yeah, you are. You're not happy."

"That's why I took a break! To figure stuff out. And now I'm ready to come home. All better!"

"It took you two weeks to get your shit together? Ha. You only want to come back because you're too lazy to do the work."

"I am not!"

"Sorry, but you are. You're lazy. I'm lazy. Coupla jellyfish, right? Only it's not funny anymore. I got to figure my life out too. And I can't do that with you here distracting me."

"But you like being distracted."

"Not anymore."

"Jesse. Please."

"Sorry, Neens. You stay there, look after Petra, and figure yourself out. I'll stay here, look after Don, and do the same. We need to go our own way for a while."

"And never the twain shall meet."

"I'm not saying that. Someday, the twain very well could meet."

"But what if we're not on the same twack?" I needed him to laugh, but he didn't.

"Then you'll know you did the right thing."

"You mean, the wight thing." I couldn't help myself. My lip was quivering but I was still so hopeful.

"Fine. We did the wight thing. Now I really gotta go. Say hi to Petra for me. Reassure her that at no time during this entire conversation did I ever picture her nude."

A joke. Sort of. A crack in the wall. I put on a snappy voice and said, "I'm so relieved. I was—"

"Gotta go. Will you call Don occasionally? He misses you."

"I miss him too. I miss us. Jesse? I—"

He hung up before I could say, "I love you."

GORD

The kids are racing to the tree. Legs like sticks, bare feet, ground spiky with rocks and roots—but, man, are they fast. Gord runs behind them, pushing Boubacar in an ancient wheelbarrow, his tiny body bouncing and jostling against the rough wood. The heat is ferocious and the wheel seriously bent, but Gord is not going to let him lose. At the base of the hill, he lets out a roar and then digs in. The old rugby training.

"So long, suckers!" Boubacar squeals as they take the lead. It's one of the many phrases Gord taught him that Matron isn't pleased with. That's why they both love it so much. Gord finds a last spurt of energy and rams the wheelbarrow into the tree. "No!" the other kids groan, flopping to the ground in defeat. "Yes!" Gord cheers, raising Boubacar's arm in victory.

The arm comes off in Gord's hand.

Gord woke up, panting. Always the same dream, or some version of it. They're in Mali, at the orphanage, goofing around, having fun. Then Gord musses Boubou's hair—or picks him up or nudges him with his elbow—and the boy falls apart in his hands.

It wasn't even light yet, but sleep, now, was out of the question.

Gord got out of bed, took a cold shower, and brewed himself some tea. He did an hour of yoga and two hundred sit-ups, then took the framed photos of Luke and Boubou out of his backpack and stood them on the coffee table. The boys had never known each other but they were so alike. Their faces made him smile, made him swear, and made him determined to do this. He opened his laptop and got to work.

Since Boubacar died, Gord had downloaded dozens of articles about Keith Osterlich. Features about his business dealings abounded, of course, but Osterlich had also supplied *GQ* with his favourite meatloaf recipe, *Cigar Aficionado* with his favourite smoking memory, and *Architectural Digest* with a detailed description of the one antique he'd save if his house was on fire. (An early Ngbandi spear. Not as valuable as other relics in his collection but his first major find so, to him, priceless. "Money isn't everything," he claimed.)

Depending on which magazine they appeared in, the profiles either focused on Osterlich's vocal support of philanthropic causes or his appalling behaviour towards "underlings." He'd first come to the public's attention when a video surfaced of him unironically using that word at a PhiTex board meeting. Regardless of politics, every profile mentioned his "uniform": bespoke steel-grey cashmere suit, a white Eton shirt, and handmade brogues. Osterlich had a walk-in closet full of identical garments in each of his many residences. Unless at one of his orphanages, he wore his uniform everywhere. He estimated he saved over a hundred hours a year not worrying about what to wear.

When asked if he'd gotten the idea for a uniform from Steve Jobs, he replied, "Yeah, but the tailoring's better on mine." Snider journalists often pointed out that Osterlich's tailoring included a top button half an inch higher than standard to help elongate his five-foot-seven frame.

Gord knew everything there was to know about Keith Alden Osterlich, MSc, but he liked to reread the articles whenever he felt his determination flag. Gord knew what he had to do, what he goddamn well was going to do, but it still frightened him. He looked at his boys and thought, *The spirit's willing but the flesh is weak.* That's what his grandfather Bix used to say before he poured himself yet another glass of rye. His long-suffering caretakers didn't like it, but Bix went out the way he wanted to. Gord was going to do the same.

But not quite yet.

He peeled a banana, shoved half into his mouth, and started scrolling. He clicked on an article from *Fast Company*. It was one of his favourites. It made his blood boil.

Just what he needed.

THE EXIT INTERVIEW

Fifty years ago, few would have pegged Keith Osterlich as a future CEO of an international pharmaceutical giant. A small-town boy with an undistinguished academic career, Osterlich's slow but steady rise had less to do with his scientific smarts than with his marketing insights. His focus on international sales and his ability to see novel off-label uses for established drugs helped turn PhiTex into a world player. Our business columnist Shauna Sandhu sat down with him on the eve of his retirement to talk about his wins, his losses, and the controversies that have dogged him throughout his career.

Shauna Sandhu: Let's start with the obvious: why did you choose to step down from PhiTex now?

Keith Osterlich: (*Laughs*) Because I wanted to.

SS: So it had nothing to do with the numerous harassment complaints brought against you by employees?

KO: Not at all...No. Sorry. I lie. Of course, it did! I'm seventy-three. I'm sick of bullshit. I have a temper. So what? I hurt your feelings pointing out your work wasn't done to acceptable standards? Maybe you should have done it right in the first place. Great companies don't get built on shoddy workmanship.

SS: It was slightly more than "hurt feelings." Belligerent late-night phone calls, offensive social media posts. You've been known to throw objects, issue threats...

KO: Hey, one man's threat is another man's incentivization. (*Laughs*) I grew PhiTex into a giant. Some people didn't like my methods. Lots of other places for them to work. But why are we even talking about this? I presume you did your homework, Shauna. You know those matters have all been settled. I'm leaving PhiTex in a better state than it's ever been in. I've done what I promised to do for my shareholders. Now it's my time.

SS: And I want to talk about that. But before I ask about your retirement plans, let's get back to the state of the company. Yes, your numbers are excellent, but not without controversy.

KO: You're like a dog with a bone, Shauna.

SS: Just doing my job.

KO: My type of gal.

SS: And, since you mention it, "gals" have been one of the issues over the years. Female employees who claim their progress was impeded because they didn't respond to your overtures.

KO: "They claim." Unsubstantiated.

SS: And yet, time and again, you offered out-of-court settlements to get rid of these "unsubstantiated claims."

KO: I've got money. What I don't have is time. Paying to have baseless accusations go away makes sense. I have a permanent employee at my home in St. Kitts whose job it is to keep vermin out of my garden. Same premise. I'm used to paying for pest control.

SS: Whoa.

KO: You asked. I'm no longer the spokesperson for a major company. I don't have to be politically correct anymore.

SS: You were politically correct before?

KO: (*Laughs*) Probably not. I guess I don't need to lie anymore either, right?

SS: Well, aren't I in luck! Can we talk about Pediaxyclone? It was touted as one of your most promising new medications.

KO: More than touted. Pediaxyclone represented the first major development in the treatment of many childhood cancers. It was a breakthrough drug.

SS: But also a potentially lethal drug.

KO: In very rare cases.

SS: Not so rare. Pediaxyclone didn't receive approval in any Developed World market. That must mean something.

KO: It means there are children living with a dangerous disease out there.

SS: But still living. Children in the Developing World have died from its side effects. Do you regret your decision to sell it in these markets?

KO: Do I regret that children have died? Yes. But I've spent a lot of time in the Third World setting up Osterlich Children's Villages—which I hope you'll also find time to ask me about—and here's one thing I can tell you first-hand. Kids die all the time there. Pediaxyclone at least gave some the opportunity to live. I can't be held responsible for poor administration of the drug or inadequate medical care. My responsibility was to PhiTex shareholders. Pediaxyclone was sold legally to those markets. There were no laws prohibiting it.

SS: There are now.

KO: But there weren't then. What were we supposed to do? Trash millions of dollars' worth of product that could help sick children? My job was to maximize profit and minimize loss, and that's what I did.

SS: And now that job is behind you...So let's move on to your retirement plans. A lot of your personal profit I understand is going to feed your passion for early weaponry.

KO: That and alimony!

SS: What got you interested in antique weapons?

KO: I grew up poor. Not country-music poor, but poor enough. One of my earliest memories is of my mother taking me to see an exhibit of Egyptian relics at the museum. I now know they were relatively unimportant—wine jars, amulets, that sort of thing—but seeing how excited they made my mother lit a fire inside me. She always wanted to go to "the birthplace of civilization," but that's not something you do on a salesgirl's salary. So a large part of my passion no doubt comes from her.

SS: But why weapons?

KO: She was a woman so, naturally, she gravitated toward domestic artifacts. I'm a man so, naturally, I'm more interested in the world of the warrior.

SS: Naturally? Oh, wow. Careful, Mr. Osterlich. You can't say things like that anymore either.

KO: Says who?

SS: Maybe it's time we talked about your orphanages...

KO: Finally! The kids. It's all about the kids. They're my real legacy.

That was one of the few things Gord and Osterlich agreed on. It *was* all about the kids.

It made Gord want to kill the guy. Slowly. Painfully. Publicly.

He slammed his laptop closed. He considered doing another flight of push-ups to keep his anger in check, but no time. Who knew how long Osterlich would be in town? Gord needed to get going.

And he needed Petra.

She was the only person he knew cold-blooded enough to pull this off. The only person who would understand why it had to be done, and why it had to be done the way he planned.

Gord had been keeping tabs on her. He'd read that Malcolm was dead. He figured that could work in his favour but maybe not. Maybe the fire was gone. Gord was terrified Petra would say no.

He looked at the picture of Boubacar, his emaciated body, the dark circles under his eyes, his patchy hair—but that smile. That joy! That will to live. Someone had to pay for his death.

Gord picked up his phone. All he could do was ask her.

NINA

Despite being gutted after that call with Jesse several days earlier, I'd been sleeping remarkably well. I blamed Mum's sheets. Don's wife, Ruth, had liked the convenience of easy-care polyester, but I'd found them uncomfortable. Airless. Like sleeping under a shower curtain. Mum's Egyptian cotton bedding, on the other hand, could pass for bare skin. I'd slip my arm under the down pillow, curl my leg around the duvet like a sated lover, then float up to wakefulness sometime around noon with a feeling of almost post-coital well-being.

I was therefore understandably pissed when, one morning, Mum's phone woke me before eight.

I buried my face in the crook of my elbow and groaned. *Why isn't she answering it?* This was when the bad dreams started. Nightmares, I'd found, were nothing compared to morningmares. The horror of the real, not the imagined. Dad was dead. Jesse was gone. My sisters were otherwise occupied. My mother was a stranger. It was too early in the day to be reminded how much life sucked. I rolled onto my side, clamped the pillow over my head, and tried to coax my illusions back into bed with me.

The phone stopped for a few moments, then started ringing again. It rang and rang and rang. Mum usually took her coffee on the deck below my window. It was the best place for the morning sun. She must have gone inside and forgotten to take her cell.

I slid the pillow down onto my chest and stared at the ceiling. Teen Me mentally shouted, "Mu-um, get your goddamn phone!" Adult

Me briefly considered answering it myself. Dad's estate hadn't been finalized. The call may have been from the lawyer, the accountant, the artisanal stone carver about memorial options. It may have been from a friend, phoning to ask Mum out. Dragging her away from whatever off-off-Broadway space she was currently staging her weird little one-woman show in.

But then I heard the kitchen door open, hurried footsteps, and a slightly desperate, "Hello...Hello?" A pause, then Mum went, "Oh..." A high gasp tumbling into a low, delighted laugh.

Relieved, I put my pillow back over my head and rolled onto my side. Mum had installed sheepskin mattress pads on all the beds. Something about them made me think of brawny men in kilts—*Outlander* types, only with better personal hygiene. And that made me think of Jesse. Not a brawny man or a kilt-wearer, but happy to watch them on TV with me. I pictured us curled up on the couch after we'd got Don down for the night, a midweek beer to share, a bowl of furikake popcorn resting on our thighs.

I tried to let that fantasy play out, but Mum let out another long, swooping "Oh!"

This time it registered. I jolted up in bed, heart-first.

"I can't believe it!" she was saying. "I'm. I'm so happy! Thrilled! When can I see you? I'm *dying* to see you!"

My mother's responses had always been measured. Jackie O did not "die" for anything. Polite enthusiasm was a simple courtesy, not to be taken literally. Certainly not to be dressed up with exclamation points.

This conversation, though, was spiky with them. Alive with feeling. Downright fucking joyful.

I stared at the blind as if all her girlish passion was going to come crashing through the window and pin me to the wall. I thought of the woman at the funeral. The heavy one with the odd voice. I tried to convince myself that's who Mum was talking to, but I knew it wasn't. They'd seen each other already. If it had been Bonnie—I just remembered her name—Mum would have been happy, I guessed, but thrilled? Dying to see her?

No. This was someone else. Someone unknown to me. Not a bridge partner, not a spouse-of, not a fellow member of the art gallery docents committee.

I stood up. The floor creaked thunderously. Mum stopped talking. I stopped moving. She laughed, and I used the sound of her happiness to camouflage my footsteps. I tiptoed to the window and lifted the blind an inch with the tip of my finger.

Mum was standing on the deck, the phone against her ear, a hand over her mouth. She dragged a pointed toe back and forth over the floorboards. A bashful girl being asked on a date. More flirtatious tittering.

I let the blind go. Folded my hands over my chest and pressed down hard. Tried to catch my breath.

"Ooh, a proposition!" She laughed. "Even better. Tell me more."

A pause then, "How about tonight? I could meet you at the big house at nine. You know where that is? Highway 7, just past Morganville. It's right beside Shonda's Nail Salon. You can't miss it." A chuckle. "Oh, stop. Stop! But you can find it?...Great. Oh, and another thing. Talk about risky—I'll be wearing a blond wig."

Sustained laughter now, a garbled response as she tried to talk through it, and then, just when I thought I couldn't stand another word, she pulled herself together and said, "Gord. Darling. I've missed you so much. I thought I'd never see you again. Really, Gord, I did."

NINA

"She has a lover." I was back in bed, terrified to take even one tiny step into a world where such a thing could be possible.

Mum was gone. I didn't know where ("Out," she'd tossed off happily when I'd called down the stairs) or for how long ("Whenever!"). I had an image of her in a black robe, laid out on a table, clutching the sides as she braced herself for her first-ever Brazilian. It was too awful to bear. I'd FaceTimed my sisters as soon as I heard her car pull out of the driveway.

"You don't know that." Lib was in her office. The bookshelf behind her was cluttered with plastic binders, World's Best Teacher paraphernalia, and lumpy clay pots her students churned out for her at touching regularity. She kept a red pen poised over a pile of papers, as if she was going to settle this ridiculous family business lickety-split and get right back to correcting tests. "You only heard one side of the conversation, Nina. You don't know what the other person was saying."

"Thank God," Clary said. I'd caught her out for a power walk with Arlo. She'd found a picnic table under a giant oak tree and pulled the stroller into the shade.

"It could have just been a friend." Lib spoke with the calmness of a hostage negotiator.

"A male friend?" Clary raised her coffee cup in greeting at someone walking by. "What male friend has Jackie O ever had a chummy conversation with? I'll give you The Dude. Although 'chummy' might be a stretch. Anyone else?"

"Okay, a woman friend."

"She called him Gord," I reminded Lib.

"Gord?" Clary said. "Not even Gordon? Ew."

Libby made some ticks on the page in front of her. "You're enjoying this, Clary."

"I'm enjoying being right. Not what I'm right about." She adjusted Arlo's Paddington Bear sunhat.

"Who says you're right? Nina overheard half a conversation while she was half-asleep, and now assumptions are being wildly leapt to."

"I assure you I was not half-asleep by the end of it. Mum was practically licking Gord's ear."

"You could have misinterpreted the conversation, Neens." Lib tilted her head and smiled. She just wanted me to give that a think.

"No," I said.

"You've been known to do that."

"When?"

Clary leapt in. "That time you thought that guy had invited you for 'cunnilingus' when he'd actually said 'this coming Christmas.'"

"Different scenario entirely. Crowded bar and copious amounts of alcohol versus quiet backyard. Plus...plus!..." I waited for them to stop laughing. "Plus...even if I misinterpreted a few words this time, I didn't misinterpret the tone. Mum wasn't talking to a male friend, she wasn't talking to a female friend. She was talking to someone with whom she has an intimate relationship."

"You don't know that!" Lib slapped her hand on her desk. An unprecedented loss of cool.

"Sorry, Lib. I do. People's voices change. They get lower or higher or huskier or something. The only time I've ever heard Mum use a voice even remotely like that is when she talks to Arlo."

"Ick." Clary jiggled her head as if she'd just burped up donair sauce.

"But there's other stuff too..." I told them about the singing, the nude sunbathing, the wedding china. Mum handing out Dad's fleet of five-thousand-dollar road bikes to neighbourhood kids like Halloween treats.

That's what Lib picked up on. The bikes.

"So? That's nice! Maybe this Gord person was just calling to thank her for a bike."

"Lib. You're not listening to me. That's not what this is about. It's not a bike he was riding. It's her."

"Stop," Lib said. "You might believe it, Nina, I'm not saying you don't. But that doesn't make it true. And even if it *is*—"

"Yessss..." Clary said, hearing doubt creep into Lib's voice.

"*Even* if it is, Mum's a grown woman. This is her life. Adultery, or whatever, is not against the law. She's—oh, sorry." Lib smiled and turned to the door. "Hey, Frannie. I'll be right there." Lib turned back to us. "Sorry, girls. I've got to run to a meeting. Can we continue this conversation tomorrow?" She'd lapsed into principal-speak. She was lost to us. "Absolutely." Clary lifted Arlo's little arm and waved. "Bye-bye, Wibby!"

"Bye-bye, pretty baby. Bye-bye, crazy sisters. I'll text as soon as I know my schedule." Lib took a moment to look us each in the eye. "Don't do anything until we talk. Okay? Promise?"

We promised. Lib touched her fingers to her lips and then to the screen.

Her square went dark, and Clary said, "Like hell we won't."

NINA

"Like hell we won't what?" I said.

"Do anything." Clary picked something out of Arlo's nose and smeared it on the picnic table. "Lib seriously thinks we're going to just sit around and let this happen? Ha!"

I had to nip this in the bud. "Scary Clary" could be ruthless. "But what choices do we have? Mum's already made it very clear she's going to do what she's going to do. Lib is right. Adultery is not a crime."

"In *itself*."

"What does that mean?"

"I've got a bad feeling about this. And you do too."

"Mum's a grown-up. She's allowed—"

"Oh, come on. You called *us*. You were thinking exactly the same thing as me: How did she get a lover so soon after Dad died?"

"I was not!"

"But you are now, aren't you? I mean, given all the weird shit she's been up to, you'd be a fool *not* to think it."

Clary raised an eyebrow, inviting a response. She didn't get one.

"Look, Neens. If she has a lover, fine. Well, not fine, but you know. We have to at least find out who this guy is. We can't just let Mum toddle off into the unknown with some stranger. Maybe he's a bad guy. Maybe he's after her money or—you know—worse."

"Meaning?"

"I dunno." She flicked her hand casually. "Maybe he's, like, got her under his *thrall* somehow. Maybe he talked her into doing something to Dad and now he—"

"Clary!"

"I'm not saying that's what happened. I'm just saying let's rule it out."

"Rule what out?! That the two of them conspired to...hurt Dad?" I could not say "kill." This conversation was already way out of control. "Oh, my God, Clary. Did you just shrug?"

"What do you want me to do? I don't know what happened to Dad any more than you do. But I'd sure love to narrow down the possibilities."

"And how do you propose we do that? We don't even know the guy's last name."

"We follow her." This tossed off so breezily I almost missed the implication.

"What?... No."

"Well, what else can we do?"

"Clary. There's no 'we.' There's just me. I'm the only person here. So what you're actually saying is *I* have to follow her."

"I'd be on the phone with you the whole time."

"Oh. Phew. Such a relief knowing my backup is a mere two thousand kilometres away, naked from the waist up, suckling a baby."

"It's the baby that suckles the mother."

"No, it's not."

"Yes, it is. Look it up."

"Clary. It doesn't matter. I'm not doing this."

"Why not?"

"You know why. Because this is the part in the movie where we start pitching popcorn at the screen. The part where the cheerleader goes into the attic by herself to see why blood is seeping through the ceiling."

"You're exaggerating."

"You're the one who just strongly suggested this Gord guy's a murderer."

"I did not."

She did. "I'm not doing it."

There was a short silence.

"Didn't Mum say the big house is on Highway 7?"

"So?" I said.

"That's suburbia! Malls. Fast food joints. Mattress warehouses. Hideous, but not scary, especially at nine on a weeknight. You're just going to see what's up. What's the likelihood something dangerous is going to happen? Low to zero."

"Yeah, well, yesterday I would have said the same thing about Mum having an affair."

"Okay, so call the police." Clary picked Arlo up and made faces at him.

"What? And say my mother is planning to meet a man named Gord, please arrest him? It doesn't work that way."

"My point. The cops aren't going to help. So who is? Can't ask The Dude again. He's still a little shaken from the last time he got sent out to look for one of our parents."

I was assaulted with an image of Dad's broken body, face down in the stream. I let my head drop.

"Shit." Clary exhaled through her teeth. "Sorry. Too soon." She looked away. I didn't. It was a relief to see her sad. Sometimes even I got a little dazzled by the sparkly exterior.

"You think it'll always be too soon?"

"No." She grimaced as if she hated having to break it to me. "People have died since forever. The world can't just stop. Life goes on, right?"

"Maybe that's all this is about. Mum getting on with life."

"More like getting *it* on."

"Grow up." Now she was pissing me off. "Why'd you plant that idea in my brain? Seriously. You've been making these little jabs ever since the funeral. What makes you so sure Mum's up to something?"

I was prepared for her to just say, "because I am." Clary had always been irrationally confident about everything she did, thought, or wore.

Instead, she said, "Neens. You know how you were keeping stuff from us? Well, I've been keeping stuff from you too."

GORD

Gord hung up the phone and drew in a deep breath. He felt good. Invigorated. Almost human. He smiled. Petra always did that to him. She was strong and smart and saw reality through the exact same lens he did.

He remembered her telling him once how much she enjoyed their "little folie à deux." He'd had to ask what it meant.

She laughed. "It's French for the 'craziness of two.' Or, as psychiatrists like to say, 'induced delusional disorder.'" He'd forgotten she was a doctor. Another one of her secrets. "It just means we're worse together than on our own. We cultivate the same delusions."

"About what?"

"How the world works. Or should work, I guess." She'd put a perfectly manicured finger into her Pyrex coffee cup and fished a pine needle out of the rum.

"You mean we're both crazy because we recognize this shit for what it is?

"Nooo." She gave his shoulder a bump. They were slumped side-by-side on a mouldy plaid sofa inside a tarpaper hunting camp. Bix had built it in the late forties when the area was still wilderness. "But hearing us talk?" she said. "That's what most people probably think. We egg each other on. Kids die. We should just get over it."

"Yeah, well, fuck them." Gord clinked his mug against hers and downed the last of his rum. "Fuck. Them." Petra's lovely feet were propped on the dented metal trunk that passed for a coffee table. He nudged them aside to reach the bottle and poured himself a refill.

"I'm afraid fucking them is going to have to be your job, darling." She gave his hand a motherly squeeze. "I've got to go. The Association of Professional Engineers is meeting tonight, and Malcolm's getting some award. I should be there."

She brushed a hair from a long-dead dog off her pale grey blazer and stood up.

"How do you hack it?" he said. "Having to pretend like that?"

"Pretend..." She mulled the word over as she checked her makeup in the chipped mirror nailed above the wood stove. "It's not really pretending. It's more like...turning something off. Turning myself off, I guess. At least the socially unacceptable parts."

Gord slouched back down onto the sofa, resting his tin mug on the crest of his bare belly. It pinged against his St. Jude medal like a cell-phone alert. He looked down and noticed he'd gotten fat. Disbarred, disdained, slovenly, and now fat too. It didn't bother him. "Yeah. I probably should do the same. It's like that thing in the Bible. Cutting off your right hand if it offends you. That's what Aziza wants me to do. Cut off my right hand and my left leg and both balls no doubt, because those guys *really* fucking offend her. May as well, I guess. Not like I use them anymore."

Petra laughed.

Gord said, "I'm serious," realizing he was. "Just amputate the rot. Forget about justice. Retribution. Be a good little eunuch and play nice. I probably should." He stuck his bottom lip out as far as it would go and poured a trickle of rum down his throat.

"You should not."

"Why?" He said it with a note of playful confrontation. He'd always been attracted to women who kept him on the straight and narrow.

Petra put her lipstick back in her purse. "Because it kills the soul. Too big a price to pay."

"Yeah, well, *you're* paying it."

"Only because I have to. I made a promise when I was too stupid to know any better."

"You don't have to stick to it."

"I do."

"How come?"

"'A promise made is a debt unpaid.'" She said it lightly.

"You believe that?"

"Yes. And Malcolm does, too, although I bet in his heart of hearts, he doesn't like it any better than I do. He'd never admit it of course. Not even to himself."

"So how long is this debt going to be hanging over your head?"

"Till death us do part."

"Your whole life?"

"Yeah, well. If it comes to that." She waved at him. "Now, up. Put some clothes on. I'm not walking through the woods alone."

Gord looked out the window of his fancy rental and smiled at the memory of Petra wobbling down the overgrown trail in those expensive suede boots of hers. He was pretty sure that was the last time they'd seen each other. They'd had a few stolen phone calls after that, but then she'd gone away on a big trip with Malcolm, and Gord's drinking had gotten worse, and then Aziza kicked him out, and he went to Mali. Later, when it looked as if he'd finally managed to turn his life around—when he'd finally gotten over losing his son and his wife and everything that had ever mattered to him—Gord often laughed at Petra saying that.

Fucking them is going to have to be your job, darling.

He was hopeful she'd changed her mind about that. He loved the way she'd laughed when he said he had a proposition for her.

"It's risky," he'd said.

"Even better," she'd answered.

He was looking forward to tonight.

NINA

"What?" I leaned into my laptop like a cop leaning into the face of an uncooperative suspect. "What stuff aren't you telling us?"

"I saw Mum do something." Clary laid Arlo on the picnic table and untwisted the leg of his sleeper. "Some *things*."

"Oh my God."

"Not big stuff. Just weird. That's why I didn't say anything. But then Dad dying, and the way she's been acting, and now this? I don't know. It went from being just kind of what-the-hell to seeming..." Clary pressed her lips together and thought, "...significant."

"'Significant'?" I hate weasel words. "What did she do? Just tell me."

Clary stared at the sky for a second, then said, "Remember when I was having trouble nursing?"

Of course I remembered. The FaceTime calls were nightmarish. Clary and the baby, both snot-faced and sobbing. Her giant veiny breasts with the R. Crumb nipples. I'd never been more grossed out in my life. "Sort of."

"Mum stayed with us for a while. She was driving me crazy. *What if you held the baby this way? How about a nice warm cloth to make the milk come in? Why not try squeezing your nipple with a red-hot pair of pliers?...* All delivered in that perfect Jackie O voice as if I wasn't in the worst fucking agony of my life.

"Anyway, one day, I just lost it. Mum was like, 'Sweetheart, perhaps it's time you had a little rest.' She took the baby and I collapsed on the couch. I'd just drifted off when her phone rang. You think she'd tiptoe outside to take it but no. She stays in the room, chats away like I'm not even there. I was pissed. I opened my eyes, all ready to lay into her, and I hear her say, 'Really, Malcolm? How lovely!'"—full Jackie O—then she swore at him."

"*Swore* at Dad?"

"Yeah. I mean, not out *loud*. But she rolled her eyes and mouthed *for fuck's sake*, like he was an idiot or something."

"Mum?"

"Yeah."

"'For fuck's sake'? You're sure?"

Clary squinted furiously and mouthed, *For fuck's sake, Nina.*

"Okay. Fine. So what did you do?"

"Shut my eyes. Pretended to sleep. Few seconds later, I faked one of those waking-up moans and—boom—Mum's right back into character. 'Clary's up. Bye, darling! Love you!' As if nothing had happened. It was weird, Neens."

"Why didn't you tell us?" I know to the rest of the world that might look pretty minor, but Mum swearing—Mum swearing at *anyone*, let alone Dad—was big news. I'd only seen her mad once, and that time, in an unprecedented act of rage, she'd pointedly cleared her throat. My sisters and I had whispered about it for days. (We never again used white linen napkins to wipe up grape juice.)

"It felt like my fault." Clary winced. "I'd been treating her like shit. I figured I'd driven her to the edge, then poor Dad said something totally innocuous, and she just snapped."

"You should have told us anyway." We were sisters.

"Yeah, but...I had a baby to look after, hemorrhoids, a husband who was driving me nuts. I didn't have the energy. Plus, telling you guys would have upset Lib and, contrary to popular opinion, I don't particularly enjoy that. So I told myself it was nothing. Mum and I had both just been under a lot of stress. But then something else happened."

"Okay..."

"You're going to judge me."

"I won't."

"You will."

"Fine, I will. Like you care. Just tell me."

She puffed out her cheeks and sighed. "This was a couple days later. I was trying to get Spawn of Satan here to latch on, and Mum says, 'Mind if I go for a walk?' I was like, fuck. I'm hanging off a ledge by my pinkie and she's deserting me? But what could I say? She'd just done the laundry and cleaned the whole house. So I wave goodbye, and off she goes for a few hours in the park, all made up and gorgeous. Meanwhile I'm stuck here with a screaming baby, greasy hair, and a T-shirt that was—no lie—crispy with day-old vomit, but whatever.

"I waited until her car pulled out before I broke down in tears. I told myself to get some balls. I've done Ironman. I've made my clients millions. I can handle a baby. What's the big deal, right? But then Arlo started howling and wouldn't shut up no matter what I did. I almost called Mum to come back but figured she was at breaking point too. So I did something terrible."

"What?"

"This is where you're going to judge me."

"Spit it out."

"I went to get baby formula."

"Oh, for God's sake." I laughed. "You idiot. Lots of mothers use formula. It's not the end of the world. You still—"

"I left Arlo by himself."

"Clary!"

She slapped a hand over her mouth. "I know. I know. I was so tired. I wasn't thinking straight. I thought if I could just feed him, he'd stop crying, then maybe he'd be rational enough to try nursing again. The convenience store isn't far, but I would have had to get Arlo's car seat, put him in it, put it in the car, get it out, go into the store, put him back in the car. I couldn't face it. So I strapped him into his bouncy chair and left him shrieking in the middle of the living room."

"There goes that Mother of the Year nomination."

"I know." Clary sucked her teeth. "But that's how I stumbled on Mum. I pulled up at the store, and there she was, walking into the motel next door."

"I thought she was going to the park."

"No. That's just where she *said* she was going. Totally opposite end of town."

"Did you ask her what she was doing at the motel?"

"You nuts? I jumped back into the car before she saw me and booted it home. Luckily, by then, Arlo was so crazed with exhaustion he actually latched on. He sucked me dry, both sides, and I've never had a problem nursing again." Clary gave me a big fake smile.

"Did you ask Mum when she got back?"

"Ha. I was worried if I even mentioned I'd seen her she'd somehow realize I'd abandoned my baby, and next thing you know, three burly ladies from Family Services would be wrenching Arlo out of my arms and putting him up for adoption. Stupid, but whatever. I did ask Mum how the park was. That was her big chance to explain why she'd gone to some fleabag motel instead, but oops. Missed it. She was like, 'The park was glorious!' She walked the whole perimeter, read all the plaques, skipped rocks at the beach, etc., etc. She sure packed a lot into those two hours."

"So she lied?"

"Flat out."

"Why?"

"I wondered the same thing. She'd been using my laptop earlier, so when I got up for the 3:00 A.M. feeding, I did a history search. First hit: *Directions to the Satisfaction Inn*."

"Meaning she'd planned to go there."

"Apparently."

"What for?"

"Good question. Not like it has a four-star cafe or anything. It's got free Wi-Fi and a conference room they rent out for WeightWatchers and support groups and I hope to God not weddings, but that's about it. Frankly, there's only one reason anyone would go to a seedy motel at two in the afternoon."

"Ugh. Clary." I shuddered. "Why didn't you tell us? That's, that's huge."

"Because say it out loud and it's true. Plus, who am I to throw stones? Two consenting adults versus a mother who abandons her newborn—who's worse, do you think?"

I didn't say anything.

"Exactly. But then the red lipstick and her giving Dad's stuff away? I was like, *maybe this is worse than I thought*, so I tried to, you know, plant the seed. See if either of you guys had noticed anything. She's my mother and I love her, but I just don't trust her anymore."

I nodded reluctantly.

"Neens?"

"Yeah?"

"We can't pretend this isn't happening. We have to do something."

"Like what?"

"Find out whether this Gord guy owns a gravel company."

"That's not funny."

"Didn't mean it to be. Dad supposedly spun out on gravel on a busy road, and yet no one witnessed the so-called accident. His wife seems strangely happy to have him gone. Put two and two together."

"That's not what I get."

"What *do* you get?"

"I don't know. Sick to my stomach mostly. You really think Mum could have done something to Dad? She was devoted to him."

Clary shrugged. "You have no idea the number of times I've seriously wanted to kill Krish."

"But you haven't."

"Not yet. But will he make it to seventy-one? I doubt it. I've already price-checked woodchippers on Amazon."

"Please stop making jokes."

"I'm kind of not. I've been mad enough I could easily imagine a scenario in which I do something terrible to him. Maybe Mum just reached her limit."

"Or maybe there's a perfectly innocent explanation for everything."

"Sure." Clary picked up Arlo and kissed his head. "Still—are we really going to let our naïve and emotionally fragile mother hook up with some unknown guy?"

I wobbled my neck noncommittally, and before I knew it, she'd talked me into checking out the big house next to Shonda's Nail Salon on Highway 7.

"Mum's not getting there until nine, right? So go earlier. If the place looks suspicious or whatever, we'll, ah—"

"What?" I said. "Call the cops? We already ruled that out."

"I'll think of something."

That didn't reassure me.

NINA

"It's a bar."

It was almost seven-thirty. I was sitting in Dad's Volvo in the vast parking lot of a suburban mall.

"What? Hold on." Clary hollered at Krish to take Arlo. "Say that again."

"The Big House is a bar. A prison-themed bar and grill." I read the words written in neon on the fake cinder block façade. "*Big House Chow Hall. Killer Cocktails!!* Note the exclamation points spelled out in bullet holes."

"Oh God." Clary let her voice slide down the scale. "When Mum said 'big house,' part of me was hoping she meant 'country estate.' A horse farm maybe. Even a McMansion. But a theme bar?"

"I know." I moved my phone around to show Clary the whole scene. "It's got fake razor wire and search lights and a mannequin stationed on the roof in what I presume is the guard tower. Can you see?"

"I've closed my eyes. I can't bear it. If Mum had been fooling around with some silver fox in a Cotswolds cottage, I mean, yes. It would break my heart, but repulse me? No. This is just so tacky. I mean, what kind of guy would she be meeting at 'The Big House'? I'll tell you. The kind who wears novelty briefs and glow-in-the-dark condoms."

"On the plus side," I said, racing to expunge that image, "it makes the perfect cover. Not as if any of Mum's friends would catch her here."

"Great. So she knows enough to cover her tracks. Which, when you think about it, just makes her sound even guiltier. Now go in and check it out."

"What? No. What if she sees me?"

"She said she wouldn't be there until nine."

"So why even go in then?"

"Just go, for Christ's sake. Ask the bartenders if they've seen her. Find out what they know. What's the matter with you? You're *there.*"

"And you're annoying," I said. But I went.

A hostess in a sexed-up guard uniform said, "What are you in for?" The first of many prison-based puns I'd be subjected to.

"Just a drink." *A double,* I thought.

She listlessly waved a fake security wand across my body, then led me inside.

It was worse than I'd imagined. "Cement" wallpaper, plastic bars on fake windows, and an Instagrammable electric chair in the corner with a sign that read, *The Big House: Shockingly good!* The servers were dressed like old-time convicts in striped outfits and pillbox hats. The few patrons to drag themselves out on a Tuesday night ate off sectioned metal trays like the ones frozen dinners used to come in.

The bartender was covertly wolfing down fries from a plate hidden under the counter. I sat on a stool and waited for him to notice me.

I checked the daily specials on a TV screen screwed to the wall. The designer had leaned in hard to the whole convict aesthetic. Lots of locks and bars and menu items spelled out in jail-house tattoos. Drinks with names like Bodily Harm, Mug Shot, and the Shawshank Libation.

Everything made me think of Jesse. If he'd been here, this would have been awful, but it would have been fun too. We'd always loved so-bad-it's-good. I snapped some pictures, planning to send them to him later with a little quip, nothing too polished, just something to make him smile and rethink his position. But then I remembered him saying, "I don't want that, Neens. I don't want you to come back."

The bartender had to ask me three times if I'd like anything.

"A Slammer," I said, because that's what had just flashed on the screen. "Two."

He slapped the bar. "Coming right up!" He wore his little cap at an angle, the way a monkey dancing to an accordion would. We all suffered mortifications. I tried to smile at him in encouragement but couldn't trust my face not to break into a sob.

He brought me my drinks in dented tin cups, the way cocktails are no doubt served in prison. I threw down the first one.

"Anything else?" he said.

I remembered why I was there. I wiped my mouth. "Yeah. Yes." I opened photos on my phone. "I'm looking for someone."

I showed him a picture from Clary's wedding. Mum was in a celadon silk cocktail dress, Miu Miu heels, and beige lipstick. She looked amazing. "Ever seen her?"

He leaned in close to my phone and squinted. "She looks sort of familiar..."

"She's been here before?"

"No. She looks like that actress. You know the one." He rolled his hand. "In that movie? New York? Bit of a ditz..." He snapped his fingers. "*Annie Hall*!"

"Oh, right. Sure you haven't seen her?"

"Oh, I'm sure." He looked pointedly at his clientele in their ballcaps and cargo shorts and pastel tank tops revealing overlarge tattoos of Disney characters. "I think I would have noticed someone like that here." He apologized for not being more help, then went back to his fries.

I sipped my drink. I'd made a terrible mistake. If I'd gone home to Don's after the funeral, I'd never have known what Mum was up to. She'd still be my mother. Still elegant, still reliable, still there for me. I'd have had the freedom to worry about my own life, not hers. I wiped my eyes on my sleeve.

Someone said, "You all right?"

A middle-aged guy with a beige buzz cut and the brown leather bomber jacket of a divorced dad was sitting two stools over. (In Big House parlance, that no doubt made us "stool pigeons." *Oh, Jesse. Jesse! Where are you when I need you?*) He wasn't quite smiling at me. Smiling wouldn't have suited him.

"Do I *look* okay?" I said.

"Not really."

"And you thought pointing that out would help?"

"Guess not." He took a book out of his pocket, put his elbows on the bar, and started to read.

I blew my nose and called Clary. She didn't pick up. Libby would have answered on the first ring, but I wanted outrage, not comfort. I indulged the idea that I had no one in my life to turn to. I finished my second Slammer.

The bartender asked the guy if he was ready for some "chow."

"Give me the vegan burger and a root beer." He jerked his thumb in my direction. "Get her whatever she wants too."

So that's who I was now. The type of sloppy woman a sad-sack divorcé buys pity drinks for.

I was past caring. I had no boyfriend, no job, and no future. I lifted my glass at the bartender to signal *the usual.*

"Another Slammer, Miss?"

"Yeah. Guess that makes me a repeat offender, eh?"

The divorced guy laughed. Not a big laugh. Just a little rumble of appreciation. It felt rude to ignore him. He was the prison padre, bearing witness to my sins. Plus, he was paying.

"You're a vegan?" I said, with a barely there sneer. I'd acknowledge him but I wasn't going to encourage him.

"I am now."

"A root beer–drinking vegan. That surprises me." As if I and my third alco-pop held the moral high ground here. "I would have taken you for a Budweiser-and-beef type of guy."

He frowned and nodded, not looking at me. The nerve. He was the one who'd initiated this conversation. Now I was the chatty drunk.

I'd show him chatty. "You got some ethical problem with booze and meat? Or just toning up for bikini season?"

"Yes," he said.

"Yes to what?"

"Yes to one and/or the other. You should frame your questions better."

The bartender brought our drinks. The guy raised his glass at me, like *cheers*, but without any of the goodwill usually associated with toasts.

"What are you," I said, "a lawyer?"

"No."

He took a drink. I watched him, sighed, and took a drink too. I didn't know why I was wasting my time with this guy.

Then he said, “I was. But that’s another thing I gave up. Law, alcohol, and hurting other living beings. Which, for what it’s worth, often involved law and alcohol.” He gave me a smile, a real one, as if this amused him. He had deep wrinkles around his eyes and across his forehead. He looked like an anorexic Charles Bronson.

“So what’s with the leather jacket then? The cow didn’t mind?”

“I had it before. Didn’t seem right throwing it out.”

“Could have given it away.”

“Why? To look like a proper vegan? Don’t care that much. Plus, I’d just have to buy another jacket. Wool comes from sheep. Cotton needs a ton of fertilizer to grow. Nylon, rayon, spandex, polar fleece—all just a bunch of chemicals. Better to stick with my leather jacket and let some random woman at the bar give me a hard time about it.”

I rolled my eyes.

He took another gulp and stared straight ahead.

I did the same. The Slammer was so sweet there was a real danger I’d lapse into diabetic shock before I got as drunk as the situation required.

“Why are you here?” He was pissing me off.

“Hungry. It was close. I knew they had vegan specials. You?”

“Not for the vegan specials, that’s for sure.”

“Huh.” He glanced at me. “Now *you*. You look like a vegan.”

“Oh, yeah. How?”

“The clothes. The hair. The sneer.”

I chuckled. (Even Lib found judgy puritans hard to take.) “Actually, I’m a devoted meat-eater. In fact, just this morning, I had kitten for breakfast. Soft-boiled.”

He didn’t laugh. Jesse would have laughed, extrapolated thereon.

“So just had a craving for a Slammer? That’s what brought you to the ‘burbs’?”

“How do you know I don’t live around here?”

“How do I know?” A little smile. “I was wrong about the vegan part, but you’re a city girl, aren’t you? Or maybe deep country? Something with a water view?”

“Yes…” I paused for him to get it. “Now who needs to frame their questions better?”

“Ha. How’s this: What brings you here?”

The TV screen over the bar said tonight was karaoke night. Not surprisingly, they called it *Sing-Song at Sing-Sing*. "The entertainment," I said.

"Another surprise. You look more like a foreign film type of gal to me."

I could have mentioned *Mean Girls* and *Ratatouille* and the eighties rom-coms Jesse and I gobbled up like Raisinets, but I didn't know this guy. I didn't want to know him. I shrugged and went back to my drink.

His meal arrived. He closed his book over the boarding pass he was using as a placeholder and pushed it away. He picked up his burger in two hands, took a large bite, then nudged his plate toward me with an elbow. "Have some fries." Mouth full.

"You don't have to feed me. You aren't my dad."

"I know. Just trying to get some food into you so I don't get puked on. Here." He handed me his napkin.

I realized I was crying again. Just the word "Dad" had been enough. I shook my head *no*.

"C'mon. You'll like them. The menu said vegan, but I bet they're fried in animal fat."

I accidentally laughed, so took some fries to cover it up. They were hot and salty and immediately soothing. I was like Arlo with a tit. If not immediately happy, at least distracted. The tears stopped. I took another bunch. One landed on his book.

"Sorry." I delicately wiped the cover with my greasy fingers. *African Antiquities*. That was the title. "Well, well. Another surprise, Mr..." I could just see the last name on the boarding pass. "...Bickerton. *Bickerton*? That's your name? Or character description?"

He picked up the book without answering and put it on the other side of his plate.

I snickered at his childishness and turned to the screen above the bar. *Fuck him if he can't take a joke.* I'd just finish my drink and go. The TV was showing bad old-style publicity photos of the singers in that night's karaoke contest. Another thing Jesse would have loved.

I told myself I'd apologize, I'd fix things with Jesse, I'd bring him here. We'd laugh really hard. Everything would be fine.

I snapped a few pictures of a female Johnny Cash, a slightly cross-eyed Dolly Parton, and someone calling himself Hellvis Stressly. It was all so wonderfully awful.

The next photo was of an elderly Marilyn Monroe. I was looking through the camera lens at her, working on a snappy caption to charm Jesse, when I realized I'd just taken a picture of my mother.

NINA

The hostess said, "Making a break for it?"

I barrelled out the front door without answering. I stumbled through the searchlights criss-crossing the parking lot, found Dad's Volvo, and clicked the key fob. The panic alarm went off. I hit random buttons until the noise stopped, and the doors unlocked, then I flopped inside, as exhausted—as terrified—as if I really *had* just made a break for it.

I turned on the car. I turned it off. I was too drunk to drive. I eventually realized this may mean I was also too drunk to know what I'd seen. I opened my photo library, clicked on the last picture I'd taken, and enlarged it.

The ridiculous wig, the garish lipstick drawn over the lines, and worse, the dress. Strapless fuchsia, riding low on a bony chest. The stringy neck, mercifully, was largely concealed by a rhinestone choker. I read the caption, *The seductive sounds of CherrySin Monroe singing her truth: Diamonds are a girl's best friend!* I wanted this to be a mistake, but it wasn't. It was Mum.

I lowered my forehead onto the steering wheel.

My mother. An aging drag queen.

Was she ill? Demented? Had Dad been covering for her all these years? (They'd talked about that in the Alzheimer's class Jess and I had gone to. Grown children are often unaware a parent has cognitive issues until the other parent dies.) Or was Mum some kind of imposter? Had this always been her life and we'd just never known? I felt like I'd stumbled onto her porn stash.

I found myself wondering if that's what had happened to Dad. He'd stumbled onto it too. She'd been found out, so he had to go.

I scoffed at myself. She was only singing karaoke! That's not the type of secret you kill for.

Or do you?

I really had had too much to drink.

I called Clary, repeatedly, but she didn't pick up. I considered calling Lib, but she'd just come up with another excuse for Mum's behaviour.

I was past that. I wanted the truth.

I texted Clary, Call ASAP I don't care what time ITS IMPORTANT

I lay back in my seat and waited until I was sober enough to drive. The parking lot thinned as shoppers left. People in sweatpants and fake nails with carts full of massive Dorito bags and two-fours of Coke. Couples bickering as they strapped discount mattresses onto late-model vans. Skinny-legged ten-year-olds performing private dances while their fathers finished their smokes. These were the type of people who perform at strip-mall karaoke nights.

My mother couldn't even sing. I knew that for a fact. Several times, I'd heard her belting out show tunes when she'd thought I was out. I'd been horrified she was singing so soon after Dad's death. So much worse to realize now she'd been practicing.

Had any of the people in the parking lot seen her perform? Were they talking about her? *Oh, Jesus, Mary, and Joseph. Did you get a load of that old girl in the Marilyn Monroe getup? Painful.*

Did Mum have any idea how bad she sounded? How far gone was she?

I almost phoned Jesse but the word "troubled" popped into my head. That's how he'd described her. I wasn't going to give him proof.

I sucked on an energy gel Dad had stashed in the glove compartment and compulsively checked my phone, as if, in the din of an empty Volvo, I might somehow have missed Clary's call.

I waited.

After an hour or so, I looked up and saw Mum walking out of The Big House. I slunk down in the seat, flipped my collar, and peered out the bottom of the window. She was still in her fuchsia fit-and-flare but without the wig now. Her hair was pinned flat to her scalp, and she appeared to be missing an earring. The person holding the door for her stepped out next.

Mr. Bickerton.

I should have known.

I threw back my head and huffed. Well, wasn't he suave, making way for the lady? I don't know why it pissed me off. It was just a courtesy to a stranger. A lot of guys his age would do the same thing.

But then I watched him put his brown leather jacket over her bare shoulders and kiss her forehead and I saw her smile—saw her light up in flames—and I realized she was no stranger.

At least to him.

But to me? I didn't know that woman at all.

PETRA

"You cold?" Gord asked.

Petra had insisted on giving him back his jacket. He laid it across their legs and put his arm around her shoulders. She was covered in goosebumps.

"Yeah, but I like being cold."

They were sitting on a picnic table at a neglected parkette overlooking the railyard. A place they used to meet years ago. They'd always felt safe from the world here.

"And I like being hot too. I had decades of being comfortable and, Christ." She rooted in her sateen clutch for something. "It nearly killed me."

"But you survived," he said.

"Just barely."

She waved a package of cigarettes at him. He shook his head.

"Don't smoke anymore?" She took one out for herself.

"No." He smiled. "There's a lot I don't do anymore."

"Therein lies a story." Petra lit her cigarette and blew smoke out the side of her mouth. "Let's hear it."

"You first. How are you?"

"Crazy." She coughed out a laugh. "I mean, obviously. Look at me. Sad, isn't it? After years of seething resentment, what do I do when I'm finally liberated? A bad rendition of 'Diamonds Are a Girl's Best Friend.'"

He chuckled, not unkindly, remembering her breathy sex-doll voice and awkward gyrations. "What was that all about?"

"Oh, hell. I dunno. I've just always wanted to sing in front of an audience, so I did." She took a long drag, then pulled her hand away and stared at the teetering column of ash. "I'm a panicky mess, Gord. That's the real reason. All those years, clamped down, blanked out, trying to keep things together…I missed so much. Now I'm desperate to do everything before it's too late."

She flicked the ashes onto the patchy grass. "Who am I kidding? I'm almost seventy. It *is* too late. Especially for this dress." She made a face and yanked up the drooping neckline. "What the hell was I thinking?"

He leaned back and smiled. "Looks good to me."

"Oh, quit the bullshit." She meant it, but loved him for trying. "All the truth, all the time. That's what we said, right? I'm elderly and deranged. I'm acting as if all I had to do was get rid of Malcolm and, voilà. I'd be thirty-three again and could just pick up where I'd left off—but it doesn't work that way. I should have left him when I had the chance."

"When would that have been?"

"Ha. I used to think once the kids were on their way I could be, too, but Clary was a nightmare teenager, then Libby was depressed in her twenties, and then, Nina…" Petra propped her chin on her thumb and took another drag. "Nina's thirty-six and still on shaky ground. I didn't want 'I'm leaving your father' to be what pushed them over the edge. Although weirdly, I thought they'd be fine with him dying of something quick and painless. I knew I'd be. Kind of the perfect solution."

She winced but just for show. They both understood ugly truths.

"I even fantasized about him leaving me for another woman. I loved that idea. I'd be free *and* blameless. But that never happened either, despite all the attractive clients and eager young engineering students I pushed his way. Honestly, I could not get rid of the man. After a while, I pretty much put it out of my head. When I'd want to kill him, I'd just get out my fabric swatches and redo another room. The house became my booze. I wasted my life on it."

He took the cigarette from her, held it briefly under his nose, and handed it back. "You're too hard on yourself. You accomplished a lot."

"Like what? Organized a few house tours. Put on some galas. Did the avid-volunteer thing. Hardly the life I'd dreamed of. But who cares? I want to hear about you. Where have you been all this time?"

"Mali." He raised his eyebrows like *can you believe it?*

"Mali? Really!" She drew her hand along his face. "Did they not feed you there? You're skin and bones."

"They fed me fine. I just decided to give up meat and alcohol. Started exercising again."

"Such a man thing." She unclipped her earring and laughed. "Malcolm did that too. You guys all think you can starve grief or outrun it. Did it work for you?"

"For a while." He shrugged. "The job helped too."

"What were you doing?"

"Working at an orphanage."

"An orphanage. Wow." She turned her back to him. "Sorry—can you undo this damn choker? I'm suffocating."

He fumbled with the clasps. His cool, dry fingers grazed her neck and she shivered. The thrilling memories it stirred up. Then, just as quickly, sadness. She'd been desirable once. Now all she could do was put on a blond wig and pretend. If people saw her grieving, that was why. She was pretty sure she'd missed last call.

Gord slid off the choker and handed it to her. She rubbed her neck and smiled. (*That's what you do. You damn well smile and get on with things.*)

"So...How did some ruthless, hotshot lawyer end up working at an orphanage in Mali?"

He laughed, then told her about the fight with Aziza, about landing in the snow, about the magazine with the story on hometown hero Keith Osterlich.

"Keith Osterlich," she said. "I know him. Well, I'm *acquainted* with him."

"Just acquainted? I saw you two in the society section a couple of times."

"Yes. And he came to the funeral, but Malcolm's the connection, not me. Osterlich bought the old McKelvie mansion. He wanted an ocean view so spent a small fortune moving it from Young Avenue to The Point. Malcolm did the structural work. Osterlich was apparently very happy with it. Which is unusual. He's notorious for his temper."

"And other things," Gord said.

"You don't like him?"

He wiped the corners of his mouth with a knuckle. "I hate the guy."

"Gee. I thought once you deprive men of red meat, they become docile. What did he ever do to you?"

"You heard of Pediaxyclone?"

Petra shook her head. "But Osterlich was PhiTex Pharmaceuticals and it starts with 'pedi,' so I'm guessing it's a children's med of some type."

"Yeah. A cancer drug. It was supposed to be PhiTex's next big hit. Huge excitement about it—until evidence showed it destroyed the liver."

"Oh, right. I seem to recall that now."

"The results pooched any chance of it getting approval in the Developed World. PhiTex was getting hammered so Osterlich did what guys like that do. Cut his losses and started selling Pediaxyclone in countries where it wasn't banned."

"Oh. Let me guess. The poorest ones."

"Yup. That old story. Save the stockholders and screw the brown kids."

Petra snorted in disgust, then something hit her. "The cancer ward at the Children's Hospital." She turned to Gord, her eyes round. "It's named after Osterlich."

"Yeah, well. Got enough money, you can buy anything."

"God, that makes me mad." Petra thought of the malfunctioning fetal monitors some company had pawned off on the clinic she and Bonnie worked at outside Butembo. The babies who died. She ground her cigarette butt into the picnic table as if it was Osterlich's right eye. She'd known Congolese warlords with higher moral standards than those white-collar bastards.

"Why is this still happening?" She banged her fists on her lap. "Honestly. I could just *kill* the guy."

Gord let out a loud laugh.

"What?" She turned on him. Nothing about this was funny.

"I'd been worried you'd lost your edge now that Malcolm was gone—but guess not."

"Me? Never. Still more than enough fury to go around." Petra remembered how quickly it had flared up when she'd seen Sharon, standing there in that purple dress, looking for forgiveness.

"I'm really happy to hear that." Gord patted her knee and smiled lovingly. "Because I have a project that might interest you."

NINA

As soon as I got home, I went to my room, opened my laptop, and typed *bickerton lawyer*. Fourth entry: *Gordon E Bickerton, LLB.*

The famous Gord.

The Gord Mum missed so much. The Gord she never thought she'd see again. Some sad, leather-wearing vegan at a tacky bar.

The first image to come up must have been ten years old. Gord was bigger and broader back then and hadn't buzzed his hair. In the photo, he was adjusting the sleeve of his expensive suit as if he was about to step into a high-level meeting. His smile suggested he'd just cracked an off-colour joke. You could practically hear the boom of the photographer's laugh behind the scenes. Good old boys, causing some poor assistant to pull her clipboard close to her chest and cringe. Gordon E. Bickerton had way more twinkle in the photograph than the guy I'd met at the bar, but it was definitely the same person.

Not Mum's type, I thought, although she'd have appreciated the suit.

He was a partner at Levi, Karchava and Bickerton: *a full-service law firm specializing in patent law, corporate law, and mergers & acquisitions.* I scrolled through photos of him holding a client's arm up in victory, playing rugby, at a New Year's Eve ball with his pretty, dark-haired wife. An all-round guy. Scanning his list of clients, I got the impression Gord was the man to call when you needed a migratory bird habitat paved over or a low-income neighbourhood razed.

I almost cheered when I read the headline, PROMINENT LAWYER DISBARRED. I clicked on the link.

> The Barristers' Society is calling for the disbarment of senior lawyer Gordon E. Bickerton, recently found guilty of professional misconduct.
>
> "We recognize Mr. Bickerton has been dealt a staggering blow by the death of his child," Society counsel Luana Ruel told a disciplinary panel Monday. "The Barristers' Society has made health and addictions supports available to him, but he has refused all offers of help. His erratic and at times violent behaviour means he is no longer capable of performing his professional duties to the standards required. As a result, we must move to disbar him. We do not do this with any pleasure. For many years, Mr. Bickerton was a strong and effective advocate who...

I read the whole article, but the only words that registered were "at times violent..."

It had been hours since I'd seen my mother leave arm-in-arm with him. She still wasn't home. Was this one of Gord's violent times? I phoned her cell, but no answer. I pictured her terrified, unconscious, bleeding out. I hit redial, then redial again. Moments later, a text came in.

Don't wait up, darling. I'll be late.

I texted back, It's after one. It already IS late. Where are you?

She replied, Goodnight, Nina, and added three kiss emojis. Instead of fighting to the death, I now pictured Mum and Gord cavorting naked. (Thanks to Clary, glow-in-the-dark condoms featured prominently.)

It was all too horrible. I went back to scrolling, hoping that might help dispel the image.

I soon stumbled upon The Luke Bickerton Foundation for Research into Wilms Tumour. Luke, a sparkly, dark-haired boy with enormous brown eyes, was apparently Gord and Aziza's son. He died at five of a rare cancer. I actually found myself getting a little tearful, and it wasn't just the residual effect of the Slammers. The website had lots of candid heart-warming photos of the family laughing, playing, and hugging throughout Luke's short life. The pain of losing him had to have been excruciating. I gave Gord a pass for some of his bad behaviour (but not for the condoms).

Then more bad news. DOCTORS SEEK RESTRAINING ORDER AGAINST DISBARRED LAWYER. I clicked on a cellphone video of three cops wrestling Gord out of a hospital lobby. This Gord had the neck beard and doughy white belly of a basement-dweller. He was screaming about butchers and hacks and baby-killers. A cop pushed down his head and shoved him into the squad car.

Something twigged. I paused the video and zoomed in. I recognized the cop. Back then he was sporting a mustache I could have done without, but Ryan Al-Haddad was still every bit as gorgeous as the day he'd shown up at Mum's with the accident photos.

I remembered him asking if Dad had any enemies. My heart thumped. Al-Haddad knew Gord. Did he suspect something was going on between Gord and Mum? Had Al-Haddad actually been on a reconnaissance mission? Is that why he'd come to our place?

I needed to talk to Clary. I texted her repeatedly, but nothing. When did Arlo get up to feed? Two A.M.? Three?

I couldn't just sit there waiting—Theatre Nina was still showing *Porn with Petra!* on all screens—so I searched the house. For what? I wasn't sure. I checked the kitchen drawers, the hall closet, Mum's purses. A package of flavoured cigarillos in with the dishtowels. A diamanté strapless bra, still in the delivery box. What may or may not have been a vibrator. Hardly damning evidence. By this point, I'd gotten used to stuff like that.

I ran upstairs to her office and found her laptop.

Mum was still using the same password we'd set up for her decades ago. The folders on her desktop appeared to be exactly as labelled. Garage blueprints. Photos of Arlo. Minutes of the Historical Society. I checked her emails. Mostly condolence letters and special offers from upscale catalogues. I checked her search history. *How to apply Marilyn Monroe makeup. Karaoke tips. Antarctic cruises. Learn to sculpt in soapstone.* Nothing from or about Gordon E. Bickerton. No *Five Easy Steps to Kill Your Husband.*

I went to her bedroom and scoured her bureau, her bedside table, the top shelf of her closet. I found nothing to bridge the gap between the woman who'd been devoted to my father for forty-five years and the alien lifeform in love with Gordon E. Bickerton.

NINA

It was after three when Clary finally called.

"Neens?" she whispered. "This can't be good."

I sat up in bed, a hand splayed over my eyes. "You're not going to believe this." I told her all about The Big House and karaoke and Mum and Gord.

"Jesus," she said. "A disbarred lawyer with a violent streak? Was he at least attractive?"

"Who cares?"

"I want to understand what she's doing with him."

"Like it would be okay if he's smoking hot or something?"

"Just tell me."

"I don't know, Clary. Not un-attractive. How's that?" I rubbed my forehead. "He has a bit of an ex-con vibe."

"You just said he wasn't unattractive."

"Yeah, well. Daniel Craig. This is so beside the point."

"It isn't. I'm looking for motive. Is he the type of guy you thought La Bouve would end up with?"

La Bouve. I hadn't heard that one in a while. It was short for Bouvier, Jackie O's maiden name, but as teenagers we'd liked it because it was sort of icky. It sounded like it could have been JFK's pet name for Jackie's vagina. No coincidence Clary had dredged it up again now.

I sighed. "I didn't think she'd end up with anyone."

We were quiet for a while. I felt weirdly guilty, talking about Gord like that.

"He was actually kind of nice," I said. "I was crying. This was before I knew who he was. It was all just so depressing. Mum. The shitty bar. Dead Dad. No Jesse to make it better. Gord asked me if I was okay. Bought me a drink."

"You think that means he's *nice*?" Clary snorted. Arlo squawked. "He spotted a victim, Neens. That's how pimps pick up lonely girls at bus stations. They buy them drinks, then hook them on drugs and force them into the sex trade...I probably shouldn't have let you go on your own."

"Let me? *Made* me."

"You think that's what he's doing with Mum?"

"Forcing her into the sex trade?" I pictured Mum's nipples dangling off the ends of her old breasts like knots on deflated balloons. There's a sexual appetite for almost anything, but really? I just couldn't see it.

"No. What's the matter with you, Nina? I mean, using her. For a source of income. You said he's disbarred. He's probably broke. Why else would a guy twenty years younger than her be interested?"

That was so insulting and dismissive of everything that made Mum appealing. "Lots of reasons," I said although none sprung to mind.

"He's probably emptying Mum's bank accounts as we speak."

"So? It's her money. If she wants to give it to him, she can." Just playing devil's advocate.

"*Wants* to give it to him? Some lowlife gold digger in a bad jacket? That sound like someone our mother would want to associate with?"

"No. But what do I know? I'm starting to think I'm a terrible judge of character."

"Well, I'm not. Something's different about Mum and has been for a while. Remember Dad's speech at my wedding? How he hoped our marriage would be as happy as theirs? When he said that, I turned and smiled at Mum. I was just so full of joy. She smiled back, but there was this weird flicker behind her eyes. It was like a scene from an M. Night Shyamalan movie. I knew something wasn't right even then."

"Stop, Clary. Don't ruin everything. Mum was happy. She was."

"No. I saw it. The same way I saw her go 'for fuck's sake,' the same way I saw her lie about that skeevy motel...I don't like this, Neens. I want my father back, but I want my mother back too."

We both did.

I pictured Mum the day I'd broken up with Jesse, telling me she'd be making choices I might not like. The look on her face. There was nothing tremulous about it. Nothing apologetic. She was steely. She'd been planning this for a while. We'd all just been too self-centred to notice.

I realized how little time we'd spent thinking about her. Actually *seeing* her. Mum had always just been Mum to us. As flawless, unchanging and, frankly, uninteresting as a statue of a Roman goddess. You'd no more have questioned what was going on in her head than you would Venus de Milo's. I wondered how many tells our arrogance had caused us to miss.

I heard the front door open.

"She's here," I said. "Talk tomorrow?"

"Yes, yes, yes, yes, yes." Clary signed off.

I waited a couple minutes, then stepped out of my room, squinting as if I'd just woken up. Mum was tiptoeing up the stairs, her cheap dress scrunched around her thighs to allow her knees to bend. Her lipstick was smudged. Bobby pins were criss-crossed over her head like X's marking the days left in a prison sentence. She was losing an eyelash. How long had I been sleeping with Jesse before I'd let him see me look that bad?

Years. More proof this was not a new thing between Mum and the mysterious Mr. B.

"Just getting in?" I said, faux-drowsily.

"Yup."

"Have fun?" I braced for the answer.

She looked away, as if this required some thought. She bit her lip and chuckled.

"The word 'fun' doesn't do it justice."

PETRA

Petra stood in front of her bedroom mirror, one arm cocked over her shoulder trying to get at the zipper from above, the other coming at it from below. She arched her neck. Her fingers scrabbled up and down her back. She wasn't even close.

She should have known this was going to be a problem. She'd needed help getting into the dress before her performance too. Polly Darton had tried, but those ridiculous nails of hers. In the end, Petra inhaled, Polly pressed in on her ribs, and Hellvis Stressley yanked up the zipper. They'd all laughed. Jokes about it taking a village and suffering for beauty and how unlikely there'd be a "whole lot of shaking going on" in a dress that tight. Despite all the wigs and Spanx and makeup, it had felt wonderfully, joyfully natural. Real life at last. Petra had thought her night couldn't get any better, but then Gord had made his proposal.

She dropped her arms and shook out her tingling fingers. Nina would still be awake. She could unzip her.

Petra took two steps towards the door and changed her mind. Nina would pry, want to know what her elderly mother had been doing until three in the morning. Petra's heart flipped. *Wouldn't you like to know?* She remembered Gord, that charming half-smile on his face, playfully demanding physician–patient privilege. He wouldn't tell her a thing about his "project" until she'd promised, hand raised, to keep their conversation strictly confidential.

She gave up on the dress, sat down at her vanity, and started on her hair. Not that she'd ever, ever in a million years tell Nina what went on—if there was one thing Petra had learned, it was how to keep a secret—but still. Why risk it? She felt almost drunk with happiness. There was a danger she'd get sloppy. Something could slip out.

She looked at her reflection and thought, *Wipe that smile off your face. What's the matter with you?* This was about children dying. About revenge. Justice, at any cost. But she couldn't help it. She felt alive again. She leaned in close to the mirror and rubbed at some fuchsia lipstick on her chin. (She actually quite liked the colour, although next time she'd go for a less glossy finish.)

How long since she'd felt this good? How long since she'd laughed this hard at stupid jokes? How long since she'd cried?

She ran her fingers over the back of her head and pulled out three more pins. She'd cried when Duncan died, of course. Non-stop and for a good year, at least. Tears of pain and sadness and red-hot rage. Rage at that damn Sharon—thinking her live kid was somehow worth more than Petra's dead one—but at Malcolm, too, for going along with it. For "being reasonable." (Like wanting to kill the person who'd killed your kid wasn't reasonable? Says who?)

But since then? Petra had dabbed at a few tears as Clary walked down the aisle, but she was pretty sure tonight was the only other time. It was seeing Gord break down that did her in.

They were still at the parkette. He'd been telling her about the orphanage. Because of his assault record, he hadn't been allowed near the kids at first, but he'd worked really hard. Built huts, cleaned latrines, went to all the church services.

"Open-heartedly, eyes to heaven, the whole bit," he told her. "God was in me, Pet. I'd forgiven Him for taking my son. I'd forgiven Him for taking Aziza. I was repentant and grateful and anxious to make up for lost time."

When he eventually did get to work with the kids, he'd fallen hard for one little guy who'd reminded him a lot of Luke. They'd both had cancer, but it wasn't just that. It was their energy. "Two little whirling dervishes of joy," he said.

Petra tried to remember the boy's name. She headed into her bathroom.

It starts with B.

She tapped her index finger against a tooth. She didn't like this. She'd always had a mind like a steel trap. Bonnie took weeks preparing for an anatomy exam, but Petra could memorize the name of every ligament, muscle, and tiny inconsequential toe bone in a single run-through. She wasn't going to let herself turn into a doddering old lady. Not when she was finally on the verge of doing something with her life.

She switched on the bathroom light. *What was his name?*

Gord told her the boy had been responding well to treatment until one day he took a sudden turn. Someone threw Gord the keys and said to get him to the hospital. He drove like hell, screaming over his shoulder the whole way. "You're going to be okay. Hang in there, buddy! I'm going to get you there, I promise."

That's when Gord had choked up. Petra put her hand on Gord's knee, but he shook it off. He wanted to finish the story. She used the hem of her dress to wipe her eyes. Last thing he needed was her crying. He gave his head a hard scratch and kept going.

Gord got to the hospital, opened the car door, and knew right away the boy was dead. The way his little neck was bent.

Petra peeled off an eyelash.

Boubacar, she remembered. *Boubou.*

The boy's death was heartbreaking, but Gord had carried on. He knew losing Luke hadn't given him a get-out-of-jail-free card. The Lord giveth and the Lord taketh away. He'd lose other people he loved. Gord thought he'd made peace with that until the day, a few weeks later, he ran into an expat doctor at a village market.

He told her about Boubacar. She'd recognized the symptoms. The ashen skin. The sudden weakness. The confusion. It wasn't cancer that killed Boubou, she said. He must have been on Pediaxyclone. She'd seen it often enough to know.

Peace was no longer an option.

In his old life, Gord had been an investor in PhiTex. He knew about the Pediaxyclone trials. He knew Osterlich was CEO. He connected the dots.

"And that, Pet, was the end of my religious conversion." Gord gripped the edge of the picnic table and looked off into the darkness. "Osterlich visited the orphanage once when I was first there. I was still just a lowly latrine cleaner so wasn't granted an audience, but I saw him get out of his helicopter, converse with the nurses, take pictures with the kids, and I thought, someday that'll be me. I'll pull myself together. Make money and do good with it. Then I found out this so-called philanthropist—this *hero*—was making money selling lethal drugs. Kids in his own orphanage were dying because of him. And that was it. You can't ignore that kind of evil."

Petra put her head on his shoulder. "Aw, sweetheart. I can see why you'd hate him."

"Can you see why I'd want to do something about it?"

That had made her laugh. "Yes."

"How'd you like to help me?"

She leaned back to get a better look at him.

Why, you scoundrel, she thought. She immediately stopped worrying about how skinny he'd become. She knew it didn't matter what you did to Gordon E. Bickerton—starve him of meat and booze and women—he'd stop at nothing to get what he wanted. She'd always liked that about him.

"Help you do what exactly?" she said.

"Take Osterlich down."

"Yes." Not a moment's hesitation.

Gord laughed, then his face went serious.

"There's something you should know before you sign up for this." He took her hand, looked her in the eye. "Osterlich didn't break any laws selling Pediaxyclone in Mali. The drug was legal there."

"Okay..."

"That means our only hope of getting justice is to do something *extra*judicial." He raised his eyebrows and waited for that to sink in.

"You mean illegal."

"Yes."

"Even better." Petra had no patience for what the legal system considered fair and reasonable punishment, and Gord knew it.

The scoundrel, she thought now, with a smile.

She found a pair of nail scissors in the bathroom drawer and cut herself out of the dress.

God, she felt good.

NINA

Mum was at the kitchen table when I came downstairs a few hours later looking for painkillers. She'd changed into her housecoat, but there were still smudges of black eyeliner swooping drunkenly toward her temples.

"Couldn't sleep?" I asked.

"Didn't want to." She sipped her coffee.

"How come?" I rummaged through the cupboard where she kept her non-prescription drugs. Everything was all-natural. I needed chemicals. Something just this side of toxic. Those Slammers were brutal.

"We have just one wild and precious life, Nina. I don't want to miss a second. And neither should you." She stretched her legs out on the chair beside her. "Which reminds me, darling. I wanted to talk to you."

I turned to her, hopeful. My hangover disappeared. All would be explained. I sat down at the table. "Fire away."

"You think it's a good idea to be living with your mother at your age?"

She wanted me out. She was moving Gord in. I immediately thought of the neighbours. Clary. Even Lib would be appalled.

"I do." I wasn't going to let her get away with that. "I mean, I'm not thinking of it as a long-term arrangement, but at the moment, I'm happy here."

"Really? Shouldn't you be—"

"Really." I hoped my smile didn't look as fake as it felt. "I've made choices you might not like either."

Mum sighed, looked away, started to say something, then laughed. “I suppose I can’t be meddling in your life when I’ve told you in no uncertain terms not to meddle in mine.”

“So I can’t ask where you were last night then?”

“Correct.” She patted my leg. “I’m here now, darling. I’m safe. I’m smiling. What more do you need to know?”

“Well…”

“That was rhetorical.” She stood up. “There’s coffee but you might like to make a fresh pot. It’s hours old. Now I’m going to have a shower. Clean myself up.”

The conversation was over. Nothing had been explained. Mum slipped her phone into the pocket of her housecoat and turned to go.

“Ah. Can I borrow your cell? Mine’s dead, and I have to talk to Jesse about something.” I was turning into Clary. I’d become sly.

She tossed it to me.

“Same password?”

“Of course. I’ve got better things to do than make up new passwords.”

“Just one wild and precious life, right? Internet security be damned.”

“Exactly.”

I waited until she’d gone upstairs, then searched her recent calls, shared all the contacts with myself, then scrolled through her apps. Mum only used her phone to call, text, google, or take the occasional photo. The other apps, Dad had downloaded for her. She’d probably forgotten she even had them.

One such app was Find My Phone. I linked it with my email address and imagined how proud Jesse would have been of me. Outdated gender norms, I know, but he’d always handled my tech problems.

All my problems.

I couldn’t let myself think about that right now.

I went upstairs and put on my navy-blue funeral dress and a houndstooth blazer Clary must have left in the closet. I remembered Gord saying I looked like a vegan. I twisted my hair into a bun and put on lipstick. I checked myself in the mirror. Maybe not quite Meat-Eating Captain of Industry, but plausibly Flexitarian with a Business Degree.

I left Mum’s phone on the kitchen table with a Post-it note saying I was out for the afternoon. I got into the Volvo and headed off to find out more about the man of her dreams.

PETRA

Petra walked into her room, naked, her wet hair wrapped in a towel. She was relieved to finally have the house to herself. Nina was cramping her style.

She wiggled into a pair of shapewear. *Cramping my style?* Did people still say that? She did up her bra and manoeuvred her breasts until the nipples were more or less aligned. She'd probably last used that expression as a teenager, when her parents had tried to impose rules about the length of her skirt, the length of her boyfriend's hair, how late they could be out.

Malcolm had cramped her substance. A much greater crime. All those years, making her hide her true self. Fake it. It was a wonder she wasn't riddled with cancer.

She undid the towel, bent over, and rubbed her hair dry.

It had been fine for him. He was the king of compartmentalization. He'd damn well compartmentalized his whole life away. She thought of all those neatly labelled cardboard boxes, heading to the shredders.

"Stupid man," she said out loud. "Stupid, cowardly man."

Then immediately regretted it. Lying to others was one thing, but lying to yourself was unforgiveable.

It wasn't Malcolm's fault. She knew that. They'd both been adults when Duncan died. They'd had responsibilities. They didn't have the luxury of falling apart. They'd had to survive for the girls. The tragedy—she refused to call it an accident—had already claimed too many lives.

It hadn't been easy. They'd gone to therapists, lawyers, doctors, yogis, priests, and outright quacks. They tried meditation, medication, primal screaming, and booze. What worked for Malcolm didn't work for Petra and vice versa. They cried and fought. They went for the soft spots. They hated the universe. They hated each other. They were headed toward mutual assured destruction.

They finally decided there was only one way forward. (Malcolm's idea, yes, but Petra had agreed.) They had to wipe the slate clean. He'd give up his family. She'd give up her job. They'd move away and forget this had ever happened. They made a promise—made it out of love, she reminded herself now—and took a "vow of silence." They'd both kept it.

Malcolm was no more to blame than she was. He'd just been better at living with it.

Petra opened her closet and paused at some of the garish outfits now taking up prime real estate. All the loud patterns and revealing cuts. Had she lost her mind? It was like she'd traded in one costume for another. This wasn't the real her either. Anything pink, pastel, or polyester was heading to St. Alban's tomorrow.

She reached into the back and took out a linen suit. Stone-grey. Beautiful lines. Understated. She thought of Gord and his newfound calm.

Before she'd driven him home the night before, she'd asked for details. "How exactly are we going to take the bastard down?"

Gord wouldn't answer. "First, you need to do some research into Osterlich yourself. You're a doctor."

"Were."

"Okay. Were. You understand this stuff. Read up on him. Decide how far you're willing to go. If we're on the same page after that, we'll discuss next steps. Until then, I'm keeping my mouth shut. I don't want you knowing something it would be better not knowing."

They drove the rest of the way in silence. He asked her to stop a few blocks from the condo tower where he was staying. They leaned awkwardly across the armrests and hugged goodbye. He moaned. "I've missed having someone I could trust."

"Me too. It's a lonely old world."

"No shit."

He opened the car door. He was halfway out when he said, "Oh, I should warn you."

"There's more?"

He clicked his teeth as if unsure about telling her. "Osterlich was also involved in developing Narcontine."

Warn me? Or rile me up?

Remembering it now, Petra suspected the latter. Gord was no fool. Whatever worked.

She'd just slipped on her favourite pair of Dior slides when the doorbell rang.

NINA

Levi, Karchava took up the top two storeys of a glass high-rise on the waterfront. Dad's firm had probably been involved in building it. The elevator was full of tall, lean people with glowing skin and expensive suits. Clary's tribe. My funeral dress was fooling nobody. Flexitarian, maybe, but definitely admin staff.

The lobby was vast and impressive: marble floors, pale wood, the wine-dark sea sparkling in the background. Several well-dressed people were seated in the waiting room, reading actual newspapers. Two receptionists occupied a desk roughly the size of the Star Trek flight deck. They raised their chins and smiled.

"May I help you?" the male receptionist said. The female went back to collating papers.

"Um. Yes..." I suddenly understood where the expression "cap in hand" came from. I didn't know exactly what I was going to say but suspected it would require some grovelling. "Odd question, perhaps..."

The receptionist's smile took on a congealed quality.

"...but I'd like to speak with someone about Gordon Bickerton." I pronounced the name slowly as if speaking through a Plexiglas shield at the DMV.

A lawyer, striding through the waiting room, turned when I said "Bickerton."

"He's not at this firm," the receptionist said.

"Yes, I know he doesn't work here anymore, but I was hoping to get some information about him."

"I'm sorry." The receptionist frowned, a clown acting out *sad*. "We have no connection whatsoever with the person you're interested in." *He who shall not be named.*

"It's an important personal matter. Even if you knew someone I could talk to about him? Someone who—"

"Afraid not. Sorry we couldn't be of more help." A quick show of teeth, then back to his paperwork. I'd been banished.

"Oh. Ah. Well. Thank you."

I slunk into the hall and waited for the elevator, my heart pounding. These people wouldn't even admit they knew him. Gord was worse than I thought.

I heard the door to the law firm open behind me and the click of high heels on polished stone.

"You dropped something." The female receptionist bent down and handed me a scrap of paper, folded in half. The elevator dinged. "It looks like it could be important."

I stepped into the elevator and opened the note. It said, *Be at Cara's Coffee Stop in 10 minutes.*

I looked up just before the door closed. She raised her eyebrows to make sure I understood.

Ten minutes later, I was sitting in the window of a nearby cafe when the receptionist walked by. She gave the slightest nod in my direction. I took that to mean *follow me*. She didn't slow down so I also took it to mean *but not too closely*.

After about a block, she turned into a mall my sisters and I had frequented as teenagers. Most of the storefronts were empty now. The rest housed Jamaican patty stands, off-brand tech equipment, and headless mannequins wearing the kind of shapeless floral dresses Jesse's mother trotted out for church tea-and-sales. The receptionist beelined through the centre court, then took a left at a door marked *TO PARKADE*. I followed a few moments later. I found her sitting on the bottom step of a concrete staircase.

She was one of those middle-aged women who must have been gorgeous once upon a time but now appeared breakable. (Keeping under 115 pounds is hard on the face.) "Sorry for the cloak-and-dagger stuff, but Avery's a bit of prick. I didn't want him getting suspicious."

"Avery?"

"The other receptionist...So? What's Gord up to now?"

"You know him?"

"Very well." She smiled. "Ever since he was a baby lawyer. Is he in trouble?"

"No. I mean, not that I know of. Kind of the opposite in fact."

"As in he *is* the trouble?"

"Yeah."

"Phew." A rattly smoker's laugh. "Back to his old self then! Scared me when you came in asking about him. What'd he do this time?"

"I think he's dating my mother."

"Well, I'll be." She slapped her thigh. "Never knew him to go for the older gals."

"Should I be worried? I googled him. His reviews aren't great. I just want to know if he's an okay guy."

"Short answer?" She patted the step. I sat down beside her. "Gord Bickerton is definitely *not* an okay guy. 'When he's good, he's very, very good, and when he's bad, he's horrid.'"

"Horrid?"

She jiggled her hands, like *calm down.* "I'm just saying he's a man of extremes. Arrogant but loveable. Smart but crude. Everyone liked him. The admin staff, because he was funny. The partners, because he won cases. He was a beast when he had a trial, but you just learned not to take offence. When it was over, there'd be drinks all around. Everybody's best friend again."

She took a package of mints out of her purse and offered me one. I accepted. Clary says my breath stinks when I'm stressed.

"Look." The receptionist took one too. "I don't know if Gord would be your cup of tea or not. But don't judge him too harshly. He's had a rough time. His kid died."

"So I heard."

"It destroyed him. The cancer Luke had isn't usually fatal. But you know, if there's an eighty percent survival rate, that means twenty percent don't make it. Gord couldn't accept that. He blamed the hospital, the doctors, his wife, everybody. The firm told him to take off as much time as he needed but he insisted on coming back. His files were a mess. He was drunk most of the time. He got arrested for fighting, issuing threats, being an asshole. Eventually, he got disbarred. The firm did their best to distance themselves from him, but it took a lot of expensive dinners to convince clients that Levi, Karchava was not responsible for went on at Levi, Karchava and Bickerton."

"Is he violent?"

"He smashed up a few offices, got in the odd fist fight, but nobody got hurt." She shrugged. "I mean, *much.*"

Oh, great. "You think he'd steal from Mum? We're a little worried he's after her money."

"No." She scoffed. "Gord always liked money but only as a way of keeping score. It wouldn't feel like winning if he cheated."

"So he's honest, then."

She laughed. "I didn't say that. Gord's not *dis*honest, but he had no problem pushing limits. He could be a bit of a snake." She crunched her mint. "But, hey. He might have changed. I heard he went to Africa and found God. He sent his ex a nice letter when she remarried. Her husband's a partner here—one of Gord's best friends—so that couldn't have been easy. They read the letter at the wedding. Very funny but touching too. That's the Gord I remember. He was so sweet after my divorce. He'd drive me home. Drag me out on drinks night. Make sure I was all right. And for what? Just because he cared. I had nothing Gord wanted. No status, no connections, and I was too old for sex. Or at least that's what I thought until I heard about your mother." She winked. "I better go. I'm supposedly picking up dry-cleaning for one of the partners, and that can only take so long."

She stood up. "Mind waiting a sec until I make my escape? All I need is Avery catching me 'trading firm secrets.'"

"Can I ask you one more question?"

"Shoot."

"How'd you feel if Gord were seeing your mother?"

"Thrilled. But my mother's eighty-four. If she can attract a guy like that, maybe there's hope for me."

AL-HADDAD

He'd only done a preliminary search that morning, but Ryan Al-Haddad had found nothing suspicious in either Malcolm's or Petra's backgrounds. No unpaid debts. No disgruntled former clients/employees/lovers. No whiff of scandal. The Ffordes appeared to be pillars of society. Al-Haddad hadn't spotted a single red flag.

So there was no reason for him to be parked under a large oak in an unmarked car, surveilling Petra's house. And he wasn't, really. He just happened to have a craving for the beet salad at the nearby Osprey Café and was taking a few moments on a quiet street to enjoy it before heading back to the office. Or at least that's what he'd say if anyone asked.

He'd uncovered nothing suspicious in his search, but that didn't mean there was nothing surprising. Al-Haddad had found literally dozens of images online of the Ffordes at galas, house tours, charity golf tournaments, barn-raisings, and art openings. Mr. and Mrs. Worthy Cause. He'd been starting to think his gut had been wrong about Petra when something hit him.

The way she was dressed.

Al-Haddad was a bit of a clotheshorse himself so her wardrobe naturally caught his eye. Her gowns were particularly impressive—simple silhouettes, sophisticated colours—but even swinging a hammer for Habitat for Humanity or flipping pancakes at St. Alban's Shrove Tuesday Dinner, Petra had always looked elegant. He couldn't imagine the woman in the photos ever even owning the type of tasteless sundress she'd had on when he'd met her.

So why was she wearing it then?

He considered the possibilities. *Petra was home alone. It was a hot day. She forgot I was coming.* None of them rang true. To a clothes person, it's never just an outfit. It's a statement. *What was she saying?*

The daughter had clearly thought something was up too. Al-Haddad remembered the horror on her face at the sight of all that bare skin. She'd become even more alarmed when Petra said she was going by her maiden name now.

That prompted him to delete *Fforde* and search *Petra Astbury* instead. The very first thing that came up was an announcement from the medical society archives stating that Petra Jane Astbury, MD, had relinquished her licence.

MD.

That did nothing to explain the dress, but it sure piqued his interest.

Petra was a doctor, or at least had been until thirty-six years ago.

He wondered why she'd stopped practicing. Petra would have been young then. There was no suggestion of wrongdoing. The announcement simply said she'd relinquished her licence. In other words, given it up voluntarily.

But how voluntarily? Al-Haddad knew the medical society would occasionally make deals to save money or face. *Hand over your licence willingly now, or we'll drag you through a very public inquiry. Your choice.*

Is that what had happened with Petra? Did she just not enjoy medicine, or had she retired rather than face censure? The fact that nowhere in all the hits—even the medical galas and hospital fundraisers—had Petra ever been referred to as "Dr." felt significant. Al-Haddad's experience was that people relinquished the licence much more easily than they did the professional title. Status is a hard thing to give up.

Something about Petra Astbury-Fforde made him itchy. He had more pressing cases to solve, but this was the one that niggled. That's why he'd chosen this shady spot to enjoy his lunch.

He cupped his hand under his chin so he wouldn't drip beet juice on his trousers and studied the Fforde house. Malcolm was an extremely successful businessperson. Petra had plenty of money. Friends in high places. An impressive address. Maybe that was all the status she needed.

Al-Haddad had to admit that his suspicions may have been based on nothing more than simple jealousy. He and Alex could barely afford their new-build suburban townhouse, and that was on two salaries. He was just guesstimating what it would cost to paint a house the size of the Ffordes' when the front door opened and a man stepped out.

Petra stood in the doorway, chatting with him. It all looked very neighbourly until she suddenly leaned forward, wrapped her arms around the man, and pulled him close. He nuzzled his face into her neck. Their bodies shook. After a few moments, Petra stepped away, took him by the hand, and led him back inside.

Al-Haddad only realized he'd knocked over his salad when he felt dressing seep onto his thighs. He'd seen that guy before, but where?

He found a wet wipe in the centre console. He couldn't remember, but it was somewhere recently. He scrubbed at his pant leg.

The feta was going to stink, especially on a hot day like this. By the time he'd cleaned it all up, he looked like he'd pissed himself.

Oh, well. Small price to pay. His case had just gotten a whole lot more interesting.

PETRA

Petra thought Wayne would never leave. He was always popping in to see "how she was doing" when, really, he just wanted to cry on her shoulder. He seemed to think they had some kind of bond now. Malcolm's two closest confidantes, devasted by their shared loss.

She felt sorry for him. She really did. Wayne was not her type—the bad hair, bad jokes, and that awful monster home—but he was a decent soul. He'd been an engineering classmate of Malcolm's. They'd been friendly if not particularly close. When Duncan died, though, and the family needed an escape, Wayne had made room for Malcolm at his firm, no questions asked. Petra was grateful, but Christ. She couldn't have him sobbing on the front step every second day.

She'd dragged him back inside and poured them each a drink of the expensive Scotch Malcolm claimed to like but never drank. Wayne blubbered away about Malcolm's integrity, his kindness, his blah-blah-blah. Petra lasted about fifteen minutes before dabbing showily at her eyes and saying, "You've got to stop, Wayne. You're going to make *me* cry!"

That did it. He pulled himself together for her sake, then Petra all but pushed him out the door. She had things to do, people to destroy. She had to get moving.

She changed her top—there was a mucus stain on the shoulder—and headed to the city library.

Despite being almost seventy, Petra wasn't completely inept technologically. She had little use for most of the apps Malcolm had installed on her phone, but she knew her way around the internet. Years and wasted years of home renos had made her a bit of an expert. She'd read enough mysteries to know, too, that if Gord wanted her to do something illegal, she'd better not have a digital record on her devices.

She sat at a public terminal on the library's second floor and looked up *Keith Osterlich*, *PhiTex*, *Pediaxyclone*, and *Narcontine*. She skimmed the headlines. Anything potentially interesting, she sent to print. She paid the copy charges in cash. When she was finished, she put the hundred or so pages into a manilla folder, then slipped the folder into her leather satchel. She took out a few books on Scandinavian furniture just in case anyone asked what she'd come for. She realized that was probably overkill—is there anything less conspicuous than a well-dressed senior at the library?—but better safe than sorry. (*Ha,* she thought. The irony was not lost on her. Playing safe, of course, was what had made her sorry all those years.)

Nina was out when she got home, but Petra holed up in her office to read the articles anyway. The last thing she needed was Nina getting wind of this.

The information on Pediaxyclone was bad but not shocking. Selling off discredited medicine in Africa was a time-honoured strategy. ("They won't know the difference. They'll be happy to have it!") The practice was rife in Congo when she and Bonnie had been there a thousand years ago.

What shocked her was that there were still no laws against it. Where were the embargos? The public outrage? Some tycoon pats a female staffer's bum, and he gets pilloried. He makes millions selling toxic drugs to impoverished nations, and he gets a building named after him. What the hell was the matter with the world? Gord had every right to despair.

She saved the articles on Narcontine for last. Just seeing the word in print sickened her. She felt a sharp spike of anger then became very calm. Cyborg calm. That's what you do in an emergency. Even as a young resident, Petra had impressed senior medical staff with her sangfroid. She took a breath to ground herself, then began to read.

Little of the information was new to her. Developed by LaFontaine Laboratories, Narcontine had been touted as a PMS miracle drug. Girls loved it. It eradicated period pain and mood swings, plus it kept their weight down. What the girls knew—and the company categorically denied—was that if you took it during the rest of your cycle, Narcontine gave you a euphoric high. Its street name was "Sweet Sixteen." That was both the age most kids got hooked on it and the length of its effect. Sixteen glorious who-gives-a-fuck hours. Crushed and snorted, its impact was shorter but even more powerful.

What Petra hadn't known was that Osterlich had been part of the team that developed Narcontine. By the time it had come to market, he'd left LaFontaine and moved to PhiTex. According to a *New York Times* exposé she'd found, Osterlich had been fully aware of researchers' concerns about the drug. Rather than address them, though, he went around them. He gave Narcontine the snappy brand name "Freeling" and developed a PR campaign aimed directly at teens. Bright pink packaging. Product placement in fashion spreads. A peppy jingle commissioned from one of the year's biggest popstars. He'd personally concocted the "scientific facts"—i.e. utter bullshit— that Freeling was both safe and effective.

Petra finished reading, closed the folder, and stared out the window. Her face remained composed, but her brain was on fire. That rage again.

She thought about Duncan. His little body, the face they wouldn't show her.

Then she thought about Sarabeth, almost with compassion. She'd never really liked Malcolm's niece—Sharon and Randall had spoiled her—but Sarabeth, she realized now, hadn't been a killer. That was Osterlich's doing. *He* was the one who'd killed her boy.

Petra took the papers downstairs and burnt them in the living room fireplace.

She didn't know exactly what Gord had in store for Osterlich but she hoped it was painful. As a doctor, she knew first-hand the worst ways to go. She'd be more than happy to offer suggestions. Strychnine. Rabies. Ebola. She'd once treated someone who'd been mauled by hyenas. She looked into the fire. Burning him alive would be good, too, although there'd be logistics to consider. The smell, the noise. She doubted he'd go quietly. They'd need some place remote. The fire would also have to be hot enough to—

Stop.

She picked up a wrought-iron poker and dispersed the flames. This was no time for fantasizing. She had a decision to make. Gord needed an answer. Was she was going to go ahead with this?

Yes. Of course.

But then she thought *extrajudicial* and reconsidered. A xeroxed image of the team behind Narcontine flared up, then curled in on itself and collapsed. She had a family to consider. What if something went wrong? The girls were still recovering from Malcolm's death.

She couldn't be rash. She worried she was being selfish. She needed a second opinion and knew exactly who to call. Gord had asked her to keep this quiet, but Petra figured it was okay. Physician–patient privilege applied here too.

First, though, she texted the landscaper and apologized. She wouldn't be having the pond filled in after all. She was just too busy with other things at the moment.

NINA

I went back to Cara's Coffee Stop and bought myself a cup of the cloudy beige suds they boldly marketed as "cappuccino." I texted Clary and told her about meeting the receptionist.

Clary: she called him a snake?
Nina: but with a sense of humour
Clary: oh well that's okay then
Nina: she didn't think he'd steal
Clary: gold diggers don't steal. Their love just comes at a price
Nina: doesn't it always?
Clary: deep
Nina: maybe he's not so bad
Clary: a snake but not so bad? Nina listen to yourself. We need to get mum away from this guy

"We"—by which, again, she meant "me." I was frantically trying to come up with a way out when dots appeared.

Clary: i'll call and say I'm having trouble with Arlo. ask her to stay a couple of weeks. mum won't say no to that

I squealed mentally, then texted a thumbs-up. I didn't mention that Gord and his glow-in-the-dark condoms would probably just hang out at the same cheap motel as last time and wait for Mum there. I figured she'd still be spending most of the day with Clary, and Clary could bend anyone to her will. It wasn't a bad plan. We signed off.

I got into the car and headed home, my mind almost clear enough to consider food. I hadn't had anything to eat since stealing those french fries from Gord at The Big House the night before.

I pulled into our driveway. A podcast was on but just as background noise, so I didn't notice at first that a new voice was speaking. I only realized something was odd when I heard the woman say "Petra."

This isn't a podcast.

It was like being slapped awake.

This is someone talking to my mother.

I checked the dashboard and saw I was picking up Mum's phone on the car's Bluetooth. She must have been inside the house on her cell.

"I know it was hard," the woman said, "but you did what you had to do and now you're free."

I recognized the voice, the weird high pitch, but couldn't identify it.

"But are you sure he can be trusted?...Pet? Yoo-hoo! Did I lose you?... Damn. I'll try again." The line went dead.

I sat there stunned for a moment, then I bolted. The woman said she'd call back. I needed to catch Mum on the phone, hear her side of the conversation.

I tiptoed in the door, through the foyer, up the stairs, past Mum's bedroom, then up another flight of stairs to her office. The door was open a crack.

"Sorry, Bonnie," I heard her say. "I lost you. You were just saying...Oh, hold on. Someone's here."

Before I could recalibrate, Mum stuck her head out the door, a hand over the phone. "Nina?" She looked concerned. "What's the matter?"

I was panting, panicked, stunned.

Bonnie. That voice. The big, dishevelled woman who'd smiled when she talked about Dad on the dance floor. Mum was talking to Bonnie from the funeral.

"Nina?" She touched my arm. "Darling?"

What was hard? Trust who? Two terrifying questions.

Mum spoke into her phone. "Got to run, Bon. I'll call you later. I'm fine...Yes, of course. Bye."

She pushed the hair off my face, put both hands on my shoulders, and looked into my eyes. "Nina, are you okay?"

"I…I was just really worried about you." Tears welled up. My lip quivered. Either I was a better actor than I'd given myself credit for or the truth was finally hitting me. *Did what you had to do?* What the hell did Bonnie mean by that?

"Oh, sweetheart," Mum said. "Why?"

"I don't know."

"I'm fine. See?" She stepped back and gave a twirl. "You're just having an little aftershock. When you lose someone suddenly, it unsettles things. You worry it's going to happen again."

I nodded tearfully. "I think…I think it's because you were out so late last night. It scared me. I didn't know where you were." My lying had become disconcertedly fluid. Almost Clary-esque. "What were you doing?"

She gave my shoulders a pat and stepped back. "Living my life."

"Were you on a date?"

She began to organize the papers on her desk into stacks.

"Are you seeing someone?

"Nina." I could hear the period. "I'm sorry I scared you, but I've looked after other people for over forty years. Am I allowed a little privacy? A life of my own?"

I opened my mouth to reply, but she held up her hand. "The answer is yes. I'll come to you when I need you. I promise. In the meantime, please back off." She smiled sweetly. "Now, apologies, but I've got things to do. You mind?"

I shook my head. We kissed and I went downstairs. Twenty minutes later, my phone pinged. Clary was trying to reach Mum. She hadn't replied to her text about helping with Arlo.

Nina: she's in her office working. Try again.

I considered telling her what I'd just overheard but was still too rattled. Clary would fan the flames, then leave me to fight the fire alone.

Clary: kk. meantime I just read something interesting. Guess where Mr. Bickerton went to law school. Correct. Mount Heber.

Don must have been one of his profs. Call and ask what he thought of him

Nina: don doesn't like talking on the phone

I wasn't dragging Don into this sordid mess.

Clary: so visit him then. Grill him. He might know something important

Like I'd grill a ninety-six-year-old man. I was just about to say "Drop it, Clary" when I thought, *visit.*

Where there's Don, there's Jesse.

And where there's Jesse, there's salvation.

I waited a couple moments, then sent back a generic OK emoji. Clary didn't need to know how thrilled I was. I texted Jesse and said I'd be arriving the next day to give him a break. He sent back fireworks, three grateful hands, and a Hooray!! word bubble.

Last time we'd talked, he claimed he didn't want to see me. Ha! Mere posturing. I knew he hadn't meant it. I gathered up my best underwear and threw on a wash. That boy wasn't going to know what hit him.

When Mum came downstairs an hour later, I told her Jesse and I might be getting back together. "I'm going to go stay with him for a few days. See if we can work things out."

"Oh, that's wonderful, darling! I'm so happy for you." She tilted her head—her mouth bent in an upside-down smile, her eyes twinkling—and stretched out her arms. We hugged. Blame it on the familiar cloud of Crème de la Mer, but for one blissful moment, everything seemed right in the world. Here was my mother again. Jesse wanted me back. Bonnie was just talking nonsense. Gord was forgotten. I could have stood like that forever, but not Mum. She stepped away, adjusted her blouse, and touched up her hair. She had to get going.

She didn't say where, but she didn't have to. An hour later, Find My Phone pinpointed her location as the bluff overlooking Chebucto Sound. The Lookout.

I knew it well. Everyone did. It was the local make-out spot.

I refused to let it bother me. I had some serious exfoliation to do.

GORD

Gord stepped out of the shadows at the Lookout parking lot and climbed into her car. Petra didn't waste any time on small talk. "I'm in," she said.

He leaned against the passenger door and nodded, not quite suppressing a smile. "You sure?"

"Never more sure of anything in my life. I want to destroy the guy."

Petra's second call with Bonnie that afternoon had dispatched any doubts. They'd talked it all through—Osterlich's crimes, the legal system's inability to deal with them, the possible risks and rewards—and Bonnie had finally succumbed. She was still a little concerned about Gord being so cagey on details, but she knew Petra could take care of herself.

She also knew Petra was going to do it no matter what. "Better I'm on your side," Bonnie told her, "just in case you need me."

That made Petra tear up. Good old Bonnie. Petra was sad they hadn't kept in touch over the years, but that was another difficult decision she'd had to make. After Duncan died, it was all or nothing. It would have been too hard to hide herself from the world with Bonnie looking on. Bonnie wouldn't have stood for it.

Petra had composed herself and said, "I knew you wouldn't let me down."

And now, mere hours later, Gord was saying the exact same thing to her.

She waved it off. "I want this as badly as you do." She flicked off her shoes, leaned her back against the car door and pressed her bare feet onto his thighs. "How can I help?"

Gord settled into his seat. This was going to take a while. "As you know, Osterlich considers himself a philanthropist."

Petra huffed in disgust.

"Don't knock it." Gord winked. "We're going to make it work for us."

"How?"

"You're going to ask him a favour."

"Me? I don't know him that well."

"So? He said *if you ever needed anything...*"

"That was at the funeral. Everybody says that."

"Yeah, but you're going to take him up on it. You're just asking him to put his money where his mouth is."

She chuckled. The irony appealed. Using the man's own duplicity against him. "And do what?"

"Help raise money for a scholarship in Malcolm's name. Osterlich was thrilled with Malcolm's work on that big fancy mansion of his. I thought a charity house tour would offer him an excellent opportunity to 'pay it forward.' It'll be the event of the season. All the best people, clamouring for an up-close and personal view of his landmark home. Osterlich will love it. Nothing he likes better than wallowing in his own glory."

"Organize a house tour." Petra clucked non-committedly. "That's what you're asking me to do?" She felt heat roll up her torso. She pretended to cough into her sleeve.

"You okay?"

She nodded but she wasn't. Some part of her had actually believed she was finally going to get to be the main character. An agent of change, not an accessory. Instead, here she was, typecast yet again. Lovely Petra Fforde and her good works. That it was Gord doing the typecasting only made it worse. She moved her feet away from his thighs and sat up straight.

Gord spread his hands. "I know that sounds like a lot of work, but I promise this will never get as far as the actual tour. It's just a ruse to get you into Osterlich's inner sanctum."

"What for?"

"To plant evidence."

The car was silent. Petra didn't dare hope.

"Damning evidence," Gord added, as if afraid he'd lost her. "We're going to take him down, Pet. Bury the murderous bastard in his own shit."

She should never have doubted Gord.

"I'd like that," she said.

They shared a smile, then cracked the car windows a couple of inches. They needed air. They had lots of details to hash out. Who, what, where, when. How to broach it. What they needed. Two friends with a dream. Judy Garland and Mickey Rooney getting the barn ready for opening night. The odds were against them. The whole thing was crazy. They'd never been happier.

Petra had the sneaking suspicion Gord was still keeping something from her, but she let it go. She didn't want to break the spell. Gord would tell her what she needed to know when the time was right.

NINA

I was on the highway when my phone rang.

Clary didn't even say hello. "Nina. She's out of control."

"Are you trying to make me go off the road?"

"She's not coming."

"Who?"

"La Bouve. I told her I needed help with Arlo, and she said no."

"No? Just, like, no?"

"*I'm busy. So much to do. Daddy's estate. The garden. Blah-blah-blah.* Essentially no. *Maybe next month.* Next fucking month! She did, however, offer to pay for a babysitter because Krish and I, as you know, are just barely scraping by. How much work could she possibly have to do? Hire a goddamn landscaper! And as for 'Daddy's estate'—I know for a fact he nailed it down years ago... Fuck. I don't like this."

I didn't either. I wobbled into the other lane. The guy behind me honked. I swerved back. (My life in a nutshell. A lane-straddler. A hazard.)

"Should I go home? Talk to her? I'm almost at Don's. I said I'd stay over."

I wanted to stay over. I wanted make-up sex with Jesse, the relationship re-established, that part of my life back on track, then I could deal with this. I'd be happy to deal with it. Not really, but I would. "He's expecting me, but if you think—"

"No. No. Go ahead. I mean, what can you do? Have a chat with Mum about saving herself for marriage? That ship has sailed."

"Enough with the sex stuff. Seriously, Clary. It's grossing me out."

"Me too but, like, exposure therapy, right? You want to get over arachnophobia, you gotta face the spiders."

"This isn't about spiders. This is about our mother."

"Same principle. We can't hide from what's going on here. I'm worried by the time Mum wakes up from her post–boy toy euphoria, all her money will be gone, and she'll be mortified, and that'll be the end of her. We've got to do something before that happens. Talk to Don. Find out how big a threat he thinks Gord is to Mum, slash us, slash civilization in general."

"Will do," I said, although only to shut her up. Shamefully, Mum's situation was no longer my top concern. I'd already turned onto Laurier Crescent, and there was the giant elm and the roses in full bloom and the Saab in the carport and Jesse, shirtless, in all his feeble glory, giving the front door a shiny new coat of mid-century mustard. I thought, *Home. I'm home. Everything is going to be okay.*

"I'm here now. Can I call you back later?"

"Sure. I want to pee before Arlo wakes up anyway. Might be my only chance to get a full wipe in." We made kissy sounds and signed off.

I pulled into the driveway. When Jesse saw me, he covered his nipples with the tips of his index fingers. It was a sight gag from *Gregory's Girl*, one of our favourite Scottish movies of the 1980s. I took it as a good sign, even if he did put his T-shirt on immediately thereafter.

"Ach. Look at ye," I said, getting out of Dad's Volvo. I was terrible at accents, but he'd always found that funny.

He didn't laugh.

"Nice ride," he said, patting the hood.

"Yeah, well, play your cards right and all this could be yours one day."

"Don't play cards anymore. Someone took the deck and went home."

"Jesse." I tilted my head and frowned. "Don't be that way."

He mouthed, *Sorry*, then said, "C'mere," and held out his arms. I hurried into them, burying my face in his chest. He was sweaty in a way that smelled like summer, and I could tell he'd washed his T-shirt but left it damp in the machine for a while. I imagined everything inside the house hinting of mould and neglect and food long past its best-before date. I was so happy to think he needed me.

"Well, come on in," he said, pulling away. He made it sound like I was a guest.

"Why, thank you." I stepped inside. "Lovely home you have here." He didn't pick up on it.

Don was sitting in his orange chair, overdressed for the warm weather in a tweed jacket, open-necked shirt, and flannel trousers, but he was neat and tidy, his hair trimmed, his shoes polished.

"Nina, my dear!" He leaned forward, pressing down on the armrests, and struggled almost to his feet.

"No need to get up, Don." I ran over to him.

"Actually, no chance." He laughed and flopped back down. His giant knuckly hands were shaking. I held one up to my face and knelt beside him. "I've missed you so much. How are you?"

"Very well, thank you. My man here has been doing a top-notch job keeping me this side of the grave. He's not the cook you are, but he's a better chess player, so there you go. You're looking well."

"That's because I'm happy to be here. I'd have been happier if you didn't look so well yourself. I hate the thought that you can get along without me."

"*Can* get along and *want* to get along without you are two quite different things." Jess had gone to clean himself up. Don leaned forward and whispered, "I believe I speak for both of us."

I squeezed his hand and sighed. "I made a mistake."

"Young people do. Not too late to fix it."

Moments later, Jesse came back wearing a nearly identical T-shirt, his face washed, his jeans still a little grubby. His hair needed shampooing. His beard, trimming. He was thinner, which I previously wouldn't have thought possible. I decided over the next few days I'd make cheese fondu and boeuf bourguignon and an incredibly vulgar concoction we'd seen in one of Ruth's old magazines called "sausage cake." I would restore him to vigour. He would love me forever.

"How about drinks on the deck?" Jesse said. He helped Don up. We each took an arm and got him outside.

"Oh, my." Don chuckled. "This makes me feel as if I'm being tossed out of a tavern for unruly behaviour. Just like the good old days."

I laughed. "You used to get thrown out of bars?"

"No, I don't believe so. Mind you, there's always the chance I did and just forgot. The wonderful thing about old age is I can portray my past any way I damn well please, and who's the wiser? You poor things still have to stick to the truth for a while."

We settled him into his chair. I offered to get drinks, but Jesse waved that away. He'd do it. I was a guest again.

"How's your mother?" Don asked with enough gravity for it not to be simple courtesy.

"I don't know. We all thought she'd be crushed but she's not."

"That's a good thing, isn't it?"

I wiped some leaves off the deck with my foot and smiled. "Sure."

"You're not convincing me."

"It just feels odd. She and Dad were together for ages. She could at least be a little sad."

"How do you know she's not?"

The lipstick. The nudity. The staying out late with strange men. I shrugged as if he may be right.

Jesse appeared at the sliding doors with our drinks on a tray. Two pitted olives for Don, a twist of lemon for me. He didn't quite bow when he served them, but otherwise Jesse's presentation was perfect. He even had cocktail napkins. He went back into the kitchen to get dinner ready. Don took a sip of his martini and sighed.

"Glorious. Now, back to your mother. I think I can be of some help to you."

"Oh, yes?"

"I was once an expert in legal ethics. I suspect old age has robbed me of that. On the other hand, it's made me an expert in something else. Death. I've seen survivors who could barely stand their spouses fall apart when they died. I've seen other people, who'd seemed very much in love, blossom in widowhood. You can't predict what anyone will do or why. I remember a friend saying of her beloved husband, 'he kicked the bucket and I kicked up my heels.' She suddenly felt young again. Your mother isn't sad enough for you? That doesn't mean she didn't love your father."

"It just seems so...insulting."

"Oh, pfft! Life's too short to take offence when none is intended. I had many long talks with your mother. Don't be too hard on her."

"Long talks?" When would the two of them have had long talks?

"Don't tell me your memory's going too?" He winked. "She stayed with me when Jesse's brother got married. Your whole crew took off and deserted me, so Petra stepped in to 'look after the old man' for a few days."

"Oh, right. I remember. In fact, I remember her being *delighted* to look after the old man."

He patted my hand. "We had a marvellous time—especially since she's not as bloody stingy with the booze as you youngsters. We'd sit out here under the stars and have our heart-to-hearts. I have very fond memories. It had been many years since I'd been alone with a beautiful woman."

"What are you saying, Don?" I tried to keep it light, but the implication was terrifying. *Don't tell me Mum got it on with him too.*

He chuckled. "You flatter me! There was a connection there, certainly, but purely a meeting of minds. Petra and I understood each other."

I gratefully banished the image of Mum incorporating Don's diapers into foreplay. Jesse called us in for dinner. He'd made Ruth's quiche Lorraine and a chopped salad. The quiche could have used a little more salt, but otherwise the meal was very good. His pastry, in fact, was better than mine. It broke my heart.

We talked about Jacques Brel and threats to democracy and the viability of free-content providers, then it was time for Don to go to bed. Jesse took him upstairs. I did the dishes, cleaned up the gunge that had accumulated behind the kitchen tap, then slipped downstairs to our bathroom to tidy myself up.

Our "quarters," as Don referred to them, were always the last to be looked after. No one saw them except me and Jesse, and we didn't care that much. I was expecting oozing toothpaste, hair in the sink, wet towels on the floor—but the place was spotless. It was like we were dating, and this was our first sleepover. Jesse had cleaned up for me.

It usually took about forty-five minutes to get Don into bed. I jumped into the shower. Moisturized. Spritzed. Dabbed concealer under my eyes and the tiniest bit of mascara on my lashes, just enough to look good, but not enough to look like I'd tried. I knotted my hair into the messy bun Jesse liked. I used his deodorant because he always used to accuse me of stealing it and then he'd sniff me like a suspicious dog and I'd deny, deny, deny until we were laughing and goofing around and had all our clothes off again. I slipped on a thong and one of his old button-down shirts. That's all I'd be needing. I was conjuring up a feeling. Memories of the happy, easy, sexy life we'd had together. I bounded upstairs just as Jesse was coming down from Don's room.

"You look good," he said.

"Oh? Huh." I touched my hair like *really?* "Just had a shower."

I sat down on the chesterfield with my legs curled, a hand placed coyly on my bare ankle. He didn't take the bait. He sat on the armchair across from me.

"Things okay at home?" he said.

I made a show of surveying the room as in *whatever do you mean?* "Looks fine to me!"

"I mean with Petra."

"Oh, geez. Where to start? You wouldn't believe what's happening."

He took out his phone and checked the time.

"You in a rush?" I said.

"No, no. Sorry. What's going on?"

"She's apparently seeing someone."

His jaw dropped. "Like, a guy?"

"Yes. A *younger* guy. A disbarred lawyer named Gord."

"Wow. Plot twist. Is she happy?"

"You're asking if she's happy? Not has she lost her mind? Dad just died!"

"I know. I know. I'm sure it's hard on you and it's shocking, but—"

"But what?" I was suddenly mad at him. "You're thinking about Roz saying Mum is troubled, aren't you? Something *was* troubling her, i.e. Dad, and now that thing is gone and she's happy."

"Well...not exactly but, um. You know." He was red and flustered and, of course, right.

I took a breath. Composed myself. Nodded. "I know. The only question really is whether it's causation or—what's the other thing?"

"Correlation."

"Yeah. Is she happy because Dad's dead? Or he's dead and she just happens to be happy? That's slightly less offensive, but not by much."

"Have you asked her what's up? Maybe it's something else."

"I've tried. She shuts me down pretty quick. None of my beeswax, apparently. She's finally 'living her own life.' And I get it. Fair. Women deserve their own lives. But, you know, she's my…my, like…"

"Aw, Neens. You okay?"

Clearly not. The trembling chin, the shaking shoulders, the jellied saliva swaying from my lips. I was a heartbroken grade-schooler. Unloved. Abandoned. An orphan.

Jesse took my hands. "Oh, oh, oh." He pulled me up, wrapped his arms around me, rocked me like the child I was. I pressed my ear against his heart. "Nina. Neens. C'mon."

And, instantly, devastated sobbing gave way to happy sobbing. Fear, gone. Confusion, gone. Hurricane Petra, downgraded from Category Five to a mere tropical storm. Soon we'd be playing in the waves.

"You all right?" Jesse moved back, dipping his chin to look at me. A hint of a smile on his face. "You good?"

I nodded, still crying a bit, but laughing now too. I was a mucus-glazed disaster of a human being, but he loved me.

He wiped my eyes with the hem of his T-shirt. "Mascara."

"Caught me," I said, hoping he'd know what I'd meant by wearing it.

"Got most of it, but you could probably use a Kleenex."

"Oh well. It's just us. Not as if you haven't seen it before."

"True."

He stepped away, shoving his hands into his pockets. A bashfulness I hadn't seen since we'd first met.

"What do you want to do tonight?" I said, bouncing onto the chesterfield. I stretched out on my side, one hand propping up my head, lots of bare leg, an invitation if ever there was one. "I purloined a nice muscular cabernet from the parental cellar. We could just curl up on the couch." I stroked the upholstery suggestively. "There's an Italian soap opera on Netflix that's supposed to be good, by which I mean bad. Might get us—"

"Um. Neens? I made plans."

"Plans?"

"You said you were coming back to give me a break, so I made plans."

"You're going out?" I sat up.

With whom? You didn't want to see me? You didn't want to use this time to mend our relationship, rekindle the fire, have sex?

"I'll be back tomorrow morning. First thing if you want to leave early. Whenever. Just text me."

"Where are you going?"

There was a long pause. He bared his teeth and sucked in his breath.

"Sorry, Nina." He put one hand out to the left. "Your beeswax." Then his other to the right. "My beeswax."

"Jesse." I stood up. "Why are you doing this? I'm here. I'm back. Don't go."

"You aren't back."

"Yes. I am."

"No. The person I thought I knew, left. I know you're hurting, Nina. You lost someone you loved but so did I. What we had before? That's all I ever wanted. I was happy with you. With *us*. This whole thing has made me realize that you weren't. You looked at our relationship as a phase—something you'd grow out of, or, like, fix. I didn't think it needed fixing. I don't want to be your problem—"

"You aren't."

"I kind of am. I don't have the right job. I'm out of shape. I start things I don't finish. You love me but you really wish I'd get my act together."

"I want to get *my* act together!"

"Exactly. And you're not going to be happy until you do. Part of me is like, that's okay. Come back anyway! I'll take you any way I can get you. But I know that would just be putting off the inevitable. So do me a favour and leave me alone for a while. Okay?"

Leave me alone.

That's what you say to a pest, someone you loathe, someone you have no respect for. My jaw wobbled but no words came out.

Jesse opened his mouth to be kind, to be Jesse, and I knew if I didn't stop him, he'd make me feel even more pathetic, so I pulled myself together and smiled, or at least sort of.

"Sure. That's fine. I'll spend the day with Don. So, midafternoon okay? No need to rush back on my account. Enjoy!"

I snapped him a salute and headed downstairs to our quarters. He'd changed the sheets. I couldn't even smell him on the pillowcase. I finished the bottle of wine on my own.

GORD

Gord fixed a cup of green tea, then allowed himself a single Biscoff from the package his host had supplied. *What the hell*, he thought. He deserved a little treat. Things were coming together. Petra was in, at least thus far. He had the weapon. His friend in Mali had made preliminary contact with Osterlich. Now Gord just needed to decide on the drug.

He pulled a stool up to the counter, opened his laptop to the PhiTex website, and considered the options. He wasn't a scientist—he'd only squeaked through grade twelve chemistry because his girlfriend wouldn't put out unless he passed—but he couldn't risk asking for expert help. The fewer people who knew, the better—including, at this stage, Petra. With her medical training, she really should have chosen the drug, but it was too soon to involve her. He didn't want to scare her off. He'd figure it out himself.

He scanned the list again. He'd narrowed it down to three.

Benzoflox. A powerful sedative but used almost exclusively in psychiatric facilities. *Why would someone have it then?* Gord ruled it out. Too hard to justify.

Anexypenol. A common sedative with good anesthetic properties, so initially the front-runner, but further research had Gord wondering. It rarely caused slurred speech and often didn't show up in autopsies. He took a sip of tea. He liked the painkilling aspect but couldn't risk the drug going undetected in the bloodstream. He scratched it off too.

Serenetol seemed the best option. A widely available sleep-aid, tasteless, easily detected in the blood, and a known date-rape drug.

He googled the list of adverse effects: excessive sedation, impaired balance, dependency, death. He laughed at the last one.

Bingo, he thought. *Serenetol, it is.*

Now, where to get it? Gord obviously couldn't get a prescription in his own name. Buying off the street would be problematic too. After years away, his street connections weren't great. He didn't know a dealer he could trust. What if they sold him a fake? The pills had to come from PhiTex. Gord allowed himself a second Biscoff and tried to think this through.

NINA

I felt like hell the next morning and must have reeked, too, but Don didn't mind. Probably didn't notice. His sense of smell was almost gone. I wished mine was.

I struggled to get him on and off the toilet, up and down the stairs, but he was sanguine about it. He generally regarded old age as a prank the universe was playing on him. He'd lived a happy enough life that he could be a good sport about what was left of it.

I got him to the dining room for breakfast twenty minutes later than Jesse would have done, but we both regarded that as a huge success. I made us pancakes and sausages. (Don liked a "lumberjack's breakfast," despite his dietician sternly reminding him he hadn't swung an axe in years. "If ever!" he crowed.) We lingered over coffee, discussing fly-fishing (of which I knew nothing) and contemporary French literature (more my wheelhouse). Eventually I said, "Did you ever have a student named Gordon Bickerton?"

Don put two fingers behind his ear. "Richardson?"

"Bick-er-ton."

"Oh. Bickerton." Don looked off into the distance. "Bickerton. Hmm." His hand shakily touched his cheek. "Oh, Nina. I may have taught him at some point, but things are awfully foggy for me these days. Any idea when he might have been at law school?"

"Twenty years ago? Twenty-five? He's in his late forties now, I'd say."

Don pointed to a bookshelf by the fireplace. "There are the yearbooks. Have a peek. I might remember if I saw his face."

I got out a few that I thought might be the right era. I flipped through three before I spotted Gord. It was the classic studio grad shot. The gown, the three-quarter-profile pose. I pointed him out to Don. He put on his reading glasses and craned his neck.

"Oh. That fellow." He leaned back in his chair, shaking his head. "Never liked him."

"Why?" I asked, although it wasn't hard to guess. Young Gord was smirking in a very punchable way.

Don took off his glasses. "Ruth would roll in her grave to hear me say this, but he was crass. A hoodlum. The type who'd win you with his easy charm, then sock you in the kisser with his brass knuckles. I reluctantly gave him an A, as I recall, despite suspecting his keen interest in legal ethics had more to do with how to get around them than how to honour them. Why do you want to know?"

"I think my mother's seeing him."

"Seeing, as in...?"

"Yes. Dating."

He took a sip of coffee. "He'd be quite a bit her junior, wouldn't he?"

"Yup."

"Hm. Well, your mother is a smart woman. I'm sure she can take care of herself."

"You are?"

"I am in fact. Petra was only here for a short time, but we got to know each other quite well. She's strong. Much stronger than I ever was. Did you know I left my first wife for Ruth?"

"Jesse told me."

"I figured he would have. It was the scandal that defined my life. I left my wife and my job and my security for one of my students. The last thing Helen, my first wife, said to me was, 'You'll live to regret this.' I guess that's still a possibility. I'm not dead yet. But I'll be ninety-seven in September, and it still feels like the best decision I ever made. Your mother, as you know, also made a huge sacrifice for someone she loved, but it was harder for her. Losing a child like that. Giving up her career. I think she deserves her happiness now, even if it is with this Mr..." He waved his fingers in irritation as he tried to recall his name.

"What?" I was struggling to understand what I'd just heard. "Losing a child?"

"I beg your pardon?" Don looked at me, startled.

"You said my mother lost a child, made a huge sacrifice for someone she loved. What do you mean?"

His jaw bounced.

"What child?" I said, trying to keep the panic out of my voice. "What sacrifice?"

"You...You didn't know?"

"I don't know what you're talking about."

"Oh, dear." Don's shoulders sank. He suddenly looked incredibly frail. "Then I have done a very bad thing. I didn't realize your mother told me that in confidence. Although maybe I did and forgot." He shook his head. "I'm too old to be trusted anymore. I apologize."

"That's okay. You didn't mean to. But you have to tell me now. Who did she lose?" I smiled encouragingly. I had to know.

"I'm going to have to apologize again, Nina. I'm sorry, but it's not my business to say. You'll have to ask her yourself, or better yet, wait until she chooses to confide in you."

Don wasn't that frail. He wouldn't budge. He changed the subject, and I poured him another cup of coffee.

NINA

I'd just gotten Don down for his siesta when Jesse showed up, wearing the same clothes he'd left in the night before.

"Hey." He climbed the stairs three at a time, dumped his backpack, and smiled, a great, big Jesse smile. "How'd it go?"

I knew that smile. I knew all Jesse's smiles. The polite smiles. The sorry smiles. The inside-joke smiles, the you're-going-to-love-this smiles.

This was a great, big I-just-got-lucky smile.

My heart banged its fists against my sternum and wailed.

He'd slept with someone else.

Some random girl he'd met at the library, in a coffee shop, online. Someone younger, prettier, smarter, more accomplished than me. A blond. Or maybe grey-haired and older, but hip. Super-hip. A woman of the world. A divorcee. Susan Fucking Sarandon. (I was suddenly hyper-alert to the appeal older women had on younger men.)

He just rolled out of her bed, threw on last night's clothes, and thought I wouldn't notice?

"All good?" he said.

Fuck off, I thought.

"Fine," I said. "I mean, you know." I looked away and shrugged. "Great to see Don."

"He was excited to see you too. He kept on talking about his 'big date.'" Jesse lifted an eyebrow suggestively.

"Yeah, well..." *Don and I aren't sluts. We're not out boning anything that moves.* "We enjoyed ourselves."

"So, nothing to report then?"

My life is over but otherwise no. "You should order some more of his heart meds."

"Picked them up on my way home!" Jesse gave his backpack a little shake. "Want me to put the kettle on? I got some of that lemon verbena tea you like..."

"Thanks, but no. Gotta run. Lots to do."

He didn't ask again. He could have insisted—*c'mon, Neens, one for the road!*—but he didn't. He kissed me goodbye (on my head, like I was a Labrador retriever), then we did this awkward wave thing, and I left.

I drove to the Coffee Time overlooking the highway and parked. I crossed my arms on the steering wheel and cried for a while—about Jesse and Dad and Don and the thesis I never finished and the guys I never dated and that pathetic novel I never wrote and the years I'd wasted and the state of the environment/the economy/the skin around my eyes—then I blew my nose on a shirt I'd stolen from Jesse and phoned my sisters to talk about Mum.

My lying, cheating, possibly unhinged mother was easier to talk about than the mess I'd made of my life. That's where I was.

AL-HADDAD

Sergeant Blair Zinck wasn't convinced.

"Of course, I know who he is. Wayne Dudek. So?" He peeled the paper off a morning glory muffin and took a bite.

They were in the station breakroom, looking at a photo on Al-Haddad's phone of two couples taken at last year's World Wildlife Gala.

"Ew. Coconut." Zinck put the muffin back in the box.

Al-Haddad suppressed a shudder. "That's who I saw her with."

"Yeah, well. Dudek & Fforde Engineering. Mr. Dudek has no doubt spent a little time with Ms. Fforde over the years."

"I realize that." When googling Petra, Al-Haddad had often seen the Dudeks photographed at the same galas as the Ffordes. That's how he'd recognized Wayne on Petra's porch earlier that day. "But this wasn't just 'spending time' with her. This was—"

"Oh, please. You're thinking some secret tryst? Would you look at the guy?" Zinck waved derisively at the photo. Wayne Dudek was a short, plump man with a Richard Simmons pouf of unnaturally chestnut hair. He was wearing a zebra-striped tuxedo and an oversized red bow tie. "You really think Petra Fforde has the hots for him?"

"Stranger things have happened."

"Not in my lifetime." Zinck picked up another muffin. "This look like blueberry to you?"

Al-Haddad shrugged.

Zinck took a bite and kept talking. "A young stud such as yourself might have trouble believing this, but not everyone gets to pick and choose. Looks mean something. Charming as I am, Beyoncé's never leaving Jay-Z for me. Likewise, Petra Fforde would not kill her husband for Chuckles the Clown here."

"So maybe Dudek's the instigator. Maybe he—"

"Or maybe you just caught him consoling her. They've been friends for a long time. She just lost her husband. Widows have been known to break down and, for that matter, occasionally wear outfits not up to your exacting standards."

Al-Haddad knew he shouldn't have told Sarge about the sundress. Zinck was the type of guy who only had one tie. (He kept it knotted and hanging off his office doorknob in case he "needed to impress someone.") Fashion nuances wouldn't register. Zinck was similarly unperturbed by the name change. Even his own wife had kept her maiden name. Al-Haddad's hunches weren't flying with him.

"Look, Al. I applaud your diligence, but you're wasting your time. My guiding principle has always been, if it walks like a duck and quacks like a duck, it's probably a duck. This is a duck. An old guy lost control of his bike and bit the dust. That's what the evidence indicates. Sad story, but there it is."

He put up his hand to stop Al-Haddad from responding. "And, yes, I know Dudek found the body, which I suppose could look convenient, but not this time. If I recall rightly, Dudek was at a line dancing class—*with his wife*—when Petra called him asking for help finding Malcolm. Nothing suspicious about that. Obvious guy for her to reach out to."

Zinck crumpled up the muffin liner and put it back in the box. "I'll grant the lack of witnesses is a tad problematic. It would only take a couple seconds to flip over the guardrail, so it could be easy to miss, but still. Busy day. Any record of a traffic stop? Some reason there'd be no cars on the road then?"

"None that I know of but I've got a call into the highway department."

"Good. There's no doubt some logical explanation. Maybe do a little more digging into that, then move on to more important things. Speaking of which, any progress on that B and E?"

NINA

Clary answered right away, but it took me three tries to reach Libby.

"I'm refereeing a game, Nina." I could hear screaming in the background, the wind howling. Tinny nineties music on a boom box.

"Well, stop. This is important," I said, then ordered an iced coffee, extra whipped topping, at the Coffee Time drive-through mic.

Lib blew her whistle, hollered at someone named Obediah to take over, then murmured, "You okay, Neens?"

"Yeah." That was a stretch but whatever. "Don told me something I thought you should—"

"Gord's a psychopath!"

"Hold on, Clary."

"He is, isn't he? I knew the guy was bad. Did he—"

"I said, hold on." A sullen teenager in a brown polyester uniform custom-designed to make him hate life leaned out the window and handed me a plastic cup full of chemicals. *Fuck the environment*, I thought. *Fuck everything.* I took a slurp, put the cup between my knees, and headed toward the highway on-ramp.

"Nina! What did he say?"

"Jesus, Clary. Can you wait? I'm driving!"

The Volvo was better than Don's Saab—it could at least manage highway speeds—but I was still a nervous driver. I had to remind myself not to close my eyes when I merged. I saw a gap in traffic and hit the accelerator. A minivan swerved out of my way, cars honked, but I was in.

I caught my breath, decided on a lane, then said, "Okay. Yes. Don did teach Gord, but it was ages ago. He didn't remember much, other than he didn't like the guy. Said he was 'crass.'"

"*Crass*." Clary snorted. "Now, there's a euphemism for ya."

"But that's not why I'm calling. I have some shocking news to report." I paused for effect, relishing the normalcy of tantalizing my sisters with the promise of salacious gossip.

Clary went, "Oooh."

Lib was quiet, as if she was above such nonsense, but I could sense her listening.

"Did you know Mum had a child who died?"

I expected squeals, gasps, shocked exhortations—but nothing.

"You *knew*?" I said.

More silence.

"You *both* knew?"

Lib said, "I didn't know you knew, Clary."

Clary said, "I didn't know *you* knew."

"Why didn't anybody tell me?" I growled.

"I didn't think it was a big deal."

"Clary! A *secret* dead sibling?" I shouldn't have been driving. The trucker behind me laid on his horn. "How could you not realize that was a big deal?"

"I don't know. Hormones? I was pregnant. That's how I found out. Krish and I accidentally chose the same name for the baby as the dead kid."

"Arlo?" I said.

"No." Like I was an idiot. "Malcolm Duncan Fforde the Second, after Dad. I thought Mum would be thrilled, but she got all weird. I was like *what's up with you?* Took some badgering, but she eventually told me they'd had a son with the same name. Two Malcolms would have been confusing, so they'd called him Duncan, just like we were going to do. He died before I was born. She thought hearing the baby's name again would upset Dad, so I was like fine, we'll call him Arlo Malcolm. That was our second choice anyway. End of story."

"Duncan died as a baby?" Libby asked. "You sure?"

"Pretty sure. I got the impression it was SIDS or something. 'Nothing genetic.' I remember Mum saying that. Arlo's heart was doing crazy things in utero back then, so I kind of freaked out when she mentioned a dead baby."

"Weird." Lib made a clicking noise. "I heard Duncan died when he was five."

"Why didn't *you* tell me, Lib?" At that point I didn't care when the kid died, I was just reeling from the betrayal.

"Dad made me promise. Said it would upset Mum."

I went, "So Mum tells Clary not to say anything because it would upset Dad, and Dad tells Lib not to say anything because it would upset Mum?"

Clary said, "I smell a conspiracy."

"It's called love, Clary." Lib tutted. "They were protecting each other."

"If it was such a big secret," I said, "why did Dad tell you about it?"

"I asked," Lib said.

"How would you even know to ask?" I could hear Clary roll her eyes. "*Hey, Dad, any dead siblings you've neglected to mention?*"

"Someone told me."

"Who?"

"I've already said too much, Neens. I promised Dad I—"

"Dad is dead," Clary said. "Just spill."

"Yeah, Lib. Spit it out."

A pause, then a sigh. "Fine. I met a guy at a conference a few years ago. I noticed his nametag. 'Nick Fforde', two Fs and an E. I went, 'Wow, think we're related?' He said, 'My Dad's Randall. Any chance your Dad's Malcolm?' And I was like *yes*! I never even knew we had cousins. He suggested we go to a bar to catch up. We get there and he admits he'd seen my name on the attendee list and arranged to bump into me so he could 'clear the air about Duncan.' I was like, 'Who's Duncan?' No idea what he was talking about. Nick was shocked. Told me everything. How our parents were living in Ottawa—"

I said, "They lived in Ottawa?"

"Yeah. Near Nick's family. Duncan was five, Clary was little, and Mum was pregnant with us. Nick's older sister, Sarabeth, used to babysit. She was the one looking after Duncan when he was killed."

"Killed?" Clary and I squeaked in unison.

"Hit by a car. He just darted out. Nick said it caused a big rift between the families."

"That's not what Mum told me. She—"

"Yeah, well, Lib's telling us now, Clary. Go on."

"The families stopped talking. Mum and Dad left town and never came back. Sarabeth became a drug addict. She died of an overdose a few years ago. Uncle Randall died, too, of cancer. Nick's mother is still alive—Sharon, I think her name is—but she was never the same after the accident."

"When did you talk to Dad about Duncan?" I said.

"That night. I FaceTimed him, and you know how happy he always looked when one of us called? He was like, 'What's up, Kitten?' I said, 'I met Uncle Randall's son,' and his smile, like, *vanished*. I told him what Nick told me. He just went, 'I'm sorry you had to find out that way.'"

Clary snorted. "Well, maybe he should have told us himself then."

"Do you know why he didn't?" I asked Lib.

"He said Duncan's death had already destroyed too many people. He and Mum couldn't let it destroy us girls too. So they left town, started a new life, wiped the slate clean. That's what he kept saying. 'We wiped the slate clean.'"

"We're in our thirties," Clary said. "I think we could handle the truth now."

"But maybe they couldn't."

Lib had a point. I remembered Dad crying the first time he'd held Arlo. Really crying. It horrified me. He'd always seemed so unshakeable. Mum said, 'Arlo could use a change,' and whisked the baby off. Dad stepped outside for a few moments, then came back in smiling. His old self.

Something hit me. "Why would Mum lie to Clary about how Duncan died?"

"Maybe she didn't. Clary said she wasn't exactly sure what Mum told her. She could have just misunderstood."

"Hold on now." Lib should have known better than to make it sound like Clary was wrong. "Mum might not have specifically said 'baby,' but I know for sure she said, 'nothing genetic.' What does that imply to you? I obviously wasn't worried my kid would inherit a propensity to be hit by cars. Mum knew I was thinking Duncan died as a baby and did nothing to disabuse me."

A whistle sounded in the background, followed by a new round of shouting.

"Sorry. We've got a disputed call." Libby's voice had taken on the tone ER docs use when vital signs are crashing. "Better go. Don't ask Mum about this."

Clary made a humming noise. Not quite agreement.

"I mean it. She just lost Dad. She's not herself. Duncan died decades ago. We can wait a couple more months to find out what happened. Okay?"

I said, "Okay."

"Clary?"

"Fine."

"Thanks really have to go love you bye." Lib hung up.

"Are you going to ask Mum about Duncan?" I said to Clary.

"Ordinarily I would, but Lib's right. Timing's not great. And, anyway, I'm much less concerned about Duncan than I am about Gordon Fucking Bickershit. He's who I'm really worried about—and you, of course."

"Me?"

"You think I don't know why you were so desperate to get to Don's yesterday? You wanted to see Jesse. And you haven't mentioned him once. How'd it go?"

"It didn't."

"Meaning?"

"I offered him a night of wild sexual congress, but he decided to try his luck elsewhere."

"Ouch."

"Big ouch."

"You okay, Neens?"

"Bloodied but unbowed."

"I'm proud of you."

"Yeah, well. Not like I had many options. 'No means no,' right?"

"And I'm proud of Jesse too."

"What the hell, Clary."

"He's finally showing some backbone."

"Great. Something for his resume. 'Planned and executed breaking of girlfriend's heart. Initiated sexual relations with random stranger.'"

"Not what I meant but, hey. Progress. You both need shaking up. You can't just schlep along for the rest of your lives."

"Not everyone's like you, Clary. We *like* schlepping. We're good at it."

"Nina." Her voice was softer. I knew I was in for it. "You think I'm just nagging. That I'm disappointed in you, but I'm not. I'm worried about you. I want you to be happy."

"I *was* happy. I don't know what got into me. I ruined everything. I was happy!"

"No, you weren't. That's why you broke up with him."

I gripped the steering wheel and pulled my chest toward it. If I said anything, I'd cry. Fall apart.

"Jesse's a great guy. But for the last couple of years, that's not why you were with him. You were with him because you didn't have the guts to leave."

"That's not true!"

"You know it is."

"Shut up, Clary."

"Nina. You're smart and funny and gorgeous. You don't have to settle. If it's not Jesse, it'll be someone else. You're the best."

"A little-known fact."

"Well, it shouldn't be. Go out and show the world what you've got, Neens. Stop hiding. Quit being such a wuss."

She was going to break me down. She was going to make sure I never saw Jesse again.

"Can we please talk about something else?"

I'd driven past several power poles before she relented. "Fine. Bickershit. Did Don say anything else about him?"

I sighed in relief, put the car into cruise control, and told her everything I could remember.

NINA

I'd just told Clary how Don called Gord the type of hoodlum who'd smile 'then sock you in the kisser with brass knuckles.'"

She said, "Have you considered the possibility Gord killed Dad?"

I wobbled out of my lane again. More honking. "Don't go there, Clary."

"Why? Because it might take us someplace unpleasant?"

That was exactly why. I'd already consumed a near toxic dose of unpleasant that day. I concentrated on the road and willed her to stop, which was of course useless.

"And it's gonna," she continued. "The obvious conclusion is not pretty. Mum and Gord have been involved for a while. Long before Dad died."

"Says who?"

"You. You're the one who overheard their phone call. You're the one who said they sounded like lovers."

"*Sounded like.* That's all I said."

"Then you saw them kissing."

"When?"

"The Big House."

"He kissed her on the forehead. Once!"

"Then stayed out half the night with her. Talking? I don't think so—especially since I'd previously seen her sneaking into a motel for a little afternoon delight with him."

"You don't know that's who she was meeting." I was gripping the wheel so tight my fingers had gone white.

"Are you suggesting our mother has more than one lover?"

Clary paused to let that sink in before adding, "Then on a hot, sunny Sunday soon thereafter, Dad dies on the only road to a popular beach. Not a single person witnesses it. That doesn't seem suspicious to you?"

"You're making it seem suspicious." I noticed I was speeding, trying no doubt to get away from the inevitable conclusion.

"Then Mum trashes anything even vaguely connected to Dad and 'wipes the slate clean.' Once again, she's starting a new life. This time, though, it's with a violent, unethical low-life with no plausible reason to be interested in a sixty-nine-year-old woman other than the shitload of money she just inherited. Lib might be able to make that sound innocent, but do *you* really think Gord had nothing to do with this turn of events? Personally, I'm terrified of what else he's got in store for Mum."

I used to love this part of the drive home. Green fields dotted with black cows. Classic white clapboard farmhouses next to giant elms. A winding river. It was a scene from a picture book. Clary was ruining it for me.

By being right.

I drove a few more kilometres in agony, then I made a decision. "I'm going to call the cops," I said. "Tell them what we know."

I felt my shoulders release. The authorities would deal with this. I couldn't be expected to worry about my father's death *and* figure my own life out too. "I'll do it as soon as I get home."

"Great idea. I mean, as long as you're sure Mum's not involved too."

Shoulders back up. "Clary. Don't."

"Because I'm only about seventy percent sure, and that's on a good day. I love her but I don't trust her. I'd hate to call the police and have them catch her doing something she shouldn't."

Mum, face down on the sidewalk, a boot to her back, some burly cop clamping on handcuffs as the neighbours crane their necks to watch.

I couldn't let that happen. "So what are we going to do then?"

"Hire a hitman?"

"Clary!"

"Relax. I'm just blue-skying here. But we have to get rid of this Gord guy somehow. Got any better ideas?"

NINA

It was almost four by the time I got home. All I'd had to eat that day was the single pancake I'd managed to get down before Don dropped his bombshell about the dead sibling. I was hungry, tired, and after an hour of listening to Clary catastrophize, almost ready to consider the hitman option.

I had just gotten out of the car when I noticed Mum, picking peonies in the backyard. She was dressed in a lovely ivory linen shift and clunky-chic sandals. Her hair was neatly pulled up into a modified French roll. She saw me and gave a big, happy wave. She was still quite far away but I was pretty sure I detected Bobbi Brown beige.

I had exactly five seconds of *Hooray! She's back to her old self!* before doubt set in. Mum had ditched the sundress, covered her cleavage. I should have been rejoicing. But all I could think was, *What's she up to now?* I waved back and walked toward her, guard way up. Clary's suspicions were like headlice. You don't know you've picked them up until you've got the creepy-crawlies, and by then, you're infested.

"I was just going to put on some tea." Mum linked her arm through mine and led me into the kitchen. "I stopped at Osprey Café this afternoon and bought a slice of that delicious caramel torte of theirs. I was going to save it for dinner but let's celebrate, shall we?"

"Celebrate what?" I sat down at the table. She got out the kettle.

"You and Jesse! All patched up?"

The silence made her turn around. "Oh, dear." Her eyes went wide.

Jackie O rarely put her foot in her mouth. "I thought you'd maybe just come back for your things. Did. Um. Did something happen?"

A tiny nod. My chest burned like I'd been underwater too long.

Mum put down the kettle and slid in next to me. She took my hand.

"He left," I finally managed to say. "I lost him."

She pulled my head onto her shoulder and let me cry and cry and cry. I burbled out the details. "My heart's broken," I said.

"Oh, darling." Mum dabbed at my eyes with a linen napkin. "Love's a bitch. A nasty, backstabbing bitch." I leaned back and gaped at her in shock. She just shrugged. "Get used to it, kiddo."

I sat there for a few moments, stunned by this latest incarnation of my mother, then I laughed and wiped my nose on my wrist. For the first time since Dad died, I didn't doubt her sincerity. I also agreed with her.

"I hate life," I said, "but wouldn't mind some tea."

"Good idea." She patted my leg and got up, catching a glimpse of herself in the window. "Oh, look at me. Time for a tune-up." She fluffed her hair with a sigh, then smiled. "Why don't you and I go on a little mother-daughter date? Get a facial? Buy some new clothes? Might be just what we need."

"Might be." I smiled back. "I'm free tonight as it happens."

"Oh, too bad." She started filling the kettle. "I've got to go soon."

"Where?" The creepy-crawlies of suspicion again.

"I'm taking the bridge ladies out. They've been so good to me since Malcolm died." She got out the cups. "Will you be okay on your own? If not, I could postpone..."

"No, no. I'm fine. I'll catch up on BritBox and have an early night."

"There's a wonderful crime series I watched...What's it called?" She got out her phone, I got out mine, then we were lost in a happy flurry of back-and-forth recommendations until she gasped at the time and said she had to run. She freshened up—more beige lipstick and an artfully knotted silk scarf—then kissed me goodbye.

"I shouldn't be late, sweetheart, but just call if you need me. I'll be home in a jiffy."

I changed into pyjamas, got into bed with the caramel torte, and watched the first episode of a police procedural she liked. During the intro to the second episode, I checked Find My Phone. I wanted to know what fancy place she was taking her bridge ladies to.

Find My Phone said she was at the Lookout.
Bridge ladies don't go to the Lookout.
She'd been lying to me again.

PETRA

It was a knife, Petra could see that, although a crude one. The iron was dark and corroded, but the blade looked sharp enough. It was lying on a piece of flannel on Gord's lap.

She sucked her teeth. "You're not going to attack him with that, are you?"

"No!" He laughed. "I'm going to sell it to him. It's a"—air quotes—"'priceless antique.'"

"*This*?" Petra went to pick it up, but he blocked her hand.

"Watch it. We don't want fingerprints." Gord switched off the overhead light. They were in Petra's car parked at the Lookout behind a tangle of alders, but it didn't hurt to be careful.

"It looks like it's from the dollar store." She shook her head. "You actually think Osterlich's going to fall for it?"

"For our purposes, it doesn't really matter—but, that said, Ebbie's pretty sure he will."

"Ebbie?"

"Oh, sorry. Ebenezer Ballo. A Malian guy I worked with at the orphanage. He gave it the okay. He's ripped Osterlich off many times."

"Won't he be on the alert then?"

"Osterlich? Nah. He goes to the orphanage every year ostensibly to 'see his kids,' then spends half the time whispering to the locals about finding him rare antiquities. He's dumb as doughnuts. Ebbie paid a guy a few hundred West African francs to bang out some 'prehistoric' swords, then sold them to Osterlich for a small fortune. Osterlich's either so confident in his own expertise or so terrified of the anti-smuggling laws that he never gets anything appraised. Ebbie's made enough off him to buy all his siblings houses."

Petra smiled. "I love a happy ending."

Gord wrapped the knife back up in flannel and tucked it into a paper gift bag.

"So that's your plan? Sell him garbage for a pile of money?" Petra had been hoping for something flashier but was open to seeing where Gord was going with this.

"That's part of it. Eb's already been in touch with him to say he has a colleague—me—with a relic to sell. Might be time for you to reach out to Osterlich about the house tour. We need to strike while the iron's hot."

NINA

The next afternoon Mum said she was going to Petronelli's to pick up some groceries. Find My Phone confirmed it. Their food's fabulous, but the service is shit, so I knew she'd be a while. I FaceTimed the girls. I had news.

"Bobbi Brown beige," I said as a teaser.

"Meaning what?"

"Lib. Geez. Her lipstick! That's what Mum was wearing. Linen dress, subtle gold accessories, and Bobbi Brown's finest. The world's oldest mallrat has packed up her neon crop-tops and gone home. She's Mum again."

Clary snorted. "I'll believe it when I see it."

"Well, I did see it," I said undeterred. Clary's concerns about Gord—and Mum's lies about the Lookout—were hard to discount, but equally so was the change I'd witnessed. The person comforting me yesterday was definitely our mother. A new, dirty-mouthed reboot, but definitely Mum. The backstabbing bitch called Love had stolen Dad from her. It had undone her for a while, given her an edge, but she was coming around.

"And then today," I went on, "I overheard her on the phone talking about doing a house tour. She wants to raise money for a scholarship in Dad's name." That was the real kicker. Proof that Petra Fforde had returned.

Lib gasped. "What a great idea!"

"Should have heard her. She was so excited. I thought, *this isn't what someone having an affair does.* She really loved Dad."

"Of course she did," Lib said. "You guys got all worked up for nothing."

"She loves *houses*," Clary said. "That's what she's excited about."

We both yelled at her. She didn't care.

"It's true. And know what else is probably true? Gord's not out of the picture yet. House tours and sleazebags are not mutually exclusive passions."

Lib scratched her eyebrow. Clary was annoying her.

"I'm not sure she'll have much time for Gord," I said. "The tour will be a lot of work, plus I'll be helping out, so can keep an eye on her."

I decided not to mention that Mum had seemed less than pleased about my participation. I'd offered to help as soon as she got off the phone.

"This isn't really your thing, darling." She rummaged around in the junk drawer and pulled out a pack of cigarettes. "Lots of phone calls and busywork and rallying the troops." She put the cigarettes back and picked up a banana.

"I can do other stuff!" I mentioned PR and posters, and when that didn't get me anywhere, threw in electronic ticketing too. I knew Mum wouldn't know how to set that up. (I didn't either, but figured YouTube could help.) "Plus, it's for Dad. I'd love to do something for Dad. It would be weird if I *didn't* do it."

Mum took a long time finishing her banana before replying. "You're right. Of course. I'm sure you'll be a big help." She smiled, but I could almost see the thought-bubble over her head: *How the hell do I get rid of Nina now?*

"I'm really looking forward to working on it," I said to my sisters. "I always figured I'd be good at advertising."

"You would," Clary said. "You'd be good at a lot of things if you'd just frigging do them. Whose house are they using?"

"That guy. You know, the one from the funeral. The one you were so excited about."

Clary's jaw dropped. There was a moment of silence, then she went, "Osterlich? Keith Osterlich?"

"Yeah, him."

"Oh my God. Even I'd help out on *his* house tour." Clary had apparently been an Osterlich groupie ever since she'd done a case study on PhiTex in an MBA class.

She was just extolling some of his sleazier business moves when Arlo started crying.

"Oh, Christ, not again." Her shoulders slumped. "I got seventeen minutes' sleep last night and a brief I need to get done today and a dump I'd really, really like to take but so much for that." She huffed out a sigh. "Honestly, sometimes I just want to kill the kid."

Lib said, "You don't mean that."

"Of course, I don't." We both realized with horror that Clary was crying. "But I do too. Wait until you guys are mothers. Then you'll understand. You can love someone like crazy but still really, really want to kill them. I've got to go. Wish me luck...and self-restraint."

We said all the right things, then we kissy-faced and signed off.

I found myself thinking about Mum and Duncan. Had she wanted to kill him too? Had she felt guilty for feeling like that after he died? Was that why her story and Dad's didn't match up?

Or was there an entirely different reason she wanted to cover her tracks?

Those headlice again.

I wondered if I'd ever know what drove Petra Astbury-Fforde. I looked around the sunroom and was struck by how little of our lives remained. A few artfully posed black-and-white portraits. An impressionistic painting of us in the garden as kids. Tiny handprints embedded in the cement sidewalk. But that was about all. Our parents were always paring down, clearing out, packing everything up in boxes. Wiping the slate clean.

And then I thought: boxes.

Lots and lots of boxes.

Maybe that's where her secrets were hidden.

NINA

I checked Find My Phone. Mum was still at Petronelli's. With any luck she'd want to pick up a nice wine to match whatever she had in mind for dinner. The Lively Grape was on the other side of town. That might keep her out of my hair for a while, but I couldn't count on it. I'd have to be quick.

I ran up to her office and nudged the door open. The click of the hinge made me jump like a cat burglar caught in the act. A reminder I was not supposed to be there. Nobody was. This was Mum's private domain. She would have been pretty confident no one would be nosing around in here.

I stepped inside and started nosing.

The place was pristine, as per usual. Antique desk, Persian carpet, soothing art, gorgeous light. A Remodelista feature titled something like "The Aspirational Office."

On the north side, the high-pitched ceiling sloped down to a pony wall. A row of three-foot-high doors accessed storage space under the eaves. I opened the first door and switched on the light. Stacks of banker's boxes were neatly numbered and labelled. On the back of the door was a chart listing each box and what it contained. I took a quick look. *Preschool drawings/report cards. House inspection/warranties. Vaccinations/dental records.* One box was labelled *Baby photos.* I felt hopeful about that one but inside were only familiar pictures of my sisters and me.

I checked Find My Phone again and could see Mum was on the move.

As expected, she seemed to be heading toward the wine store. I didn't know how much time that would give me but probably not enough to go through each box individually. I decided to get a quick overview, note anything of interest, then check again next time she was out.

I opened the doors one-by-one and read the list of contents on the back. Boxes had been stored in chronological order. We grew from newborns to purported adults as I worked my way to the back of the house. The list on the final door was all in Mum's handwriting except for the first three entries which Dad had written. Seeing his tidy engineer's caps rebroke my heart. He really was gone, never more to develop and implement an efficient new organizational plan. My eyes filled with tears, so it took me a second to notice the last line on the list. A box Mum had recorded simply as *MDF 2.*

I remembered being in Dad's home office the day she was packing it up. She'd shocked me when she said Dad was like a Nazi commandant but then rallied by explaining she'd only meant in his penchant for documentation. She was putting all his papers in boxes for poor Wayne Dudek to deal with.

So why hadn't she given Wayne this one?

MDF 2.

A bell went off. My sisters. Talking to them on the drive back from Don's.

It hit me. Not the second box of Malcolm Duncan Fforde.

The box of Malcolm Duncan Fforde *the Second.*

The dead boy.

Our brother.

I pulled the box out of the closet and looked inside. A photo album was on top. Swirly green cover, brass-ring binding, yellowing acetate holding the photos in place. The first photo was of Mum in a hospital bed, a long braid over her shoulder, smiling at the sour-looking baby in her arms. Dad—fat Dad—was crouched beside her, beaming, a finger held out like a perch for the baby's tiny hand. On a slip of paper underneath, Mum had written, *Malcolm Duncan Fforde II. The legacy continues!*

I flipped through the album, watched Duncan get chubby and long and smiley and red-haired. He crawled and walked and climbed and seemed to laugh a lot. Mum got skinny and then plump and soon it was obvious she was pregnant again. Then Clary was born. Interspersed were photos of another family, one I came to recognize as Uncle Randall's. His wife was a tiny pretty woman with crazy-curly dark hair. The kids took more after him, I thought, but the daughter was pretty in her own way. She seemed to be fond of Duncan and Clary. She was often photographed with them.

There were blank squares, too, where pictures had obviously been removed. My guess is they were ones that didn't include Duncan. Our parents could pretend he'd never existed, but to have no baby pictures of Clary would have looked suspicious. Those photos must have been moved to another album. One we'd been allowed to see.

I went through the rest of the box. There were blue baby clothes and birthday cards and a single sneaker which I knew couldn't be good and then below, in a grim, officious, plain brown folder, the clippings. A newspaper article about a boy struck by a car, unnamed pending notification of next of kin. The death certificate. The obituary. (*Untimely death. Beloved son. Cherished brother. Adored nephew and cousin.*)

Another article saying charges wouldn't be laid. *Child died under care of young relative. Distraught driver. Babysitter in shock.*

An op-ed about law enforcement's failure to police drug use amongst teens.

And, finally, an article on a drug called Narcontine. I'd never heard of it, but I had heard of Freeling. That was its brand name. Lib did a project on misogynistic advertising when we were in high school. Ads from the sixties, seventies, and even eighties were truly mind-boggling. Wives spanked for serving the wrong coffee brand, wives crying over dish soap, ads telling women to douche with—no joke—Lysol.

I remembered Freeling because it was for girls our age. Something to do with your period, although we had to deduce this ourselves because, back when it came out, you couldn't say certain obscene words on television such as "shit," "fuck," "cocksucker," and "menstruation." The commercial showed a girl in a long white dress dancing euphorically through an Instagrammable field of daisies while a folksy voice sang, "I'm free! I'm free! I love the Freeling feeling!" The girl ran into the arms of a tall, dark-haired man, waiting at the top of the hill. (Pause to barf.) For a while, Lib and I used to sing the Freeling jingle when we burst out of school at the end of each day.

I don't know how long Mum had been in the house before I realized she was back.

"Nina!" she called, her feet clattering up the stairs.

I shoved everything into the box and the box into the cupboard and flicked the door shut with my heel.

"Nina? You home?"

I rushed out to the landing and leaned on the railing. "Hey." Very casual.

Mum looked up at me, smiling. "What are you doing up there?"

"Oh. Ah. Just looking for supplies. Got some time on my hands so thought I'd try doing a poster for the house tour." I pulled that one out of my ass.

"The house tour?"

"The one for Dad."

"Oh, right." She touched her forehead and laughed. "So you're honestly interested in working on it? You don't have to, you know. You must have better things to do than help a bunch of seniors convince another bunch of seniors to walk through someone's house. That's all it is, darling. Doddering old folks."

"Please. You gals are spring chickens compared to Don and his buddies. It'll be like going to a rave. I'll love it."

"Really? Don't you—"

"Really."

Mum paused, tapping the banister, then laughed. "Well, okay. Find what you were looking for?"

"No. Just got here. Not even exactly sure what I need. Some Sharpies, I guess. Drawing paper. I thought I'd try doing one of those little house sketches I used to do."

"Great idea. I always loved their quirky charm."

Quirky charm. She'd had to dig deep for that. Drawing was another thing I hadn't stuck with long enough to get any good at.

"Paper should be in the top drawer of my desk and Sharpies? Hmm... Let me look."

She started up the stairs.

I turned and noticed the cupboard door was half-open. "Stop!" I said, eyes flying around the room. "I...I see them." And I did, thank God. "In the mustard pot on the bookshelf."

"Oh, right. If they're dried out, check the filing cabinet. There might be a fresh pack."

"Thanks. I probably won't get much done tonight anyway but you know. Strike while the iron's hot!"

"Indeed," she said in an oddly serious voice.

PETRA

"No, I get it," Gord said.

It was midafternoon, not a time they'd generally meet, but Petra said it was an emergency. They'd chosen a rocky part of the beach where they'd be unlikely to run into anyone, especially on a rainy day. Just to be safe, though, they both had ballcaps on and hoods up. They leaned their elbows on the concrete breakwater and stared out to sea.

"I understand why you're concerned. I wouldn't want my kid involved in anything illegal either. But there's nothing illegal about the house tour itself. Nothing dangerous about it. It's not even going to happen!"

"But what if someone connects Nina to what *we're* doing?"

"They won't. They can't. She's just making a poster. She's never going to know about the rest. We'll make sure of that."

Petra sat with that for a moment, then almost laughed. "Oh, well. Not like I could talk her out of it. She's going to do it anyway. Clary always calls her a jellyfish but, truth is, Nina's surprisingly stubborn."

A wave crashed against the breakwater. They jumped back, laughing, and shook the water off. Gord waved Petra over to a dryer spot.

"You're still worried," he said.

"I am."

"Why?"

"The truth?"

"Petra. Geez."

"Okay. I'm worried about what you're not telling me."

"About Nina? Nothing."

"I mean about your plan. Our plan."

He didn't reply.

"I want to get this prick too," she said. "As badly as you do. But you've got to tell me everything, or I'm walking away. Let me assess the risks myself. I can't handle this uncertainty."

Petra's voice was calm, but her insides weren't. She hadn't considered what she'd do if Gord said no. She realized it might destroy her.

He curled his lips inward, thought for a few seconds, then said, "You're not going to like this."

Petra was shaken and that didn't happen often. Since Duncan's death, she'd prided herself on her composure. Cold, hard reason had been her armour, but cold and hard isn't a good look for a woman. The presumption is you're angry, dangerous, and/or hiding something. So she'd softened up her edges—some highlights, a breathy voice, silk blouses—and carried on. She made herself acceptable, unnoticed.

She sat in the car and watched Gord scramble up the pebbly path and onto the road. He'd refused a drive. He was shaken too. He'd said he'd wanted to ease her into it, but she insisted. Now or never. He'd hesitated, then told her everything.

"But no pressure," he said. "You can walk away, Pet. At any time. For any reason. No hard feelings. I can figure out how to do this on my own."

He was very clear about that. He was going through with it. He'd made up his mind. Now she had to make up hers.

A memory from her time in Congo popped into her head. She'd been caught in the crush of a street market when shooting broke out. She'd been too scared to move, too scared not to.

She put her hand on her chest. That's how she felt now. The enormity of Gord's request was giving her palpitations.

Time to call Bonnie again.

Bonnie understood how messy the real world is, how few decisions come without risks or consequences. She'd know what to do.

Petra's call went to voice mail. She didn't leave a message.

She had to talk to someone. But who? Deb Dudek? Ha. She'd die. Wayne? Likewise. Her bridge ladies? They fell apart at the seams if someone so much as reneged on a bid. Her daughters? Never, never, never. Petra's world suddenly felt very small. Impostors don't make friends. There was no one else to call.

Boo-fucking-hoo, she thought. *Get over it.* She'd gotten over worse. She opened a window. Fresh air might help.

She thought of Don. They'd barely spoken in years, but their conversations the week she'd stayed with him had been so helpful. His insights, his compassion, his moral clarity. He was, after all, a legal ethicist.

She searched her phone for his number. Not under M for Meisner. Not under D for Don. Had she put him somewhere else?

Yes. There it was. *Nina. Landline.* Ninety-seven-year-olds don't have cellphones.

She'd typed in half his number when her words came back to her. *Legal ethicist.* What was she thinking? Don would give her a hard no. There were few things less legally ethical than Gord's plan.

She called Bonnie again. This time she left a message.

"Bon. It's me. Call me please. ASAP? It's, um, important. Thanks."

NINA

"You look like a wet kitten," I said when Mum stepped in the door. Such a Dad expression.

"Not the best day for a walk, but I was desperate to get out." She hung up her jacket and ruffled her hair in the mirror. "What are you working on?"

I'd been busy. Having a project again had turned out to be surprisingly invigorating. There were sheets of white paper all over the kitchen table, more crumpled into balls on the floor. Mum smiled, but I knew she couldn't be happy about the mess.

"I found pictures of Osterlich's house online. Thought I'd try drawing it."

"Oooh." She put a hand on the back of my chair and pointed at a cartoony sketch that exaggerated the building's Victorian excesses. "I like that one. Something a little"—she wiggled her fingers—"Ronald Searle-ish about it."

"You mean *wonky*. Leaning Tower of Pisa or what."

"Yes, but that's what makes it—" Mum's phone buzzed. She checked the screen, then squeezed my shoulder. "Sorry, darling. I should take this..."

I shook my head like *no problem* and went back to my sketch.

"Bonnie?" Mum's voice dropped to a whisper. "Thank God. I have to talk to you about something...Yes, yes. The same issue. Give me a second."

She headed upstairs to her room.

I stopped drawing. Waited a few moments, then followed her.

PETRA

Petra heard footsteps on the stairs. "Hold on," she whispered into the phone. She opened her bedroom door a crack and saw Nina disappear into the bathroom across the hall. Seconds later, the shower turned on. Petra shut the door and sat on her bed.

"All clear."

"So what can I do you for?" Bonnie asked.

"I need help making a decision."

"Oh, Christ." Her big, yapping laugh. "And you're calling *me*? Fine. Just let me undo my bra. This about that rich bastard again?"

"Yes."

"I've thought a lot about him since our last conversation."

"And?"

"I've decided his head should be presented to the village children to use as a soccer ball."

"Not an option unfortunately."

"Pity. It's what he deserves."

"He deserves worse."

"Agreed. Got any ideas?"

"That's what I want to talk to you about...My friend told me the rest of his plan."

"The tone of your voice suggests some unease on your part."

"More than some. It's illegal."

"Hmm." Not shocked, just making a note of it. Classic Bonnie.

"And maybe immoral."

"Oh, great."

"But it could be our only chance for retribution."

Petra wasn't just saying so. At the beach, she'd made Gord walk her through all possible legal options again. None would work. As far as the law was concerned, Osterlich was an innocent man. They'd never get justice if they relied on the courts. Other illegal options Gord had considered were either messier, less dependable, or too morally suspect even for him.

"He wants—we both want—a punishment that fits the crime. Not a slap on the wrist. Not a 'cancellation.' An eye for an eye."

"Let's hear it, Pet."

"Okay, but first there's something I've got to tell you about Gord."

NINA

I left the shower running, threw a towel around myself, and tiptoed out of the bathroom. I pressed my head against Mum's bedroom door and listened. She was whispering, so I didn't catch everything, but I clearly heard her say "it's illegal" several times and "but I don't care." An unsettling combination.

I picked up other snippets here and there too.

My training.

Justice, or maybe she said *just us*?

Mercy.

Something about *patients.* Or *patience*?

There was silence for a while—Bonnie must have said something—then Mum replied, a little louder than before, as if she was frustrated. Not getting what she wanted.

"But it *is* grievous and irremediable. *Something something something.* He needs me. And here's the thing..."

What's the thing? I leaned forward. The floor creaked loudly. I ran back into the bathroom, shut the door, and jumped into the shower, heart pounding.

A few minutes passed. I turned off the tap and put on a robe. When I heard her door open, I stepped into the hall, rubbing my hair with a towel. Steam billowed out after me.

"Well, you certainly indulged yourself!" Mum said, smiling. If she'd been upset, she wasn't now.

"Don's shower is pathetic. Zero pressure. This one is such a treat, it's hard to leave."

"Well, good. I know we're supposed to preserve water but, in the scheme of vices, a long, a hot shower ain't the worst. Now why don't you get dressed and let's go out. I've barely eaten all day. I'm starving!"

I said sure—I never turned down a free meal—but something about it made me deeply uncomfortable.

What was she so happy about?

NINA

The next day, I found the business card he'd left at our house and called to set up a meeting with Detective Ryan Al-Haddad.

I had a good reason to call, or at least a pressing one. Mum had been smiling and sweet the evening before, but I just couldn't shake the sense that something was up. I know you can't judge what goes on in a phone conversation when you only hear one side, but *yes, you fucking can.* You hear a person you know well—or at least thought you knew well—suddenly start saying things like *it's illegal but I don't care*, you judge. You worry.

Normally that would have meant I'd call my sisters.

But normally, the night before, I wouldn't have been at a very nice, very hip little restaurant with my mother. I wouldn't have been seated at a corner table looking out over a sea of beautiful people, all more or less my age, none of whom were dining with *their* parent. They were all dining with someone who turned empty wine bottles over in ice buckets and gestured at servers for more. Someone who ate off their forks and held their hands and kept holding them even when the busser tried to clear their plates. Someone who they got dressed up for and, later, no doubt, *un*dressed for.

To compound my misery, when our little mother-daughter date was over, I retreated to my childhood bedroom and scrolled through social media. After fifteen years with me, Jess had decided to replace the grey generic head with an actual profile picture. He was on the move. I was not.

My life was a mess. I could not deal with The Mother Issue on my own anymore. I needed help.

Professional help. And I don't mean a hit man. I didn't want Clary convincing me otherwise.

"Ms. Fforde," Al-Haddad said when he met me in the lobby. "Nice to see you again. I got us a conference room." I followed him down the hall to a windowless cubby with a vinyl table and matching chairs.

"Have a seat," he said. "Tea? Coffee?"

"I'm fine, thanks."

"Sorry I can't offer you anything as delicious as those squares of yours." He patted his slate-flat belly. "I still dream about them."

He remembered me, or at least the Hello Dollies I'd tossed on a plate for him. I smiled coyly. "Had I known, I would have brought you some!" My cheeks warmed. I felt like I was auditioning for a Doris Day movie.

"Very kind." He sat down. "You're probably wondering about your father. I wish I had something new to report, but I'm afraid things move much slower in real life than on TV."

"Actually, I'm here about something else." A pained smile. "It's my mother. I'm...well. I'm concerned about her."

"In what regard?"

"I think she's seeing someone."

"Really?" He raised his eyebrows and nodded as if she'd taken up competitive eating or camel racing. Quirky, but no real cause for alarm.

He wasn't getting it. "I'm worried he's after her money."

That hit home. Al-Haddad took out his notepad. "Has something happened to make you suspect that? Are large sums missing from her account? Any irregularities with her banking?"

"I wouldn't know. I don't have access to her bank accounts. But something's strange. She goes out a lot. I have no idea where. She's always whispering on the phone. She *swears.* That's new, too. It's like she's low-grade possessed or something."

"Do you know who she's seeing?"

"Um..." And that's when I heard it: My internalized Clary, shrieking at me. *What are you doing, Nina? You're not actually going to rat her out, are you? Our own mother?*

My breath caught. Had I lost my mind? If Al-Haddad found Gord, he'd also find whatever Mum may or may not have been up to.

I shook my head. Went red. “No. No, I don’t. And, um, truthfully? I’m not even sure she’s seeing anyone. She’s just behaving a little oddly. I’m probably overreacting.” My mouth smiled. “But grief, right? Makes people do strange things!” Like me. Here. Now. Babbling. Such a bad idea.

Al-Haddad tapped the table. “So this behaviour is out of character for your mother?” His fingers were neat and rectilinear, like an illustration from a book on how to draw hands.

“Yes. I mean, no. Her husband’s never died before—so, hard to say!” *Wrong time to crack wise. Recalibrate.* “But you know. The poor thing!” Sympathetic pout. “She just suffered a terrible tragedy. Of course she’s not herself.”

That got a slight nod.

“I feel silly now.” I touched my hair, hinting I was normally more pulled together than this. “I was just worried. Ignore me. I shouldn’t have come.” I pushed back my chair.

“No, no. I’m glad you did.” Al-Haddad tilted his head like he wanted me to stay. He really was incredibly handsome. And the way he was looking at me? The man cared. “I’m always interested to hear your concerns or suspicions.”

“No suspicions! Seriously.” I laughed prettily. (I hoped. Something about those dark brown eyes. I couldn’t go yet.) “Just me being overprotective. I mean, even if she were seeing someone—which she’s not—she’s a grown-up. It’s her money. She can do with it as she pleases.”

“True.”

“*I’m* the one who’s acting oddly.” Here was my chance. I bit my lip. Rom-com shorthand. “I bet that’s what you’re thinking.”

He laughed politely. “No.”

“I am. I kind of understand where Mum’s coming from. It’s confusing when you suddenly find yourself alone.” I went for it. Clary would have been so proud of me. Taking risks. Grabbing the bull by the horns. Getting myself out there again. “I’m actually back on the dating scene myself these days.”

This was where he was supposed to raise an eyebrow, suppress a smile, and ask if he could call me sometime.

“Oh, yeah? Been there, done that.” He stood up. “Well, best of luck with it, and with your mother. I’m sorry I couldn’t be more help today.”

I stood up, too, suddenly mortified. A major misread of the situation. I felt like I should be looking down at my hands, clutching a small vinyl purse, and apologizing to the boyish parish priest for having wantonly thrown myself at him. (I'm Irish in this image. It's the mid-sixties. I'll be boarding the boat for Liverpool the next day, never more to bring shame onto my family.)

"We'll get back to you and Ms. Astbury as soon as we have any news about your father." Al-Haddad opened the door and showed me out.

AL-HADDAD

Constable Heather Briglio noticed the flustered young woman leaving the police station. She waved Al-Haddad over and whispered, "Another member of your fan club, Al? You're like our very own Biebs or something." Al-Haddad smiled, then shielded his hand with the Fforde file so people in the waiting room couldn't see him give her the finger. The pretty-boy jokes had gotten tired years ago.

He headed back to his cubicle. His colleagues knew he wasn't against using his looks in the name of justice but, this time, he hadn't been trying. ("Doesn't even have to try!" The jeers.) He opened his desk drawer and put his rainbow pin back on. He should never have taken it off. It would have spared Nina the embarrassment. Last thing he wanted was to scare her away. Blair Zinck might roll his eyes at the idea of Petra Fforde having someone on the side, but Nina clearly didn't.

Odd, though, all the back-pedalling. It was like she'd wanted to tell him something, but *didn't* want to tell him too.

He considered the possibility Briglio was right and Nina was just another fangirl. Wouldn't be the first time someone had come in on a trumped-up excuse to see him again.

But, no. He ruled that out. Nina randomly making up an affair when Al-Haddad was actually investigating one? Too much of a coincidence.

So let's say Nina's concern was legitimate. Why wouldn't she have mentioned Dudek? She obviously knew him. Al-Haddad reached a hand over his head and cranked his neck toward his left shoulder. All this sitting was hard on his upper trapezius. Maybe, he thought, Nina was used to seeing Dudek around the house over the years. She might have noticed the change in her mother's behaviour but just never connected it to her father's old partner.

His short, fat, old partner.

He pictured Dudek in the zebra-striped tux. Sarge had a point. Petra and Wayne would make a pretty weird combo.

Al-Haddad took a sip from his water bottle, then checked the time. It was his boyfriend's birthday. If he hurried, he could get to the mall, buy the fancy tennis racquet Alex wanted, and still be back for his 13:30 meeting. He was chockablock all day, so better go now. He couldn't come home empty-handed. A late birthday present would be the final straw. Things were pretty rocky between Alex and him at the moment.

He stood up to check his pocket for car keys and wondered: *What if Alex died in a bike accident? How sad would* I *be?*

The answer came painfully fast. *Not very.* If it weren't for the dog and the house, they probably would have broken up years ago.

He reconsidered Petra. His spider senses had tingled like crazy the day he met her. A worse flirt than her daughter and barely able to contain her glee. But so what? Lots of relationships die before either spouse does.

True. But what better reason to get rid of him? No love, no use having him around anymore. A husband would just be in the way. A classic crime of passion.

Al-Haddad sat back down and keyed *Petra Astbury Fforde* into the National Repository of Criminal Records. Petra didn't strike him as someone with a criminal past, but you never knew. There'd been a case a few years back involving a lovely churchgoing granny who'd just happened to lose six husbands under mysterious circumstances. Black widows aren't always easy to identify.

No hits for *Petra Astbury Fforde* but lots for a *Sarabeth Fforde.*

A pseudonym, maybe?

No. The dates were wrong. Sarabeth was almost twenty years younger than Petra, not to mention dead. She'd died of an overdose eleven years ago.

Al-Haddad tapped his pen against his chin. He remembered Petra saying Malcolm's brother had a kid with addiction issues. So maybe a relative?

He looked at her mugshot. Sarabeth's hair was curly like Nina's but otherwise he didn't see a resemblance. Hard to tell, though, given the blank stare, the black eye, and the tattoos. Lots of jailhouse skulls and crosses. *Duncan* written in caps across her throat.

He read on. B and Es, disorderlys, a sad attempt at cheque kiting. A parole report mentioned her ongoing guilt over the death of a young cousin in her care. Some indication that Sarabeth may have been high at the time, although no toxicology report.

Then something hit him.

The tattoo.

Duncan.

He glanced at the manilla Fforde file.

Malcolm Duncan *Fforde.*

The name Duncan was obviously important to Sarabeth. A neck tattoo was a major commitment, even for a junkie. Would she have tattooed her *uncle's* name on her throat? Unlikely—plus, why? Malcolm didn't go by Duncan. So maybe a boyfriend then? Not a super-common name, but Al-Haddad couldn't rule it out.

He googled several variations of *Malcolm, Sarabeth, Fforde,* and *Duncan* and three obituaries came up. No new information in Malcolm's or Sarabeth's but the third one was interesting. It was a microfiche newspaper clipping from almost forty years ago, confirming that Petra and Sarabeth were indeed related.

Duncan Fforde, aged five, beloved son of Petra Astbury and Malcolm Fforde, died tragically in a car accident...

He thought of Petra in that ridiculous sundress. Beautiful house, beautiful daughters, and shit luck.

It made him think of a guy he'd arrested years ago. Gordon Bickerton. Lawyer at one of the big firms, gorgeous wife, lots of money—then his kid died, and he lost everything.

Lost? More like he threw it away. Al-Haddad had liked the guy but, man, talk about bent on destruction. Gord's heart was broken, and he wasn't going to be happy until everything else was too.

Al-Haddad reached over and stretched his neck in the other direction.

Petra, in comparison, didn't seem so bad. She'd lost her kid, too, and now her husband. She was acting a little strange but so? Who was he to judge?

A disc cracked loudly. He groaned in satisfaction.

A cop, that's who. Al-Haddad could feel sorry for Petra and still suspect her.

He was just about to put Wayne Dudek's name into the crime repository when he saw the time.

Shit. He grabbed his jacket and raced to the mall.

NINA

The ultimate walk of shame. Having to make my way past all the felons and scofflaws and late payers of traffic violations after Al-Haddad showed me the door. I saw him whispering to the desk cop as I left. My face burned. I was fourteen again.

What had I been thinking? Coming on to the cop investigating my father's death? Willing to sic him on my own mother in the hopes of getting a date? I'd reached a new low. I scurried down the sidewalk toward the car.

There was a ticket on the windshield. I snatched it up from under the wiper and threw myself into the driver's seat. On top of everything else, I hadn't put enough change in the meter. I was irresponsible too.

I leaned back against the headrest and stared at the ceiling. Tears seeped down my face, around my earrings and under my collar. I was running out of ways to fail. No boyfriend. No job. No skills. Google "loser," and I'd be the first image to come up.

I wallowed in that for a few moments, then said, "I am not a loser. I am not irresponsible. I'm going to fix this." By which I meant everything. "I am strong."

Clary would have puked, but it worked. At least sort of. I wiped my face on my elbow and called Mum. I was going to talk to her, adult to adult. Find out once and for all what was up.

"Hello, darling."

"Are you home?"

"Not for long. Just heading out to meet Deb Dudek for a late lunch. Why?"

"There's something I need to talk to you about."

"Oh...Okay. I'll be back in a couple of hours. Can we talk then? I should run now. I'm late."

"Sure. Absolutely. Say hi to Deb for me."

"Will do. See you soon, darling."

It wasn't much, but it was something. I'd at least tried. Not my fault she was busy. First step in a thousand-mile journey, etc. I wasn't going to call it an excuse.

Ten minutes later, I was home. There was a red Audi in the driveway and someone on the front porch.

The big hair, the leopard-print scarf. Even from behind, I recognized her right away.

Deb Dudek.

She heard the car door close and turned around. "Why, Nina! Aren't I lucky? How are you, sweetheart? I was just leaving some orchid show tickets in the mailbox for your mother. She said she'd sell some for me."

I bounded up the stairs. "I thought she was meeting you for lunch today."

"I wish! I can't drag her out anywhere these days. She's still so busy with your dad's estate. Don't let her run herself ragged, will you? Wayne and I are worried sick about her. She's just go, go, go." Deb checked her phone and made a face. "As I should be. Got reams of tickets to drop off before the traffic starts."

We air-kissed. I waved goodbye, then ran inside and opened Find My Phone. According to the app, Mum was not seated at a sunny linen-covered table at Café Bijou, looking out over the harbour, wondering if perhaps she'd got her dates mixed up. My lying, cheating mother was actually way out in the boonies at a highway motel called Shady Rest. I looked it up on Google Earth. It was every bit as sleazy as it sounded.

I'd finally reached my breaking point. I got back in the car and drove like hell.

The cover of a pulp novel entitled something like *A Spirited Vixen* or *Naughty Comes the Lady*. That's the picture that came to mind. Mum tarted up in a sheer nightie and a black beehive. Gord in a grubby singlet, leaning against the doorframe, with a glass of whiskey in his hand. Cigarettes, etc., smouldering.

I was furious. She'd gone too far this time. I was going to knock some sense into her. Some decency. Having sex in the middle of the afternoon with a younger man at a scuzzy motel?

Having sex when I wasn't?

Having sex, period?

The gall.

I pulled into the motel driveway and saw her car in front of 5B. I parked mine across the lot, next to an overflowing garbage bin with a stencilled sign reading *Visitor Parking*. How apropos. I checked out the scene through the rearview mirror.

The other rooms looked like they had permanent renters. Some had faded plastic lawn chairs out front. Two had makeshift clotheslines strung between rusting metal posts holding up mossy roofs. A grocery cart full of empties had been left outside another.

This is where my mother chooses to conduct her affair.

She had to be stopped.

I threw back my shoulders, took a fortifying breath, and stepped onto the steaming black asphalt. The roar of the highway, the stink of the bin—they just egged me on. I locked the car. It would probably be sitting on blocks by the time I got back.

I strode across the parking lot to her room. The door had once been white but grime had settled into the faux wood grain, turning it a bleak greige. Dents on the bottom right suggested it had been kicked in more than once.

Should I knock?

Identify myself in a loud, authoritative voice?

Just barge in?

What was the protocol here?

I put my ear against the door and listened. I braced for animal noises, passion, even amorous murmurs, but all I heard was the low rumble of normal conversation. I couldn't make out words, but I recognized my mother's laugh. I thought of Jesse and me in bed: Happy, goofy, sexually satisfied. It would kill me seeing my mother like that.

I almost turned back. But then Mum spoke. Louder than before. I could hear her plainly.

"I don't like what you're making me do, Gord, but I'll do it. I'll do it for you."

Fuck protocol. I kicked in the door.

AL-HADDAD

Al-Haddad was eating a bulgar salad at an outdoor food court beside the Dudek & Fforde building. Wayne Dudek was several tables away having lunch with three women. He'd hugged each of them effusively when they'd arrived.

And that was about the most incriminating thing Al-Haddad had been able to dig up about Wayne Dudek. He was a hugger. These days, that could get you in some serious trouble professionally and socially, but not criminally. (At least, not yet.)

Neither Google nor the National Repository had come up with any other infractions. In the last thirty years, Dudek hadn't even had a traffic violation. His business was booming, his online reviews were glowing, he even seemed to love his wife.

So? Could just mean Al-Haddad hadn't done enough digging.

Dudek said something and the women all laughed. A server arrived, carrying a cake covered in sparklers. Dudek reached over and hugged the brunette. She made him stand up and do it again.

Al-Haddad's phone rang.

It was Ivany Gaetz, his contact at the Department of Transportation. "Hey, Al. I think I figured out why there were no witnesses in the Fforde case."

NINA

I put everything I had behind it—all 127 pounds of flesh and bone and wobbly, untoned muscle—but I didn't need to. Either the door wasn't locked or the lock was shit, because one bump, and it gave way like a saloon door in an old Western. It slammed against the inside wall. With no resistance, I barrelled Jim Carrey–like into the room. Feet slapping ass, arms windmilling, lips rippling open as if caught in a wind machine. I was shocked and terrified and yet all I could think was, *Jesse. He'll be laughing about this for months.*

I could hardly wait to tell him. Even in extremis, that's where I was.

Mum let out a short, sharp shriek. Gord pushed her behind him and dropped into a half-crouch—arms out like wings, teeth bared.

I knew instinctively he had a gun. I closed my eyes, clapped my hands over my ears, and swung my face away. My head filled with noise: one long, loud interior wail and, beneath that, a sad little rumble of drums muttering *nononononononononononono.*

This couldn't be happening. I wasn't ready to say goodbye to youth and life and unfulfilled ambition. I wasn't ready to leave Jesse, miss out on Arlo, beat Don to the grave. I had stories to tell, places to visit, children to have, books to write, layers to grow out. It was both too soon and too late for me. I realized Nina Antonia Fforde would not live on in any way, shape, or form. Violins screeched. I was being expunged.

Nothing in my life ever turned out the way I wanted. That was my last thought.

But then, silence.

No bang, no impact, no white light at the end of a tunnel. The violins stopped. Highway noises resumed. An overhead light buzzed. I was suddenly aware how tightly my shoulders, belly, and teeth were clenched. Sometime later—a few seconds? A few minutes?—Mum said, "Nina?" I opened my eyes and slowly turned towards her.

She'd stepped out from behind Gord and was looking at me in either horror or rage. Gord was looking at me, too, but more in confusion. I'd caught a glimpse of them on my way in, but it was only now that I realized they were both fully dressed. The beds, I noticed, too, were untouched, their shiny floral coverlets pulled up neatly over pillows, flat as sheet cakes.

"You?" Gord wagged his finger at me, as in *haven't we met?*

Mum snapped to. "How do you know Nina?"

He looked at me, then looked at her, then said, "This is your daughter?"

"What are you up to?" Mum said.

Gord and I both went, "Me?!"

A long silence followed. Clearly, none of us was quite ready to reveal our hand. Our chests rose and fell in time. (We'd synched up so quickly. Roommates menstruating.)

Mum brushed a strand of hair off her forehead. "Why don't we make ourselves comfortable?" Classic La Bouve. "Have a seat."

She pointed to the bed on the left. I hesitated, as if this might be some kind of trap, but did as I was told. She sat next to me. Gord shuffled through the narrow gap between the two beds and sat across from us.

"Nina, how about you start? You seem anxious to chat." Mum gave a small, joyless smile. "Tell us why you're here."

"I followed you."

"Obviously. But why?"

"I called and you said you were with Deb, but then Deb came to our door"—Mum grimaced as if she should have thought of that—"so I knew you were lying again."

"Again?"

I'd offended her. I didn't care. "Yes, *again.* You've lied over and over to us since Dad died."

She lifted her chin. "I've tried not to."

"Yeah, well, not very hard if you ask me."

"I didn't ask you, Nina. We talked about this. I need to live my own life. I asked you to butt out. You didn't. Lying just seemed easier than constantly fighting you."

"I'm sorry but I'm not going to 'butt out.' It's our job to look after each other. That's what you've always told us. It's our job, in fact, to butt *in* and that's what I'm doing."

"I don't need looking after."

I jumped up. "You sure about that?" I swept my hand around the horrible little room that, despite eyewatering amounts of pine air freshener, still stunk of countless strangers sharing cheap cigarettes and bodily fluids. "You're almost seventy years old and you're having sex with some down-on-his-luck nobody in a highway motel. Someone here isn't making good choices."

Gord put his hands over his eyes and his elbows on his knees and started to laugh.

"It's not funny! She could lose her reputation. She could lose her money. She could get...bedbugs"—I was going to say crabs—"in a place like this."

"Darling. Even some of the nicest places have bedbugs." Mum started to laugh too.

"This isn't funny! It's very upsetting! You carrying on like this, days after Dad dies. Maybe even before. Did you know Gord before? You did, didn't you? Were you cheating on Dad? How long have you two been together? Did you—"

She cut me off before I could say the thing I didn't want to say.

"Sit down, Nina. Sit. Down."

I didn't.

"I'll explain, but not with you hovering over me like that." She gave my hand a tug. "Please."

I sat down but I wouldn't look at her. If I looked at her, I'd believe her. Just like I'd believed her every other time.

NINA

Mum said, "Gord and I have known each other a long time."

"I knew it."

"We met at a grief support group for parents of dead children. Your father and I had a son who died."

She was playing for sympathy. She wasn't getting it from me. "Yeah. Another thing you'd been lying to us about."

"You knew? Who told you? Clary?"

"No. And Lib didn't either. Don did. By mistake. Somehow you felt you could tell someone you barely knew, but you couldn't tell us."

She rubbed her thumb over my hand. "Telling a stranger a secret is often easier to do—although, if it makes you feel any better, for the longest time your father and I didn't tell anybody. Not a soul. Just too painful…But I'll tell you now, if you'd like?"

I nodded like a teenager. Yes, I wanted her to tell me, but I didn't have to be happy about it.

Her story matched the one Nick Fforde had told Libby. Mum was pregnant with us. She got Dad's niece Sarabeth to babysit one day so she could take Clary to an appointment. Duncan got hit by a car and died.

"It was my worst nightmare. What made it even harder was I'd known something like this could happen. I hadn't wanted to hire Sarabeth. The girl was a spoiled brat. She was stoned half the time. That glazed look, the giggling. But she was Malcolm's niece, and Randall and Sharon—her parents—had been having a hard time with her. There was this idea a little responsibility would do her good. It was only for a couple of hours. What could possibly go wrong? Sarabeth was 'a good kid'"—Mum gave a sour laugh—"so I got talked into it."

She looked away. Gord reached across and patted her knee.

She wiped a little something off her blouse and turned back to me. Jackie O. Calm, pleasant. "I wanted Sarabeth to burn in hell or, at the very least, die in prison. She was high when it happened. She wasn't watching Duncan. She was sleeping or having sex or counting daisies. We never found out what.

"Malcolm's family were horrified I wanted her charged. Sharon came to me, begging. Sarabeth felt 'terrible.' Her punishment was 'going to be living with it for the rest of her life.'" Mum shrugged. "So? That was my punishment, too, and I wasn't stoned when I should have been looking after him. I lost my son, I lost my career, and I was in very real danger of losing my marriage."

"You lost your career?" *What career?* I hated to tell her, but "housewife" didn't count.

"Yes. Another thing I lied to you about." She adjusted her collar. "I was a doctor."

"What?" Had Bonnie been right?

"A pediatric emergency specialist, in fact. I knew exactly what my thirty-seven-pound son would have looked like after having been hit by a VW van. I'd dealt with bodies like that before. I knew I'd never be able to do it again, so I quit."

"Why didn't you tell us you were a doctor?"

"Because I would have had to tell you why I'd quit, and that meant I would have had to tell you what happened, and your father and I decided not to do that. I was so angry at Sarabeth and her family, and Malcolm was caught in the middle. Your father and I knew we couldn't compound the tragedy of Duncan's death by sacrificing you girls to it. So we made a deal. I quit my job, we cut ties with Malcolm's family and moved away. Put the pain behind us. Forgot about it."

She raised her eyebrows as if that would ever happen. "Your father got comfortable skating on life's surface. I pretended to, but inside I was furious. Grief became a spectator sport for me. Every so often, I had to sneak off to watch other people rail against it. That's how I met Gord."

She told me about watching Gord trash a meeting room at a grief counselling session and realizing she'd finally met a kindred spirit. They both laughed at that.

Then Gord told me about the death of his son. I feigned ignorance. They didn't need to know how long I'd been following them. He told me about losing his wife, getting kicked out of his law firm, and heading to Mali to work in an orphanage.

"I'm a changed man," he said.

"A vegan." I smirked.

"How do you know that?" Mum asked.

So then I *did* have to admit how long I'd been following them. I recounted overhearing their phone call and thinking she was meeting a lover at "a big house" near the highway.

"I got there and found out it was this tacky bar, and I was so upset I started to cry, then this guy tried to pick me up—"

"I did not! Don't listen to her, Pet! I had no idea she was your daughter," Gord said. "She was just this sad person at a bar."

My new Tinder profile: Nina Fforde, just some sad person at a bar.

"Ugh." I flopped down flat on the bed, and one of its legs fell off. The mattress hit the floor, and I slid ungainly into the wall. We all cracked up. The tension, I guess.

Gord helped me onto my feet, then knelt down and wiggled the bed leg back into place.

Mum said, "This is why you should never stay in cheap motels."

I chuckled out a "yeah," but then I wondered. "Why *do* you stay here, anyway?"

"I dunno. Handy, I guess." Gord stood up and dusted off his knees. "Have a seat, ladies."

Mum busied herself straightening the coverlet, then sat down.

Handy, my ass, I thought. To what? The train tracks? A ready supply of rusty oil drums? The off-ramp to oblivion?

If this little get-together was as innocent as they claimed, why did they need to be sneaking around?

"Mum," I said. "What are you up to?"

She couldn't Jackie O her way out of this one.

AL-HADDAD

Blair Zinck was in full sermon mode. The wise old man, imparting judgment. Al-Haddad just had to sit there with a falsely receptive look on his face and take it.

"I know it's disappointing, Al, but we're not the Mounties. We don't always get our man." Zinck plunked himself on Al-Haddad's desk. "And PS, not always a man to get. Case in point: Malcolm Fforde. 'Death by misadventure.' Just like I told you. You got your answers now, and they add up. Stupid teenagers plus an old guy on a bike plus a dusting of gravel and bingo. Case closed. Be happy! You might not like the Widow Fforde but, hey, I don't like a lot of people. Still not allowed to lock 'em up."

Al-Haddad laughed dutifully, then cast a pointed glance at his computer as in *work to do.*

Zinck took the hint and heaved himself off the desk with a groan. "And anyway, there's still hope. You're young. Lots of time to get her for something else. If she's as bad as you think, she's bound to screw up at some point. They always do."

"Thanks, Sarge." Ivany Gaetz at the Department of Transportation had provided a very credible explanation for the break in traffic on Highway 3 the day Malcolm died, so it looked like Petra was off the hook. Al-Haddad was reassured, though, to think that someday he might get her for something else. "I mean it."

That woman didn't seem right to him.

NINA

"You guys are doing something you're not supposed to, and I want to know what."

Mum pursed her lips. Gord cleared his throat.

"Now," I said.

They were caught. Deer in the headlights. They looked at each other silently for a few seconds, some message was exchanged, then Gord turned to me.

"I could argue the 'not-supposed-to-be-doing thing' with you, but I'll set that aside for the moment. You need background first. The drug Sarabeth was on is called Narcontine. It was marketed to young girls for PMS symptoms, despite numerous internal studies showing it to be both psychotropic and highly addictive."

I made a face.

"Exactly," he said. "There's another drug you should know about too. Pediaxyclone. A pediatric cancer med. Because of potentially lethal side effects, it couldn't get approval in First World markets, so PhiTex—the company that developed it—cut its losses and sold the drug in Africa. A perfectly legal, if absolutely immoral, business move that resulted in the deaths of dozens of children, including a little boy I knew and loved, called Boubacar. The man behind both these drug strategies is a local captain of industry called Keith Osterlich."

It took a second for the name to register. "Osterlich?" I said to Mum. She nodded.

"Like, house-tour Osterlich?"

She nodded again. Her poise enraged me.

"Why would you want to have anything to do with him? Why are you connecting Dad's name to some scumbag?"

"She isn't," Gord said. "The house tour is never going to take place. It's a feint."

"A feint," I repeated derisively. "Who are you? Miss Marple? No one says 'feint.'"

"A ruse, then. Better? It's just part of our plan to bring Osterlich to justice."

"Hold on. Bring him to justice? I thought you said what he did was 'perfectly legal.'"

"Correct. The law can't get Osterlich." Gord allowed the slightest smirk. "But that doesn't mean we can't."

"Now you're vigilantes or something? Going to go all tiki torch and hunt the man down?"

"Not quite. But what we're doing is not strictly above board."

"As in *illegal*."

"Yup." Gord frowned, but just for show. "No other choice."

"Absolutely none," Mum said. "Osterlich is immune from prosecution."

"But *you* aren't! You're talking about committing a crime!"

They shrugged and tried not to smile.

"Oh my God, guys!"

Mum sat up very straight. "Do you think Osterlich deserves to get away with murder?"

"No, but—"

"Well, then, Nina, extrajudicial is the only option."

"How *extra*? How far outside the law are you going?"

A pause. Mum tapped Gord's thigh. *You do the honours.*

"Okay. Here are the bones of the thing." He told me how Osterlich founded the orphanage Gord had worked at in Mali. Osterlich styled himself as a philanthropist, but his real interest in Africa was for its antiquities. "He thinks he's an expert but, ha. The locals have been ripping him off for ages, selling him cheap marketplace trinkets for huge sums of money." Another smirk, but bigger this time. "I'm just going to do more of the same."

"So, a scam?"

"Basically."

"And Mum's involved how?"

She shook her head modestly. "House-tour stuff mostly. Nice volunteer-lady activities. Don't worry, darling. It's not dangerous."

"It isn't." Gord raised his hand, Scout's honour. "Even if this all goes to shit, I will make sure that no one ever connects Petra to what I'm up to."

"Even if?" I said. "Things go to shit all the time, and the worst type of shit is the kind you don't anticipate."

"You're right, darling. But again, it's my life. We've had this discussion. I've lived forty years with the agony of losing a child because of Osterlich. I couldn't even talk to my husband about it because my rage would have destroyed us both. I don't have to worry about that anymore. I'm finally free to right the wrong. So, thank you for your concern, but I'm doing this. I'm a big girl. And I'm going to make Osterlich pay for what he did."

She took Gord's hand. They looked at me serenely, the way a loving couple might look at their grown children when breaking a cancer diagnosis. *We're fine. It's all good. We're in this together.*

After a while, I said, "I get it."

I did. Of course, I did. There was nothing I wanted more than to feel that much love and passion and purpose. I envied them but still had questions. "Fine. But I want details."

"Sorry." Gord shook his head. "Can't do that."

"You have to."

"I can't."

"He can't," Mum confirmed.

"Why?"

"Because the less you know about it, the better."

"Thanks for the vote of confidence."

"Not *you* in particular. I just mean there'll be fewer opportunities for slip-ups if nobody knows everything."

"Jesus. You're starting to sound like a terrorist organization."

They grinned.

"Wrong reaction," I said. They laughed. "What's the matter with you guys?"

Mum's face went serious. "Nothing's the matter, darling. We're just laughing because...oh, I don't know." She looked at Gord and smiled again. "After all this time, to have a solution? Even the hope of a solution? It's a little intoxicating."

"Great. Drunk and criminally inclined. Aren't people supposed to slow down in their seventies?"

"I'm tired of doing what I'm supposed to do, Nina. Plus, I'm not seventy yet. I still have a couple of months to kick ass."

La Bouve kicking ass. I laughed. She'd won.

She put her hands on my knees, looked into my eyes, and I was a child again.

"Please don't ruin this for us, darling. Please don't ruin this for your brother or all the other innocent kids Osterlich killed."

Try arguing with that. "I won't."

"Thank you." She kissed my hand and didn't let go. "There's one more thing we need you to do."

"Okay..."

"Promise you won't tell anyone anything about this. Not your sisters, not Jesse, not anyone. Will you do that? *Can* you?"

I nodded, but they both kept looking at me until I said the words out loud. "I promise. I won't tell anyone."

It would be a first for me, but hey. Suddenly everything was.

PETRA

Petra had just closed the door behind Nina. She didn't turn around. She couldn't. She was mortified. She'd thought she had a face in her repertoire for every situation, but clearly not.

"Pet?"

She drummed up some sort of smile and looked at Gord. "Sorry. Sorry. I was as surprised as you were to see her. Honestly."

"I know. Forget it. Nina seemed okay with it. You all right?"

"Not like I have much choice, do I?" She plunked herself on the bed beside him. "Is this a non-smoking room?"

"So the sign says."

"Oh well. Shouldn't anyway." She lay down on her back. "Nina." She looked at the ceiling and shook her head. "Of all the girls, she'd be the last one I'd expect to figure this out."

"Why?"

"She can be a bit…I don't know, out of it. Spent the last fifteen years living in a bubble with her equally charming and impractical boyfriend. I didn't think she'd ever get her wits about her. I've been so worried about her."

"And there's the answer to your question, Pet." He lay down beside her. "Push over."

"What question?"

"The one you were asking before we were so rudely interrupted."

"Gord. I'm too frazzled for Buddhist koans. Just say what you mean."

"Why I'm doing this. You have people to worry about. You have a life. A future. A reason to keep going."

"A raisin." She laughed, but sadly.

"What?"

"That's what Malcolm used to call me. Raisin. Because I was his 'raison d'être.' Ha. Ha. His reason for living." She remembered the goofy guy she'd fallen in love with. How long since she'd thought of him? "Malcolm actually used to be fun."

"Yeah. Me too. But I'm not anymore. I guess that's what happens when you lose everything except the screaming need for justice. That's my raisin. My one and only." He shrugged. "I'd love for you to help, but if you can't, I understand. I'll find another way. It just might not hurt Osterlich as much as I'd like."

He'd find a way to make it hurt. Petra knew that. Gord always got what he wanted. She'd been that type too. The type the gods destroy. They let you think you're in control then bam. They go and kill your kid.

Petra turned on her side and draped an arm across Gord's chest.

"What?" he said.

"I'll do it. You knew I would. You've always known exactly what works on me."

He tried not to smile.

She put her leg over his and pulled him closer.

"But I'll kill you if anything happens to my girl."

NINA

I texted my sisters: GOOD NEWS. They FaceTimed me immediately.

"I've got eight minutes," Lib said. "I should be preparing notes for a meeting, but the hell with that. Good news. Finally. What is it?"

"And would *I* call it good?" Clary was in her backyard, topless, nursing a naked Arlo.

"Yes. It's about Dad's accident. The mystery has been solved." Al-Haddad had come by to speak to Mum and me that afternoon. He had an amazing poker face. You'd never have known only days earlier I'd been seconds away from offering him a lap dance.

"There are many, many mysteries," Clary said. "Which one?"

"Why no one saw it happen. Turns out some kids had a bunch of wakeboards tied on the roof of their car. They lost them going up a hill just before the beach. Traffic heading that way stopped for, like, five minutes while they picked everything up off the road and tied it back on. That's why there were no cars going by when Dad hit the gravel and flipped over the guardrail. No cars were going the other way because it was Sunday morning. Who'd be leaving the beach then? Everyone was heading *to* it. Dad was just in the proverbial wrong place at the wrong time."

"See?" Lib said happily.

"I can't believe you're gloating over how Dad died." Clary pretended to be appalled.

"Oh, and there's more good news," I said.

"Is this about Jesse?" Lib was sweet.

"No. I met Gord the other day."

"What?" In unison. "How?"

"Good old Find My Phone. I saw Mum was at a park and followed her there. I gave them quite a fright, let me tell you." I'd lapsed into Dad cadence. His way of adding a little folksy charm to a pedestrian story. Lull them into believing the harmlessness of it all.

"And?"

"Two points for Clary. Yes, they've known each other for years but—three points for Lib—it's totally innocent."

"Totally" was an exaggeration but otherwise I stuck to the facts. I reeled off the story Mum and I had decided on before I'd left the motel two days before. She and Gord had met in a grief counselling session after they'd both lost a child. Their spouses found their anger hard to deal with so they got together in secret to vent. Gord eventually divorced and moved to Africa. He came home just after Dad died. They reconnected when he got in touch to offer Mum his condolences.

I left it at that. The girls seemed to buy it.

Clary took Arlo off her breast and burped him. "So, why the secrecy now?"

We hadn't discussed that. I shrugged. "You know La Bouve. She thought it would look inappropriate. Her out with someone so soon after Dad's death."

"Seriously?" Clary squinted.

"People are funny," Lib said.

"Yeah," I said.

"So what did you think of him?" Clary asked.

"I liked him. A bit gruff for Mum's tastes but a decent guy. He had a rough time after his son died. It took him a while to get back on his feet. Mum helped him."

I'd made Lib's day. Not only had we been wrong about an affair, but Mum came out looking like the hero.

There was a knock. Lib turned her face from the screen and lifted a finger. "One minute, Frannie. Sorry. Tell them I'll be right there." She turned back to us. "Gotta run. All good otherwise, Neens? I know it's greedy even asking after this veritable cornucopia of blessings but any word on Jess?"

I opened my mouth to say something glib, but my lips froze in an agonized square. Lib shook her head. "Don't worry about him, Neens. Shouldn't have asked. What about the house tour?"

"The house tour?"

"For Dad?"

I pulled myself together. "Oh, yeah. Yeah. I've been working on the PR." Which was true. "Just a little poster and news release. But I'm enjoying it. I mean, I can *write.* Maybe it's something I could get paid for? I don't know. Just an idea."

"A wonderful idea! You'd be great, Neens. Really. You'd—"

I could feel her attention drifting toward her next appointment.

"Go, go." I said. "You'll have lots of opportunities to butter me up later."

Clary groaned. Arlo had just barfed down her back. "I gotta go too. Sorry, Nina. Kisses."

They both had lives to return to. For once, I felt like I did too.

GORD

It had been surprisingly easy to pull off. Ebbie, Gord's friend from Mali, had called Osterlich and left a cryptic message about a child who "needed a new home but was too old for the orphanage." This was their agreed-upon code meaning he had an ancient relic for sale.

Osterlich got in touch right away—on a burner from an undisclosed location—and said he wanted to know more.

"With pleasure, Mr. Keith," Ebbie said warmly. "I have a friend who knows the little one very well. He'll call you to arrange a meeting. You'll like him. You have many things in common."

"Such as?"

"A shared love of...children."

They both laughed.

On the phone later that day, Ebbie told Gord he wished he'd recorded the conversation. He loved how it made Osterlich sound like both a fool and a pedophile.

"And here I thought he couldn't get any worse." Gord joked around with Ebbie for a while, then called Osterlich. They set a meeting for nine the next night.

Gord chose an industrial park just outside the city. When he was young, the area had almost been wilderness. Kids walked through wooded trails to swim, kayak, and make out. Now the forest was replaced with parking lots. Concrete benches overlooked lakes weedy from runoff. Bewildered deer often held up traffic. Osterlich was no doubt an early developer of the park. (Humility check: Gord himself had had the opportunity.)

At 8:55 P.M., Gord parked his car next to the recycling depot and took the "woodland trail" to Eisenhauer's Heating and Air Conditioning. It was an unexceptional brick building, surrounded by a giant parking lot, overlooking a pond. Two benches faced the water. Gord sat on the one with a brass plaque dedicated to Roland Fassbender—*an adequate golfer, a good mechanic, and a great dad. Donated by his friends, family, and clients.* Stupid, but it made Gord tear up a bit. He wouldn't be getting a brass plaque. He thought he'd come to terms with that.

He pulled up his hood and put the gift bag on the bench beside him.

At exactly five past the hour, Osterlich arrived from the opposite direction. He was wearing a navy-blue tracksuit (obviously new) and dark sunglasses. He had a small fluffy terrier on a leash. *Just the type of dog you'd expect a guy like Osterlich to have,* Gord thought. A rat with an expensive hairdo.

"Mind if I sit here?"

"It's a free country," Gord said, just like he said he would.

Osterlich nodded. They sat in silence for a while.

"Am I supposed to say something now, or are you?"

Gord laughed. "You mean, how does this international smuggling thing work?"

"Jesus Christ." Osterlich took a quick look over both shoulders.

"Relax." Gord rolled his eyes. "No one's here. Plus, if you're worried about attracting attention, lose the sunglasses. Nothing says eighties pop star or inept criminal like sunglasses at night."

Osterlich put his glasses in his pocket and tried to laugh, but it was obvious Gord had embarrassed him.

"You have something for me?" he said.

Gord pushed the gift bag toward him with his fingertips. It was pink with a word-balloon saying, *Don't get your hopes up. It's the thought that counts!* Gord loved how perfect that was.

"You shouldn't have." Osterlich's attempt at humour.

"I'd take a look before I said that."

"Here?"

"I have a no-return policy. You buy it, it's yours. So better check."

"But here?" Osterlich looked over his shoulder again. The parking lot was still empty.

"What are you so afraid of? The place clears out like a shot at five.

Anyone still around is doing something worse than we are. So open your present, honey. It's your special day."

Osterlich put the bag on his lap and pulled out the crude metal knife. Gord's luggage had been searched at customs, but when the border agent saw the *Made in the Philippines* tag, he'd let him go. Gord had removed the tag and sharpened the blade but otherwise done nothing to it.

"Nice," Osterlich said, bouncing it on his hand. "Heavy. What can you tell me about it?"

"Iron," Gord said. "Two to three hundred thousand years old." Total bullshit of course.

"I figured as much. Provenance?"

"Discovered circa 2012 in a burnt-out field by a guy who used it until a couple weeks ago to chop plantains. That enough provenance for you?"

Osterlich tested the blade with his thumb. "Nice story, but I'm going to need more."

"What? Like an appraisal? Sorry. I'm not getting busted for smuggling. You could sell a few of your fancy suits and pay your way out of jail but the rest of us don't have your resources. We prefer to keep our business on the downlow."

Talk of his money and handmade cashmere suits flattered Osterlich. He let out a little snort of laughter and held the knife handle in his fist. He moved it back and forth in the light.

"How do I know it's real, then?"

"You either know or you don't. But, hey. No pressure. I only contacted you as a favour to our mutual friend. You don't want it, no skin off my nose. I make one call, and it's in a private collection before midnight."

Gord picked up the gift bag and held it open. "You all done with that?"

"Actually," Osterlich made a stabbing motion, "I don't think I am. This might round out my collection nicely…Our friend said two-fifty, I believe?"

Gord snorted. "Well, if he did, he was sadly mistaken. Try three-fifty, and that's only because I like Ebbie."

"Three hundred and fifty thousand." Osterlich shook his head at the ridiculous number and put the knife back in the bag. "Oh, well. In for a penny, in for a pound. How would you like it?"

"Cash. Unmarked euros."

"Euros? There a reason?"

"Yes."

When Osterlich realized that was all the explanation he was going to get, he said, "Fine. And when?"

"Wednesday. Gives you four days. Can you do that?"

Osterlich huffed, as in *of course*.

"Good. I'll leave a message confirming time and place." Gord picked up the bag and turned to go.

"Got anything else for sale?" Osterlich said.

"Look who's getting greedy."

"Not *getting* greedy. Greedy's how I got here."

Four years ago, Gord would have pounded the smirk off Osterlich's doughy, rich-boy face. Now he just catalogued it for future reference. "You come through first on this one before we talk about other deals. In the meantime, pick up after your fucking dog."

Gord pointed at a mushy turd on the path and walked away. He loved the thought of Osterlich stooping to pick it up.

As soon as he got home, Gord sealed the knife in a plastic baggie and tucked it under the living room couch. He was careful not to smudge the fingerprints.

NINA

When we were little and sad, Dad would snuggle us on his lap and tell us not to worry. "Everything looks bad at the moment, but you just need one thing—one tiny thing—to go right, then everything will feel sunny and bright." He'd let us do his makeup or win at checkers, then he'd time us while we ran around the block and cheer extravagantly when we broke all previous records "by a mile."

And he was right. That was usually enough. One step toward the light, and the darkness receded.

Likewise, this house tour. I knew it wasn't real, but it didn't matter. It felt good even pretending to do something for Dad. Something he would have been proud of.

I took the project on. I drew endless sketches of Osterlich's house. I taught myself to use a graphic design program. I worked on a bio for Dad and a mission statement for the scholarship and a bunch of catchy titles for the tour. I was forgetting to eat. I was forgetting Jesse and sadness and the thought that my life might amount to nothing. I felt grateful.

I called Gord.

"Who?" he said at first.

"Gee thanks," I said. "Nina. You know, your co-conspirator's daughter?"

He laughed. "Sorry. Just wasn't expecting you. What's up?"

"I owe you some fries."

"Fries."

"Yeah. I ate all yours when we were at The Big House."

"That's okay."

"It's not. Never let it be said that I don't pay my debts. I owe you a couple of drinks too—"

"I don't drink."

"Root beer then. I also owe you some thanks."

"For what?"

"Your little scam. You made my mother happy. And me too. I'm enjoying myself again. Working on this imaginary house tour has weirdly given me a sense of purpose."

"Well, good to hear. But no thanks necessary. Seriously. My pleasure."

"I want to take you out to The Big House."

"You don't need to do that."

"Sorry. Not taking no for an answer. I owe you. Plus I have nothing else to do. My mother—my one and only playmate—had to fill in as a fourth at bridge tonight. So The Big House at six? That'll get us there in time for Early Release Cocktail Hour!"

He didn't answer.

"I'll pick you up. I have my car."

A pause, then, "No. That's fine. I'll make my own way there. Six P.M. at The Big House." He signed off.

I got dressed up, at least by strip-mall standards. I found a long knit skirt that Clary must have worn waiting for her tummy to recede, a button-up white linen shirt that belonged to Mum (she had dozens), and a pair of clunky sandals. I put my hair in a loose bun and wrapped a scarf around my head, letting the curls bubble out the top. I put on a pair of big gold hoops but felt too Carmen Miranda, so traded them for a pair of small agate earrings. I curled my eyelashes, put on mascara and a little lip gloss too. I wasn't doing it to seduce Gord. I was seducing *me*. Luring myself back into the land of the living.

Mum was heading straight from the hairdresser's to bridge, so I didn't bother telling her I was meeting Gord.

Bother?

Hardly le mot juste. I didn't *want to* tell her I was going out with Gord, although why, I couldn't say. She wasn't interested in him romantically, and neither was I, but still. Always that sliver of doubt, right? I was happier not having the conversation.

The Big House was busy. Nothing like two-buck beer to bring out the crowds. I craned my neck and spotted Gord in the corner by the electric chair. I waved happily. He nodded discretely. He was one of those.

He stood when I got to the table.

"Well, aren't you well brung up?"

"Just stretching my legs," he said and pushed my chair in for me. He sat back down. "You're looking good."

My mind raced to come up with some jailhouse comeback, but I had nothing. Nerves, I figured. "Thanks. It's fun to get dressed up every so often."

"My wife used to say the same thing. I'd bitch and moan about some black-tie event we'd got roped into, and all I had to do was put on a suit. She'd get special underwear and special shoes and need me to zip up her dress and she couldn't have been happier." He rearranged the condiments. "I'm making her sound like a bimbo, but she wasn't. Super-smart, super-competent. She just liked to get dressed up."

"Hey, you don't need to tell me. Look at Amal Clooney."

He laughed, but I could tell he had no idea who that was.

A server/inmate arrived and put two drinks on the table.

"I ordered you a Slammer," Gord said. "Hope that's okay."

"Perfect." We clinked glasses. "Here's to bad guys and good times."

He raised his eyebrows and took a sip.

"Just made that up on the spot," I said proudly. "Seems fitting."

"Oh, right. The Big House," he said, as if that was the connection.

"No," I whispered, "I mean Mr. O." I checked to make sure he got my drift, then continued in my normal voice. "He's a monster—clearly—but he's the roundabout reason I'm working on the house tour, so not all bad. It's made me feel like I can do something again. Like I'm good at something." I shrugged, embarrassed but not.

Gord gave a little hmph of a laugh. "Funny how that works, eh? I wish I'd never lost my son, but losing him knocked the arrogance out of me. Got me heading in the right direction. Whatever it takes, right?"

"Another Slammer, perhaps?" The server was back.

"Indeed," I said.

While I polished off the next one, I talked to Gord about Dad, and he talked to me about his grandfather, this mouthy little guy called Bix. He sounded awful—I didn't say that—but I could tell he'd meant a lot to Gord. "A man of his word," he said. "Wouldn't take shit from nobody."

I decided against a third Slammer and opted for a glass of white. My stories were getting longer and wobblier and, I was pretty sure, ever more charming. Gord insisted we eat. He ordered the veggie burger. I ordered the baby back ribs because, short of bunny sushi, it was the worst thing I could think to order while dining with a vegan. The ribs hung off either side of the plate and came impaled with a plastic shiv. Gord and I had a good laugh about that.

Laughing made me think of Jesse, so I told Gord about him too. By then the drinks had kicked in and the ribs were messy, so I had sticky red sauce all over my face and hands and Mum's beautiful linen shirt. I went through our whole relationship, from the moment Jesse and I first bonded over Lord Byron's sexy striped turban in Romance Lit 101 to the moment he said, "I don't want you to come home, Neens." I was sort of laughing and sort of crying too. Gord listened intently. He wiped the grease off my chin and moved my plate so I wouldn't put my elbow in it. He said, "Aw, honey" at exactly the right time.

I eventually pulled myself together. "Sorry. Sorry. Geez. Here I was, supposed to be treating you to a nice night out and look at me. Crying again. You must think that's all I do. Go to bars, drink too much, and sob. But I don't. I'm actually a lot of fun!"

Which made me think of Jesse again. My eyes screwed up in pain. A rictus jittered on my face.

"Anything else?" the server said.

Gord handed him the plate of ribs. "A doggy bag and a few more wet wipes?"

"Wet wipes," I said, almost laughing. "A new low, even for me."

"Hey. Love'll do that."

"I was talking about my table manners."

"No, you weren't. Nothing to be ashamed of. Take it from me. I lost everything—career, money, status—but love's the only thing I miss. I bet Jesse misses it too. You're a great girl. He'd be a moron not to want you back."

"Men have been known to be morons."

"Really?" Heavy sarcasm.

"Yeah. But he's the moron I want."

"Well, here's hoping you get him then." He clinked his root beer against my almost empty wineglass.

"I think I'll have another," I said, turning to look for the waiter.

I didn't get my drink. I don't think I paid the bill either. We talked some more about his grandfather and the orphanage and shenanigans my sisters and I got up to when we were teenagers, then I was in a cab with leftover ribs in a box on my lap and the warm, happy feeling you get when someone, especially a man with no apparent ulterior motives, gives you a really good hug.

Dad's Volvo was parked in the driveway when I woke up the next morning.

PETRA

"One o'clock today? That would be lovely!" Petra was on the landline talking to Osterlich about the house tour when Nina came down to the kitchen for a coffee refill.

"I'll come too," she said when Petra hung up.

"That's okay, darling. You don't have to. He sounds game. It's just a preliminary walk-through."

"I'd love that."

Petra leaned back against the counter. "I'm not sure you should come. I really want to minimize your connection to this thing."

"You were the one who said it was perfectly safe. No one would ever connect you with Gord's scam. Why would they connect me?"

Petra opened her mouth to disagree but found nothing.

"Excellent." Nina bit into an apple. "So we leave here at, what... twelve thirty?"

Petra laughed despite herself. Some jellyfish. "Fine. Don't talk with your mouth full."

"Oh, wow." They both had the same reaction when they turned up the driveway and saw Osterlich's house. The amount of money he'd paid to have it moved was revolting even by Petra's standards but hard to argue with. He'd bought a promontory at the mouth of the harbour, tore down the old army barracks there, and sited the Victorian twelve-bedroom mansion so that it looked out to sea. It was a tourism ad. The opening shot in a Merchant Ivory film.

Petra parked next to the carriage house and checked her makeup in the visor mirror. The beige lipstick she'd worn for years seemed too blah for the occasion. She dotted some hellebore gloss on her lips and her cheeks. The dusky pink was actually quite nice.

She smoothed down her suit and took a large leather bag from the back seat.

"Whoa. Planning on staying awhile?" Nina said.

"Too big?"

"A tad."

"Oh, well. It's what I brought." Petra tried to sound nonchalant. The last thing she needed was Nina getting suspicious. They headed up the walkway.

The front entrance had two enormous oak doors, leaded sidelights, and the name *Ashdale* written in the stained-glass transom. Far too Christmas rom-com for Petra's taste, but she appreciated the workmanship.

She rang the doorbell, and chimes sang out as if there'd been a royal birth. She and Nina had to kick each other's ankles to stop from laughing.

Moments later, a young woman with long shiny hair and the tightly fitted suit of a *Succession* extra opened the door. "Mrs. Fforde?"

"Petra, please. And my daughter Nina."

"Come in. I'm Alexis, one of Keith's assistants. He's in the drawing room."

"Isn't this magnificent?" Petra said, looking around the foyer. The carved oak staircase, eleven-foot ceiling, ornate gasolier, florid wallpaper. *Whorehouse*, she thought.

"Yes. Keith went to great pains to restore *Ashdale* to its former glory."

Alexis led them down a wide hall over acres of Persian carpets. Just before knocking on the drawing room door, she whispered, "Keith has set aside five minutes for you."

"Lovely," Petra said. That would be about all she could stand.

Keith Osterlich was sitting in a deep wingback chair. He put his book on a mahogany side table and stood up when they entered. He was wearing his standard uniform: grey cashmere suit, white shirt, black loafers, no tie. He was not an attractive man by any means, but he knew how to dress. Someone had obviously taught him. *A wife*, Petra thought. *Too bad she hadn't stuck around to help with the house.*

"Petra," he said, shaking her hand. Alexis would have reminded him of her name. "So glad we can make this happen for you."

"As are we! This is my daughter Nina."

"Pleasure." He gave no indication of recognizing Nina from the funeral. Just another nobody to him. Petra didn't mind the slight. The more he pissed her off, the easier her job would be. Fewer scruples.

"We know you're busy," she said, "so don't want to take up too much of your time. We're hoping just to get the lay of the land today, then we'll come back to you with a proposal."

"Sounds like a plan. Alexis, of course, will be quarterbacking it from here, but let me show you some of the highlights."

The four of them walked through the house. If anything, Osterlich was taking up their time. Endlessly detailing the pains he'd gone to, the money he'd spent, the compliments he'd received.

He led them upstairs. Bedroom, bedroom, bedroom. A study. A library. A conservatory. And then, with a spectacular view out to the ocean, his "chambers."

"The armoire! The fauteuil! The canopy bed!" Petra said. "Oh. Aren't they magnificent?" She threw around a few more synonyms before looking puzzled and asking, "But closets? Do you have closets?"

She had a moment of panic. What if he kept all his clothes elsewhere? She and Gord hadn't discussed that possibility.

Osterlich smiled. "That's the thing about these old houses. Even ones as splendid as this. The Victorians just did not have the closet space we require." He pressed a wall panel and a hidden door opened. Behind it was the ultimate modern dressing room: light, bright, and organized. Osterlich's famous identical suits and shirts hanging neatly on a brass rod, his shoes lined up underneath on polished wooden risers. He must have had thirty pairs. A whole wall of bleached oak drawers for what? Underwear? Accessories? Hankies? Even Petra didn't need that much storage space.

She lightly slapped her chest and gasped. "I'd kill for a dressing room like this!"

"Not true to the period, of course, but a man has his needs." Osterlich laughed. "I'd have a valet, too, but apparently manservants aren't kosher anymore."

"May I take a closer look?" Petra said. "I have this weird fascination with closet systems."

"Fill your boots. It's custom-made by a master carpenter I brought in from Italy. I've got him booked again in the New Year. You might like to talk to him then."

"I just might." Petra walked into the dressing room. She opened doors, inspected hinges. "Mind if I take a few pictures?"

"Go ahead. I'll leave you to it. Alexis will show your daughter the view from the other side."

He headed downstairs. Their time was apparently up. Nina and Alexis headed to the library. It couldn't have worked out better.

Petra felt oddly calm. The last thirty-six years of her life had turned out to be very good preparation for this little caper. Not showing her true emotions. Being blandly pleasant. Jackie O, as she knew the girls secretly called her. She'd honed her skills on windbags, petty snobs, and garden-variety thugs. She was dealing with a killer now but, really, it was only a matter of degrees.

She stuck her head out the dressing room door, just to be sure no one was watching, then stuffed one of Osterlich's suits and a pair of his shoes into her large leather bag. She covered them with her scarf, then met up with Nina and Alexis in the library. They were gushing over the view of the outer harbour when they heard a phone ring downstairs, and moments later, Osterlich angrily cursing.

Alexis bared her teeth apologetically. "Keith has got a bit of a temper."

"Powerful men," Petra said, waving it off, then whispered, "Anything I should be careful about when dealing with him? I wouldn't want to upset him."

"You won't be dealing with him," Alexis said. "I'm your person. Direct all your concerns to me, please."

"Lovely. You've been very kind. I got so much out of this little walk-through today. I'm really getting very excited about this project."

GORD

The next day, Gord called Osterlich. "You ready?" No intro.

"Yeah. Where we doing this?"

They were both trying their best to sound tough.

"Be outside the south door of Tech Loft, tomorrow, 9:00 P.M. Bring the money in a plain black backpack. And, for Christ's sake, don't wear a costume again."

"What are you talking about?"

"The sunglasses. The 'athleisurewear.' You looked like you were going trick-or-treating. Wear what you normally wear."

"I normally wear a suit." Like that made him special.

"Fine. Then wear a suit. I'll tell you more when you get there."

"I'd prefer to know—"

Gord hung up. He had an appointment at the blood donor clinic that afternoon at four but first he needed to clean the apartment. The lease was up at the end of the week, and he wanted to leave it spotless.

He got out a rag, a mop, and some disinfectant, then started on the bathroom. It reminded him of his work at the orphanage. For the first time in eight years—maybe longer, maybe ever—he felt truly at peace. He was finally doing what he was supposed to be doing with his life.

NINA

The day after my dinner with Gord, I'd called Meg Mancini. We'd worked on the school newspaper together. She'd gone into advertising right out of university. Started as a receptionist and now was creative director at a big agency. We had a good chat. She said there was nothing to it. I could write. I just needed a portfolio.

"Pull some stuff together, then come see me."

I told her I didn't have anything.

"Make it up, Nina!" she said.

So that's what I was doing. Making it up.

I'd set up my laptop on the kitchen table. Mum was heading down to a quaint if touristy town on the coast to meet Bonnie who'd flown in for a conference earlier that week. They were going to have lunch, maybe do a little shopping. Before she left, Mum leaned over my shoulder and read an ad I'd written for a fake moving company. She laughed at the headline and said, "I love what you did with the elephant. Very clever." She pulled my hair into a bun. "I think you've found your calling, darling."

I felt like I had too.

I went back to work. Hours passed. Occasionally, I'd get up to stretch or pee or make a pot of coffee. When I did, I'd think about working for Meg. I'd think about the clothes I'd wear, the awards I'd win, all the nice things people would say about me. I thought of The Dude giving his eulogy again, but now I was the sister everybody knew about. The one with the money, the one who did the pro bono campaign for UNICEF that moved the whole world to tears. I thought of Jesse in the pew, squeezing my hand in pride. I thought of him home with Don and our babies while I worked at my high-powered job.

Problem solved. I just needed to get the job. I went back to work.

At some point late in the afternoon, the phone rang. I was expecting Mum or maybe Clary. I wasn't expecting Jesse. We hadn't spoken since my disastrous visit.

I saw his face appear on my phone. Happiness whooshed up, then my heart stopped.

"No!" I said.

"What? Nina?"

"Is it Don? Don't tell me it's Don. Please."

"No. No. Don? No! He's fine. Better than ever. Doctor says she's already bought a dress for his big one-hundredth birthday party."

"Oh my God. You scared me."

"Didn't mean to. I didn't want to email you or, you know, *text.* Thought it would be better if we spoke in person."

"What do you mean 'in person'?"

"You know, like face-to-face."

"I know what it means, but why?" I pushed my chair back. I stood up. "What do you need to tell me in person, Jesse?"

A long pause.

"You met someone."

"Who told you?"

"No one needs to tell me anything about you, Jesse. I know you. You met someone, didn't you?"

He didn't answer.

"What's her name?" I said.

"You don't know her."

"Her name, Jesse."

"Anneka."

"Anneka what? Or is she one of those women who goes by one name? Beyoncé, Cher? So fabulous that's all she needs?"

"Anneka Sabot."

"Oh, God. Sounds like a Bond girl."

"Nina. She's not like that. Look. I didn't mean this to happen. I—"

I read when a patient first learns they have cancer, they often don't hear another word the doctor says. He could be saying, "It's mild, it's merely cancer of the earlobe," but all they hear is "cancer," and they think "death."

That's what this was like. Jesse went on for some time. He might have told me where Anneka was from and what she did for a living or as a hobby or in bed, but it breezed right past me. At some point, I realized he was telling me he loved me and always would and how our fifteen years together were the most precious whatever and that's when I said, "Yeah, well, see ya, bye" and hung up.

I called Clary. She picked up, but I didn't get a chance to tell her.

"Sorry. Can't talk. I'm in the hospital with Arlo. He was having trouble breathing, and I just thought it was a cold so I fucking wended my way here—like, I mean, stopped at the liquor store—and now the doctor's telling me it might be respiratory-something-something-virus, and it could be dangerous. He's just gone for...oh, hold on, the doctor's here. Gotta go. I'll call you as soon as I know."

Then I called Libby. Three times. No answer. Then she texted: In all-day meeting with mayor. Can I call you later? Xo

I did circles of Mum's office. I sat on the floor. I looked out the window. I thought about jumping. I thought about smashing my head into the wall. I thought about the mess that would make and everything Mum had already been through.

I had no one.

Except maybe Gord.

GORD

Gord had had a productive day. He'd cleaned the apartment until it glowed. He removed his hard drive and destroyed it. He dropped his laptop off at the Sally Ann, along with anything he wouldn't be wearing in the next twenty-four hours.

At 3:30, he took an Uber to the blood-donor clinic.

He was just about to check in for his appointment when a guy he recognized walked out. They did a double-take, said hi, then both laughed when they realized how they knew each other. Ryan Al-Haddad had arrested Gord several times.

"No hard feelings," Gord said, and he meant it. "I was an asshole."

They talked for quite a while—about sobriety and Mali and Al-Haddad recently making detective—then they wished each other well. They even hugged. It couldn't have been more perfect. It was the type of conversation that makes you feel good about humanity. It also established Gord's timeline. Al-Haddad wouldn't forget running into him.

Gord had a good chat with the nurse too. She asked about a scar on his arm. He said he got it playing rugby. Turned out she used to play in high school, which surprised him. She was a little bit of a thing—no bigger than Aziza. He couldn't imagine her tackling anyone. No one could, she said. That was her superpower. The element of surprise. He said he'd love to take her to a game sometime. She said she was married. He apologized. She said she was flattered. She took out the needle, gave him a cookie, and asked him to wait fifteen minutes before leaving. He figured she'd remember him too.

Petra met Gord as arranged at a bus stop five blocks away. They drove to the Lookout. They barely talked on the way there, but they held hands. She parked behind a scrim of trees, just to be on the safe side. She put on a pair of latex gloves, removed the Band-Aid from the blood-donor clinic, and inserted a needle into the same hole.

"It's been a while since I've done this." She drew the blood, then replaced the Band-Aid.

"Haven't lost your touch." He rolled down his sleeve. "Before I forget." He handed her the baggie with the knife in it. "Never touch it without gloves on. Osterlich's fingerprints are all over it."

She nodded.

"Did you get the pills?" he said.

"Yes." She rummaged in her purse and pulled out a yellow vial. In the end, they'd been easier to source than Gord had thought. Dr. Bonnie Peters had prescribed Serenatol to relieve Petra's sleeplessness after the death of her husband. It was PhiTex's version of Rohypnol—its own brand of roofie—a tasteless, odourless nervous system depressant.

She tapped six pills onto Gord's outstretched palm. "You won't need that many. But just in case. Try two first. Take a couple more when you get there. Make sure you're out cold. Okay? Please. Do that for me?"

"I will. Don't worry. I really appreciate this, Pet. You know that, right? You're the one person in the world I could always count on."

"Gord." Her eyes welled up. "I'm here and I'm always going to be here. You don't have to —"

He raised his palm, like a priest giving a benediction. "Please, Pet. We decided."

"You decided."

"Yes. My life. My decision."

She smiled sadly. "Yes," she said and turned on the car.

She dropped Gord a few blocks from the apartment. He stopped at a takeout place nearby and bought a pizza.

He'd just walked in the door when Nina called. He'd wanted to rest or meditate or rewatch *Planes, Trains and Automobiles*, but she was upset. She needed someone to talk to. He didn't want her rattling Petra. He gave Nina his address and told her to come over.

And now she was here, a sodden, sobbing mess. He put his arms around her and let her cry. When she stopped, he made her tea and shared his pizza. She didn't notice her vegan saviour had ordered pepperoni. That's how upset she was.

"Aargh," she said, dabbing her eyes on a greasy napkin. "I bet you're sorry you ever offered to buy me that drink. Now you're shackled to a nutcase."

Gord shook his head. "You're not a nutcase. You're crushed. I was just as bad."

"I bet."

"I was. I could always find a way to fix something before. Throw money at it. Bend the truth to fit it. Beat the shit out of it. Then I got my heart broken. No fixing that. You can't talk someone into loving you. You just have to suffer."

Nina laughed. "Gee, thanks, Mr. Sunshine."

"Sorry."

"I think I would have liked you better when you were still bending the truth."

He took another slice of pizza. "I doubt that."

She remembered googling his name. Seeing the pictures of him with that expensive suit and annoying smirk.

"Probably right." She picked something out of her teeth. "Want to watch something?"

Planes, Trains and Automobiles was one of Jesse's favourite movies too, so she said no to that. They agreed on *The 40-Year-Old Virgin* and snuggled up together on the couch.

When the movie ended, Nina said, "Can I stay with you tonight?"

NINA

I had no pride. I pleaded, I begged. He said, "Nina, no..." and put up his hands, like *walk away.* "Your mother wouldn't like this."

"My mother won't know. No one will. You'd be an anonymous benefactor, selflessly alleviating a little of the world's misery."

"My middle name is 'misery.'"

"Oh, please," I said.

"That was a joke. It's a line from an Elvis Presley song."

"Never heard of it."

"That's because you're too young. Another reason you should leave."

"Gord." I punched the couch. "Please. I'm not going to do anything to you. I just can't go back to my mother's house, to my old bedroom, while Jesse is off getting fellated by some babe named Anneka. I can't do it, Gord. It's you or some random stranger. Your choice."

"My choice?"

"Yeah. Yours. Here with you, or I take my chances downtown with some syphilitic scumbag."

"Nina."

"Pleeeeease."

He looked at the floor, then looked at me. "Fine. You can stay."

I kissed him. I mean, kissed him on the cheek, the way I used to kiss Dad when he gave me what I wanted too.

Gord made me call my mother, as if I was a child. I left a message saying Jesse had a new girlfriend and I needed some alone time. Not to worry. I'd see her in the morning.

I brushed my teeth with my finger. Gord made up a bed for me on the living room couch. He ruffled my hair goodnight, then went to his room. I took off my skirt and slipped my bra out through my sleeve. When I saw his light turn off, I got up and climbed into bed with him.

"No," he said. "Nina."

"I'm not going to do anything! I'm lonely."

"Go."

"I'm really lonely!"

He sighed. "You're a brat." He let me in.

He rolled over. I spooned against his back.

"Nina."

"We're just cuddling. I cuddle with my sisters all the time. It's perfectly innocent."

He accidentally laughed and I knew I'd won.

"Makes all the difference in the world, doesn't it?" I squeezed his hand.

"It does," he admitted.

We started talking about best cuddles. He told me about his first girlfriend. Stephanie Philpot. How they used to meet at his grandfather's cabin out in the woods. Put the fire on. Have sex. Walk around "naked as wood nymphs." It was heaven—better than anything he'd ever imagined—until he cheated on her with his best friend's girlfriend.

"Stephanie was the one who gave me this." He rolled over and pulled a chain out from around his neck.

"I can't see."

He took his phone off the bedside table and shone it at an oval medallion.

It was portrait of a bearded man in a blue robe with a flame coming out of his head. A lot of the paint had rubbed off. It was like something you'd find in a bin at a souvenir shop.

"Some saint?" I said.

"Good guess."

"The halo was kind of a giveaway. Which one?"

"St. Jude."

"Patron saint of hopeless causes!" The only saint I knew.

"Exactly. Stephanie gave it to me because that's what we were. Hopelessly in love. She dumped me when she found out about the other girl. She took all her stuff back but told me to keep the medallion. 'Because there's no cause more hopeless than Gord Fucking Bickerton.'"

"That's a pretty good parting shot for a teenager."

"Yeah. Especially since it was true." He kissed the medallion and slipped it under his T-shirt. "I've worn it ever since. Keeps me humble. I rubbed it raw over Luke and Boubacar, cursed it a few times, but I never took it off. Never will."

I asked him to tell me more about Stephanie. He did, then seamlessly rolled into appalling stories about his "tomcat years." I told stories, too, but mine were mostly pathetic. We traded breakups and crushes and unrequited passions. We laughed over wildly inappropriate decisions. There are so many ways love can go wrong. We talked most of the night. It was the best pyjama party ever. I fell asleep around four.

I woke up at nine when my phone buzzed. A text from Clary. Arlo had just been sprung from emerg. He was going to be fine. I sent back hearts and fireworks.

I got up and peed. I said, "Gord?" No answer. He must have gone out. There was a fresh bagel on the kitchen counter. He'd written on the bag:

Thanks for nothing, Nina. I needed that. Your friend always, The Hopeless Cause

PS Just pull the door closed behind you when you leave.

I ate the bagel and put the empty bag in my purse for a keepsake.

GORD

Osterlich phoned Gord that evening, just after nine. "I'm here." The mall was closing, the parking lot clearing out.

"I see you." Osterlich was standing, as promised, by the garbage bins near the south door of Tech Loft. He was carrying a black backpack and, Gord was relieved to see, wearing his usual grey cashmere suit.

"Where are you?" Osterlich was moving his head from side to side as if watching a tennis match.

"Doesn't matter."

"What am I supposed to do now?"

"You have the money?"

"I told you I'd have the money."

"You know The Ship's Anchor?"

A pause. "The bar out on the Old Guysborough Road?"

"Yeah. Meet me there in half an hour. Take a table near the back. I'll find you."

"Okay."

"Now put your phone in the garbage bin."

"What? No fucking way. I need my phone."

"Not tonight you don't. Put your phone in the bin or the deal's off. I don't want this transaction recorded."

"What if someone takes it?"

"You're a rich man. You can buy another. This is non-negotiable. Do it."

Osterlich sighed and took out his phone.

"Hold it up so I can see it. Turn around." He did. "Now put it in the bin."

Osterlich shoved the phone through the slot with significantly more force than required.

"Okay," Gord said, "Now, off you fuck."

He watched Osterlich drive away, then slipped on a latex glove, left his hiding place behind the chip wagon, and walked over to the garbage bin. He fished out Osterlich's phone and put it in his pocket. He called an Uber on his burner. It was there in two minutes.

Just before his Uber pulled up to The Ship's Anchor, Gord popped a couple of Serenatols, the sedatives Petra had given him. He picked the gift bag up off the seat, thanked the driver, and got out.

"How you doing?" he said to the hulking bouncer seated on a stool just inside the entrance to the tavern. "Quiet night, eh."

"Yup."

"Good thing. I got a little meeting with an old guy. Not sure how good he hears." Gord saw Osterlich, seated at the back as instructed. "Oh, there he is."

He slapped the bouncer on the arm and headed over.

"Mr. Osterlich. You came prepared." Gord nodded at the black backpack on the bench, then sat down. "Hope you don't mind me dragging you all the way out here. Not your usual stomping grounds, I guess."

"You guess correctly."

The server came over, a round aluminum tray resting on her hip. "What'll it be?"

Gord ordered a pint of draft and a shot of rum. He was looking forward to them. It had been years since he'd had a drink, and he'd never truly lost the desire.

Osterlich said, "I'd like a craft beer."

"Then you're in the wrong place." The server jutted her chin toward the chalkboard above the bar. "There's our beer list. Ten-Penny's the coldest."

"Ten-Penny then." He dropped his jaw and shook his head. "Whatever."

"Whatever," she said, unfazed by his rudeness, "coming right up."

Gord leaned back in his chair and smiled at Osterlich. "This is exciting. I've followed your career for a long time. I was an early investor in PhiTex."

Osterlich clearly didn't know what to make of this sudden change of tone. He considered Gord for a few seconds, then decided just to roll with it. "You must have done okay."

"Better than okay."

"I guess drinks are on you then." Osterlich smirked and tapped a coaster on the thickly lacquered table.

"Absolutely. My treat!"

The server returned with their orders.

"Cheers!" Gord said and lifted his glass.

"Cheers," Osterlich replied. He took a sip and winced.

"Shall we get down to business?" Gord put the pink-and-yellow gift bag on the table. Osterlich reached for it.

Gord wagged a finger at him. "Cash first."

Osterlich removed a manilla envelope from the backpack and slid it over.

Gord bounced it in his hand. "Feels a little light to me."

"Are you accusing me of ripping you off?" Osterlich wasn't sure if this was a joke.

"Wouldn't be the first time you ripped someone off. Like I said, I've followed your career for years. You've done worse."

"What's that supposed to mean?"

"All the kids you killed."

Osterlich was alarmed now. "What the fuck are you talking about?"

"Those African kids who got treated with Pediaxyclone? You killed them."

"Me?"

"Yeah, you. Just business, right. I mean, you had to look after your bottom line. You had stockholders to consider!" Gord smiled, then took a haul of beer. It was so good. Cold and crisp and tasting like girls and youth and hope. He was amazed he'd ever been able to give it up.

"Who the fuck are you to talk to me like that? Some low-life smuggler. Like you're a paragon of virtue. I'm getting out of here." Osterlich grabbed the gift bag with the knife in it and got up to go.

"Shouldn't you check and make sure it's what you wanted?"

That stopped Osterlich momentarily. He didn't like being told what to do, but he didn't trust the guy either. He opened the bag and pulled out the knife. He shrugged. It looked okay to him.

"Turn it over," Gord said, his eyes twinkling.

This copy of the knife had the *Made in Philippines* sticker still on it.

It took Osterlich a few seconds to understand what that meant. His face went white, then red. His eyes went big, then very small. He leaned over and pointed the blade at Gord's chin. "What the hell is this?"

"A piece of shit. Just like you. It's the thought that counts, right?" Gord jerked his head toward the caption on the gift bag.

"What are you playing at, asshole?"

"Not playing, Mr. Osterlich. I'm deadly serious."

"Give me my fucking money."

"Sorry. Too late. No backsies!" He took another sip of beer.

"Give it to me."

"No." Gord laughed. "What are you going to do about it? Call the police? *This man promised to illegally sell me a priceless artifact, officer, then he welched on his deal!* Try it. See how that flies."

Osterlich lunged for the envelope. Gord threw up an arm and blocked him. "Careful, old man. You wouldn't want to get in a fight with me."

Osterlich made another grab for the bag. "I'm going to kill you! I am going to fucking kill you!"

He'd forgotten about using his inside voice.

The bouncer at the door moved surprisingly fast for such a big man. He clamped a hand on Osterlich's shoulder. "Fun's over, buddy. Time to go home."

Osterlich tried to shake him off. Gord laughed.

"I am going to tear you to fucking pieces," Osterlich snarled, inches from Gord's face.

The bouncer said, "Okay, that's enough. Off you go," and muscled him out the door.

It had all gone perfectly.

Gord put the money into the gift bag with the knife and shoved it into his pocket. He was already feeling a bit woozy, but he popped two more Serenatol, and washed them down with the shot of rum. He finished his beer and Osterlich's, too—no use wasting it—then walked up to the bar to pay the tab.

"You know who that guy is?" he said to the server as he got out his wallet. "Keith Osterlich."

She shook her head. Never heard of him.

"One of the richest guys in the country! Made millions selling pharmaceuticals in Africa. Shit pharmaceuticals that killed kids."

"You serious?"

"One hundred percent." He snorted. "Guess I shouldn't have brought it up."

"That why he got so mad?"

"Yup. And now look who's stuck paying the tab. Little old me."

"Typical rich guy," she said. "Mooching off the rest of us."

"Amen." Gord smiled. "Keep the change." He handed her a fifty.

On the way out, he slipped the bouncer a twenty. "Thanks for your help there, eh. That guy's a maniac. Didn't know what he was going to do to me."

"He wasn't going to do nothing to you. Not with me around, buddy."

They fist-bumped. Gord stumbled.

The bouncer caught his arm. "You okay?"

"Yeah, yeah, but whoa. I had, like, one beer and a shot. Don't know why I'm so dizzy."

"Want me to call you a cab?"

Gord waved that away. "I'll get an Uber. I'll be fine."

He headed out into the parking lot, walking under the streetlight to be sure the CCTV camera picked him up. He felt pleasantly drunk. A high-school type of drunk. He texted a thumbs-up to Petra's burner, then staggered down the road.

During the day, this area was relatively busy. There were second-hand-car dealerships and warehouses and a military base nearby. After five, though, it cleared out. Unless The Ship's Anchor was having a fifty-fifty raffle or an open-mic night, it was a ghost town.

Gord walked along the deserted road, then turned up the gravel driveway of a former muffler shop. Someone had started renovating but must have run out of money. The windows were boarded up and new shingles were already falling off. Gord headed over to the far side, as planned, and sat on the ground, his back against the wall.

He was finding it hard to keep his head up. That made him laugh. For the first time in years, he thought of the foolishness he and his law school buddies used to get up to. They were wild and they were jerks and there were no doubt more than a few girls who'd have some choice words for them today, but he realized how innocent they'd been. They thought they could win. They thought there was a prize at the end. They had no idea how much evil there was in the world and how easy it would be to slip into. If Gord had been a better man, he'd have stayed and fought, but he wasn't.

The last thing he thought of before his head hit the ground was Bix raising his glass of rye and saying, "The spirit's willing but the body's weak."

Good old Bix.

He'd have been proud.

NINA

I closed the apartment door, bought a large latte at the nearest coffee shop, then stopped at a park to call my sisters. I told them Jesse had somebody new but didn't mention I'd spent the night at Gord's. They would have probed. I wanted to keep it pure.

Clary said she was going to send us both plane tickets and Lib was going to take off work. We were all going to hang around in pyjamas for a week—"or longer, a month, however long it takes, Neens!"—but I said no. I needed a little solitude to get my head straight. Libby said that sounded like a good idea. Clary thought a little solitude was the last thing I needed, but gave in.

I texted Mum to tell her I was fine but wouldn't be home until later. She texted back to say she'd be out most of the day, too, and added a hug emoji. I went to a movie by myself—something sad and Croatian—and slept through most of it. Then I bought myself sexy new underwear which I thought would make me feel better but just depressed me even more because all I could think about was what type of underwear Anneka wore (if any). I kicked myself for not having made an effort to be sexy back when it might have made a difference, rather than now, when there was no hope.

And then I thought of hopeless causes, and St. Jude, and Gord, and wondered if I'd missed my chance there too.

I thought, *no* and *ick*. What we'd done—talked and laughed and cried (at least I had)—had been perfect. I hooked my pink bag full of thongs and breast-enhancing bras over my elbow and called him from the mall to tell him that. He didn't pick up, and I was instantly awash in loneliness again. I went to a little restaurant I knew, called The Cabana, got a table in the corner, and had dinner by myself. I decided I may as well get used to it.

I got home around nine, wanting to talk with Mum (or anyone, really). I waited up for her until ten but by then I was tired. Tired but wired. I'd had very little sleep the night before, but my brain was buzzing.

I went to her bathroom to see what she had in the way of sleeping pills. Years at Don's had taught me a thing or two about pharmaceuticals. I checked her medicine cabinet and found the usual suspects. Stuff for rashes and constipation. A couple of anti-inflammatories. A bottle of something called Serenatol. I didn't recognize it, so I read the label. *Take one before bedtime for occasional sleeplessness.* I took out two, just in case, and put the cap back on. I noticed Dr. Bonnie Peters had prescribed it. I hadn't known Mum was having sleep problems, but I wasn't surprised.

The Serenatol knocked me out cold. It was mid-morning by the time I got up. I staggered down to the kitchen, bleary-eyed. Mum was on the phone with Alexis. She wiggled her fingers at me and kept talking. She looked exhausted and very pale. She really was better with makeup.

"...mind if I took a walk around the grounds today? I won't bother you. I'd just like to get some pictures. I was thinking a little garden party might be a nice addition to the tour."

There was some back and forth about where they could set up the tables and what to do if the weather wasn't ideal. Then Mum thanked Alexis profusely and said she'd be over in the next half hour or so.

She hung up and said, "Hello, darling. Sleep okay?"

I nodded. "Wow. A garden party now too. This imaginary house tour is getting pretty fancy-pants."

I poured myself a cup of coffee. I had a wicked hangover from that sleeping pill. "How long are you going to keep this so-called feint up?"

"Not much longer. Gord just wants me to case the grounds."

"Listen to you. 'Case the grounds'! People are going to think you're a gangster's moll." I started rooting through the cupboard for a painkiller.

"Hardly. One of the benefits of being an aging, white, middle-class hausfrau is that nobody suspects you of anything. What are you looking for?"

"A Tylenol or something? My head's killing me."

"Let me." She pushed past and found me a green and suspiciously organic-looking bottle. "Take two. Now, I have to run. I've got a million things to do this morning." She kissed my head, grabbed that giant leather bag she'd recently started using, and headed out.

I waited for the painkiller to kick in, then went back to work on my portfolio. Meg had suggested I make up ads for children's charities and social justice issues. "Creative directors love campaigns that pull on the heartstrings." I wondered if anyone had ever done anything about companies selling dangerous drugs to the Developing World?

I was playing around with some ideas when it dawned on me that I had no idea how this scam was supposed to work. I knew it had something to do with smuggling antiquities and planting evidence, but nothing more. I'd never managed to squeeze any details out of either Mum or Gord.

"What you don't know can't hurt you," they'd said ominously.

I didn't know about Anneka and that hurt me.

I went back to my sketchbook. I couldn't think about that. It was killing me.

Mum returned around two that afternoon. She called up the stairs. "I think I'm coming down with something. I'm going to take a nap."

I stepped out on to the landing. She looked like hell.

"You okay?"

"It's nothing. Just tired. Wake me if I'm not up by five. I took the scallops out of the freezer. I'll make that risotto you like."

I scribbled out some more ideas, then lost a few hours down the rabbit hole of "World's Best Commercials." By then, it was five-thirty, and Mum was already at the stove.

I put on an apron and started grating cheese. We poured some wine. The radio was on. The newscaster said a body had been found just off the Old Guysborough Road. Identification was withheld pending notification of next of kin.

Mum burned the risotto. We ended up ordering in Thai.

We didn't find out it was Gord until the next day.

NINA

Mum was a mess. Sobbing and crying in a dark room. Not eating, not sleeping, not talking. Inconsolable. The way I'd thought she'd be after Dad died.

I brought her tea, which she left to grow cold, and sat on the bed beside her. I tried to comfort her.

"It's not your fault," I said. The news was reporting Gord had had an argument "with an older man" at The Ship's Anchor the night he died. "Over dead babies in Africa," the server was quoted as saying. "Some rich guy who gave them bad drugs."

Gord had obviously met up with Osterlich, and something hadn't gone to plan. St. Jude had let him down again.

The agony Mum must have been in. I was sure she regretted ever getting involved. Ever encouraging Gord. Not saying no to his crazy scheme. She'd always been so cautious.

I stroked her head just like she used to stroke mine when I was upset. She buried her face into her pillow. Her body shook. It's awful when someone you love is in such pain and you can do nothing to help them.

I'd called my sisters earlier and told them what had happened. At least, some of what had happened. Gord was dead. It looked like it had something to do with Osterlich and smuggling and Pediaxyclone. No mention of the scam.

There was shock, of course, that Gord and Osterlich had any connection, and lots of questions about Pediaxyclone, but otherwise their reactions were predictable. Basically, "yay, Gord's dead!" from Clary and "Oh, dear..." from Lib.

"The house tour," she said a few moments later.

"My guess is it's off," Clary said.

"No, I mean, who knew about it?"

"Nobody," I said. "I mean, Mum, me, and Osterlich's assistant. That's all. We were still just talking about whether it was even possible."

"Oh, phew."

"Why'd you want to know?" I asked.

"Well, just think what it would have looked like."

"Lib! I thought you didn't care what things looked like."

"I try not to, Clary, but we're talking about Dad here. Osterlich sounds evil. I don't want people thinking Dad had anything to do with the guy. Imagine how upsetting that would be for Mum."

"She's pretty upset as it is," I said. An understatement, but they would have been horrified if they knew the state she was in. Over *Gord.* It was, to use Clary's word, unseemly. "She cries a lot."

"Probably a delayed reaction to Dad's death," Lib said. "She had to hold it together for us, but now everything's coming out. She's probably exhausted. Is she sleeping?"

"No."

"Could you talk her into taking something for it? Not sleeping is enough to put anyone over the edge."

"I'm living proof," Clary said.

I said I'd try.

I looked at Mum now, lying face down on the bed, convulsed in sobs. I remembered the sleeping pills in her medicine cabinet. I tapped a few into my palm and poured a glass of water.

I rubbed her back. "Mum?...Mum?"

She sucked in her breath and turned toward me.

"You need some rest. How about you take one of these?" I offered her a Serenatol.

She knocked my hand away. "Go, Nina. Just go!"

NINA

I was shocked by how many people came to the funeral. Not quite as many as turned up for Dad's, but still. The cathedral was packed.

I squeezed into a pew near the back where I could cry discretely. A bishop, four priests, and a phalanx of altar boys put on a full mass: incense, chanting, the whole bit. I took my cues from the crowd about when to stand, sit, and respond. I'd always wished I'd been born Catholic. The true-body-of-Christ thing and pedophilic priests make it a bit hard to commit to as an adult, but all the genuflecting and abject pleas for mercy still appealed to my romantic nature. Watching the ceremony, I doubted they would have appealed to Gord's. The robes alone! He'd seemed so no-nonsense, so sure of himself. Not a genuflector. But then I remembered that medallion of his with the paint rubbed clean off. Maybe he'd been a man of faith after all.

The mass ended. The altar boys and priests filed out. The bishop was level with my pew when he turned, raised his hand, and intoned, "Go in peace." It seemed like an insensitive thing to say at the funeral of a murder victim. A reminder that Gord hadn't. A new wave of tears. I never brought enough Kleenex to these things.

Stepping out through the cathedral's enormous oak doors, I spotted Detective Ryan Al-Haddad standing unavoidably at the bottom of the stairs.

"Ms. Fforde. I'm surprised to see you here. You knew Gord?"

What to say? "A little. He helped me once when I needed it." True enough. "You here on police business?"

"The murder investigation? No. Not my file. Just here to pay my respects. I always liked Gord. He had a tough go—although he'd be first to admit he was at least partially to blame. I told him once it might be wise to curb his drinking. He said thanks, but 'wise wouldn't get him what he needed.' I'm guessing that might have been a factor here too. The not-wise thing. He had a problematic attitude, but I liked him."

"Me too."

"How's your mother?"

"Oh." I frowned and shook my head. "Bad. The Dad thing. It's finally caught up with her. It's like she was manic at first or something. Now she's crying all the time. She's very upset."

"I'm sorry to hear that."

"Grief sneaks up on you, I guess."

"That's probably what it is."

We nodded at each other. "Going to the reception?" I said, hope rearing its ugly head once again. But why not? The case was closed. We knew how Dad died. I didn't have to worry about getting Mum in trouble anymore. And Al-Haddad really was insanely handsome. I wondered if funerals were as good as weddings for picking up single guys.

"Afraid not. My boyfriend's waiting in the car. It's our anniversary."

So much for that idea. I smiled. "Congratulations!" Gord would have been proud of me for at least trying.

NINA

The reception was held in a restaurant nearby. Castonguay. Very bougie. Lots of sparkling lights, brass fittings, and impressive greenery. The coat check person took my jacket. I gave myself a quick dusting in the lobby before stepping inside. I considered turning around immediately and going home. I shouldn't have worn my funeral dress. This was definitely not a Banana Republic crowd. Comme des Garçons or Mark's Work Wearhouse. Nothing in between.

A server came by and offered me a glass of champagne.

To the unwise, I said to myself and took a drink. It was very bubbly. It went up my nose and stung my eyes, and I decided if I got tearful, I'd say that was why.

I wandered through the crowd. Lots of laughter and low-contact hugging. It felt like a cocktail party, or a networking event, very much like something Gord would hate.

I found a spot at the end of the bar, near massive windows looking out on the water. Other than the receptionist from the law office, I didn't recognize a soul.

I was just about to head out when the familiar strains of "Another One Bites the Dust" came on over the speakers. Conversation stopped. Everyone laughed. The crowd parted, moving like lead filings towards the edges of the room. One of the many handsome, well-groomed men there got up to speak.

He was the Levi of Levi, Karchava and today's emcee. He assured everyone he was not in charge of picking the music—Gord himself had suggested it years ago—and then welcomed us all to this sad, sad event. He gave a short eulogy to the hard-hitting lawyer he'd come to love and respect, then ceded the floor to those who knew Gord better.

Lots of people took the mic. Law school buddies who choked up halfway through funny stories that made Gord sound like a jerk. (He'd been right. I wouldn't have liked him then.) A childhood neighbour who talked about how good Gord had been, not just with his own cantankerous grandfather but with all cantankerous old people. A guy named Ebbie who'd flown all the way from Mali got everyone laughing describing how hopeless Gord had been when he'd first arrived at the orphanage, then crying when he talked about the little boy named Boubacar whom Gord had befriended.

Then Aziza got up. She was small and beautiful with a severe black bob that I would have loved to have been able to pull off. Her husband—tall, broad, and handsome—stood beside her, one arm over her shoulder, the other at her waist. She was pregnant.

"I don't know why I'm up here," she said, holding back tears. "Gord drove me crazy. He probably drove you all crazy too."

Laughter at that, although I had the feeling it wasn't a joke.

"He had so much going for him. He was so clever and driven and—I think you all know this—so kind. Like *pathologically* kind. But he was also an idiot. He made my life a living hell. He just could not do anything by half. He couldn't say 'too bad about that, it sucks, but let's move on.' He was a total stranger to the concept of harm reduction. Luke died and, as far as Gord was concerned, nothing was ever going to be okay again. It broke his heart and then it broke the hearts of everybody who loved him. And we did."

She turned to her husband. "Sam and I both loved him." He nodded.

"We thought his time at the orphanage had really helped him. We were so happy when he agreed to be our baby's godfather. Because, I mean, how great would he be at that? Fabulous, right? But the guy was an asshole. He could not let things be. And now he's dead."

Sam pulled her face against his chest as she cried. He leaned into the mic. "But we loved him. So cue the music. Let's get this party started. Once upon a time, Gord loved a party. This one's for him."

More eighties rock on the speakers. More champagne. The most over-the-top buffet I'd ever seen. Mounds of lobster. A sushi chef. A giant side of beef. For my friend the vegan.

I was standing by the dessert table trying to decide between the pavlova and the buttered-rum crème brulée when Sam came back up to the mic.

"Have you checked your alerts?" he said, waving his phone. "Keith Osterlich has just been arrested for the murder of Gordon E Bickerton."

NINA

I was in the kitchen the next morning, considering toast, when Deb Dudek rapped at the back door. I pulled my T-shirt down over my butt and waved her in.

"Sorry to barge in on you like this, honey."

"You're not barging in!" Although it did strike me as unusual. This had always been an 'invitation only' kind of house. Deb knew that. "Like some coffee? It's fresh."

"An inch," she said, pulling up a chair. "I can't stay long. Just concerned about Petra. She missed bridge last night. I called and called but no answer." An awkward smile. "Is she okay?"

I got our coffee and sat down. "She's been better." I didn't know how I was going to spin this. Mum missing bridge, Mum not responding—hell, Mum not sending a handwritten apology—clearly, she wasn't okay. Deb just didn't need to know by how much. "She's having a rough time."

"Wayne and I have been a little worried she was doing *too* well, frankly." Deb pouched out her lips. "Never good to keep things bottled up like that."

"No," I said. That bottle should have blown sky-high decades ago.

Deb took a package of Sweet'N Low out of her purse, gave it a shake, and stirred it into her coffee. "How can I help, honey?" She leaned across the table and took my hand. I was hit with an overpowering waft of White Linen and hair product which I found both slightly tacky and deeply comforting. A real grown-up. A mother. Hope. She whispered,

"I don't mean to nose in, Nina, but"—she jerked back into her seat—"Ooh. Sh. Sh."

I heard it too. Footsteps coming down the hall. We widened our eyes at each other—two kids caught with a cigarette and nowhere to toss it—then turned our cheeriest faces towards the door.

Mum walked into the kitchen, thinner and paler than usual, but wearing makeup and a flattering sea-green linen shirt.

"Deb. What a nice surprise! What are you doing here?"

"Had to find out why you weren't at bridge last night! You didn't answer my calls. You okay, hon?"

Mum sat down, laughing a little.

"Yes. Yes. I'm always forgetting to charge my damn phone. I've been..." She stopped so abruptly and so absolutely it felt like a buffering issue.

"Mum?"

She looked at me, then at Deb, her face blank. "No. I'm not going to say that. I'm not going to tell those kinds of lies anymore."

"Mum?"

She folded her hands, lifted her chin, then smiled briefly. "I've been upset, Deb. Terribly upset about this whole Osterlich business. It's brought back bad memories."

"Oh, Pet...Losing Malcolm so tragically, I'm sure that—"

"No." Mum swallowed. "No."

A long, spiky pause. Silent but not. I didn't know what was going on inside Mum's head, but there was a scrum of hecklers inside mine shrieking at me: *Don't just sit there! Say something! Lie, for Christ's sake! She's your mother! Help her!*

I got as far as opening my mouth. Mum touched my arm. I closed my mouth.

"There are a lot of things you don't know about me, Deb."

"Oh?" Deb sat up a little straighter.

Mum said, "Get me a coffee, would you, Neens?" and then she told her. About Duncan and Sarabeth and Narcontine and what Osterlich had to do with them all. She explained she'd been a doctor—that nearly floored Deb—and how she'd had to give it up to survive. How Dad had to sever ties with his family. How they'd just had to do what they had to do to keep moving forward for us girls. How it was Wayne who'd saved them, offering Malcolm a job, keeping their secret all these years. Mum didn't mention anything about Gord or the house tour or the scam, and Deb had no reason to ask.

Around noon, Deb stood up. "Well, so much for just an inch of coffee! Now I really have to run." They hugged. Deb said, "You're amazing, Petra. Just amazing. But we've always known that," and then she left.

Mum bit her lip and made her eyes big. "Well, that wasn't as bad as I thought it was going to be."

"Wish you'd done it earlier?"

"Oh, Nina." She put two slices of rye in the toaster. "I don't have time for regrets. Onward and upward, right? Do we have any jam left?"

It was hard to believe this was the woman who'd spent a week sobbing uncontrollably in a dark room. I was trying to frame a question delicate enough to address her radical mood change, but I didn't have to.

"Look." She turned to me, bread plate in one hand, butter knife in the other. "Gord dying broke my heart, but it isn't a tragedy. He was profoundly and irremediably depressed. He'd lost everyone and everything he cared for, including the will to live. Osterlich has been arrested for his murder. With any luck, he's going to go to prison for a very long time. It's not for killing Boubacar—or Duncan for that matter—but it's something. I know Gord would find that incredibly satisfying. Something good came from his death."

Her toast popped. We both jumped, then laughed at ourselves.

"I feel like Gord's finally at peace," she said. "Now I'm going to try to be too."

She smiled and slathered an obscene amount of butter onto her toast.

OSTERLICH FOUND GUILTY
By Staff

Cheers erupted in the courtroom today when the jury foreperson pronounced Keith Alden Osterlich guilty of the first-degree murder of Gordon Ernest Bickerton.

The jury deliberated for less than an hour on a case involving a black-market deal gone wrong.

Mr. Osterlich, former CEO of pharmaceutical giant PhiTex and an avid collector of African antiquities, maintained his innocence despite a substantial body of evidence against him. He claimed he'd been misled to believe that Mr. Bickerton was a reputable antique dealer and had agreed to purchase an Iron Age knife from him for $350,000. When they met at The Ship's Anchor tavern on the evening of June 8 to complete the transaction, the artifact did not have documentation proving its provenance. As a result, Mr. Osterlich rescinded his offer, but Mr. Bickerton refused to return the $350,000 he'd been paid.

Mr. Bickerton's body was discovered the next morning at a deserted muffler shop nearby. He'd been stabbed in the neck. Wound analysis revealed the disputed knife to be the murder weapon. Forensic experts also confirmed footprints at the scene of the crime matched shoes found at Mr. Osterlich's residence. Traces of Bickerton's blood were detected on the shoes, on one of Mr. Osterlich's custom-made jackets retrieved from a nearby dumpster, in his car, and on several doorknobs in his home. Phone records showed Mr. Osterlich had been at the muffler shop around the time of the murder.

Defense counsel, Andrea Fahey, argued that it would have been physically impossible for a man of Mr. Osterlich's age and size to subdue the younger and fitter Mr. Bickerton. The jury seemed to believe the prosecution's assertion that the presence of large amounts of Serenatol in the victim's blood was proof Mr. Osterlich had planned the murder. Serenatol is a powerful sedative made by PhiTex, the company of which Mr. Osterlich had long been CEO. The prosecution suggested Mr. Osterlich added the tasteless medication to Mr. Bickerton's beer in order to be able to overpower him. Chad LeRoy, bouncer at The Ship's Anchor, testified Mr. Bickerton visibly staggered as he left the bar.

Mr. LeRoy and server TashaLynn Grieves also testified they'd heard Mr. Osterlich threaten to kill Mr. Bickerton several times that evening. It was for this reason, in fact, that Mr. LeRoy removed Mr. Osterlich from the premises.

Sentencing is scheduled for next month. Mandatory jail time for first-degree murder is life imprisonment with no chance of parole until twenty-five years served.

As well as the murder charge, Mr. Osterlich is facing increased scrutiny regarding his business practices as PhiTex CEO. During his tenure, he authorized the sale of pediatric cancer drug Pediaxyclone in Africa despite internal studies proving its potentially lethal effect on the liver. It is estimated that dozens of children died as a result of the drug. He was also involved in the marketing of Narcontine (brand-name Freeling), which caused a wave of teenage addictions in the 1980s and early 1990s.

NINA

TWO YEARS LATER

The baby's crying again. I grind my palm into my forehead. I've got to finish the pitches today for a client meeting this week. I look up from the dining room table and groan.

Mum stops skimming the chicken stock. "I've got her, darling!" She turns down the stove and heads up to Don's old room. It's bigger than ours but Jesse and I decided to make it the nursery anyway. It just felt too weird sleeping in the room where Don died. I prefer our old "quarters" downstairs, especially now that Jesse has sworn he and Anneka never did it there. (A convenient lie, perhaps, but I didn't challenge it. I was just so relieved he'd come to his senses. I also flipped the mattress and bought new sheets.)

"Sorry," I say to Mum. "I only need five minutes."

"Lucky me! Five minutes alone with Aurelia!"

(Yes. That's what we called the baby. Aurelia, Latin name for our favourite species of jellyfish. It's an inside joke, but we also thought it was pretty.)

I'm working on a campaign for a local fast-food chain. Not quite the big time, but there's a lot riding on it. As in, a full-time copywriting job for me at Meg's agency. I scribble down a few thoughts so I'll have something to come back to. I can still hear Aurie mewling. My breasts are hard as rocks. I start undoing my bra as I head upstairs.

The baby is naked and lying on the changing table. Mum is holding her ankles in the air and inspecting her angry, red bottom.

"Oooh, poor thing," she says. "Neens, I picked up a new diaper cream today that might help. It's in my bag. Can you grab it for me?"

"Where is it?"

"Over there." She jerks her head toward the corner of the room.

Since the baby was born, Mum's started carrying that big leather satchel again. It's the perfect size for all Aurelia's diapers and sleepers and toys and what have you. It's packed full. I rummage through it.

"Where?" I say.

"Somewhere. It's there."

I'm getting agitated. Milk is dribbling down my belly. Ideas are evaporating. I don't have time for this. I dump the bag on the floor. I see the tiny tin of Healthie Heinie Cream but I see something else too. I forget about my leaking breasts and my career. I pick it up.

"Mum," I say. "What are you doing with Gord's St. Jude medallion?"

PETRA

THE NIGHT GORD DIED

Petra checked herself out in her full-length bedroom mirror: back, front, and sides.

Perfect, she thought, smoothing the linen tunic over her hips. She'd always liked the elegant roominess of Eileen Fisher casual pantsuits, but especially now. No one would ever know she was wearing surgical scrubs underneath.

Bonnie had delivered the scrubs a week earlier when they met for lunch on the South Shore. She'd just flown in for the day. They sat on an artfully weathered deck, enjoying the view and a surprisingly good chowder, and talking about nothing much at all. They weren't intentionally avoiding the obvious topic. They'd moved on. They were both the type who made decisions and stuck with them. They were content just to take in the sunshine and the company.

They were saying goodbye outside the restaurant when Bonnie went, "Oops!" and reached into her satchel. "Can't forget this! Your uniforme de la guerre, madam."

She handed Petra an unsealed courier package, pre-labelled with the return address. Petra peeked inside and was immediately hit by the unmistakeable odour of industrial-grade hospital bleach.

"The ER!" She sniffed dramatically and laughed. "Boy, does that transport me. It's like I'm suddenly twenty-five again and ready to save the world."

And then, just as suddenly, she was thirty-three and her world had ended. Petra clutched the envelope against her chest. The corners of her lips pulled down to her chin. Her eyes widened. Her chest heaved. Her soul was making a break for it.

Bonnie hugged her hard. "You don't have to do it, Pet. You can stop any time. Really. Gord would understand."

Petra held her breath to keep from sobbing. She shook her head against Bonnie's shoulder and eventually said, "It's not that."

She made herself pull away from all that love and comforting flesh. "It's Duncan. The day he died. That's what it smelled like." And then she sort of laughed. "So, no, I can't stop."

Bonnie tilted her head and took Petra in. "No. I guess you can't."

Petra had snot all over her face and her lipstick was smudged, but Bonnie, as always, had a hankie for her. Petra cleaned herself up. They kissed goodbye.

"I won't call you," Bonnie said as she struggled to squeeze her belly in behind the wheel of her rental car.

"Good idea. We'll reconnect when the time is right."

"We don't need to, Pet." She shut the door. "We've never *dis*connected. Never will."

They both teared up at that, then kissed again, and Bonnie left.

Petra took one last look in the bedroom mirror. Gord was right. Their situations were different. Petra wasn't alone and never had been.

At 9:00 P.M., Petra picked up her big leather bag and headed out the kitchen door. She stopped. She'd almost forgotten about her phone.

"Petra!" she said out loud. It was the voice of her father, Rear Admiral Douglas Astbury. Imperial. Impersonal. Unflinching. The voice she'd railed against throughout her teens. The one she'd internalized in med school. In a single word, it said, "Enough. Do what you have to do. Officium super omnia. Nothing else matters."

She was a doctor. This was a crisis. People's lives depended on how well she controlled herself.

She took her phone out of her leather bag and left it on the kitchen counter so it couldn't be traced.

She got in her car, then ran through a quick mental checklist:

Envelope pre-addressed to hospital—yes.

Envelope pre-addressed to Ebenezer Ballo—yes.

Knife—Gord had given it to her earlier that day when she'd extracted blood. She reached under her seat, pulled out the plastic baggie the knife was sealed in, and put it in her purse—yes.

Osterlich's shoes and jacket. Latex gloves and booties. Wet wipes. Her burner. They were all in her bag too.

Petra still had the small plastic vial the blood had come in. She'd smear the contents discretely on car handles and doorknobs when she did the grounds tour of Osterlich's mansion the next afternoon. That was perhaps overkill, but they'd prepared for everything. Other evidence might be missed or compromised in some way. Gord's blood in Osterlich's home would be hard to dismiss. She hid the vial under the car seat until then. She'd rinse it out and drop it in a random garbage bin later.

She drove to the giant twenty-four-hour warehouse store on the Old Guysborough Road and wandered the aisles, just your average invisible homemaker hunting for a bargain.

She didn't think about Gord or Duncan or Osterlich or what she was about to do. She thought about hypoallergenic mattress pads, discounted thrillers, and one-litre jars of pickled asparagus spears. She checked out the six-packs of white cotton T-shirts. She sampled some baba ghanoush, a vegan chorizo, and a gluten-free pain au chocolat. Most people lost their appetite under stress, but she'd always had an iron stomach. Even Bonnie couldn't face spaghetti and meatballs after a chainsaw injury.

She found herself humming along to the piped-in Muzak, another vestige of her medical training. Surgeons often had music playing in the OR. Helped with nerves. Removed you enough from reality to allow you to focus on it.

Petra was aware of an insistent thrumming in her chest but, otherwise, she was fine. She headed over to small appliances. Deb had mentioned she'd gotten a great deal on a compact cappuccino maker. Halfway there, Petra realized she recognized the song being played. It had taken her a second because it wasn't Bob Dylan singing it this time. It was some girl with a big voice and a backup orchestra, but every bit as moving.

Petra's lungs spontaneously filled. She'd always loved this song. She stopped in the aisle and looked up as if she'd see the singer herself belting it out from the steel rafters of the cavernous warehouse. *Nothing that I wouldn't do,* Petra sang along in her head, *to make you feel my love.*

The words assaulted her. The thrumming turned to a pounding.

Nothing, she thought.

Her lip trembled. She suddenly felt the enormity of her love. It was too big for her. She stared at the display of air-fryers and tried to make it go away.

An older man with an earring and a baseball cap tapped her on the shoulder and asked if she'd mind moving. Petra looked at him blankly, no idea who he was or what he'd said, then the Admiral spoke up again. *Keep your wits about you.*

"Oh, sorry!' She touched her temple. "Lost in space!"

The man said, "This place'll do that to you," and helped her push her cart out of the way.

She turned around and headed back toward the dairy section. The last thing she needed was another cappuccino maker, although she could use some butter.

Moments later, just after 9:40, her burner buzzed. A thumbs-up text from Unknown Caller. She abandoned her cart and headed to her car. She drove north with Dylan playing on a loop in her head. A piper leading her into battle.

The Old Guysborough Road was home to some of the cheapest real estate in the city. It was a dimly lit secondary highway with no shoulder and numerous failed businesses. She'd been driving for about six minutes when she saw the sign for The Ship's Anchor. Lots of weedy evergreens, then the almost obscured entrance to the abandoned muffler shop. As per her instructions, Petra kept going to the next driveway. It led to an empty lot. Whoever owned it had recently done some clearing. She parked behind the large mound of earth Gord had described and got out. She could see the muffler shop through a break in the trees.

She stayed in the car and removed her linen suit. She was down to her scrubs. She put on the latex gloves and booties, then slipped on Osterlich's handmade Italian loafers. He really was a little man. They were almost too snug for her. She grabbed her leather bag, got out of the car, and quickly walked to the muffler shop.

Gord was sprawled on the ground at the side of the building. He'd fallen over, his face in the mud, his left arm awkwardly bent beneath him. *Aw, sweetheart...*,she thought and rushed to help him up, as if he'd only hurt himself. She was tempted to kiss him, cradle his poor aching body, but there was no time for that. Three minutes, they'd both agreed. It couldn't take her any longer.

She cleaned out his pockets. She put Osterlich's phone and Gord's burner into separate sterile plastic baggies, then into her leather bag. She found the last two Serenatol and put them in her bag too.

She patted Gord down but knew she wouldn't find anything else. He was smart, efficient, and determined to make this work. He had it all planned to the letter. There was nothing more to do except get on with it.

She took Osterlich's jacket out of her bag, then laid it on the ground next to Gord. She gingerly pulled the knife out of the baggie. It dawned on her that she didn't know the correct way to hold it. Carving knives, paring knives, scalpels—she knew how to use them, but this was new to her. She'd just have to wing it. She held it in her fist. *Like a killer*, she thought, and was hit by a wave of nausea.

She shook her head. *Enough. Get on with it.*

She leaned in close, told Gord she loved him, and then in one swift move, severed his carotid with the knife.

Blood sprayed out like a geyser. Petra squeezed her eyes shut. This was what he wanted, she reminded herself. These are the fireworks. Gord going out in a blaze of glory.

This is my blood, she thought, *shed for you and for many.*

For Duncan and Boubacar but also, it hit her, for Sarabeth and Sharon and all the other victims. For Malcolm and herself. Redemption at last.

She was not a religious woman, but something about that felt right.

She threw the knife into the woods as far as she could. She checked Gord's pulse but just out of habit. He wouldn't have survived that. She stuffed Osterlich's blood-sodden jacket into her bag. She noticed she'd severed the chain holding Gord's St. Jude medallion when she'd slit his throat. She knew she shouldn't, but she threw it in her bag too. She blew Gord a kiss and left, making sure to walk through the blood.

She only managed to make it to the car without vomiting because it would have ruined everything.

Robot, she told herself. That's what she was now, what she had to be. No stomach, no brain, no heart. Just get it done. The worst was over.

She put Osterlich's shoes, soles up, on the floor of the passenger side. She wiped her hands, face, and neck on the wet wipes. She stripped out of her scrubs, booties, and gloves and threw them into the courier envelope with the wet wipes and leftover pills. The envelope was pre-addressed to Bonnie. She'd dispose of them in her hospital laundry. No one would bat an eye. Petra got back in her Eileen Fisher suit. She put the knife, Gord's burner, and the euros in the envelope pre-addressed to Ebenezer Ballo. Gord had briefed him. Ebbie would know what to do.

She turned on the car—no headlights—and glided down the driveway to the highway. When the coast was clear, she switched on her lights and headed south. She pulled into the parking lot of a large supermarket and dropped Osterlich's bloody jacket into the dumpster Gord had identified. He knew from an enthusiastic freegan Facebook group he followed that there was a dumpster-dive planned for later that night. They'd be sure to find it. She got back on the road, drove to a nearby drugstore, and dropped the pre-addressed envelopes into the mailbox out front. Then she drove to Osterlich's home.

High up on the hill, she could see lights still on in his bedroom. She pulled over and hid Osterlich's phone behind a bush at the base of his driveway.

That was all she needed to do that night. She had another walk-through arranged with Alexis for the next day. She'd pick up the phone on the way in and leave it somewhere in the house. She'd leave a few discrete smears of blood on doorknobs. She'd also have to find a spot for his bloody shoes. She'd just ask Alexis if she could use the washroom. Easy enough to do.

Petra headed home.

The Volvo was in the drive. The house was dark. Hopefully, Nina was asleep. Petra turned on the car's interior light to make sure there was no blood on her face, then turned it off without checking. She couldn't stand to look at herself.

She needed to get clean. She couldn't walk into the house like this, couldn't contaminate her home. She got out of the car and headed to the backyard. She felt lucky their property was so private. She stripped off her clothes and slipped into the pond naked. She swam until she felt purified.

For the first time, Petra appreciated why Malcolm had loved the pond so much. It really was lovely.

Dear old Malcolm, she thought.

Dear, dear Malcolm.

He really was a wonderful man.

PETRA

When Nina asked about the medallion, my heart stopped. I'd been a fool. A sentimental fool. (Not my brand at all.) Why hadn't I thrown it away, hidden it, buried it out back behind Bix's cabin, instead of leaving it untouched and unseen in the bottom of my purse for two years?

I'll tell you why. I couldn't bear to. Couldn't bear to look at it, couldn't bear to lose it.

And now it was going to take me down.

Luckily, I was busy with Aurelia's bottom so had a few moments to compose myself.

"Gord's what?" I said and went back to cooing at the baby. "What a nice tummy you have! Yes, you do. A nice—"

"Gord's medallion. His St. Jude medallion."

Nina barrelled toward me, her hand outstretched. I was going to have to look at it now.

"Careful. You'll step on something." I said it to stall, but it was also a legitimate concern. The contents of my leather purse were strewn all over the floor. Bobbi Brown wasn't making my favourite blush anymore, so if Nina broke my compact, that would be the end of it. (Granted, not a particularly important concern but a useful one. I'd always found, when under stress, I could maintain calm by focussing on small, controllable things. Which is why all the renovating worked. Until, of course, it didn't.)

Nina shook the medallion under my nose. Her face was an unflattering patchwork of mauve and grey. "Mum. Why do you have it?"

I kept holding Aurie's ankles with one hand and took the medallion from Nina with the other. I'd moved into cover-up mode. I reasoned there might come a time I'd have to explain why my fingerprints were on it.

I rubbed inconspicuously at a speck of dark brown residue in the grooves of the cheap metal setting. Nina wouldn't recognize that as blood, but a cop would in a second.

"I have no idea." I shook my head and frowned. "It was in my purse? I've never seen it before. Who knows how it got there. That bag's always stuffed to the gills. I should probably clean it out occasionally. Would *Gord* have put it there, do you think?" I raised my eyebrows at Nina. She wasn't buying it. As if I hadn't cleaned out my purse in two years! Talk about 'not my brand.'

"I can't imagine him wearing it. Can you? Religious medallions don't seem like Gord's style at all. Although if they were, St. Jude would have been a good choice, given how this all turned out." I smiled sadly, then turned the medallion over to look at the back. "No inscription. Why do you even think it's his? Did you see him wearing it?"

That started out as another delay tactic and turned into a real question. I'd seen Gord shirtless many times but when would Nina have?

The mauve drained from her face. Her jaw bobbed. There was something she wasn't telling me. She didn't need to. I knew a guilty face when I saw one.

There was an awkward moment when neither of us could quite summon the guts to lie as extravagantly as the situation demanded, then Aurelia peed on me—a direct hit—and it became moot. We both laughed. Criminals should always have a baby with them. They're excellent cover.

"Oh, Mum! Your shirt! Go clean yourself up. I'll deal with Aurie." Her relief was almost comical. Nina isn't much of an actress. Thank God we hadn't told her more about what we'd been up to. She'd have been the weak link.

"This calls for a shower. Another one, that is," I said, holding my silk blouse away from my belly.

"No kidding. Take your time."

Maybe I was just being sensitive, but I got the feeling Nina was hoping a woman my age would have some deficits in short-term memory. I'd get out of a nice long shower and would be like, *Medallion?*

What medallion? Now that I was well and truly into my seventies, I was much more aware of ageist jabs.

"May I keep this?" I rolled the medallion between my thumb and forefinger. "I don't have much to remember him by."

"Oh, yeah. Sure. Whatever." Nina was using the baby's bottom as a distraction too.

I put the medallion in my pocket and headed downstairs.

My wedding gift to Jesse and Nina had been installing a new bathroom on the ground floor. Something a bit luxurious for them to decompress in. Their lives had become so busy since Don's death. He'd left them the house and enough money to retrofit a disused church as a centre for active aging. Thanks to Don's gift, Jesse suddenly had a career. But that and a wedding and a baby and Nina's freelance work had left them exhausted if, at long last, fulfilled.

I stripped off my stinking clothes and stepped into the shower. It's a cliché, but a shower really is an excellent place to cry so I made the most of it. I cried for Gord, of course, but I cried for me too. Nina had slept with him. That was obvious. My guess was it had happened the day she'd found out Jesse had someone new. The day before Gord died. Nina hadn't come home that night. She'd said she needed some alone time, and I'd believed her then too. (She lied better over voice mail.)

Was I jealous?

I'm not going to answer that. I'm not going to think about it. I'll just say my feelings were complicated. I soaped up my body, lifting my breasts to clean under them, lathering the sparce hair on my almost bald pudenda, leaning a hand against the shower wall so I wouldn't fall over when I did my toes, and thought how much I hated being old.

And then I thought, *suck it up, buttercup*. I should be happy. Gord had had the comfort and joy of bedding a beautiful young woman the night before he died. I hoped the earth moved for him—and for her too. They'd both been hurting. Fragile little lambs. Love, even just the physical facsimile, is a great healer.

I stepped out of the shower and dried myself off. And who was I to complain anyway? I put on a lilac lace bra and panty set, then looked in the mirror. Not bad. At least Tom seemed to think so. He was my latest "guy." (Not boyfriend, not man, and please God, not partner. This was no business venture. It was a fling. A palate cleanser. An ice cream sundae after years of meat and two veg.) A few years younger than me, very fit, very smart, very fun, and totally irresponsible. Definitely not marriage material. I liked that about him. He was what I called my Hazelton Diversion. I only saw him—or thought about him, frankly—while I was in Hazelton helping Nina and Jesse with the baby. I'd be seeing him later that night. My heart (or something) did a happy little flip.

I found some bleach under the sink and rinsed the medallion, then I finished dressing and went upstairs. Nina was in the rocking chair, nursing the baby.

"Well, don't you look gorge. Seeing Tom tonight?" The fact that my girls liked him was nice but hardly essential.

"Yes. But not for a while. I think he said seven, but you know Tom. If he's here by nine, I'll be happy."

She smiled knowingly. Jesse and Tom had a few things in common.

I said, "About the medallion..."

She stopped smiling.

"I think I know where it came from."

"Oh, yeah?" She wrestled Aurie unnecessarily off one breast and onto the other.

"I accidentally picked it up at Osterlich's house. That's the only thing I can think of. I was there the morning after Gord died. Maybe Osterlich had taken the medallion as a 'souvenir' or something. Killers do that, or at least they do in detective books. I could have grabbed a bunch of stuff and just didn't notice it. What do you think?"

Nina rocked her head. "Could be. Sounds reasonable."

I nodded, she nodded back. We'd made our pact. Neither of us would raise it again.

"Now why don't you toddle off and let me put Aurie down for you?"

"Oh, thank you!" Nina handed me the milk-drunk baby and ceded the rocking chair. "I need to get at least another page written and would love to—"

"Go, go, go." I waved her away.

She kissed Aurie's head, then she kissed mine and left us alone.

I haven't sung in public since that disastrous performance at The Big House, but I do love singing to my grandbabies. I stick to a few old classics I remember my mother singing to me and some slowed-down hits from the artists of my youth.

That night, as a promise to Aurelia and in honour of Gord and Duncan and my girls and—yes—Malcolm, I sang Dylan.

There really was nothing I wouldn't do for them.

ACKNOWLEDGEMENTS

Thank you to my agent, the gracious and lovely Samantha Haywood, for believing I could write for big people.

Thank you to the perspicacious Whitney Moran for spotting the missing link in the original manuscript. This story would never have worked without your eagle eye and keen insights.

Thank you to my family who have always been so supportive of my writing. Keep it up and you'll have nothing to fear.

And, finally, thank you to all the people out there who have annoyed me over the years. Having a deep well of rage to draw on came in handy while writing this book. It was great fun getting it out of my system.

Vicki Grant is the author of twenty-one books for children and young adults, including *36 Questions That Changed My Mind About You*, which was translated into seventeen languages, and *A Green Velvet Secret*, which was selected as a White Raven notable book by the International Youth Library. Her middle-grade legal mystery, *Quid Pro Quo*, won the Arthur Ellis Award for best juvenile crime fiction and was a finalist for a Mystery Writers of America Edgar Award. *These Are the Fireworks* is her first adult book. Vicki lives in Halifax, Nova Scotia.

Photo by Studio Umlah